A
River
Called
Time

A River Called Time

Courttia Newland

Published by Akashic Books
All rights reserved
©2021 Courttia Newland
Map ©2021 Courttia Newland

Hardcover ISBN: 978-1-61775-926-0
Library of Congress Control Number: 2020947303

Published in Great Britain by Canongate Books Ltd, 14 High Street, Edinburgh EH1 1TE

First printing

Akashic Books
Brooklyn, New York
Twitter: @AkashicBooks
Facebook: AkashicBooks
E-mail: info@akashicbooks.com
Website: www.akashicbooks.com

For Sharmila, my rock in rough waters

Geb Time Line

5900 BC	First Ta-Seti (Kushite) kings recorded
5600	First Kemetian pharaoh recorded
2500	Foundation of Kerma, Ta-Seti
2300–1500	Origins of Hinduism grow from the Indus Valley
1600	First Ta-Seti pyramid
1500	First Kemetian pyramid
1000	Emergence of Abraham and beginning of Judaism
900	King David forms Jewish Empire in Israel and Lebanon
463–383	Lifetime of Confucius
304	Birth of Ashoka Maurya, Buddhist king
3 BC–AD 27	Lifetime of Jesus Christ
50	Buddhism introduced to China
213	Christianity tolerated in Roman Empire, emperors favoring religions based on Kemetian cosmology (*maat*)
470–532	Lifetime of Muhammad, founder of Islam
553	Qur'an written
1245	Rise of Aztec civilization in Mexico
1291–1375	First Dalai Lama in Tibet
1369–1439	Lifetime of Guru Nanak, founder of Sikhism
1392	Christopher Columbus lands in Guana. Trade and intercultural relations begin, lasting centuries.

1434	Henry VIII declares himself head of the newly formed Anglican Kemetic Temple, separating from the Roman Kemetic Temple
1635	Beginning of Hasidic Judaism
1800–65	Lifetime of Professor Harman Wallace, Kemetic scientist
1814–18	The Flash War, or War of Light. Dinium City devastated for 123 square miles, known as "the Blin"
1830–1910	Construction of the Ark
2000–20	Hanaigh E'lul's tenure as governor of the Ark

Wender

Iseldown

Vaun

Watkiss
and
Regents

Marvey

The Blin

The Ark

Fitts

Milton

The
Heights

Baba

Vaynan

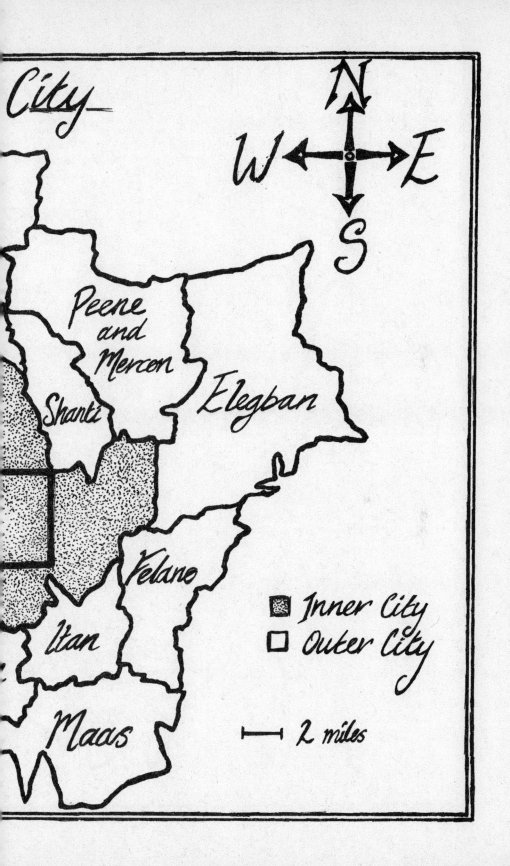

Part One

Being and Becoming

"The golden light of a candle flame sits upon the throne of its dark light that clings to the wick."
—*Sefer ha-Zohar*

1 May 2000

1

V oid. Hum.
Three hundred and sixty degrees' expansion, pervading known
and unknown matter.
Breath.
Existence.
Him.

The first time he was struck by a spontaneous nambula, Markriss
Denny was eight years old. Feet pushing hard on pedals, body leaning
against handlebars, the wheels of the bike ahead glistening with
sunlight. His attention was seized and for a moment he saw the
heavens in that shimmering rotation. He couldn't take his eyes away.
There was pain in the center of his forehead. He was falling from
his bike before he knew it.

He must have blacked out, because the next thing he was lying
on the pavement, elbows and knees raw, the bike a resting animal a
yard or so from where he'd fallen. His friends stood over him. T'shari,
Karis, Nesta. Markriss let them wrench him to his feet, limping back
to his fallen metal steed, waving away their concern, their insistence
he looked pale. Soon they rode in unison again, creaking gears and
turning wheels a random symphony beneath them.

They stopped outside rusting gates propped open with fallen
masonry. Flakes of orange made the once-grand entrance look

diseased. Grass and weeds stood as high as their waists. A slight breeze made the strands rustle like a whisper of ghosts. They sat on their bikes, staring at the blighted metal. Silent.

Nesta edged forward, thin bicycle tire nudging the gate. He rolled over crumbled stone, standing and stamping on the pedals to gain more power until he was over the obstruction, inside. They followed, one after another. Markriss, Karis, and T'shari, the skinniest child, always last, lifting his chin toward graffitied walls, brow arched, fearful.

The building was huge. Not compared to the Ark of course, though it towered above their heads, four stories high. They rode through warped frames of wooden doors into the main entrance hall, craning their necks to look at the roof. Fallen glass left the dusty brown sky exposed. Their school picture books showed chandeliers and birds wheeling overhead, but the boys saw neither. They got used to being alone, speeding up and down once-polished marble floors, performing wheelies and long skids, creating miniature desert storms. When they grew bored, they explored alone.

Markriss rode past closed ticket booths and parades of empty shops, to the platforms where sleek grand trains once stood. He left his bike against a marble bench and jumped onto the tracks, among long grass. Some of the weeds were long green strands that looked like wheat. He lay against cool steel, trying to imagine what it must have been like. The olden days. He closed his eyes.

The mute disk of sun hadn't moved by much when he woke. Markriss guessed he hadn't been sleeping long. He climbed back onto the platform, studying the multicolored lines of the Dinium route map, wheeling his bike into the entrance hall. There was no one. He thought they might have left, panicked for a moment, and then heard voices. Relief made him sag against handlebars. He smiled and hummed a soft tune, wheeling his bike in that direction.

An open corridor, doors long ripped away or kicked down. Black-edged shadows. He paused, biting his lip. The rectangle of light at the opposite end was small, and far. Gloom seeped. Markriss called into the expanse. No answer. Partly, he was glad.

The faraway voices of his friends reached beyond dark. Spun-cotton wisps, distant. He made up his mind, rolling over broken glass and wood, careful, into the solid length of night. Daylight seemed consumed by that murky length of corridor. He saw nothing, his own physicality mythical; the only knowledge he existed came from the warmth of his handlebars beneath his fingers, his own harsh breath. The beat inside his chest, hot blood. The corridor smelled musty, damp, and old. Markriss could taste the odor. He covered his mouth, pushing with one hand, which made the going even tougher; the floor beneath him, thick with dust. He repeatedly bumped his tire against what felt like heavy blocks of concrete.

His bike wheel stuck. He pushed again. Still nothing. Again. No luck. He climbed aboard the pedals, resolving to do what Nesta had, stand up and push down hard.

There was a moment before he did this when Markriss had an inkling of what was to come. An image of himself and his friends, sprinting on bikes, screaming faces static. Metallic banging from a place he could not find, like a football smashing against a chain-link fence. A peal of laughter somewhere beyond his peripheral vision. He felt the sound in his stomach, an ache.

He snapped back into the moment, back in the dark corridor, sniffing. Urine. His nose wrinkled. Gotta get out of there. He rose, smashing down with both feet.

The roar came from everywhere, echoing, bouncing from unseen walls. He was pushed violently, hitting something sodden yet hard, recovering to wrench the bike around and back the way he'd come, pedaling fast. He heard shuffling behind him, running footsteps and mushed words like a foreign language, obvious curses. He sprinted toward the light, shooting into the entrance hall and screaming for his friends at the top of his lungs, surprised to see them rapid-pedaling away, until he saw the vagrants behind him. Grimy faces of shining tar, they stumbled and wheezed, trying to run even though their lungs wouldn't serve them, their clothes in tattered strips, clawing empty air like old view-screen monsters. They chased the boys for yards before they gave up, legs faltering, hands on knees, shaking from rasping explosions of lengthy coughs. Markriss caught one last sight over his shoulder—the vagrants lying in dust, spotlit by shards of light from the broken ceiling, shuddering as though undergoing a group fit.

He turned away, sprinting harder.

They directed their bikes toward the gates, T'shari, Karis, Markriss, cheeks and foreheads damp with effort, tendons thick in their arms.

Far from the Ark Station, almost two blocks away, they realized.

"I thought he was with you!" Markriss screamed over the handle-bars. Karis trembled, sweat gluing baby-corn hair to his forehead.

"Don't shout at him, we all went off on our own!" T'shari's neck stretched taut, tendons protruding, a late entry to any argument, as was his way.

No one dared go back. They waited a heart-wrenching fifteen minutes before Nesta returned, shoulders hunched, riding slow.

"Ra . . ." Smiling when he saw their surprise, their worry. It angered Markriss, though he said nothing. "You lot was scared, right? You shoulda hid. They got sickness. They can't hurt you."

An ice cream truck a few blocks from the Ark Station, the young vendor leaning on his counter, tattooed and bored. A dig for change, excitement from Karis and T'shari, echoed in miniature by Markriss and Nesta. The joyful-bought whipped-cream cones, slow-melting vanilla; the somber orange and lemon ice poles that bled sweet juice. They rolled their bikes toward a grass verge behind the truck, to a bench where they could sit.

"You lot never seen a sickie before, yeah?" Nesta licked at his ice pole, watching faces. "My uncle had it. He died. Only took three months. I was there."

T'shari, the only boy still mounted, rocked his bike back and forth, eyes cast at the pavement. "My cousin had it. He died. I wasn't there. My parents wouldn't let me see him. He was old anyway."

"My dad doesn't believe in sickness," Karis piped up.

"So what d'you think killed them?" Nesta, leaping to his feet, waving the pole. Orange spatters flew. The youths backed off.

"Dunno . . ."

"Dunno . . ."

"Dunno . . ."

"Maybe cancer . . ." T'shari's offering, limp, useless.

"You don't catch cancer, so it can't be . . ."

Markriss, sitting higher on the verge, lost interest. He stared across the street at a broken building wedged between the One Tic store and a shop called Mama's Day that sold maternity wear. A sliver of storefront lit by red fluorescent lights placed above the awning to form letters, the letters creating words: *TEMPLE OF SEBEK THE MEASURER*. Twin symbols—three circles placed inside each other housing a small triangle—bookended the name. Men and women clothed in long white robes drifted in and out, holding thin black books to their chests. A sign was placed on the pavement, green chalk on blackboard, imploring passersby to *Find the Neter Within. Join us in worship: 11–3 / 6–10. All welcome.*

His mother, Willow, called them Kushites, or Nubians like herself. Some noticed the ice cream truck and crossed the quiet road. Markriss didn't want to stare, though he was fascinated. A man, broad in his cheap suit, smiled as he bought a cone for his pebble-headed son. Markriss's lips twitched. He looked away, caught.

Willow didn't go to temple, though she had a shrine in her podroom. She believed in Neter, not religion. He wasn't quite sure how his mother separated the two, and never had the courage to ask. Markriss considered himself lucky that she didn't force him to pray twice daily, like his friends whose parents were Ila, Nandi, Yoruba, Abaluyia.

He lifted his head, searching beyond the ice cream truck, the temple and its followers. Above, the skyline undulated in a frosted brown haze, a broad smudge that stained the horizon.

That evening he played World Cup outside with his brother while the filthy sun descended, casting dusk like a curse. As Ninka was five he couldn't play to the best of his ability, though Markriss still enjoyed the game. Their street was a discreet row of redbrick houses, backed against one another like continuous Siamese twins. His brother was born on the living room floor, his mother's moans climbing the stairs to his podroom, where he'd been banished with a neighbor to await Ninka's arrival. Markriss himself had been born in the local hospital after his mother's waters broke and he didn't arrive. When he was ventoused into the world, some eighteen hours later, his parents had lived in the house for less than a year.

Chasing the ball, running, he had an abrupt vision of a sleeping face lit by restless candlelight, eyes cast heavenward, blind; more flickering lights, larger than the candles, the ancient stutter of a cinema reel projected onto the blank screen of their eyes. He saw himself, his mother and father standing to attention beneath the wailing screech of gears, the everlasting blast of a train horn. Unknowing, Markriss was granted his second premonition.

His brother began to splutter and cough, overheard by Willow, who called the boys inside. Markriss trailed behind. He wanted to dismiss the pictures in his mind, alarmed after what he'd seen that afternoon, those lurching, failing bodies. He couldn't tell his mother he'd been playing in the derelict station; he'd be grounded, possibly beaten, and he wasn't even sure his assumptions were correct. Ninka always coughed, fell over, bumped his head. Most infants did. It wasn't worth the risk of a beating to tell his mother what he'd seen over what was probably just grit in his brother's throat.

The boys ran straight into the kitchen, believing dinner was about to be served, only for Willow to hurry them through the tiny space and push them into the garden. Unlike the confines of the house, the garden was their mother's refuge. Three times the size of her kitchen, twice the size of their living room, it was where she grew spinach and mint, parsley and oregano, which often ended up on the family plate. A fruit-bearing apple tree stood on the far left. A fence at the farthest end was wrapped with a black currant bush, plants that sighed with the wind. Willow never stopped reminding the children of their luck. Many nights saw their mother on her deck chair, long slim legs straight as pool cues, smoking a cigarette constructed, in part, from one of the plants grown in her airing cupboard.

Long accustomed to Willow encouraging use of the garden, the boys followed her wishes with little protest. At the bottom of their mother's haven, just past the berry-laden fence, in a man-made valley two hundred meters from where the boys stood, lay a rusting, dirt-brown train track. The majority of the city's poor were found in regions much like the town where Markriss, Ninka, and Willow lived, while the rich lived nearer Dinium's center, a bare desert of dark earth leading to high walls surrounding Inner City—the Ark. Karis told Markriss that beyond those walls were streams of honey, all the computer games a boy could play, even nudie magazines given by generous men on street corners. Markriss argued white-heat dismissal, never knowing whether to believe him. At night, in his sleeper, he dreamed it was true.

His mother called them to this spot once every six months. For once every six months the train transporting the lucky to Inner City ran along the track at the end of their garden. Being "lucky" seemed to mean you had to make an exceptional amount of money, be a renowned artist of any kind, or a teacher, or a great fighter, or adept at any skill that could benefit the world within those walls. Though many complained it was slave labor in disguise, few of the poor found courage enough to decline the opportunity, if or when it came.

Willow agreed with the optimists, for on those nights she walked them down the garden until they were immersed in the smell of mint and the buzz of insects. Pollution soaked the clouds like mud-stained cotton wool. In all the picture books he'd read the sky was blue. He'd often wondered why book characters never wore the ugly black masks that covered the faces of people on the streets of his town. When he'd asked his mother why, she said he thought too much and told him to go outside and play.

He watched the bullet-shaped train ease past government houses, so old its former gray metallic exterior had turned copper in places. The Excellence Award logo, an E slashed above an A, was long faded. A stubborn layer of dust coated the windows. Smoke seemed to emerge from every crack in the metal, every loose panel, though it didn't bother the occupants, who were delirious with joy, screaming with laughter, hanging from open windows, yelling how they'd made it, how happy they were, of the new lives they would lead. Families in various gardens waved and wished further luck. Try as he might, Markriss couldn't contain his envy.

Willow eased herself between her sons, taking their hands, a strange look on her face. She seemed tall enough to tear a handful of rotten cloud from the sky. Feeling his eyes, she managed a smile.

"Remember what you've seen," she said as always. "That's your ticket out, and don't ever forget it."

Ninka was too young to grasp her words, of course, though Willow seemed relieved when Markriss nodded. As his brother grew bored and found a neighborhood cat to play with, she kneeled beside her elder son until her face was level with his. Her thin, pretty features were elegant, her eyes like the tawny orbs of a lioness. Her skin reflected red sunlight, giving Willow a warm tint that made him love her more than he thought possible.

"It's up to you." Her whisper scratched at her throat. "Understand? You're too young, though when you're older you'll ride that train. You can be anything you want, Markriss, you're the only one. I'm too old, and your brother . . . Well, he isn't quite strong enough. So it's you."

He watched Ninka grasp for the tabby's tail and felt hollow, cold. His brother could never ride that train by his own power, no matter what changes he was destined for. His natural IQ was low since birth, and recent schooling seemed to indicate little would change. Markriss was a child, and yet he already knew the results would mean Ninka growing up to become a burden, maybe someone that he, as his older brother, would be forced to carry. It didn't make him love him less, yet the fact remained. It was something known without words.

"Yes, Mum."

"Good. Now go and get your dinner."

He ran inside, clipping Ninka on the ear to make him wail, a success, then collecting his steaming plate of spaghetti Bolognese from the oven top. Markriss remembered the meal as one of the best he'd tasted. Full, he kissed his brother on the forehead to apologize. Willow smiled, pleased with them both.

In full night, after wiring him into his sleeper, she closed the lid and loaded a Nocturna program, telling Markriss how proud she was. He could have wested and gone straight to Aaru.

Markriss fell asleep to a baritone vibration of comfort, until some-time during the night he was wrenched from his familiar projection of playgrounds and climbing frames to find, when he opened his eyes, he couldn't see. There was pressure on his chest. He couldn't breathe. He tried to fight, yet the more he struggled, the worse the pressure seemed, and he knew his eyes were open because he could feel himself blinking; still, he *couldn't see*. He tried to open his mouth and scream. Nothing came, so he fought to kick and punch, only it was useless and his breath was leaving so fast that soon he wouldn't have any left. A voice rasped in his ear, deep, creaking with age—an old man's rattle—whispering words he didn't understand. He fought harder, pushing and tearing at the pressure, lashing out—though not with his limbs, which seemed paralyzed, with his mind. He couldn't quite work out how he managed this, fighting until he woke up.

Everything remained as it was when he had gone to bed. His toys were where he'd dropped them, his clothes were where he'd folded them, and his brother lay in his deep, humming sleeper on the opposite side of the room, faceup, arms flat by his sides. Markriss lay back on his pillow, curled into a ball, shuddering from the remnants of his sleep cycle. It would take another few hours for him to realize that Ninka's breathing had ceased, to leap from the bed and shake his brother, first gently, then more frantically, for Markriss to scream for his mother and Willow to burst into the room moments after, breath caught in her throat, tight fist clutching her dressing gown, pushing her elder son aside in haste. Shoulders colliding, unaware of the other, they pushed and pulled at Ninka until Willow lifted his limp body from the pod, knowing he would never be warm again.

2

The machine is stilled. Coffin-dead, cold, awaiting a second chance. Quiet breath surrounds it. The podroom door remains closed. Her elder child occasionally wanders inside, although he doesn't stay. She never does; she hates it.

The machine is stopped. Perhaps forever.

The doctors refused to, or couldn't, explain what happened to Ninka. He was in perfectly good health, by medical accounts, up until that chilly spring morning. They made grand statements, citing ailments Markriss and Willow had no knowledge of and were sure Ninka hadn't suffered from. E-Lul Corporation, universal manufacturers of the sleeper pods, spoke in grave voices about complex states of transcendental being, using terms neither understood. Few experts mentioned the sickness. Ninka's body was subjected to numerous tests until they ascribed his respiratory failure to some vague form of crib death. The experts returned, gave Willow a certificate stating the flimsy fact, and left in a collective of frowns and sympathetic words that held very little meaning for mother or son.

When Markriss remembered Ninka in those early days, he saw convulsing, faltering vagrants, puffs of dust and light that caught spinning motes in wide, angular shafts. Tattered figures collapsing to the floor, unable to chase. His brother's cough, thick and dirty as a derelict Ark Station. He knew.

At first it was all Markriss could do not to give in to the pain, to be strong for his mother, who veiled herself behind blank eyes and a robotic normality he could never match. After the funeral, attended by friends, neighbors, and very little family as there weren't that many, they wandered the corridors of their house, sometimes not speaking for days. Willow's visits to her beloved garden ceased. No smoke curled from cigarettes. One day, Markriss stamped open the kitchen bin to find twin packs concertinaed into a formless lump; after, there were none. Shopping in the local market and mall, they walked with their eyes straight, never acknowledging yet feeling the stares and sympathetic whispers of neighbors. Markriss became subdued, the subject of child psychologists and concerned acquaintances. This last even included his school lunch lady, who thought giving him extra helpings might ease his pain in some small way.

Though buffeted by circumstance while he made sense of his new beginning, his new life, thankfully for Markriss the world sometimes makes children supple enough for such strain. The loss of his brother soon felt like an amputated limb. Though the pain was largely gone, he often felt a nagging itch that reminded him of what had once been. Like days when he felt Ninka close in his ear, a ghost of warm breath on his cheek. Or before he went to school, playing with his brother's toys in the passage, when he would go into the kitchen for a cool glass of milk and return to find the toy on Ninka's pillow, as though it had always been there. These occurrences were ordinary as sunshine, and so Markriss immediately told his mother. Willow gave a faint smile. She felt Ninka too. That was the first time she cried in front of him following Ninka's death, the moment they first shared their experiences of his presence.

Although Ninka never entirely left his mind, by the time Markriss was eleven, secondary school and the joy of being in a grown-up world was more than enough to keep his attention. There, he discovered that his natural curiosity was linked to an aptitude for study that made him one of the brightest students in school. Of course, he had no intention of being a geek or a swot, so he combined his passion for learning with a passion for people, soon becoming part of the school's ragged social elite. In those days Inner City was enough of a lure for people to understand his reasons for knuckling down, even if they didn't share his prowess. He joined the football and rugby teams in winter and the athletics club in summer, scoring straight As in his academic subjects. He became especially skilled in English language and literature, writing stories and songs he'd perform for eager school friends whenever out of adult earshot. Markriss wasn't alone in having such a talent, and pretty soon a small group of them were having friendly competitions during the hour lunch break, surrounded by cheering spectators who formed a noisy circle around them.

He developed a special bond with some kids and was advised by Nesta, the only friend who joined him from primary school, to buy a pad and carry it at all times to write down lyrics and thoughts. Following this advice, Markriss found that he couldn't go anywhere without the pad, and therefore, without his schoolbag. His rucksack became the trademark he was known for, always strapped to one or both shoulders.

Such activity was bound to get him noticed by a certain section of the student population. By thirteen, he'd noticed them too. The young women who roamed playgrounds, hallways, and classrooms were something like the sweets to be found at the Great and Wonderful Confectionery Store; though actually seeing them, being with them, walking past them for hours on end was like having keys to the shop and being told to eat until your teeth rotted. Markriss, along with a good few of his male counterparts, discovered the opposite gender with a vengeance that was almost an obsession. Each watched their opposite number develop with fascinated glee. Markriss discovered a new pain, a new itch; only this one was deep, a swelling tumor.

Nesta became his running buddy in this quest of new discovery. He hailed from Priory Street, one of the roughest, darkest back alleys in Regent's Town, the area they'd grown up and gone to school in. He'd become tall and berry dark, his smooth skin reflecting a shimmer of light that seemed to glow a faint electric blue. Nesta was notorious for fights, stolen goods, backchat, and a general give-a-damn attitude that was overbearing for most adults. Their teachers spent years imploring Willow to keep her son away from him, as it was taken as given that Nesta would come to a bad end. Willow had none of it, reminding tutors that Markriss hadn't failed an exam to date. More to the point, she always found Nesta pleasant and full of generosity in her own home.

He was formed by the usual Regent's Town stories, though his seemed worse than most. A family of dealers, ranging from mother and father, to the uncle that died of the sickness. An upbringing that revolved around the blocks and corners of Priory Street, where kids on bikes were the biggest road teams and adults crossed the road when they rode by in their hundreds, a predatory flock of birds. Nesta's own philosophy was to become the hardest, like his father and father's father. Not long before his tenth birthday, Nesta's mother had walked the Regent's Town streets alone after a night drinking with girlfriends. Singing with all her strength, stumbling from pavement to curb to lonely road, barely able to stand, until she was spotted and mugged. Her assailant, armed with a simple length of rope, claimed he killed her accidentally, pleading guilty while on trial. Locals discovered his trussed and nodding body on the banks of the River Azilé not long after being released from prison; weights meant to sink him had broken free. Nesta's father was arrested and eventually freed when no evidence linked him to the murder. Some said it had been done in the family home. That Nesta saw everything.

At fifteen, when the boys cast their eyes on the school's most coveted prizes, Nesta was well on the way toward being expelled. Early that summer, he'd been spotted with a gun. Although he hid the weapon where it couldn't possibly be found, he'd been hauled from his first afternoon lesson and kept in the head's office for the remainder of the day. The only thin ray of light in his dark future was the consolation that Misty Ahmet and Raymeda Khuti, the school's most gorgeous young women by far, had agreed to meet the boys for an after-school date. Days earlier, they had planned a trip to Burbank Park, the imitation woodland of trees, plants, and small animals not far from the blinland that stood between Inner and Outer City. After all the deliberation and game playing between them, Markriss was hardly able to believe the girls said yes. He resigned himself to the belief that they would never meet by the school gates like they agreed, especially after Nesta's antic with the weapon.

He left the building at the electronic bell, walking the through road that led to the adult world, unable to deny the duo standing beneath the *Regent's and E-Lul Secondary School* sign. Faint disappointment lurched. If they hadn't turned up, at least he couldn't be blamed if things didn't go well.

Misty and Raymeda were tiny beauties who bore as close to matching complexions as Markriss had seen. They were direct cousins through their mothers, who also shared that burnished gleam of vitality and life. Misty stood slightly taller than her cousin and closest friend. Raymeda's eyes and lips looked like they'd been shaped with an artist's perfection. They were top of their classes and forwards in the volleyball team. Both walked the school corridors completely aware that they starred in every adolescent fantasy the male students could muster.

As is often the case with men, Markriss and Nesta were torn between each girl, neither knowing which they preferred. Fortunately the cousins were more decisive, or maybe less greedy, than they. Over the past few weeks Raymeda had expressed a tardy desire for Markriss, even as Misty made moves for Nesta through half smiles and lowered eyes. Clearly the girls long discussed any differences in taste. This suited the boys.

Markriss approached the gate, working for a casual manner, though he couldn't stop his excitement prompting a smile. He was heartened when Misty and Raymeda returned matching grins. They stood in silence together as e-cars whined by on the main road, a trio of satisfied faces joined in agreement. All decisions had been made. The battle was over. This was the time for counting spoils. A new teaching assistant drove along the through road, catching sight of the students as she joined the rush-hour traffic. Recognizing the scene for what it was, perhaps thinking of her own school years, the TA smiled as Markriss, Misty, and Raymeda, all students she knew, underwent an ancient ritual in her rearview mirror.

"So you can't speak?" Raymeda said, after they had stared enough.

"Hey, Raymeda. Hi, Misty."

Kisses for both girls on both cheeks, dry lips meeting soft flesh; Markriss felt heat, even from that limited contact.

"When's he comin out?" Misty burst between quick pops of gum.

"Dunno. They came in class and got him, didn't say anything to us lot. He's been there all afternoon."

"Well, we can't get to Burbank without him, so . . ."

Misty gave the gum a last pop before turning to walk a few steps toward the gate. Raymeda took the cue, stepping forward and slipping her hand into Markriss's, positioning her face beneath his.

"What kind of lame kiss was that?"

He obliged, keeping it brief even though his every impulse was to let his hands move, hold her tight. When he lifted his head she was studying him, lips pouting.

"That'll do, but you better be more romantic when we get there."

It was forty minutes before Nesta came strolling down the through road, that hard face etched with thought. He visibly collected himself, arranging his features into a smile even wider than the others. Markriss caught a glimpse of muddy-brown coloring overtaking his fluid blue sheen, even as he envied the smooth and comfortable manner in which Nesta drew Misty to him. The confident way he looked at her from head to foot. The way he dared to squeeze her body and kiss her lips until she had to scream and fight him off, fist pounding at his chest, not too much.

The boys bumped fists while the girls threw questions, Nesta guiding them toward a battered little car parked farther along the main road. The vehicle was scuffed and dented, no logo between the dull eyes of headlights, no name on its rear. To Markriss, the little car looked squat and hardened by elements, much like Nesta.

Chauffeuring the girls inside, he faced Markriss, shaking his head before he spoke.

"I bin expelled."

Even though he'd guessed as much, reality caused Markriss to gape. "But they never found the—"

"So? They don't give a shit about that. This was the perfect opportunity to get me out."

Nesta's fear was apparent enough to make the sadness of his eyes unbearable. It had nothing to do with what teachers or even his hustler father might say while bathed in piahro smoke. It was certain

Nesta would never live to see beyond Outer City; with no qualifications there was little chance he would ride the train to the inside world.

"Better tell Raymeda and Misty . . ." Markriss followed Nesta around the back of his car toward the driver's door, keeping his voice low. "They waited ages."

"Nah, Mars."

"What, you're just gonna leave—"

"I said no!" Nesta's words seethed between twisted lips, sharp enough to alert the young women staring out from the mucky glass of the car window. "It's all right for you lot, innit, wid yuh Excellence Award shit; I got nothin! They don't care about me, I just make their life less boring . . ."

"Yeah, but, if they felt that way surely—"

"People like them don't stay with Outer City people. They could fail their exams and live on the street; they'll always have that option— some Inner City guy will bring them in. The only people who stay with Outer City people like me are *Outer City people like me*. You too stupid to see?"

He didn't wait, wiping his face with one hand, wrenching at the driver's door. Markriss closed his eyes, too late to block what he'd seen. Nesta's tears obeying gravity's rules, not those of teenage boys, falling to the concrete regardless of his wish. Markriss saw the girls interrogate the youth, knowing they'd get nothing from the set of his face. He made sure his own was set in similar fashion and ducked into the backseat, slamming the door hard enough to rock the car.

Predictably, the journey was tense, filled with a silence too thick to penetrate. Nesta was stiff jawed. His lips moved in mute conversation, none aimed toward his friends. For the first five minutes Misty was concerned and unblinking. After ten she gave the occasional sympathetic glance, until she began nodding along to the radio. From that point she paid Nesta little attention, head moving and fingers absently tapping her thigh.

Raymeda's expression betrayed that she'd possibly overheard their argument. She gave Markriss lingering glances. Unlike her cousin,

Nesta's music selection, machinelike drums and lithe bass, wasn't enough of a distraction. Midway, she slipped a hand into Markriss's. He jumped as though woken, feigning a closed-mouthed smile that bore no resemblance to his former grin. Soon he was looking out of his window again, thoughts churning as Regent's Town slid by. Raymeda eventually retrieved her hand, although it was difficult to tell whether Markriss noticed or not.

They rode a mostly straight route to Burbank Park. Regent's and E-Lul Secondary, half state funded, half owned by the corporation, was located on the farthest edge of Outer City, a forgotten star in a faded galaxy. Watkiss and Regent's was one of sixteen boroughs surrounding the inner enclave of the prosperous, and seven of those were poverty-stricken hellholes. In the previous year Regent's had won the title "Worst Place to Live," according to a headline in a local daily. The article, spanning ten pages of community testimonial, police and government-official accounts, and off-the-record stories of road-team leaders, detailed the drug and gun culture, rapes, and teenage murders that prompted Nesta to come to school with his pistol.

Boarded, graffiti-laden shops went by, clouded by an idle, carbon-monoxide-spewing cruise. The only bright spot came when they drove along the high street and past the bustling Ark Station: there, things managed to look almost normal until they left the main road, back where the real people lived. Beyond that point they witnessed the usual Outer City transactions; road teams, partygoers, drunks, and dealers all emerging while the sun, a grubby copper coin in a matching sky, disappeared behind the buildings.

The brown above turned black, lined with streaks of red that seeped across the darkening sky like dilated veins. It was strange to see the contrast between that temporary beauty and the degradation of their city below. Then the scenery changed again. They entered a world of comparative prosperity, fashion boutiques and wine bars where they heard laughter and the musical tinkling of glasses. An array of masked people, mouths and noses covered by the protruding metal snouts of face masks, walking with hurried purpose, never a pause. This was Marvey, richest borough of Outer City. Eastward from the elite region lay a section of Dinium's sprawling business district, Central Circle, the corporate hub that enclosed the Blin citywide. Within the circle of trading blocks, nothing other than wasteland, and the Ark. Marvey's proximity wasn't simple geography. Everyone knew 90 percent of Inner City immigrants moved inside from that borough.

Markriss only ventured as far as the River Azilé on rare occasions, mostly traveling to Central Circle with his friends by car after dark. Each time he'd been stung by the stark office blocks, water fountains, smooth concourses, and needle-thin skyscrapers populating the sleeping business sector. Glass and bright lights, glittering diamonds of ambience and wealth. The serene emptiness of locked buildings, desolate streets. Lip curled, breath clouding glass as the car turned its back on the borough, Markriss watched Marvey's financial district perform a graceful slide across his passenger window into dusk. Jealousy wasn't good aura, though he couldn't help feeling confused by the disparity between their lives. Wasn't he smart, didn't he work just as hard? Why were they granted more? This district looked much like the world portrayed in his childhood picture books, of dreams he'd believed writers created to give kids like him an imaginary world of escape. Always, he told himself it wasn't real. Nesta's comments echoed in his thoughts, a taunt. Misty and Raymeda were Marvey born and bred.

Burbank Park stretched for close to a square mile, boasting a lido, a man-made forest area, six football fields, and a host of other attractions that made it a summertime paradise for all. Open-air plays and concerts took place in warmer months. The entrance had walls and gates, but long ago someone had decided the concrete jungle needed some form of oasis, and the gates stood forever unlocked. At night, the more exotic animals (like the almost extinct peacock and the aptly named ray bird) were kept in a vast underground menagerie, just in case any local Iseldown degenerates attempted a sting. In these darkened hours, the park was also an obvious choice for courting couples.

Nesta found a parking spot near an open gate. They got out in silence, standing in an awkward group on the pavement until he beckoned at Markriss. Markriss followed him to the back of the vehicle, watching him raise the trunk. After some shuffling, Nesta emerged.

"Got a bleeda?"

Markriss shook his head. Something cold touched his hand. A scuffed knife. Stifling disquiet, his fingers closed.

"Ra."

"In case of nutters, you know?" Nesta cast his eyes at the wrought-iron gate. Thin lengths of metal formed a ten-meter arch. Two words, *Western Forest*, were chiseled into the wall beside it.

Markriss grunted thanks. "You got one?"

"What do you reckon?"

Nesta returned to the trunk. This time he emerged with a thick woolen blanket. "There you go. Gets chilly at night, trust . . ."

"Thanks . . ."

"Better have your own doms!"

They slapped palms, mates again. Nesta waved a hand beyond the car. "Come we go."

In their absence, neither date was looking pleased. Misty's mouth exploded like a popgun while Raymeda wouldn't look at anyone, anger making her face glow. The boys homed in on their respective partners, escorting them through the gates. Nesta must have known his roads well, for he'd parked next to an entrance that led directly to the outskirts of the forest. They followed an upward path lined with white sodium lamps. When they reached the peak, Markriss couldn't help but notice Misty's hand firmly within Nesta's own.

He glanced over at Raymeda. She had a stubborn, chin-held-high look of pure attitude that surely meant she was still angry. Markriss found himself cursing Nesta's ability to shrug off a mood when it suited him. He had no such talent and was now suffering.

In silence, he absorbed forest sights and sounds. The sky was clear. Night birds called. A rustle of small animals came from darkened bushes. Less frequent was the murmur of deep voices. Men sometimes met in this park. Markriss wasn't sure if Raymeda had known—the first time they heard whispered conversation she stopped in the center of the path. He eventually managed to cajole her into moving, her eyes wide, staring at the bushes in fear. She jumped when a squirrel ran across their path, hooking an arm into his, pushing close. They settled into friendly conversation, talking quietly, trying to put each other at ease.

Misty and Nesta had left the path some way back, while Markriss and Raymeda decided to continue. The forest of trees grew thin. The mirror surface of a pond reflected the quarter moon that had risen during their walk. A massive hut to their right housed the boats and deck chairs that came out during summer months. Grassy earth gave way to tarmac, and the trees fell back as if in awe.

Raymeda let go of Markriss's hand and ran to the water's edge, looked up at the sky, then skimmed pebbles over the pond. He laid their blanket near the edge of the forest.

"*This* is romantic!" She strolled back, happily swinging her arms. "Don't you think?"

"Yeah, it looks good. The way the moon hangs over the pond and everything."

Raymeda frowned into thick night. "Not that bit. I think the moon looks kind of sick. All skinny and brown like it's gonna fall. It scares me, especially when it's full."

"I like it. It used to scare me as a kid, but now I don't mind. My mum likes it on the hot nights when it goes kind of beige."

"My mum doesn't like it at all. She reckons the darker the moon gets the crazier people seem."

"She might have a point."

"Yeah . . . Mummy's clever like that," Raymeda said, as though surprised.

When they ran out of conversation there was nothing left to do besides sit on the blanket and kiss. They continued for some time, passions developing until the cool spring breeze caressed their naked bodies with a feathered touch. Neither was new to the experience, all too common in a place where the young were forced to ripen sooner than they should. Afterward, they ate.

Markriss had only brought sandwiches, fruits, fizzy drinks, and small cakes, yet Raymeda was pleased and they feasted as though it were a banquet. They blew cigarette smoke over the pond and attempted to break open the hut in order to row a boat, though the locks were too strong and they ended up back on the blanket. They talked for an hour or so about school and all its social ties, until Raymeda started to doze, fell asleep. He eased her onto the blanket, smoking and watching the quarter moon. He didn't expect to sleep until there was a forceful tug from somewhere; before he knew it, he was gone.

A split second later he found himself high in the air, surrounded by gloom that meant he was deep in the trees, far from the path. He didn't know which way was up or down, although he could hear grunts and sighs that meant he wasn't alone. Markriss tried to move his body toward the sound; kept trying, even though he got nowhere. When he flapped a hand in front of his face he could see nothing, presumably due to the intense dark. Curiosity invaded him. He wanted to know where he was, and what was making those noises. Those thoughts had only just become a voice in his mind when he found himself falling so fast he thought he'd die. He saw branches and leaves slap where his eyes should be, though strangely, he couldn't feel them. All he felt was his heart, rattling in his chest. Fright had frozen him solid. He wanted to scream, and opened his mouth to try, only for nothing to come out. He wanted to stop . . .

And he did. Halted beneath the lowest branches of the trees, Markriss hung above a scene that was near insanity. Directly beneath him, in a clearing surrounded by dense forest, were Misty and Nesta. They were making love, writhing, his friend on top, pinning her to the ragged blanket. Nesta's sheen of color was more vivid, and had changed again, glowing a bright, angry green. Alarm went through Markriss when he saw what was happening.

Nesta wrapped his hands around Misty's neck, starting to squeeze. Her eyes opened. He continued to choke the girl, his movements growing rigid, more frenzied. She tried to fight, but the youth was bigger and stronger, her panic seeming to make his fury worse. Her arms flailed. Color seeped from her features. Markriss tried to yell at Nesta; instead, he dropped.

It was the strangest experience of all. Rather than plunging onto their bodies, injuring everyone, he had time to witness Nesta roll over in shock before his world turned into complete night.

It lasted for some moments—five seconds at the most—until he found himself back by the pond, yelling Nesta's name. Raymeda jumped to her feet, poised to run, thinking they were being attacked. Markriss wasn't even sure what he had seen: Surely it couldn't have actually happened? His own fear was reflected raw in Raymeda's eyes, and he wanted to make her feel better about being in his company. All he could tell her was something about a bad dream.

They packed the blanket and food into his schoolbag, deciding to look for the others. Markriss kept much of his terror to himself, making sure Nesta's ratchet was secure in his palm. Halfway down the path, Nesta and Misty emerged, saying they'd been disturbed. Both seemed keen to leave, and as Nesta was driving, no one was about to disagree.

Raymeda told them what had happened, including Markriss screaming his best friend's name. He walked, mouth closed tight, not looking at anyone, wishing she hadn't. Prickles of cold ran up his back, and he noticed Nesta watching him from the corner of his eye with thoughtful, wary speculation. Though that was disturbing enough, a more unsettling discovery came with the walk toward the western entrance, along the path lined with lamps. There, they all saw the rise of growing bruises, ten imprints, on either side of Misty's throat—a somber flesh necklace. Fattened and pale in the dark.

3

He stands against the open door, latch protruding into his chest, their podroom a place that Markriss locks in every conceivable manner. He'd take the machine apart—nuts, bolts, and panels—had he known how to safely. They've discussed this over many hours. Somehow, without voicing why, Willow and Markriss know they can't.

On a tiny side road beyond Watkiss High Street, just past the greasy-spoon café and ever-popular One Tic shop, stood Mr. and Mrs. Lee Tsoi's Great and Wonderful Confectionery Store. The fact that Mr. and Mrs. Lee Tsoi owned the store was without question. Whether it was indeed Great and Wonderful was a little more tricky to answer if you were an adult, though was Neter's truth to the thousands of children who had flocked through its open doors over the years. Mr. and Mrs. Tsoi were purveyors of fine elixirs that, when boiled, left to set, or baked until they hardened, formed sweetened narcotics delicious enough to please even the most critical young taste buds. The couple had emigrated from Shanxi province to Dinium over fifty years before and had been creating sweet delicacies for most of their lives.

Markriss'd joined the Tsois' paperboy task force when he was twelve, a job inherited from a neighborhood friend whose family paid an extortionate sum—the equivalent of a lifetime's earnings—to move inside. He'd spent many longing afternoons in the store before that, mostly waiting on his mother as she bought the daily paper and made idle chat with Mrs. Tsoi. As they talked, he'd gaze all the while at the hundreds of jars containing jellies and sherbets and gum and chews and bite-size fairy cakes, all glistening like cave minerals, unable to stop his mouth watering. Huge digital scales sat on the counter just to the right of Willow, dusty with frosted castor sugar coating not only sweets, but everything in sight.

Poster-sized advertisements for E-Lul Corporation products, including the Ark, were on every wall. An unobtrusive stand to the left of the shop counter housed a register for the Ark prospectus. Though the Tsois sold newspapers, magazines, and tobacco of all kinds, it was homemade confectionery that made their name in Watkiss Town. Markriss couldn't have been more than six in those early days of wanting, and in later years the store became a place symbolizing happier days of childhood. A place where he remembered everything as good.

That day, almost a man and not quite a child, Markriss felt anything but well. He'd been helping out in the sweetshop after school for the last year, riding in on his bike and taking a few hours to sweep, serve customers on occasion, sometimes even stock-take in the damp basement if things were quiet upstairs. It didn't bring in much money; still he turned half over to Willow on a weekly basis, and because she agreed to take it, he continued. Over time, he'd grown close to the Tsois, staying behind after work to eat with their daughter and son on a number of evenings, for, at fifteen and eleven respectively, they attended the same school. Markriss was glad of the money and the chance to help his mother put food into their cupboards and fridge, something he knew often wasn't easy for Willow. Inadvertently, he also knew she worried less when he was busy at work in the Great and Wonderful Store.

That late in the afternoon, the sign bearing twinkling bells and wind chimes that so amused Watkiss Town children was reversed, so *Closed* faced the darkened street. Markriss swept the wooden floor, soothed by the swish of the broom, mindlessly herding dust into a corner to be disposed of later. The shop floor was silent and empty of customers. Lee was in the basement stock-taking, while Wai Chee, Mrs. Tsoi, was upstairs in their four-podroom flat, either sleeping or watching VS—her two favorite pastimes. Unaware of his immediate surroundings, Markriss worked. The bristles automatically gathered dust and minuscule portions of outside world as he swept, head down, his mind lost in that windless night at Burbank Park, trying to decipher what he'd witnessed. He had yet to learn what had happened on that strange evening two weeks ago. Whether he'd seen reality or a dream.

A rattle of clogged breath, familiar and abrupt, made him jump, holding the broom to his chest in defense. Yi-Kei Tsoi's slim figure stood beside the shop counter. He relaxed, feeling stupid.

"Why . . . so jumpy?" Still, hardly blinking, her jaw fell a little, forming a snatched gasp every time she inhaled, exhaled. Fluid rattled in her chest, loud then softer as she breathed. Her lungs sounded submerged in low water.

He put the broom down. "You scared me. I didn't hear you come in."

Yi-Kei beamed, success. "Mum's napping . . . We have to be quiet . . . on those stairs. She's . . . a light sleeper."

Something lived in her eyes, so wide and dark and fathomless he drifted away right there, to Burbank and the Western Forest, to Raymeda's warm body and the steady lap of water. Birds disturbed leaves above. The skin of his neck rose, an army of pinprick bumps.

"Are . . . you okay?"

"Huh?"

He was on the shop floor with her again. Yi-Kei's clear unblemished face stood unchanged, apart from the tremor of a wrinkle flitting across her forehead.

"You look . . . like . . . something . . . bothering . . . you."

"Oh." He stared at the broom. Yi-Kei was often the subject of hushed school conversations about her sickness and lack of availability, despite an unconscious beauty that belonged to her as much as her husked voice, or hiplength black hair. He didn't like to think of her that way, because all he could see was Nesta squeezing and moving, Misty's eyes looking blind into his. It made him queasy.

"Well, I've got things on my mind."

"I . . . tell." A dwarf-star smile, gone before fully formed. "Are you . . . sleeping?"

"Not much. No."

"You look . . . bad as me."

He finally noticed the dark circles around her eyes.

"Doesn't your sleeper help? I thought Nocturna had a program?"

"I doze . . . Few hours . . . Cough wakes me."

He winced, remembering. Of course, how would she sleep each night with a racking pain in her chest, the pressure, that feeling of suffocation, like she might die? Like he did all those years ago, sleeper vibrating beneath him, the low hum of mechanics and electrics. His brother opposite, a mirror image.

"I don't really like sleepers. Most nights I lie awake for hours." Markriss eyed dust again. He hadn't said that to anyone.

"I might . . . be stress . . . about . . . you know. I try to stop worrying. But sometimes I can't, think too much. At school . . . What will happen . . . if I can't take . . . exams . . . ? I wonder if someone will like me . . . like this . . . I like people, and I don't know . . . if they like me back. Mum and Dad. They always try to do things. Lift this. Take that. Help me down . . . stairs. Don't sit in the shop. How am I supposed to run the business? If they won't let me? How am I supposed to take care of them when they're old? Or be independent like they keep telling me? How can I—" She caught his eye, saw the smile. Her lips rose slightly. "What?"

"You stopped breathing like you normally do."

"Oh!" Yi-Kei wheezed laughter, coughing three sharp bursts. A fist clutched at her throat. The other held the counter. Markriss stepped toward her.

"Can I get you—?"

A rapid shake of the head, a raised palm. He waited. Above, a thump against ceiling. The creak of furniture, imaginary old bones.

"What you . . . stressed about?"

His arms moved, but he pushed the wooden broom handle without strength, not sweeping. A pretense. Bristles scraped floor.

"Nesta?" Yi-Kei's eyes were unflinching, in spite of his obvious surprise. "He's . . . funny. Looks . . . and smiles . . . in school . . . Doesn't . . . look like . . . smiling . . . to me."

Sharp pain. No way he could tell her, or anyone.

"Maybe I shouldn't make you talk like this. I gotta go."

Yi-Kei nodded finality. "Go. I'll . . . finish."

She reached out. Markriss crossed the shop floor, placing the broomstick into her waiting hand.

"Thanks. Sure you can manage?"

"You . . . owe me . . . a . . . shake."

They laughed quietly.

"I do."

He kissed her on both cheeks before going into the basement to say goodbye to Yi-Kei's father. After rising from the lower level, his bike lifted onto a shoulder, Markriss unlocked the shop door and wheeled into the night, Lee Tsoi's wind chimes singing random melodies around him.

Once his legs grew warm, Markriss knew which direction he was pedaling. Riding gave him clarity of mind, a type of mental focus where, if left alone with his problems for long enough, he'd find a solution by cruising through Outer City roads and traffic. Rush hour was on, a perfect time for unconscious cycling, e-cars and their smokier ancestors jammed one behind another while bicycles, scooters, and motorbikes weaved between. It had been a dark, moody day, made even more so by lumped brown clouds hovering over Dinium, threatening rain though never quite bursting. Streetlamps glowed soft illumination. Night was yet to fall.

He followed a similar route to Nesta's fourteen days previously—east, toward prosperity. Soon the streetlights were numerous, and he began to see police officers. Staying off sidewalks to avoid being arrested, Markriss followed the main streets until he noticed a sign for Rochester Drive, the well-to-do suburb of West Marvey. He angled his bike and rode on.

Misty's bruises had shocked everyone, even though she didn't seem to realize the full extent of her injuries until Raymeda screamed, her trembling voice and rapid steps creating a widening space between herself and the boys. She had grabbed Misty's hand and talked to her in urgent tones, seeming not to know what to make of Markriss, looking at him distrustfully, as if his outburst by the lake made him complicit, before she launched herself at Nesta, a clawing, lashing blur. It took most of Markriss's strength to keep them from each other. After an initial outpouring of tears and refusal of comfort from anyone, even her cousin, Misty collapsed into Raymeda's embrace, having to be practically dragged along the path. They walked to Nesta's car two by two, still arguing, Markriss trying to keep Nesta away from the girls. Although his friend's stare burned Markriss's cheek, daring him to condemn or condone him, he could do neither. He'd been rendered comatose by his vision. His hands shook. His skin was sticky and cold. The teenagers maintained their two-by-two formation during the ride home, Markriss taking the passenger seat, the young women in the rear.

Wordless, Nesta let them out at Rochester Drive. At Watkiss Town, Markriss expected the same, Nesta waiting until he'd left the car to stand on the sloping pavement and slammed the groaning passenger door.

"Now you see my aura. Now you see me for real."

His foot was down before Markriss could say anything. By the time he reached his front door, Nesta's battered car was just another pair of firefly taillights.

In the two weeks since, Misty, Raymeda, and Nesta had been routinely absent from Regent's and E-Lul Secondary: no rarity for Nesta, anathema for each cousin. Faced with empty desks and silence as names were called, the lingering pauses and glances of classmates stayed with Markriss until the home bell, causing Burbank Park to replace his brother's aura as he lay awake and sleepless, consumed by the dark in his silent pod. Night visions plagued him. Even as he tossed from his left side onto his back, to right and left again, eyes red, prickling, jaw aching, eventually succumbing to fatigue and seeping into unconsciousness, he dreamed of tumbling into Misty's eyes, those twin dark voids, and he would wake, jolting, the covers squeezed into a fist, skin damp from chilled perspiration, gasping wordless pleas at the bumped ceiling.

He found the street he was looking for, leaning his bike into the turn, pulling brakes. The whistle of air fell into silence. A lean, muscular e-car growled by, seashell pearlescent, presumably having just exited the open black gates yards away. He glided to a stop, climbing from his seat to take hesitant steps toward the grand detached house, pushing his forgotten bike by his side. Number 175 Rochester Drive was like a house from the movies. A modest, carefully kept driveway, ornate candlelit lamps as front-door sentries, garish yellow paint, those large black gates, and a looming hedge that walled the house from jealous eyes. Markriss followed the driveway, feeling hemmed in. The gates whined to a close.

After a long pause in which he glanced across to the neighboring buildings and took close note that yes, all the houses on this street were more or less the same, he rang the bell. High-pitched, shrill, a no-nonsense tone that seemed uninviting, all business, echoing from interior walls as if the house was vacant and had been for some time. No one answered. It felt like forever. He tried again. After further pause, footsteps approached, clipping against a hard floor with quick precision.

The door opened with a progression of tumblers and locks. A tall skinny Nubian, dressed in a well-worn butler's uniform, appeared on the other side. His face was mapped with ridges, and he seemed unsteady, barely able to stand. Loose jowls hung from his cheekbones below old-man eyes, jaundiced, sunken, red-rimmed, and heavy-lidded. Only great effort seemed to keep them open. He wore a creased suit, the shirt beneath yellow and stiff from thousands of hot washes. His lower jaw rocked right to left, as if about to speak, before Markriss realized it was involuntary. He took a gulp of air, unprepared for this apparition of a man.

"I believe . . . the gate . . . locked." The specter trembled, voice wavering.

"Not when I came in. I walked right up."

Lips pursed. Clearly, he wasn't believed. The man peered behind him.

"Um . . . My name's Markriss. I'm here to see Misty, please . . ."

The old butler's limbs performed an irregular dance for a time, before, with what looked like giant's strength, a single word escaped. This minor event took so long Markriss only just resisted the urge to thump him, in an attempt to knock the full sentence from his lips.

"The . . . Ahmet household . . . receives no . . . visitors."

"Well it's important. Very. It's about those marks . . . on Misty's neck."

Drooped eyes grew wide before the butler collected himself, Markriss in no doubt that he'd seen them. Both men, one at the inner concentric circle of life, the other at its farthest edge, regarded each other, released from subterfuge. They spoke the same tongue, peeked into the other's soul with grudging respect, no less real despite their reluctance, or the gulf age tore between them.

"We understand your concern . . . Nevertheless . . . Mr. Ahmet is confident that everything is under control. Miss Ahmet is well rested and taking studies at home. So you must not worry yourself, Master Denny. Go home. I'll reopen the gate and do my level best to pass your good wishes to Miss Ahmet."

Being addressed formally was far more disconcerting than the knowledge that he hadn't told this old man his surname. How much did the Ahmets know? Probably a lot, as even their ragtag butler knew Misty's injuries had nothing to do with him. An out-of-depth feeling lapped at Markriss's chin. He grabbed for the cold metal handlebars of his bike.

"Okay . . . Okay then . . ."

"Goodbye, Markriss. Be secure in the knowledge that the Ahmets' appreciation is sincere . . ."

He ignored that last, crunching along the gravel path, eyes on the swinging gate, which opened as he approached, pulling a face screwed up in confusion. Either the butler had undergone a major change of character since he mentioned Misty's injuries, or Markriss was suffering from latent yet acute paranoia—though he never smoked the "sleeping drug" piahro like some kids at school, or even drank the liquor they raided from parents' cabinets. Not since he'd been sick outside the school gates that one time.

A quick look over his shoulder hardly settled the unease. The front door was half closed, the right side of the old man's face shielded by the wooden barricade so that only one glassy, bulb-yellow eye was visible. As he contemplated whether to complete his turn, or perhaps go back, the door opened wider again. Markriss stopped. A thin arm protruded, flailing, waving him down the path. He sighed, turning his back on the house, hearing the brief thunder of a closing door. He'd almost reached the gates, swinging open-armed to greet him, when he heard a frantic tapping come from above and behind.

He swiveled again, on one foot this time, more fluid. Misty's face pressed against a high window, signaling from beside an arrangement of red poppies, his mother's favorite. Her viewpoint seemed precarious, as though she was struggling to keep balance. An eager smile made her look well rested, as the butler had described, her gleaming eyes and bright teeth lifting her usual shield of nonchalance with the obvious joy of seeing an outside, familiar face. A sturdy off-white bandage was wrapped around her neck many times over. His joy at seeing her in good spirits faltered. Hurt raced through him. He felt warm night air, saw the veil of leaves and branches, and knew. What he'd seen wasn't a nightmare, or hallucination. It was reality.

Misty stilled. She placed a sheet of paper against the window, just beneath her nose. Her forehead pressed pale. A small white cloud appeared, expanding and contracting lungs on glass. She pointed at the paper. He tried to focus on the dark printed words. They were difficult to make out, something about . . .

"Go?" he murmured, frowning, bike dropping to a clattered heap by his feet. A few steps closer. Misty's fingers were bleached white with pressure, the paper flattened on the window as Markriss squinted, straining his eyes from the shadow cast by the house. "Go . . . see . . . Oh, 'Ray'! Go see Raymeda, right? All right, Misty, thanks—"

He'd whispered, and yet he still jumped when the old butler appeared by Misty's side, transforming her joyful grin to shock. He grabbed her shoulders and she was gone, leaving the collection of poppies nodding. Markriss stood open-mouthed, unsure.

"Hey—"

His feet crackled, spitting stones up the gravel path until he heard barking dogs. The clamor was enough to make him turn and reach for his bike, jumping on to pedal through the gates before her mother was called.

* * *

Unlike her immediate family, Misty's divorced aunt opted for metropolitan life over the suburban comforts of Rochester Drive. Maple Court was one of seven tinted-glass, dark-metal, high-rise blocks that overlooked the banks of the Azilé, or as it was known to old-timers, "The Western River." The Courts were built as homage to the fabled Inner City dwellings everyone heard so much about, their design drawn up by Inner City's lone architect, Massell Khnemu himself. Lattice-steel balconies threw far-reaching silhouettes across early-dusk sky. Bare windows exposed spacious open-plan homes, pastel colors, and ambient lighting.

Markriss cycled at speed, forehead damp, legs a little sore, panting slightly, past security guards lined against the backdrop of the first three blocks. It would be next to impossible to get inside, though he kept sprinting. Closer to the egg-speckled concrete steps of Maple Court he slowed, smiling as Raymeda got to her feet, wiping dust from her jeans and moving toward him as though it had been hours since they last saw each other, nothing between them but the breeze.

"Hi." He wiped sweat from his brow and dismounted. Raymeda stood back, her arms crossed.

"Hi. Guess who got a major squeeze when Senef called my house while Mum's out playing oware?"

He grinned, laying the bike down to walk over and enfold her in his arms. "You?"

"Correct . . ."

She grasped him tight, so Markriss was forced to speak into her hair, the light-brown path of her center parting dotted with freckles. Four security guards stared with open hostility. They wore black jumpsuits, their relevant blocks printed on the shoulders, metallic face masks strapped around their ears, covering noses and mouths. The E-Lul-manufactured products made the guards seem part reptilian and were often worn as luxury items by residents on this side of the city.

Sharp memory of Yi-Kei's coughs, the girl bent over, holding the sweet counter with clawed fingers. Markriss had never been that close to an E-Lul Metro face mask, and he couldn't return the guards' stares. He carried too much hate for them to risk it.

"Is Senef that old butler then? What did he say?"

Her expression drew tight, almost ugly. "I didn't talk to the 'old butler,' as you call him. I think he'd prefer 'housekeeper.' I let him tell it to the answerphone and came downstairs. You ride fast for a skinny guy."

"Cheers." She squirmed against him, seeming uncomfortable, so he let her go, shooting another glance at the uneasy guards. "I just hope your cousin's all right alone. He's kinda weird."

"Senef's a sweetheart, Markriss. He loves Misty. You don't have to worry, he would've told her off and left it."

The guards had formed a tight group, heads low, their masks and helmets a series of dark, glistening globes like Dinium CCVS cameras. Clearly, they were talking about Markriss and Raymeda. A quartet of guns strapped to their waists bore silent threat.

"Uh, maybe we should . . ."

She grabbed Markriss without looking back, leading him away from the concrete steps. "Let's go by the river; everyone's gone. We can talk."

"Okay."

She led him along the main road until they reached a grimy set of narrow steps. Moss-clad brickwork, mottled handrails on either side, ancient etched graffiti. Going up, they emerged onto the man-made bank of the river, wide enough for a parade that contained a minimart, a glowing pizzeria, and a taxi stand. Only the pizzeria was open, spilling stark light and the smell of baking dough. She walked him along the parade and on until it was far behind, a walk that took them to the sleeping business sector where E-Lul Corporation reigned. The company HQ was on the opposite side of Dinium's corporate belt, the stretch of banks and stock-exchange buildings collectively known as Southern Circle; here, on the Western Circle, the computer giant still made its presence certain, with billboards high on glass tower blocks, sponsored buildings with glowing E-Lul logos, and parks adorned with corporation-funded statues of lesser gods and ancestors—generals, philanthropists, and inventors, mostly.

Rival companies fought for space and attention, next to lost among the bright sea of E-Lul Corporation vid-ads. Immune to propaganda, or perhaps subconsciously absorbing what they saw, the friends kept going until they reached an empty bench that gave a lover's view of the Azilé and the twin cities.

Along the river to the west, a glitter of luxury apartment buildings spread that, if he'd known no better, gave an illusion of everlasting wealth, fairly distributed from the financial nucleus to the farthest corners of the city. Due south, as the river turned and traveled, a twinkle of lights emanated from scattered buildings, a world of steel, spotlit logos, and glass. Beyond that, nothing. Gaps between corporate buildings awarded glimpses of a glow on the horizon, fuzzed light exposing the grim fact that only the Ark existed in that direction, not buildings or people. E-Lul, with the aid of the government, had grown their glittering circular business center to block the view of bare earth from sight and mind. Even the river had been made to disappear by the time it flowed into the Blin, forced underground by years of planning and engineering to pump through a network of Inner City veins.

Markriss often found himself thinking about the river, and whether others in the city imagined its plight as he sometimes did—diverted beneath the earth against its will, straining against demands, powerful yet robbed of strength, mighty though fallen. Whether it lamented the days when it had reached hundreds of yards from shore to shore, a width now split by arched tunnels and concrete dams into canals and underground ponds, streams, and, in some places, no more than a faint trickle of lank, bacteria-concentrated water. Life under immense pressure, even then. There was no doubt the river had fought, bellowing, twisting, and biting until its strength gave. He imagined it asleep, devoid of anger or thoughts of revenge, a self-inflicted slumber in order to rebuild the energy of old, eternally dreaming of the day when it would rise.

"Romantic, huh?"

She watched him peer over the expanse of dark water, tugboats, and solitary fishermen, her eyes lit bright with deep pleasure. Markriss leaned against the cold metal railing, finding it difficult to believe this world came to an abrupt close—the financial infrastructure, commercial hub, and recreational facilities—all becoming one and the same behind Western City Circle, the river emerging miles on the other side of the city. Beaten to submission by the World's End Reservoir that siphoned water daily, by the ton.

He leaned his bike against the railing. Raymeda looked at him with an expression of thoughtful concentration that drew him close, the force of whatever was on her mind tugging at him, favorable or not. She allowed his embrace, although she was tense and wouldn't hold him in return. Markriss recalled her warmth. It was all he could do not to smile. He rested his head against hers and they kissed, gentle and mutual, until she forced him away, eyes tight, frowning as she turned to the river.

"You were right in Burbank," he tried, quiet with dismissal. "It was romantic."

She'd wandered to the end of the lookout point. A coin-operated telescope pointed at concrete, lifeless.

"What's wrong?"

"We shouldn't."

He pondered the words that might draw her out further and unlock her reasons; remembered the security guards. He sat on a bench. "Know why I'm here?"

She twisted from muddy water, smiling a little. "Well, if I'm honest, part of me hoped you'd come to see how I was doing." She looked directly at him. "Senef said something about you wanting to talk with Misty. I reckon that's the reason."

Sweat prickled his cheeks and forehead. Unseen shards of pain. He looked at his hands. They glittered like soft earth, city night.

"Yeah . . . But I was worried about you, Raymeda. It's been mad at school not knowing where you lot are."

"Home tutors." She left the telescope, coming to sit by his side. "Our parents told the governors we weren't coming back till Nesta was arrested. Apparently they need to find him first."

"They'll have a job. I haven't seen him."

Raymeda kept her focus on the telescope. "Mum has."

"She has? When?"

"Sometime last week. Mum does voluntary stuff at this center in Iseldown, you know, the Munroe Centre in Ochosi? Every week, two nights a week she's there. She's been doing it for years, knows all the faces. Right after you guys took us to Burbank, Nesta turns up with a load of guys. My mum spoke with a few of them. Apparently Nesta and the rest got involved with some grocery store robbery in Taunton, so they had piahro and weren't shy about advertising. Mum called the police, then Nassir and Abiola—that's Misty's mum and dad. She probably wasn't quiet about it, cos some of the kids told Nesta and when the police came he was gone. There's an estate not far from Munroe where local kids hang. Mum reckons that's where the police would find him and the rest. They won't even look."

"Right. Did Misty tell you anything about what happened at Burbank?"

A massive sigh, her legs trembling. Markriss felt it through the bench.

"A little . . ."

"Why, what did she say?"

Another reluctant, constricted face. He had to know. Markriss hated to cause such obvious discomfort, but he had to.

Raymeda breathed like Yi-Kei, her eyes immediate liquid glass. "She told me that night. We didn't go straight home after you dropped us off, we went to the 24-store to cool off. They do rubbish coffee but the smoothies are all right. I bought Misty a Strawberry Twist cos I didn't want her going home with runny makeup and crumpled-up clothes. I wanted her to drink it, and I'd clean her up, and that would be it. If I'd known those bruises weren't gonna fade I would've taken her home, but I wasn't sure if it was serious. Stupid, right? Misty's done crazy things before, between you and me. I thought this might just be another of her weird things.

"So she's all quiet and teary, and I'm sitting there asking what happened just like you, and she's not saying a thing. Then she starts to talk. Telling me how things were cool, how they smoked and ate food she'd cooked at home especially, got intimate and fell asleep like we did. Then . . . I'm not sure about this, because she was crying quite a bit, and I couldn't really get what she was saying . . . But . . .

I *think* she said she woke up and saw Nesta was having some kind of fit . . . He was talking to himself, making noises, thrashing from side to side. She shook him, trying to wake him up, and that's when he rolled over and started to strangle her.

"The weirdest thing about it is she swears you were there, Markriss. Swears blind, even though she knows you were lying next to me the whole time. He was definitely trying to kill her, she reckons. First she thought it was rough sex; then it got violent and she couldn't breathe. Everything slipped away from her she said . . . The trees, Nesta . . . She really thought she was gonna die . . ." Raymeda halted, gulping emotion.

"Then she saw you. *Flying in the trees*—she said that, not me—'Flying in the trees like a comic-book person,' is what she actually said . . . Misty's convinced you were there and you saved her, Markriss. Don't ask me how. You were with me, definitely. You didn't move from that spot. I'm sure."

Her eyes widened, as though she remembered something; their glint enough to betray a calculation that threw him. "You did have that nightmare still. And you did scream Nesta's name. Didn't you?"

He stood up, crossing the lookout point, going back to the safety of the railing. His damp T-shirt stuck to his back. The wind felt colder, reaching his skin. He might have been inching closer to answers, though none that he'd wish for. A foghorn cried, long and distant.

"Maybe *you* should be telling me what happened. What you dreamt about."

"I can't remember."

"You sure?"

"Positive. I tried."

"And you weren't smoking pi?"

"I don't."

"Even though Nesta does?"

"No. I don't."

He knew that throwing rough words over his shoulder could be read as a sign of guilt. He inhaled deep breaths, closing his eyes, then turned back to the bench and saw Raymeda bowing her head toward her sneakers as though truth might be gleaned from her entwined laces and the minuscule, intimate dance of loose threads in the breeze. To lie was the worst thing, although there was no way she could deal with what he'd really seen and felt. No way. His nerves sang, his pulse beat, rapid at his wrists. He might have still been floating high above them. Everything he'd experienced that night and since remained locked in that higher perspective, that looking down from a great height. His feet hadn't felt the warmth of earth, his arms hadn't steadied his body. It was too bizarre, even for him.

"Sorry, Ray. I don't know."

Water and night shimmered in her eyes. She managed a smile. "Mum said you'd do this. She told me you wouldn't accept what happened, and we shouldn't speak with you or Nesta again. Me and Misty agreed about him in the 24-store, although we'd thought you'd get the benefit. See how brave you were. You aren't."

Markriss kept silent. He wanted to ask what it was he should accept, yet to do that he'd have to tell Raymeda everything. His lips grew tight from being pressed together.

"You should go."

A step closer, and a jolt when she pivoted her body toward the walkway that led back to the steps and her housing block. He'd held her not long ago.

"So that's it? Aren't we friends . . . ?"

The grimace, even thrown backward, disturbed her beauty, a rock that broke glass. "We're not going in the same direction, Markriss."

He wanted to argue, and had no idea how to begin, what should be said, what she might want to hear.

"Go home. Don't make me scream for the guards."

She took another two steps. Her back, her shoulders. Her hair. He waited until he was sure that she meant every word, especially the last, most hurtful. Picked up his bike, threw one leg over, rode. He pedaled until the lights on either side streaked into soft blurs and the wind grew constant, low in his ears.

Markriss kept pace, riding into Iseldown at brisk speed until the burn in his legs matched that of his heart; acknowledging anger, expression set like Lee Tsoi's treats, heart thumping. This was not a zone to be taken lightly. Already, teenagers loitered in streets and estate entrances with their older and younger counterparts; already, he'd received the stares reserved for out-of-towners, police, and others without trust, youths even spitting in his wake as he tore by, a dull tattoo of patters behind him. He had the knife Nesta gave him, previously hidden in his saddlebag, now relocated to his back pocket so they could see it as he raised himself above the handlebars. It ensured he wasn't followed, that he was a kid with business to settle. The youths let him tend.

He knew the estate. Gunnersbury, deep in the heart of Iseldown, where police resorted to driving past years ago, and road teams ruled with a fist that was usually small and semiformed. The young sons and daughters of criminals long made their presence felt. Backed by family reputation and deeds, they'd turned Gunnersbury into their own personal territory for so long, it became the estate decent people didn't mention, and a magnet for unloved, untended kids who'd come of age steeped in crime.

A squeeze of the hand, a squeak of unoiled brakes, and a slow turn to the left, Markriss searching the dark spots where bodies formed habitual flints and shadows, until there he was, as Raymeda's mother had predicted. Huddled yards beyond the estate entrance where Markriss stopped, sweating and breathing hard, among a thickened group of seething kids by the grainy underground garages. Nesta, dead center, smoking and spitting lyrics at the dark-shelled sky, blind to the approval of his team, lost in expression. Fueled by noisy animation, they bounced each other into walls whenever he said something they rated, or cupped hands around mouths, sounding off to the heavens in appreciative cries. Doubtless there were ancestors who saw, heard, and approved. Markriss watched in awe at how lineage could reach across so many years, molding its kin in ways that might only be viewed with distance—such as he was granted in that moment. Old customs performed anew. He stood by the entrance for close to ten minutes, cars passing through to stop with their windows open, halting beside the team for quick exchanges, moving on. They were so involved in what they were doing, so used to being unmolested,

Markriss could have been there ten minutes more and they would not have seen him.

He let his bike roll along the through road, feet on pedals unmoving, down the steep incline into their domain. The wind sang on the edge of nothing, receding into quiet. A chill on his forehead and shoulder blades returned, damp on his chest. The youths muttered, minimal as wind. Nesta saw him last, feeling the stiff countenance of his fellows, chin raised in his direction. He grinned, saw Markriss wasn't smiling. The corners of his lips fell, muscles gave way. He stepped from the group and came a short way up the incline, arms swinging, a faint rocking from side to side, a man at sea.

"What's up, Mars?" The tails of his bee-yellow raincoat flapped in the breeze, a thin, expensive material whispering as he stepped. Synthetic, glossy from lack of wear. "How you find me, man?"

Markriss dismounted. Lowered the bike. Nesta waited for him to kneel and rise empty-handed, grinning again, a grand show of teeth, eyes one-dimensional, on one spot.

The team all had the same eyes, minus the grin.

"I remember this estate. Came with you once, remember?"

Laughing, turning to face the underground garage. "Man's got a good memory!"

Markriss reached into his jeans pocket and pulled the knife, holding it stiff. It was important for them to see. The team screeched warning. Nesta whirled, alarmed for a rich second. His shoulders dropped. The grin seeped back.

"That's familiar." More teeth. "Markriss, wha you doin? You don't want this, I'll bleed you up. Forget what I said, your memory can't work that good, otherwise you'd know. We shouldn't be fightin anyway! What for?"

"For Misty!" he growled, anger taking him closer. Heart thumping to escape, veins hot. The team laughed, touched fists. They liked that.

"*Misty?* Shit, Mars, listen yourself. This ain one of those Coronet films. You better mind out. Anyhow, you're so bothered, how come you didn't use that in the park?"

"I would've, if it wasn't for the girls."

The grin faded. Nesta's entire face flattened. His team conferred without taking their attention from Markriss. In his lower regions, the base chakras Willow would have emphasized, Markriss began to think he might not have chosen his most favorable path. It produced a stomach twinge he tried to dismiss.

Nesta's shoulders heaved silent, disbelieving laughter. He shrugged off the bee raincoat. A mop-haired boy shot flames at Markriss and took the coat, folding it with sales-assistant patience.

"All right, Mars. You're my mate, no matter how you feel. I won't hurt you. Put down the bleeda. Let's be men. Don't do nothing permanent." Grumbles of approval. "Wha you reckon?"

"So they can do me in while we're at it?" Wincing, knife erect in a sweating fist. "No thanks. I'll fight fists, away from this lot, and I'm not leaving the knife. I won't use it on you. Okay? You know I'll keep my word."

Nesta thought, nodding, hardly pausing to make a decision. His peers were happy for the first time since Markriss arrived, rubbing hands, bouncing on toes. Fun.

"Okay . . . So I got your word?"

"Yeah. You have."

"Say it."

"You have my word I won't use this on you, Nesta."

"Cool. Come we walk. You man wait here."

Markriss raised the bike with his left hand and began to wheel farther down the incline, knife in his right, eyes on Nesta and the team of young men. He tried not to think of Raymeda, firm and warm beneath his palm, the smell of lotus mixed with oils he didn't understand, soft breath tickling his ear though he would not move. The pleasure of not moving. Her beauty, shattered by disappointment. Misty at the upper window, and not. Things he was too young to know, those he should never have known. He could not stop them entering his mind.

Nesta scuffed the soles of his sneakers on the pavement to create rhythm, digging into his pockets to produce a piahro splint. He paused, stuffed it into his mouth and lit up, trotting to join Markriss. The smell was intense, acrid, terrible. Invading everything, hanging like a vengeful spirit. Nesta had a raw, diagonal blin that ran from his temple to the lobe of his ear, lava red, probably made by a knife. The weeks they'd spent apart underlined their differences. Already, battles for his friend. How young he must seem to the boys in Nesta's company, even if most were his age. The forthcoming brawl might be difficult, faced with someone used to fighting as a man, often fighting men. Butterfly flutters betrayed him. He was afraid to do it, equally afraid what would happen if he didn't, fearful that one rash decision based on childish ideals of justice might become the ten-second instance that ended his life.

They walked deeper into Gunnersbury. Slabbed blocks, squat and weighty on either side. Hard-faced, five landings apiece, solid chunks of brickwork, as alive as the leaping dogs that ran up and down before him, groups of equally strong men in car parks, severe women hefting shopping aided by moaning infants. An open-air labyrinth where heroes and monsters took the same form. Pathways, walkways, hundreds of windows and doors. Multicolored estate maps obliterated by scrawled graffiti into fogged masses of ink and paint. Some lights worked, many were knocked out. Black globe cameras hung, cracked and jagged as breakfast eggs. The low hiss of cars on the main road fell until the only sounds were the estate. The shuffle of feet at his rear. Hoots and whistles, car horns and screams that crept a thin line between expressions of play and pain.

He was being led into probable danger, only there was no alternative. He lowered the knife to a less visible position.

An old, decrepit block where another steep incline led toward the underground car park. The few windows in nearby blocks were boarded, or no more than gaping rectangular holes. Many were bricked up. Flats had bigger holes where doors should have been, outlines of burned and broken frames. There were no lights in the car park beyond, a steel shutter pulled to the ground, lying twisted on concrete, a broken corpse. Some kid waited meters away from the dereliction, shoulders hunched, shivering. He heard them, rounded on Nesta, eyes lit up.

"Ra, Ness, Ra, wait up. Got a piece?"

"Later. Stuff to do."

"Ah come family, a little somethin . . ."

The tiny youth wheezed in Nesta's face, crowding him, ignoring Markriss. His face was murky, eyes underlined with crusted dirt. A rotten smell rose from his body, the damp musk of a mouse. His chest rattled like dried poppy seed as he breathed, similar to the noise emanating from Yi-Kei Tsoi, although louder, bubbling throughout his pleas until he paused, coughing webbed brown phlegm onto a patch of yellow grass. Markriss looked away. Nesta ignored it. The kid wiped his mouth, unconcerned.

"So what, Ness?"

Silence made Markriss turn and see his former classmate incline his head at the kid. "Sort him, it's fine."

Nesta's boys stepped to one side, completing the transaction with a flurry of hand movements. When it was over, Nesta eyed Markriss, motioning at the car park. They descended, the kid wandering off. Darkness enclosed them. A flicker of sparks; Markriss flinched in anticipation of some trick. It was Nesta's flamethrower lighter providing a rippling circle of luminosity.

There were few cars in the gaping caverns of lockups. Those he saw looked older than the building, decaying skeletons patchworked with rust, picked clean of even the simplest bolt, relics from Dinium's gas-guzzling days. The lockups housed grimy mattresses and bobbled blankets. Silhouettes crouched over fires watching husks of view screens. He wondered how anyone could stand the choking smell of oil, dirt, and sweat in that place. Hot, stifling, an odor of lost hope.

Against his wishes, though he didn't dare say it, Nesta led him farther.

"Can't we just do it here?"

"You want them man to kill you? I'm protectin you, bro."

Their steps, shivering flame, occasional darkness. Sparks, the return of orange light. The etched shadow of Nesta's broad face.

"Why'd you hurt her? What did she do to you?"

They kept on. Scuffled feet rebounded from crumbling, broken walls until they were everywhere. Feet walked above, behind, and beside them, unrelenting. He could only see Nesta's profile, imagining the contemplative expression he might have found with better light. He'd seen it often enough.

"See that kid? Ashmeed. He got sickness, man. Had it years. You an I both know that shit's easy to treat—there's a Geb of suppressants and painkillers that could help him, even some that could cure it. Thing is, you need money. You need to be privileged. If not you end up like Ashmeed, smoking piahro for pain and killing yourself, all cos of bad air an a sickness that ain't even fatal. It's not right, Mars, you know it's not right, innit?"

A subdued curse of pain as the flamethrower died. Clattering. His lighter, too hot to hold. They were so far inside the car park that distant fires in various lockups helped illuminate their direction. He felt and heard his bike squeak, barely saw the frame.

"What's that got to do with Misty?"

"She wouldn't ever have sickness. There's no way she'd suffer without medicine."

"That's not her fault!"

Anger warmed him. Strangely, he was grateful to Nesta for reigniting it, shedding light on his fear, forcing it to fall back. A shuffle, a halting scrape. Nesta stopped.

"I know, Mars, you're right. I was wrong to take my shit out on her. Wait a minute."

He was only gone a few seconds, yet Markriss feared he might go insane in near dark, blind, wondering at his agreement. If Nesta knew he was wrong, why fight? More sporadic fumbling, a switch clicked, louder than he'd thought possible. Harsh white light flooded the lockup from a single rectangular lamp fixed in the left-hand corner of the unit. The lockup itself was greasy and fairly empty. One single mattress without a blanket or sheets, a series of oily tools laid in an interestingly neat row beyond the makeshift, thin bed. Various lengths of wire coiled into lazy circles like snakes escaping the sun. Nothing else. He noted a small rectangular window on the back wall just above the mattress, covered by a mesh of metal. Negligible light. Markriss was struck by the cleanliness of the lockup in comparison with the others. Privilege indeed.

"We can deal with our business here," Nesta said. "This is mine."

They faced each other. Markriss laid his bike on one side, walking into the damp, confined almost-room, hands limp, unsure what to do. How to start. He'd fought before. Going to the school he did, in the zone he lived, he'd faced off with opponents on many occasions. It was the thought of brawling with a best friend that made him self-conscious, pressured by gravity of choice. He replayed the image of Misty, wide-eyed with pain, head craned upward, hoping it might fuel him.

Nesta also seemed wary. He made slight, unwilling movements that were hardly noticeable, no defensive gestures. Markriss came toward him.

"Why did you say I was right about Misty?"

Nesta blinked. Surprise replaced anger. "What d'you think? You were right. I shouldn't have done it. What d'you want me to say?"

Markriss waited, frowning from harsh light and confusion. "You weren't saying that out there, laughing with your team."

"What, you want me to admit it like some doobs? In front of everyone? It ain got nothin to do with them."

They faced each other off, tense. Markriss's breathing was quick and shallow. He felt his writhing heart.

"Lissen, Mars, we don't have to—"

A preemptive roar, Markriss throwing a wide, arcing punch that connected with Nesta's cheek, knocking his head to one side and propelling him as far as the roughened gray wall. He crouched a moment, catching breath until Markriss swung a hard kick aimed at his stomach. He made an airy *oof* noise and fell to his knees. Markriss stepped back.

"Get up. Fight."

Nesta spat on concrete, a dark coin, heaving phlegm from his throat.

"If I was to fight I'd kill you, Mars. What would your mum think? You don't know me."

"I don't care. Fight."

Another kick to the stomach. Nesta curled on the floor, gasping. This time Markriss stood to one side, waiting until he got to his feet. Nesta tried to look jovial, even though he was hurt and his cheek swelled with an apple shine.

"I'm trying to say, innit. You're right to be angry. It was wrong, but I wanted to, Mars. I was gonna kill her, right in the park."

"Shut up."

Markriss kicked out again, slapping him with his weaker left hand, a blow that sent Nesta reeling onto the mattress holding that cheek, looking up with gleaming eyes. He was high. Maybe the few puffs of the splint had tipped him over the edge. Predatory now, Markriss stamped a foot on his chest, forcing Nesta onto his back, retching and spluttering beneath his sneaker.

"I can't, Mars," he wheezed, a hand on his chest, his voice much like Ashmeed's. "I can't shut up, you're the only one I can tell—"

"Tell your mates. And fight back."

Another punch, a strong right. Blood flew from Nesta's mouth, splattering onto the floor. He spat the excess onto the mattress, thick tendons of red that hung for one moment, stalactite. Nesta laid his bruised cheek not far from the tools, still coughing. Markriss noticed that what he'd mistaken for oil was in fact blood, dried and dark, mostly coating the working ends of each tool. Further patches spotted the concrete, patches he'd first taken for shadows and oil spots, and began to see as something more. Something worse. He stopped, mesmerized by implication. Nesta raised himself to a seated position, mouth streaming with blood that circled his lips, a perpetual messy grin that seemed clownish.

Markriss let his hands fall, seeing the tools, the dark patches.

"You get me now? She wouldn't have been first, not at all. Can't help that, can I? It's different here: Watkiss was a different me, you lot don't know what I do."

"How many did you bring here?" His voice was flat, colorless; Markriss barely heard himself. The closest to seeing Nesta's face was his whirlpool crown.

"Six man."

Nausea, eyes swimming. The stained mattress, the wires, the cold tools, everything became as vicious as the knife he carried. Beyond his thunder of outrage Markriss heard a slight, furtive scratch that became blunt knocking, a thud. Nesta gasped, facing the mesh window.

"Seven," he giggled.

Before Markriss registered, a booted foot slammed against the mesh repeatedly, until a corner gave way and a rush of boots appeared, kicking at the dangling frame, frantic. He erupted into movement, running for his bike and jumping on as the mesh clanged to the floor and Nesta's uncontrolled laughter just about rose above the continuous thump of the road team's boots hitting concrete. Markriss stood, pedaling one-handed, making his tired legs move harder and faster than ever, twisting back on himself to free the knife from his back pocket, crying with the pain of foreign movement. A storm of footsteps battered his ears, over shouts and a wet explosion of artillery spittle splashing his back and ankles. Markriss pushed harder, wretched with fear. A hand flailed against his back. He lashed out with the knife, twisted again, feeling a thud of connection, a yelp of pain and grim satisfaction as he grabbed the handlebars in both palms, concentrating on riding faster.

Though he tried to hold it, the knife clattered to the ground with a sound like receding metallic laughter. Roars of triumph from the boys. Stamping. He kept on through complete darkness, unsure where he was headed, trying to stay away from the fires on each side, punching and kicking whenever someone came near, sprinting with his head down, neck bared, teeth grinding in panic.

A sensation of movement without progress, riding midair. No wind, a still nothing, bathwater warm. The shouts, screams, and ache in his legs fading. His feet moving and breath expelled, nothing registering. Something expanding, somewhere ahead. A swirling glimmer of constellation, pinks, blues, purples. Shifting and turning, closer. A static jewel, similar to Nesta's whirlpool crown yet bright, pretty as morning. Like the wheels of a bike when his brother was alive and they rode single file to play inside a derelict Ark Station, moons ago. Dark as narrow walls, the stench of vaporized concrete and unwashed vagrants, a cocoon-like presence of pervasive night wrapped around his body, pressing his arms tight by his side, lifting.

The bright rectangle of the outside world, streetlights highlighting a coursing flow of street kids pouring into the underground car park, like a thousand seething rats into a drain. Taunts and battle cries. He sprinted full pelt, lost but uncaring, whimpering a vow to take some with him. Above that hopeless, desperate prayer, a bang over one shoulder. Jerking panic. *That's it*, he had time to think. A high-pitched whisper close in his ear, the bike wobbling alarm, a scream from a kid, a thud, and the sibilance of someone unseen calling "Hush," rolling with the momentum of their run. Another bang, echoing, nowhere near him, and still he jumped once more, and swerved.

The road team ducked for cover, or fled for the shelter of abandoned lockups. He emerged into night alongside yet another shot, almost as if he had been fired into the Gunnersbury streets, dust and concrete showering his head. Kids and ragged adults ran in the same direction, scattering across the estate. No one seemed to know what was going on. Ignoring everything, keeping speed, Markriss left the clamor behind, waiting for the final shot that never came, even when he surged past the estate entrance, out toward Iseldown's main street, following signs for Watkiss Town.

Far from that place, a lengthy verge ran parallel to the halting flow of mid-evening traffic. He slowed, pulling over, tired legs unable to rotate, lungs burning his chest. Draped across bicycle handlebars, alive to the hum of vehicles, Markriss watched the grass spin lazy revolutions. He wrenched harsh breath into his cooling body, mouth open until his vision cleared, and he could rise.

4

A length of white cloth is draped across each machine. He can't help thinking they look like shrouds. No burnings, no burials. Just twin, humped objects at rest on either side of the room. His mother waits by a passage wall, gifting strength without her presence. "We should have done this years ago," she says afterward, sitting rigid at the kitchen table.

His day finally arrived. Seven years of dedicated study had brought him to the eve of success, and could be measured by the ticket. A simple rectangle with rounded edges, printed letters, and code numbers that promised so much, in so few words. He read the information as if it might somehow disappear. No matter how many times he looked, each character remained as bold and exciting as the flap of the mailbox and fall of the envelope, almost one week ago:

Markriss Denny: Single
Frm: Western Central St
To: The Ark
Fee: Waived

It rained; it had been raining all day. Dark bands of water keeping the city indoors, fearful of going out and being "washed dirty," as some called it. He'd argued with his mother most of the morning about going out into the downpour, and yet he savored the smell of damp concrete, wet against his tongue, and mist creeping lonely streets. People long spread rumors of water contamination. Sickness spread by microparticles inhaled, perhaps swallowed. Markriss didn't care. He entered the derelict Ark Station a few blocks from his house, picking his way through the weeds and brush that swamped rusting tracks, remembering how he'd lain there as a child. He wandered familiar streets, letting water soak him to the bone in vague hope that he would become born again, a new man rising from the carcass of the student. No more rain. No wind, no prickle of sunshine, nothing of the life he lived. Alone, apart from others dashing from dry spot to dry spot, Markriss surveyed the landscape of his hometown as though enjoying a stroll in summer heights, committing every street sign, building, and alley to memory. Hours later, when he eventually returned, he wrung half a bucket of water from his clothes.

His mother held a small party, inviting old friends, neighbors, and a smattering of college students he remained in contact with. There was the lecturer he'd become attached to, speaking quite loudly in his usual unironed blue shirt. The young Persian lady who wore nothing but black clothes, black lipstick, and painted her eyelids in heavy onyx shadow. The thin, wispy mature student from their writers' circle with round, wire glasses who stared at Markriss without pause and said "Thank you very much" almost too softly to be heard, over and over. The man who sat in a corner, insistent on wearing his E-Lul Metro mask, ignoring all.

No one from Regent's and E-Lul had been invited, not even teachers. He'd heard Nesta sold piahro in crumbling housing blocks, moving through the Gunnersbury underworld with frightening ease. On the few occasions he'd seen Misty she'd been quiet and reflective, a loner who seldom raised her head. Raymeda had become torn between the silence of her cousin and a blossoming political aware-ness. Her studies were discarded in favor of rallies and marches on behalf of the Outsiders, a left-wing organization whose principle aim was the closure of Inner City. The strain proved too much. By the time she realized what she might forfeit and refocused her attentions, it was far too late. Both young women failed their finals, shocking everyone and securing their school-going fates for another two years. They would attend college in the hope of retaking their exams, any chance of entering Inner City over, save by way of menial work. Markriss, just as amazed as the rest of their school, felt sorry for them, though he made no moves to console or help. He'd been running with an older crowd ever since Gunnersbury. Students who were studious, and less prone to lead him toward trouble.

He soon grew bored of his own party, leaving the guests (each as unexciting as the tuna-paste sandwiches his mother made for those who feared spices) and heading for the podroom he'd shared with his brother. He remained on the threshold, staring at their covered sleepers for the last time, feeling that to enter would be to give way to emotion, to swim in a grief Willow's calm mourning never allowed. To vent all the anguish and pain he'd felt when he touched his brother's body and found it cold, more butcher's meat than human being.

A shuffle of feet on stairs and familiar scent of jasmine brought news of his mother's arrival. She kept precious steps away, observing his silent tears. When he left the door to come toward her she hugged him close, both tall as the other now. She buried his head into her collarbone, stroking his neck as though he were a child. At first, when he felt damp in his hair, he thought their roof had leaked again—then caught himself wishing he hadn't been chosen. Perhaps Willow read his mind, for she held him at arm's length, wiping her eyes with the back of a sleeve.

"Are you scared?"

He'd been sitting in the living room of a college friend when the story of Ark soldiers shooting dead a trio of burglars emerged. The incident took place yards from the L1 town he'd been assigned, ironically named Prospect. He'd been avoiding the topic all morning, another reason for his admittedly foolhardy run into a downpour that could possibly make him ill. His mother had bided her time, while he'd opted for cowardice.

"A little . . ."

"Don't be. Everything that could happen there already happens here, you know that. At least you have opportunity. It's almost as if they took all the opportunity with them, hidden inside that building . . ."

He coughed dry laughter, no more than a harsh puff of air at most, guessing it might be the desired response. In that house, humor had died years ago. She squeezed his shoulders as though she'd just remembered the fact, her expression calling for gravity.

"You should take this." She passed something from her hand to his.

When he looked down, Markriss saw a thick black leather book. Gold-embossed title. *The Book of the Ark.* He raised its weight to his eyes. "What is it?"

"A book your father used to love. He was going to take it with him. Obviously, that never happened."

"What's it about?"

"It's not that type of book. It's essays, mantras, meditations. Instructions on how to live inside that place. They'll do you good."

"Thanks, Mum." He kept his eyes low, on bumped leather, caressing lines and creases.

"No matter what happens, don't look back. Do the best you can, but most of all don't dare look back. Just look after yourself. Don't think about me, okay?"

"But—"

"*Markriss.* Don't you dare look back. Right?"

He was crying too hard to free the words. "Right . . . Okay, Mum . . ."

He wiped away tears to find her already striding downstairs, strong back reflecting a thousand questions he wished he'd the nerve to ask. He closed the door on his brother's room.

The last well-wishers left by eleven, and the minibus arrived just past midnight. He wouldn't let his mother carry any of the four suitcases he'd packed, mostly with books and clothes (everything else could be found within his allocated apartment, he'd been told), even though Willow insisted she could manage. It was an hour's drive to a meeting point near Western Central Station, situated in the heart of West Marvey. For the first twenty minutes they were the driver's only passengers, until they picked up a lanky boy and his father somewhere near Taurion. Though they greeted each other cordially, no one said a word for much of the remaining journey. Willow held her son's hand, keeping her face turned toward the window.

The minibus carried them to a small building a block down from the sprawling railway station. It let them out onto the chilly night streets and drove off with Willow, who would stay at a nearby hotel. Shooting forlorn glances at the hoard of bags blocking the sidewalk, they were met by a gray-haired official wearing an unfamiliar E-Lul mask over his mouth and nose that resembled a feral animal's snout. The official informed them they would be spending the night inside the building, in a youth hostel. IDs were checked, bags gathered. Markriss bedded down on the bottom sleeper in a dormitory of fifteen bunk pods, the interiors empty, covering lids closed. Seen that way, the collected machines looked like a colonnade, still and empty, malevolent. After the youth won their coin toss for the upper pod, Markriss made a comment about business being poor. Junior laughed aloud, lit a cigarette, and proclaimed there was no business because the pods were not for rent. E-Lul Corporation owned this building, purchased solely for the purposes of the Excellence Award. Years ago it would have been packed with lucky participants, now . . .

Junior offered Markriss a cigarette. He took it, smoking without pause or thought, saying nothing as he made a pretense of wiring himself into his sleeper. He planned to keep quiet until the morning alarm, and lay with his sleeper open, looking up at the eggshell-smooth underside of Junior's pod, kept awake by memories of old school lessons. He almost felt the glazed surface of touch-screen boards, classrooms stifling despite the rumble of air con, closed windows, and the rare trill of birdsong, which always made them jump and crowd windows for a look. Ms. Haverstock, sitting on the desk, waiting for them to stop and return to their seats. No admonishment, no raised voice, just motionless contemplation.

What's wrong with Miss?

Nothing's wrong with Miss. Haverstock's expression still lake water. *Today we're not doing design tech, today we're going to talk about something you should have learned in Year 5.*

Markriss turning to Nesta, both turning to everyone, faces scrunched. *What?*

Haverstock addressing the class for what felt like hours, allowing time for questions, talking even longer and allowing more time, striding through the rows separating desks. Today she would teach "contemporary history," the facts behind the 1814 Flash War, or War of Light. Four years of military politics, atrocities, the slain. Moving her silver pointer between the class and the view screen—*How many dead?* Arms raised, flapping hands. Nesta's rictus expression, palms flat on his desk, head facing the window. Gum-chewing slow, trying not to be seen.

Markriss flapping harder, hearing his name, found by the pointer. *One hundred million.*

Actually more like one hundred and three, but close. And what was the war's nickname, something short on the tongue?

Another sea of flapping hands, bare branches in wind, fresh green leaves another organic sight they only saw in picture books, or sanctioned parks. People saying, *Don't touch the trees, they're cloned.* Rumors of skin infection, denied by the mayor. Nya's hand bobbing, braids jumping, rainbow sunshine hair, standing on tiptoes. They knew, of course. *The Light.* Three million people killed in a tenth-of-a-second EMP blast sent by one hundred million secularists a mere sea away, all dead. Inner London, far from the global southern seat of power, obliterated. The antispiritualists bested in a swift counter-attack, everything remade anew.

Ms. Haverstock continuing without pause, explaining religious reformation, biblical censorship, and the acceptance of Jesus Christ as a prophet of dualism. Cross-cultural references to Hinduism, Buddhism, Islam, a plethora of Bulan cosmology. *Maat*, as it had been known for millennia in Ancient Kemet. A compromise of a kind.

Dinium, a scarred battleground dotted with derelict buildings and unexploded bombs, barely any children left to wander that new playground. A crater the size of a rural town set deep in the center of the city like a scar. Scientists who'd exploited their knowledge of electromagnetic technology to create bombs tested the earth and told

the world it was unsafe. Some areas better than others, most unin-
habitable. The official military title: the Clear Zone. "The Blin"
coined by the populace before the name was grasped by a media
with no qualms about such morbidity, leaving pessimism to do its
work. "Blin," working-class Dinium slang for a disfigurement, or
wound. The word surviving long after officials and scientists and
politicians died, leaving the problem they'd created intact.

The need for accommodation. Marches, petitions, and inevitable
riots. Soldiers returning home to no housing or jobs, roaming the
streets committing robberies, arson, burglaries, muggings, and rapes.
The dark sky that never returned to its former glory, instead becoming
a permanent, soup-like mist. Rain that burned in those early days,
ripping human skin from flesh like plummeting razor blades. The
homecoming soldiers who caught the worst, turning into hordes of
zombie-gaited vagrants that had to be put down by the authorities.
And still there were more, as if they'd been bred in the darkest corners
of the city; those feral, sickened homeless, too devastated to be
dangerous, never left.

The dawn of 1825 saw an ousted government, a new prime
minister full of hope, the queen promising the war was worth it, new
optimism on the horizon. The land in the city center going for tender,
E-Lul Corporation putting forward plans for a unique construction
to rival the Great Wall of China, the Pyramids, the Aztec temples
and Roman Colosseum of old. Ten miles in length, four wide.
Radiation-proof, powered by the weak light of the sun. Four levels,
each a mile high. Able to house three million, maybe more, provide
work and clean air and drinking water. Indoor parks, thoroughfares,
schools and hospitals, universities. Cinemas, fairgrounds, places of
work, economic centers. The mass of gainful employment generated
by the project's magnitude. Inner City, where the best of the best
could weather the storm until the foul winds of the outside world
had had their day. Prosperity all around, they said.

The Climate Control Law passed by a fearful Eurasian Coalition,
too late to halt low-level radiation sickness. E-Lul Corporation blueprints published in every daily nationwide, from greasy-spoon tabloids
to corporate broadsheets. Tender won. Construction began on April

11, 1830, though it would be fifty years before E-Lul's proposed residents, the saviors of the kingdom, moved in. Some said more people died during the build than were relocated to the Ark once it finally opened. Unlike previous rumors, those particular tales were easily substantiated. An underground worker accidentally pierced the walls of the city's foundation, letting the river free: one hundred people consumed. Tunnels that formed the sewer system regularly collapsed on engineers and workers alike: fifty, two hundred, once three hundred, every six months or so for the span of the eighty-year build. Falling structural beams killed five hundred or more, twice over. Another one hundred lost their lives when a recovered electromagnetic particle bomb destroyed months of construction, killing a crew of night workers. That led to a fault with the electricity on a whole level, which charged everything made of metal: 1,500 instantly electrocuted, some just by drinking from the taps in newly built houses. And then there were the unavoidable on-site accidents, magnified by the size and longevity of the project: faulty tools, bad judgment, lack of experience, overwork. Men and women lost eyes, fingers, toes, arms. A sheet of glass fell from two levels up, killed twenty, injured sixty more. The foreman was relieved to go, grateful the losses hadn't been worse. When his vacancy was posted no one took the job for nearly two months, and his replacement had to be paid triple with complimentary life insurance just to step on-site.

Rumormongers whispered tales about the original visionary architect, Massell Khnemu, committing suicide when he was already an old man, hanging himself from the wooden beams that framed his garage. A Kemetic scientist who worked on the Ark, Harman Wallace, poisoned himself and his female lab assistant. Both men had regrets about their roles in the project, rejecting links with E-Lul after the build. The project was deemed cursed but was still completed with Khnemu's grandson Senenti at the architectural helm some twenty years after his death.

For a time, everything E-Lul promised came to pass. The opening of the Ark was the biggest event in the history of the country, even warranting a rare appearance by the new king. Railway stations and schools transformed into Ark stations. Advertisements lit up televisions, magazines, billboards, cinema tickets, restaurant receipts, banks, and supermarket counters. Dignitaries from around the world attended that first ceremony, and E-Lul-sponsored street parties took place every month of that first entry period. For two years, once a month, trains journeyed back and forth across the pitted bare earth that was the Blin, entering the Ark building and depositing thousands. Then the gates closed, the locks were sealed, and there was silence.

The class had listened, intent, elbows fixed to desks, chins cupped in palms. Even Nesta hunched forward, eyes bright, nonchalance forgotten as Ms. Haverstock strode between desks, clicking through images, using the pointer to emphasize details. The hush when she was finished. Weight.

Markriss rolled over in his pod, tired and red-eyed, dormitory beds cold and silent around him, floorboards creaking with the weight of years. He loaded the sleeper program, dreaming of a lush, green expanse of park. Huge trees lining dark tarmac paths bore leaves bigger than his hands and looked hundreds of years old. Peacocks strutted freely on low-cut grass. Hand-drawn ice cream carts were dotted along the paths, and children laughed in high-pitched squeals as they chased brightly colored balls. His first simulation since Ninka's death. Immersion sweeping through him, Markriss tried not to think about that, only for his brother's voice to echo from somewhere he couldn't find as he turned on the spot, whirling, seeing nothing. Still, Ninka wouldn't quiet, calling out to him, a wordless cry he couldn't decipher coming from everywhere. A reminder of the promise he'd made and kept inside his heart, to honor Ninka by shunning E-Lul and their works for all time, as his mother had. The sting of his eyes caused Markriss to rapidly blink so he could ease them. Betrayal stony in his throat, a light-headed sensation at his forehead that remained until he slept.

They rose at eight, had breakfast by nine, and by nine thirty the parents and children waited in the lobby, visibly nervous. Shared anxieties broke silence. They spoke, not to make polite conversation, only to reassure themselves everything would be fine. The bland official appeared before them, all smiles and congratulations, annoying catchphrases. They ignored his phony jubilation, letting themselves be led to a small dark car with blackened windows like a hearse. Willow balked. The official was at her shoulder in an instant with more smiles, some gentle nudging, and they were in. Doors slammed, twin crunches. The car moved.

Everything had been so low-key up until that point, his first sight of the crowds and cameras and protesters had the effect of being punched. Although they were not the thousands that had besieged the station in the early days, the crowd still numbered over five hundred and would be rounded up to eight on that night's evening news. The car slowed; people were on the roads, sidewalks, signs, rooftops, bus shelters, window ledges, parked cars . . . Anything that could hold their weight. Grateful for tinted windows, Markriss watched people beat fists against the glass in delirium, scream they were sell-outs cursed by Ra, or simply stand as motionless as they could manage in the jostling crowd, attempting to take pictures—of what, nobody knew; glass rendered their cameras useless. All through the onslaught Markriss watched, barely taking a breath, barely feeling Willow's hand on his back rubbing in gentle circles. Beside him, Senior was equally stunned by what he saw. Junior went silent for a time, then suddenly screamed loud, turned beetroot, and apologized immediately.

Eventually, all of them dreading the moment, the car came to a gradual halt. Doors opened and there were hands, a forest of them searching as the driver yelled that they should "leave the vehicle right now!" Senior went first, then Junior, then Markriss himself was pulled into the noise; the colors, the screaming, jeering, shouting, cheering, going off in their ears. Snatches of sentences from hundreds of open mouths. Everything too bright, too noisy. The tinny sound of a band could be heard from somewhere near. The air was a jungle of odors, ranging from cigarette and piahro smoke to hot dogs, sulfur, sweet nuts, perfume, frying onions, alcohol, and vomit.

Markriss stumbled, turning to see his mother flailing between two rows of E-Lul-masked, black-suited men who formed parallel lines from the car doors and beyond. Long-barreled guns drawn, they held the crowd back, saying nothing other than "Keep moving, sir, madam. Please keep moving . . ." He shouted to see if Willow was all right but there was so much noise his voice was lost, and before he could try again his eye was caught by one of the larger protest banners, luminous yellow, screaming: *Inner City Is a Lie—Let Them Stay!*

Nothing. No sound, only a silent movie playing in front of him, people jumping, screaming, punching fists into polluted air, driven by passion Markriss had never seen. That was when he noticed one particular protester bearing a smaller sign: *Today as Yesterday, Tomorrow as Today, Is Truth!*

He looked into the eyes of the young woman with the tiny placard. She wasn't shouting or punching her fist. She was motionless, mouth closed, tears rolling down her cheeks. Raymeda. It was her. Dressed in jeans and bruised sneakers, an open men's overcoat. Markriss's hearing returned just as his neck craned around as far as muscles allowed, when more hands pulled him in another direction, up metal steps and onto a bridge that took them over the heads of the crowd, onto the station platform.

The noise from their new position seemed unbearably louder. Below them, the old, powerful bullet-shaped train stood in wait, a huffing and creaking tired beast, armed guards standing beside each passenger door. On the opposite platform he spotted the tinny brass band he'd heard playing badly from outside the station. Instruments glinting in frail sunlight. Rows of well-to-do spectators sat above the band on specially made grandstands custom-built every year. The E-Lul logo—interlocked Es painted red—was everywhere.

Markriss reached for his mother. Why had Raymeda come when it was too late? Speeches were made by the mayor, their college tutors, even one via videophone from CEO Hanaigh E'lul himself, who wished them both Raspeed and welcomed them into the Ark. Nothing made any impact. He held his mother, searching the crowd, desperate for another glimpse of Raymeda. She was too far outside the main festivities. He had lost her again, this time forever.

He only remembered what was happening when he heard his name called from massive loudspeakers, echoing and rolling thunder. He looked up. Senior was smiling now even as he wept, motioning toward the train, which his son was already approaching. Markriss turned to face his mother. What he saw was devastating. Tears flooded her face, turning her strong features into a reddened, wrinkled mass. Desperate finality shrouded both their auras. The Authority, foremost governing body of the Ark, forbade contact with the outside world by any means possible. Markriss and Willow, like everyone else separated by Inner City walls, would never communicate again, though she would receive a regular portion of his wages as she had when he was a child. Still, Willow found courage enough to clasp him tight, tell him not to worry when he asked about his suitcases, push him away with a kiss and a promise that she would never forget. He promised the same, wondering why she would even think such a thing, and walked, dazzled by the glare of the crowd and flash of cameras, along the platform where an armed guard stood with his gun barrel pointed at his feet, eyes blank behind his mask. Markriss knew what this meant. He gulped and nodded at the guard, who saluted with his free hand. Empowered, Markriss saluted right back, then turned and waved in what he thought was his mother's direction, though it was impossible to tell. The crowd roared. The band played with even more fervor.

Markriss stepped onto the train.

The carriage was much the same as their shared dormitory. Junior lounged with his legs spread across two seats, drinking an ice-cold bottle of beer. They never bothered with proper names, as the young man revealed he was destined for L2, after which they'd never see each other again. The fridge, he told Markriss, was at the far end of the compartment, where the fire extinguishers were usually kept. There were no other passengers.

Markriss capped his beer, grabbed a packet of crisps from a makeshift larder above the fridge, and settled down adjacent to his traveling companion. When the train began to move, they paid the crowd no further attention, both forming false displays of nonchalance. An announcement was made, welcoming the lucky prizewinners. Junior barked more laughter, putting on headphones, closing his eyes, head nodding. Crowds, bands, protesters rolled away as though the outside world had been placed on a town-sized treadmill. Struck by guilt, he tried to see his mother even though Junior told him it wasn't worth it. He was right. The station disappeared from view. Markriss settled in his seat, the leather book Willow had given him resting in his hands.

For all the fuss made about this infamous train ride, the journey didn't last very long. Town after town went by, each filled with further crowds of people lining the dusty trackside, waving or booing depending on the lie of their politics. The farther they progressed, the fewer people. Fewer houses, fewer corporate buildings, until finally mud and soil. A man-made land of desolation. The Blin.

"Ra."

Junior and Markriss swapped nervous glances. Mince-brown earth, an eternal, emptied building site. Occasional fields of lion's-mane sunflowers, thousands of dark iris corollas watching from regulation five-hundred-square-meter patches to the north. No signs of life other than birds, and even they didn't dare land. A glinting block on the arid horizon that grew brighter by the moment. Fifteen minutes later their guard was back, telling the young men that a look from their windows would reward them with a sight few had seen. With the Ark ahead and the train coming toward it at a right angle, it was difficult to catch. Markriss and Junior tossed away casual attitudes, rushing for the train doors. There, they could look beyond the glass, even if they couldn't open any windows.

The Ark was a colossus, far bigger than anything Markriss had ever seen, man- or Ra-made. The closest thing his mind could think of that might compare was the concrete car parks of Regent's Town — even then, that wasn't nearly accurate. The Ark was a mountain range of gray stone built in the center of inhospitable terrain. It was as if a never-ending concrete glacier had fallen from the sky. The sides, though difficult to see, were largely unmarked apart from varied antennae and satellite dishes. The train tracks, a closed zipper on dark material, led right up to the seamless walls. Straining his neck, Markriss saw just how far the building stretched upward. Concrete dominated his vision as though the sky had set solid gray.

They began their approach. Markriss and his traveling companion watched in awe as huge steel gates opened, tearing cracks in formerly seamless skin, exposing metal framework, gigantic hydraulics, and hordes of jumpsuited workers, staring with quiet intent. The gateway seemed to go on for miles above their heads, yet there were still miles more of flat, unmarked surface beyond, everything growing ever larger. Steam rose. The carriage grew dark as it crept beneath the shadow of the Ark. Their guard switched on lights from some master control, and they stuttered fitfully into life. Markriss and Junior looked at each other from opposite sides of the carriage for the last time, apprehension quieting joy. It was real. They were here.

The train came to an unsure halt. More steam billowed, low and lazy mist. Sounds echoed and bounced from walls, assaulting their ears with an aural sensation that would become normal within months. A jumpsuited individual opened the train door and introduced himself, though Markriss didn't catch his name. He was too busy feeding curiosity to notice Junior being told to stay aboard, too busy to say goodbye and wish him well, or notice the gift from his mother, *The Book of the Ark*, forgotten on the seat behind him. Later, far too late, he would remember, and the shame would last him years. It prized his mouth shut, made escaping words stutter, gave his dreams the flavor of liquescent nightmares. At the time, Markriss scanned everything with a voyeur's greed. He was guided into an area the size of three aircraft hangars, looking over his shoulder to see the huge gates closing, the pale sun caught almost dead center, a flap of wings from some unrecognizable bird flying to an unknown destination. Nothing of Western Central, Marvey, or anywhere else lay in sight beyond the gates. Only the Blin, that lifeless barrier between two worlds.

While his attention was diverted, more men in jumpsuits separated his former carriage from the train. It stood isolated, sideways on, one row of windows facing him. Moving back to gain perspective, he saw that it had been maneuvered into some kind of vehicular lift. As he watched, machinery clunked into life, hoisting the carriage high, destined for L2. He caught a glimpse of Junior's bloodless face and shocked bright eyes at the train window before the young man saw him, ducking away. The gates shut with a noise like the largest prison doors known to man. Fear struck Markriss. He came to a true understanding of finality.

"Markriss . . . Markriss . . ." First Jumpsuit was back, gray hair flopping over eyes, pulling at his elbow with gentle assistance, smiling at his wonder. "Welcome to the gateway. Please have your ID ready for inspection. If you'd like to walk this way . . ."

After, there was nothing but compliance.

5

The third time it happened was the last.

17 October 2020

6

The alarm gave Markriss a jolt he blamed on his body clock at first, until he recognized the beeping. He disengaged the covering, hit stop, knocking the lightweight melatonin bottle over in the same movement, yawning as he wiped his eyes, and stepped from the sleeper before he had time to think. The tiled floor against his feet accelerated his waking state. He made for the bathroom without slippers, relishing cold. Markriss passed the living room window, fully aware of turning his head, unable to look. Feeling only partial shame.

He ignored the manual switch that controlled his ceiling Lites, normally set to his favored cloud-and-blue-sky simulation, entered the bathroom, and turned the dial on his power shower, anticipating nothing until he walked into the cubicle with a sigh, cold water touching his skin. Soon he stood beneath a fierce cascade that slowed to a feeble trickle after exactly eight minutes. He got out and, on a whim, shaved his chin bare. He found a large towel and dried himself, wrapping it around his waist while he moved toward the kitchen.

His cereal bowl was full when he wandered into the living room. The room was consumed by dark, although empty enough to cross without banging a limb against any furniture. A sofa, an easy chair, a small coffee table. A VS and music center embedded in a far wall. The allocation was featureless apart from those few items. There was next to no sign that anyone lived there at all.

He crossed the expansive living room floor, hearing dogs bark on the streets below. Rustles and the clatter of materials nosed or tugged. Scavenging, no doubt. Farther away, the high-pitched sound of an alarm echoed, faint as the drip of a tap, equally relentless. He listened, hoping the sounds would cease. When they did not, he shook his head. Markriss approached the window, pushing a button. Nothing. Cursing, he pulled at the curtains until they came apart in angry jerks, revealing more tiles, a ledge. Of course, the mainline power was cut. He'd forgotten for a moment. No neural connection or peripherals, backup generators only powering housing essentials, connection considered a luxury in his zone. He leaned forward, raising himself to take a first look outside.

The riot had only lasted a night, but the damage was extensive. Block after block of mayhem lay beneath him. His apartment allocation was on the fifteenth floor, giving an unobstructed view of the surrounding area. His adopted town was demon ugly. Smoke rose from numerous places. Cars and trucks were flipped upside down like bugs left to die. Shop windows were smashed, while in others fitful lights strobed beneath passing clouds of smoke. He tried to convince himself they gave the town a magical glow. It looked more like the end of the world.

There had been a football game, the winning supporters deciding to have an impromptu party on Prospect Road. First the people gathered, dancing to music, women hitching skirts to thighs and bending low, scuffing behinds on sidewalks. Men yelled and drank more beer, more tequila, throwing empty bottles and cans against walls, grabbing the partners they desired, moving with them. Someone climbed a road sign, shaking it hard enough to bend. The crowd pummeled the sign into pieces before throwing them at the nearest grocery store window. When glass broke, people surged inside, eager to steal. Others fought.

Markriss and Chileshe Lusu had watched the rioters burn and loot, trying to reassure each other they wouldn't be killed. Although Prospect Towers gave relative comfort, it also made them an easy target for the less fortunate. There had been riots where people in the Towers had been murdered in order to appease jealous anger.

Tied up, burned, beaten, throats cut. Since those days, extra measures were taken and residential security was tightened to an almost frustrating degree, yet Markriss never quite fooled himself into feeling safe.

They had frozen by his window, watching the crowd spread through shadowed streets, joining friends and family from nearby blocks. It seemed as though every back alley and main road was filled with people, screams, the sound of everything breaking at once. In the confines of their level, noises echoed and bounced to find them. Soon they hugged in fear, Chileshe shivering beneath him like an injured bird. She was an earnest young woman, Lotse by descent, a photographer for *Ark Light*, though she refused to record what they saw. They ate, drank, and talked until half past three, when the riots moved from their block. Chileshe left for her own allocation. He remained at the window for another half hour before retiring to bed.

Markriss ate his cereal, watching dogs lope through spilled rubbish and broken glass like conquerors, before returning his bowl to the kitchen, getting dressed for work. He left the allocation, locked the door, and made for the lift; pressed the call button, which stuck, ejecting itself five seconds later. The corridor, smooth and lifeless, a series of identical cloned doors spread into near distance. He raised his chin to the blank square above the lift doors, fingers working by his sides, unable to help stealing a look at Chileshe's locked door, wondering if she was awake, whether she'd even slept. The steel doors remained shut, firm and serious as pursed lips. He remembered—the power—and sighed, expelling pent-up tension. He tried the stairs instead.

The rioters had smashed the lobby windows, which had been specially designed so a metal shutter fell when that happened. A miniature lake of congealed blood lay just by the main entrance doors, reflecting a shallow glimmer of light, almost beautiful. Someone had apparently got caught beneath the security precaution and been killed, or at least maimed. Markriss expected Pious, their friendly security guard, to be there poised and watchful, his usual state, only the gray plastic reception desk stood empty. Stilling apprehension, he walked past the booth and into artificial Day-Lite. Quick pain as his eyes adjusted.

It was useless waiting for the 8:30 light railway. There had been no Corps presence during the riot, the crowd allowed to run themselves ragged as long as they kept their violence within the Poor Quarter. That meant there was a barricade. He pulled his ID from his wallet, kept it hidden in his palm, deciding to walk. The power would surely be on in the next town.

He followed glistening tram tracks eastward, stepping between thin metal and the intermittent yellow stripes marking the center of the road, attempting to mix a calm manner with a high state of alert. The deserted high street lay before him, the road beneath his feet speckled gray like rare eggshell; the blocks uniform grids of retail space made up of minimarts, tic stores, charity shops, homestyle restaurants, bakeries, clothing stores, street-food shacks, and discount perfumeries, each a broken, looted skeleton. The sight was frightening enough to make him wish he'd brought a kitchen knife or some other weapon, though he'd be equally scared to use either. He ignored the dogs padding toward him at first, then away when he shouted. He turned a blind eye to the vagrants and winos scrabbling in overturned bins with the animals. He pretended not to read spray-painted graffiti on metal shutters, Outsider slogans ranging from the comical (*We've Been E-Lulled*) to the commonplace (*Inner City Is a Lie—Let Us Go!*). Markriss kept his head straight, his functioning, observational brain buried in proverbial earth; it would be of no use. Although the power was off, and the sky simulation with it, Day-Lites grew strong enough for him to see the destruction in more detail. It sickened him to notice prone bodies every now and then. He squinted into bright Lites a mile above, moving faster, fearful of his own streets.

There was Mr. and Mrs. Lapido's grocery store, a trail of crushed fruits and spilled vegetables halfway across the gray road. A discount off-license raided beyond belief, fluorescent sign still blinking, awarding split-second flashes of empty shelves and broken glass and strewn liquid. Farther on, a digital VS lay with an iron bar driven through the screen. As Markriss passed the electrical store it had been looted from, he saw sparking loose cables and smelled the sting of ozone. He took careful note of the red fluorescent sign above the high street temple, one of the only buildings untouched. Fresh flowers were laid on the pavement outside its scorched wooden doors.

These were places he had known and owners he'd grown to recognize as members of his community. He'd seen other riots, living as close to the Poor Quarter as he did, though none had changed his landscape to such a terrifying degree.

He stopped. A faraway sound, the angry roar of bees. He tried guessing the origin, as that would reveal how far he had to walk until he reached the barricade. He craned his neck in the direction of the sound. Five blocks or so north, perhaps. Markriss pushed his hands in his pockets and continued to walk.

Electric scooters were the only sanctioned form of personal L1 transportation. Other than those, the Authority allowed public trams and taxis. Bikes could be rented from terminals found all over the city that also kept them charged, known to locals as "scooter stands." Ark residents rich enough could afford a bike of their own, or if they were lucky, the company they worked for provided one. Markriss had once counted himself among that number until the bike was stolen. His employer's insurance replaced that scooter, yet it too was stolen, and the one after that. He turned the next scooter down, resigning himself to catching the morning tram.

Higher levels were rumored to have access to double-decker trams, high-speed bikes, electric cars. Markriss never participated in upper-level conversations, often forcing the idea from his mind. What was the point? He'd never know.

The ten-minute walk led into Willington, located on the far edge of Prospect. He knew he was reaching the boundaries of last night's disorder when he saw Corps soldiers lined behind barricades with rifles, attack dogs, and assault vehicles. They twitched as he came closer, ashamed at failing to keep their composure iron rigid. Guilt flecked every eye. Markriss made for one standing by a lone computer terminal that looked highly out of place in the middle of a usually busy street. He handed over his ID, laying his palm against the touch screen, mute as the soldier swiped, checking the seven-digit code and his details. A brutal nod. The group of lower-ranked men pushed the barricade open and Markriss stepped into Willington.

There wasn't much difference between the towns, save the fact there were fewer allocation blocks and less devastation on this side of the barricade. The miniature mall before him stood untouched, early shoppers attempting to go about daily business and ignore the soldiers. Kids pointed in glee before they were herded away by parents. Shopworkers slowed and sometimes stopped near enough to get a view, far enough from any potential action. The LRS stop was alive with gossip, everyone talking about how scared they'd been, the animal behavior they witnessed, what the news anchorman said about Prospect. It was difficult not to be ashamed. Markriss didn't say anything, because he already knew it was useless. The Y arrived, four black-and-yellow carriages, a lumbering queen bee devoid of wings, metallic wheels whining against tracks. He stepped on, palming his ID over the reader at the ticket barrier's miniature sliding doors, easing past fellow commuters as the doors fell back, taking the first empty seat he found.

Warmth, sleep-tinged chatter. Rows of black padded double benches forced those not reading slides to stare in the direction of the entrance. Some wore medis—meditation visors—eyes made blind by plastic strips that wrapped around each temple, blue light above each ear growing brighter, fading. Medis were in effect portable pods, all the rage since E-Lul launched them the previous year. Above his head, a stunning brunette silently implored commuters to use Yukon deodorant for everyday freshness, ignored by most of the swaying people. Markriss stared out of the window, tugged by insistent fatigue. His eyes closed. The tram jerked around a corner, woke him. Before long the rocking became rhythmic, lulling him into sleep.

He dreamed himself in a doctor's consulting room, sitting up on a pod completely naked. He was alone. A nameplate on the small imitation-wood desk said *R. A. Amunda*, the name meaning nothing to him. A drip in his arm trailed upward, connecting with a bottle that contained a purple fluid. Silver wire pierced the skin on his chest, protruding outward by an inch. Markriss felt horror the first time he saw it, although he was vaguely aware of dreaming the past. It hadn't hurt back then. He relaxed. Each beat of his heart was matched by a computerized beep, and there was no indication of machinery until he heard a hiss, a slight sigh.

The large panel in front of him slid open to reveal some kind of robot. Small and rectangular, it was attached to the wall by a metal track. As the track extended and the robot drew nearer he saw syringes filled with more unrecognizable liquid, coming closer, ever closer. The computerized beeps grew rapid. He tried to get away from the pod and realized metal clamps held his hands and feet. He struggled, fought, screamed. The syringes came closer, touching the skin of his arm, a puncturing pin entering a balloon . . .

"You all right? Mate? Mate, you all right?"

He opened his eyes. The man seated next to him was poking his arm with a pen. He blinked. Everybody was looking. He saw their thoughts as clearly as the memory of last night's fighting. Trouble. They smelled Outer City all over him. He nodded at his seating companion, moving slightly toward the aisle.

"Yeah, thanks, just drifted off. Are we at 1322?"

"Two stops."

The man watched Markriss, curious. He ignored him, turning his attention out of the window. In time other passengers did the same.

After years of struggling with insomnia as a child, sleep, something he'd grown to relish during his time inside the Ark, had once again become an apprehensive part of his daily existence. Every night he lay in bed waiting to be greeted with vivid accounts of his life before Inner City. Sometimes he dreamed—as he had just moments ago— of events that had already happened. Willow reaching for him, Nesta's giggles, or Raymeda's expression of pain beneath the shadow of her placard.

On other nights he felt a strange tug, like the drop of his tower-block lift, a slow descent. He remembered the feeling. Those were moments he feared most, phantom voices in his ears, a suspension of dream and reality. He couldn't breathe, couldn't move, and smelled dangerous miasma. When he struggled awake it was difficult to erase thoughts that these occurrences had happened before, in childhood.

He reached his destination, a monolithic, flat glass building situated opposite the LRS stop. He stood on the sidewalk as the tram lurched unsteadily onward, as if unsure of its way. It was the same each day. He doubted whether it would change.

Soon after his arrival in the Ark seven years before, Markriss had started what the officials termed his "granted vocation." Proficiency in English had gotten him through college and university with grades high enough for the Excellence Award panelists. Careful grooming by lecturers in his final year had given Markriss the jump over his fellow students.

He wanted to write. It was all he'd ever wanted, although he hadn't known it until he grew older. Ancient history, contemporary, neither mattered to him. Seeing, thinking, writing. That was everything.

Thoughts of being a journalist were exciting until he spent his first day in the *Ark Light* offices. There, he'd been told his job was not to discover and report news, as he'd wished, but to transcribe prewritten information into an "exciting and believable format," as his editor, Willis Bracken, put it. Bracken had expressed no qualms when he saw Markriss's disbelief. None of the other writers seemed to mind. Most had well-paying jobs, better than they'd ever get outside. A small price to pay for relative luxury.

Seven years ago, when he'd started, there were few riots, so it became easy to embellish stories about the outside world's pollution levels, crime, and poverty. Most were syndicated to Outer City newspapers, and Markriss saw just how much of what he'd grown up reading was fabricated. Against better judgment, aided by the threat of breaching his contract, he began to do the same. *Ark Light* and its digital VS siblings, *Ark 1* through 8, were the window on a world beyond Inner City walls, a view painstakingly drawn by thousands of people who had no more idea of what was going on than anyone else. When the first Prospect riot took place during his second year inside, he watched his colleagues paint horror so biased he almost turned and left immediately. Though there had been no deaths, *Ark Light* said there were three. No soldiers were hurt, and yet the paper said one had been beaten almost to death. Markriss figuratively threw up his hands. What choice did he have? Return to Regent's Town? And so he too wrote many a lie, none as large as the latter, all equally untrue.

The *Ark Light* building had no markings or proclamation. A pole jutting out at ground level waved a red flag bearing the numbers

1322 in yellow. The windows there and on the upper floors were
darkened by tinted glass. Markriss lifted his head upward. Way beyond
the roof, blue-sky Lite simulation halted further curiosity and a view
of the metal ceiling beyond. After a quick look from left to right for
oncoming trams, he crossed the dappled road and walked through
the entrance.

He passed swiftly through armed security guards in the lobby,
who paid his ID twice the usual attention, and moved into the lift,
asking for the seventh floor. When it settled and the doors opened,
he almost wanted to turn around and go right back, get the LRS
home, stay there until . . . He didn't know what. He was only sure
he couldn't take seven and a half hours in the building. That was a
slow, meaningless death.

He found his feet taking his body through the maze of partitioned
eight-by-ten cubicles, toward his own computer and desk, his makeshift office. His mouth saying hello, his head nodding with feigned
enthusiasm, avoiding gossip and whispers of how the riots happened
in his zone, how brave he was to come in. Head straight, he made
for his cubicle praying nobody would stop him to ask his opinion,
nobody would force him to lie. Opinions were worthless, nowhere
more so than inside this very building, where their point of view was
a distant whim controlled by higher bodies. He stepped across the
office floor with the speed of a sleepwalker. Reached his work space
and fell into his chair, slumping onto the desk. Muscles sagged until
he heard her. He was bolt upright, alert and listening.

There. A vision of their office, angel of the seventh floor. Keshni
Roberts moved across the aisles with a fluid, confident stride of
understated beauty and natural poise. Since the day she walked
through those doors, a month ago, he'd been in awe. After seeing the
indifferent way she dealt with the handsome young men of that
building, she'd achieved iconic status. They'd become distant friends
of mere hellos and nods; much as he admired her, Markriss was
perfectly aware he'd never express how he felt. She was too good for
him. It would never happen. All that left him with, all he had to
replace that space she might have occupied in his life, was the vision
of her in reality and his dreams.

She was taller than him, by only an inch. Her body was lithe and athletic. Not that she was shapeless; some days she wore minis and figure-hugging tops. Her features were elegant and lovely, her skin dotted with constellation freckles, eyes green with hazel flecks. A former North Marvey resident, Keshni didn't talk to most people and seemed concerned with nothing other than the job. She avoided men, and only spoke to Markriss when no one was around, all conversation kept safely within the realms of work. Even so, talking with Keshni every day became his only working grace.

She passed his cluttered desk, looking down with that interesting smile. "Morning."

"Hey, Keshni."

"Catch you at break?"

"Sure . . ."

He peered around his cubicle, watching her glide away leaving only the memory of her low, rasping voice. He frowned.

"Looks good, don't she?"

Somayina Ukwu, the skinny Igbo arts editor with a head that seemed too large for his pencillike neck, had risen from his cubicle much like Markriss. His eyes were bright and brown, glistening with good health. His office space was neat and almost empty apart from his computer, phone, a desk-mounted Lite-box, some photos and box files. He watched Keshni go for her own cube with a look of fiendish joy.

"How come she only says mornin to you?"

Markriss shrugged. "Dunno. I'm not sure why she does anything."

Somayina hardly listened. "Yeah, well, one day I'm gonna be with her, believe me . . ."

His tongue flicked over his lips, hands rubbing in appreciation. Every man in the office said as much, while Markriss kept his desires very much to himself.

"You don't think so? Watch, my friend . . ."

"When I see it, I'll think so."

Markriss smiled at the loud burst of laughter exploding from behind thin walls, and turned to perform the task he'd been avoiding—reaching around his Lite-box, switching on his E-Lul, and looking at his in tray, set beneath the photo of his mother and brother. He turned his eyes from them. Too much, especially today. When he saw his assigned story, he was unable to control himself and groaned aloud, collapsing on the keyboard. Sympathizing with Markriss, it beeped outrage.

"Got the riot? Wondered which lucky sod would be lumbered with that," he heard from behind the wall, recognizing Somayina's pleasure.

He was right, although reporting was something Markriss might have relished, had "reporting" been even close to what Bracken had in mind. He settled in his seat, finding the optimum position, sighing as he worked hard to keep his body upright and thoughts positive. "How to make this good," he muttered, not caring whether he was heard. "How to make it flow." He scanned the brief once for overall intent, and then read it again more carefully, letting his fingers rest lightly on the keys. As he began to type he breathed in through his nose and out through the mouth, allowing his mind to drift and thoughts of Keshni Roberts to become the focus for his easily distracted mind.

7

He finished by lunch, deciding to go for a celebratory smoke before he hit the canteen. At Markriss's regular spot, a roof garden on the fifth floor, Somayina chatted with two techs from the design department while Keshni smoked by herself alongside an expanse of imitation potted plants. Chileshe wasn't there. Markriss was disappointed. His Prospect Tower neighbor usually puffed in a corner, amusing fellow workers with raucous jokes by that time of the day. He kept searching the roof, attempting to hide his displeasure. She'd more than likely stayed off work, as he'd suspected.

The view took in a crisscross of busy blocks and roads progressing in large squares. Nothing but tall buildings of glass and steel, takeouts and sandwich shops, suited men and women. If they closed their eyes it was easy to imagine they lived in the real, outer world—there were e-engines, strident voices of manual laborers, even manic screams of schoolkids carrying on still air. Eyes open, the simulated sky wasn't ideal, though still better than nothing and certainly healthier than the outside haze. On the roof itself, fake plants in giant terra-cotta pots gave the space the feel of a tropical greenhouse. There were benches and even a table with an umbrella attached, which became the butt of many jokes, seeing as it never rained.

Markriss joined the men and gave the beautiful journalist some space, especially in front of the guys. She was looking over the busy streets, expressionless. He didn't join the conversation, which seemed to have been going for some time, instead sitting on the edge of a wall a few meters away. It didn't take long for Somayina to notice.

"Mars, you all right? You look well tired."

He offered a weak smile. "Not much chance for sleep last night, but yeah, I'm fine. Got about two hours before I had to get up."

"That ain't right," Somayina insisted, warming up. "A man's supposed to get a good eight hours. If they don't sort them riots, you'll never get peace, know what I'm sayin?"

"Looks like it sorted itself from what I saw. The Corps got it sealed off and everything."

Somayina's face tightened, ready to argue. Markriss swore, lips tense and hardly moving—he'd risked being baited into another lengthy debate. Something inside him groaned. This could go on far longer than his hour lunch break.

"Yeah, but I watched the news, and this guy reckons there's gonna be more trouble tonight—"

Everyone looked at Somayina. From the other side of the roof even Keshni watched, a rare, full smile in place. Somayina opened his mouth in query before he caught himself, beginning to laugh.

"Damn! Got so used to it I fooled myself!"

They laughed. Markriss tried joining in, mirth lodged inside his chest, a bad cold. One clause in their contract was an NDA. If the contract was breached, their privileges were taken away and they were sent to live on the ground with the manual workers, most of whom became rioters after enduring such poor living conditions. Employment was difficult, near enough impossible, to find: in the Ark, it was one man, one job. Welfare didn't exist. Unemployment was a stone's throw from the vagrants Markriss had witnessed that very morning. Still, Somayina and the men he didn't know laughed as though there was really humor in their predicament.

"Well, it doesn't matter," he said through a cloud of smoke and heaving after-chuckles. "I'm having trouble sleeping even when there aren't riots. I don't get it. I've never had insomnia, now I spend hours tossing and turning . . . I've tried melatonin, lavender, sleeping pills, everything . . ."

It was ridiculous to lie, Markriss knew, still he saw no reason to admit how long he'd been suffering, or that he refused to access pod simulations. They might easily think him mad. It happened, a modern, enlarged version of cabin fever brought on by vitamin D deficiency and light deprivation, mostly affecting the poor, who were unable to afford Lite-boxes or home simulators. The condition, circadian dysrhythmia, was tentatively nicknamed "interior trauma syndrome" by open-minded doctors, ITS by everyone else.

"Sure you aren't just stressed?" Abi, an Omani design tech, eyed him. "Maybe you need a break."

"Reckon he should grab himself a copy of that poverty tome, *The Book of the Ark*, right? Have you seen that crap? If that don't send a man to sleep, nothing will . . ."

They roared laughter along with Somayina, who seemed to think his dire humor a great deal funnier than the others. Markriss shrugged the attempt off, unsmiling, pretending he hadn't spoken.

"Well, I don't feel too stressed . . ."

Unspoken fear of ITS drove them to silence, murmuring defeat as Markriss pocketed his vape. A whiff of familiar scent. His head lifted. Keshni stood just beyond their unconscious circle. Crinkles of laughter traced her lips, and her blank-eyed stare was detached. They narrowed as if she was looking at a distant point far beyond the roof, perhaps far into the future. Her proximity clearly made the men uncomfortable, though she seemed not to notice, or even mind; either way, she ignored them as usual. They watched, mouths half open, vapes poised by drying lips.

"Hi."

"Hey. How . . . how are you doing?" Markriss found himself stammering.

"Fine, thank you, just fine. I hope you don't mind, but I was listening."

"No, not at all, we don't mind, do we?"

Neither Somayina nor any of the techs bothered with an answer, which was fortunate as Keshni refused them any attention.

"If you don't mind me saying, it sounds like you have problems with your sleeper." Her voice caused his shoulders to fall, the muscles in his neck and back to unwind. "It can be the cause of insomnia, so I've heard. You should try adjusting your settings, loading new programs. That's if you haven't."

She smiled. He almost wished time would stop so he could analyze every movement of her facial muscles, the curve of her eyelashes, every dark freckle marking a trail his fingertips ached to trace.

"Nah—no." Forcing the correct word from his mouth. "No, I haven't. I wouldn't really know where to start. I'm not that much of a handyman you kno—" Halting, midword. "Do you know where I could find out how to do that?"

She shrugged, a tiny movement. "I could show you. If you don't mind. I'm pretty good with tech, I could come and have a look."

He couldn't hide his amazement, spluttering useless words. "Uh . . . sure . . . When?"

"After work sometime," she said, in a manner indicating they'd enjoyed numerous conversations at a similar friendship level millions of times before. "We could go for a drink or something to eat?"

"Fine . . ." That one word bore the weight of all his unsure emotion, even as his brain forbade him from saying any more, ruining the moment.

"It's a date!"

He looked up, shocked to see Keshni fighting a blush. Gaining courage, looking him in the eye, her smile coy, contained.

"Not a 'date' date, but . . . you know what I mean, right?"

"I know what you mean."

Her nerves gave him strength. Before he could capitalize, she nodded once his way, once more at Somayina and the design techs, turning her body toward the door.

"See you . . ."

"Yeah . . . uh . . . bye . . ."

She was gone a scant moment before the men jumped and slapped palms, jostling Markriss for a reaction. Though they screamed about luck and prana energy, how casual and aloof she was, what had happened was far too strange to thank the ancestors. Still, try as he might, even as he shrugged off Somayina's praise, Markriss found good feeling impossible to deny.

* * *

After the break, his working day normalized. He made a vain attempt at stifling hurt when Keshni ignored him, striding through office aisles with her head high, silencing Somayina's renewed banter with a disdainful sigh. He kept his eyes on the screen, his mind on assignments, wishing he could blinker his nose and ears in the same fashion. It was no use. While writing on mundane subjects like the marriage of an upper-level stockbroker to a wealthy heiress of the same standing, he thought of her. When he finished the report, moving on to the opening of a new library on his level, he wondered if she liked books. Coupled with Keshni's office jaunts, by the end of his working day Markriss was a jangle of nerve endings and confused messages. There were more assignments, though with his pleasure in an empty office dulled, he saw no point staying late watching Keshni clock up overtime. No. He would go home instead and muse over what the hell happened on the roof.

Somayina's cubicle was neat and tidy, not a trace of the puppet-headed young man to be found. He closed his document window, and noticed he'd received a v-mail. Markriss checked the sender. "From: keshni.roberts@arknews.co.uk, 12/10/20, 18:10." He moved his mouse until the little brown hand caressed "play." He double-clicked, sat back.

Keshni appeared on his monitor in front of her own desk, looking into the webcam. "Hi, Markriss," a low whisper, shifting in her seat. "I suppose you're wondering why I'm mailing like this instead of coming over. I just wanted you to know that I'm really looking forward to hanging out, getting to know you—as a friend, of course. In case you've not noticed, I haven't many friends in this place. See you . . ."

She leaned forward, clicking the button ending the recording, turning the screen black. He remained in his seat, reliving the sight of her for at least thirty seconds, telling himself it meant nothing, that her words belied her actions; hoping opposite. He replayed the v-mail four times, with a broad grin he was unable to suppress. Against better judgment, he looked over the partition toward her cubicle on the far side of the office. He just made out her bobbing curly head, the sound of fingers striking computer keys. Even in the throes of work she gave off an air of beauty. He sat down, selected e-mail, typed "I'd like that very much," clicked "send," then grabbed his jacket and walked through the office doors as he heard her computer chime.

All the way down the corridor to the lifts, Markriss wondered if she'd leave and come looking for him. He vacated the building, still half expectant. Faced with bright Lites, he cursed his naivete, telling himself to get a grip even as he spotted the Y tram. A burst of sprint and he caught up, heaved himself aboard.

The barricade was disappointing to see on Prospect Road, upheld by Corps soldiers still checking IDs. A small group stood in line on the Willington side, waiting to be checked in. Worse than the barricade were larger groups opposite the blockade, queuing farther along, waiting to exit. Most were families, young children clinging to parents' legs, staring at soldiers through dull eyes. The children were not dirty, nor did they wear ragged clothes, and yet Markriss found himself riveted. A Corp yards from where he stood argued with a hysterical man demanding to be told when he could cross. His ID was correct, he shouted, he was a law-abiding citizen. This was against human rights. The soldier pushed the man back, raising his rifle butt, while the man's son, no older than six, watched in silence. The man grabbed his boy, fading into the crowd where he became another jostling head, a flash of ill-fitting clothes.

Markriss ignored the families after that.

Going in proved far easier than getting out; the barricade opened to him and others on the Willington side within minutes. During that time, no Prospect families crossed the line. He turned his back on them, taking his ten-minute walk as slow as he dared, while others—all single men—disappeared into side roads and alleyways. Soon, he was alone.

The power remained cut, so the farther he stepped from the barricade the darker the main road became. In response, rioters had lit fires, spacing them four to every block, blooming dark flowers of soot against brick walls. No local community members were in sight, perhaps cowed by the display of brute force at the blockade. The streets waited, bare and simmering. Nothing moved; nothing was heard besides the hum of air con and miles of generators, normally too low to detect. It grew difficult to ignore last night's damage: the broken shop windows and stolen items left smashed on the pavement, the bloodstained walls and bodies.

He stopped, looking up to check the ceiling Lites. Nothing but dark. He turned around, looked behind him. No one. He waited a few more minutes. No one came. Took a last glance, placed his feet wider apart. He leaned his head back, arms outstretched behind his body, open-palmed, looking into the gloom above him. He closed his eyes and imagined gentle wind brushing his skin. The smell, soft and pungent, rich and warm. He tried to recall being struck by thin shards that fell from the sky, making his hands, face, and neck tingle with the sensation of contact, nerves alive and humming. He saw himself walk through Watkiss streets while everyone around him ran by, newspapers over their heads, hoods raised, umbrellas held before them like shields. A game he sometimes played on the Inner City streets, only at night, when he was sure no one could see. He stood in the center of the barren street, eyes shut tight, hands open wide, visualizing being drenched by downpour. He almost felt the drops of rain collect on his tongue, a regular trickle falling from his chin and onto his shoes. He almost remembered.

A sound behind him. He opened his eyes. Someone was coming. He moved past a side street where a row of looted shops trailed away to a vague outline of terraced one- and two-story buildings: the Poor Quarter. It was impossible to see any residents, even as he caught the flicker of orange light in every window: candles, he presumed. In ground-floor houses bonfires were ablaze, sending hyperactive flames dancing across bare brick walls and the black concrete of the street. Smoke became a man-made fog playing tag with obscure corners. There was the high-pitched yet distant sound of children's laughter; no sign of them or anyone else.

Deep into the maze of houses where no fires were lit, Markriss caught a sense of something. Huddling bodies, shadows captured and thrown toward the main road, the faint whisper of many gathering as one. Maybe Somayina had been right, unwittingly. *Ark Light*, in telling a lie, created truth. He walked on, coming across another prone body. Curiosity stirred.

The man resembled a grim mannequin, teeth bared in an expression that could be read as anger or pain. He was fully clothed and almost devoid of violence apart from a tiny bullet hole crusted with dried blood located behind the right ear. The wound reminded him of a worm burrowed into an apple. Only a soldier killed with such precision. Markriss switched sides to see a larger exit hole above the left ear, providing an unobstructed view into the oyster-gray interior of skull. His gaze jerking automatically down the rest of the body in fits of movement, Markriss saw ragged fingers like uncooked sausages torn open with a blunt fork. A halo of blood surrounded them. The dogs had probably been at them.

Stomach convulsing, he left the corpse where it lay, shoes clicking, producing a hollow echo on forlorn streets.

Prospect was far worse than any ghost town, for it harbored an additional nightmare: it was occupied. Moving deeper toward his home block, faster now, reminded of how dangerous his streets were, his ears picked up strange sounds. Shuffling, scraping, a ghostly swish of cloth against concrete. The light tinkle of dislodged glass, the patter of stones. He breathed hard, heart thumping, sweat stinging his eyes. Dogs appeared in ones and twos, standing firm, marking his face with their mouths open, pale tongues dangling. Once again he wished he'd brought some weapon, partly hoping that this wouldn't be his final regret. He decided to jog the last five minutes or so, and almost began when a sudden noise stopped him. The dogs pricked up their ears and vanished with a growl of confusion. Markriss stood to attention, waiting.

The sound grew louder; he realized what it was. Whistling. While he strained to catch the tune, the singing began in earnest, a baritone rolling and bouncing from concrete walls. The powerful voice carried well in the almost-silence. Two verses by the unseen man, detailing the trials of Inner City before spluttering on the words, coughing in loud, sodden bursts. Markriss suppressed a smile. He'd heard that song. Some nights he and Chileshe caught whistled melody drifting through their allocation windows. Only fear had stopped him from recognizing the tune. He'd never seen the whistling singer, though Markriss guessed he was well known and loved by Poor Quarter residents, and there was no doubt this man was one. He stepped onward, sure that he would come to no harm from the whistler-singer at least.

Then the shadow of a man spoke from a cramped alleyway between two shops.

"Don't move, don't you *fuckin* move . . ." The voice was raw, fierce words spat onto the pavement. "You live four blocks away, right? I know. I watch. Run an believe me, I'll bleed you, unnerstan?"

An unmistakable click of metal. Markriss's head moved up and down, yet he couldn't remember thinking the actual word *yes*. Though scant, this was enough to tell that the man was tall and broad, inspiring fear that made him compliant.

"I haven't got tics . . ."

A peel of growling laughter. "Should've known." Emotionless, the voice was a quiet baritone, every word deep, considered. "Should've known that's what you'd think. Typical Ivory you are, didn't take long. Should be ashamed . . ."

Markriss shrank. Ivory—Poor Quarter slang for sellout, traitor. People who lived in high-rise Excellence Award–funded blocks, "Ivory Towers." Him.

"So what? If you don't want to rob me, I've got nothing. You might as well let me go."

"True . . ." A reluctant admittance at best. "Although, supposing I had something to give you?"

Markriss's head grew light. Unease was a razor-sharp pain in his guts, an omen of an embedded knife. "You want to kill me?"

Another roll of deep-throat laughter, a minuscule rendering of thunder, the vocal outside world. "That depends on you, Markriss. That depends on you very much."

The sound of his name being spoken by this rasping, effortless voice was more chilling than his sentence: protest or questions were drowned by fear.

"Heard our singing friend? They call him Sares. Sings like the heavens. They say he's got ITS—nasty condition, you know? On the outside they'd call him mad. Give him drugs to sedate him, or lock him up, but he'd get *treated*. He'd get *looked after*. What does Inner City do? Ignore him. Give him a few tics and let him destroy himself with drink, wipe out everyone around him in turn. Let him infect Poor Quarter people with madness. Let him spread the word; we ain *nothin* . . ."

The voice paused, collecting itself. "He's not the only sick one. There's worse, aren't there? People that live in Ivory Towers, born *of* the poor and made to believe they're different. Separated. Given jobs an privileges, looked on better than the rest, exceptions that prove the rule. People like *you*."

"What d'you want?"

His words exploding before he could grasp them back, push them between his jaws and into the dark pit of his gut. The voice was silent for a moment, laughed again.

"'Today as Yesterday, Tomorrow as Today, Is Truth,'" he said, quoting the slogan with quiet force. "Heard that? I know you have. You'll write that, once and for all, so everyone can see. You're aware of what truth is, Markriss. Write it for us. For your people."

Injustice writhed in his stomach. "It's not that easy! They wouldn't let me live!"

"What makes you think I would if you don't?" At its former level, the voice was free of anger or passion, speaking cold, hard facts. "You haven't got long before I lose patience. You can't have it both ways—you can't live amongst us and write lies. If I don't see changes I promise we'll be meeting again. And I won't be so friendly."

"But I can't do anything!" He was almost in tears, pleading.

"Yes, you can." The empty, monotone conviction even more chilling than the distant click of the knife. "Now go home."

A thin whisper of clothing, the fried pop of trodden glass as the figure became shadow, Markriss twisting on himself like the idling stray dogs at play. Nothing. He was alone on the main road, shivering in disbelief. While he panted fear, regaining his composure, further whistling began to float like the nonexistent breeze, adrift from faraway streets. It was all he could take. Covering his ears, Markriss ran the remaining four blocks, head down, eyes on pounding feet, elbows rigid beneath his temples.

Closer to Prospect Towers, he slowed. By the time he reached the building steps he was still breathing hard, throwing quick glances over his shoulder. Candles were placed in block windows, while a suitcase-sized generator provided enough power for the lobby lights. The mechanical hum was loud as he stepped through boarded doors, over the ghost of blood, toward the concerned faces of Pious and Chileshe. They rose from where they'd been talking, Chileshe hunched over the reception desk, the security guard behind, moving in worried unison.

"Hey, steady, you need a seat . . ." Pious said, Markriss stumbling into their clutches. He threw a strong arm around his shoulders, guiding Markriss across the tiles.

"Markriss? *Markriss?* He's not even hearing me . . ." Chileshe floated somewhere beneath him.

"I can hear you. I'm all right. I don't need to sit down. It's shock, that's all."

They eased him toward the desk, ignoring protests. Though he wouldn't sit, he leaned his tired body against the counter, trying to slow his heart. As he calmed, Markriss told them of the man in the alleyway, unable to extract fear from his voice. Pious, huge and adorned with cuts, along with a bandaged hand that told of his encounters the previous night, ran out with a meter-long bar to find the streets empty. Markriss was too guilt ridden to repeat what the voice had threatened, saying instead that he was accosted and released when the thief learned he had no tics. Pious returned.

"An it looks like I'm working till Day-Lite again," he said. "They're getting ready for more, you can tell."

"Earlier people were saying the Outsiders are going to attack the Corps." Chileshe's voice trembled. Her mouth shut tight.

"They wouldn't take the chance." Pious, in heavyset contrast, was tense and ready.

"Not tonight—one day they might."

Markriss pushed upright. "If that happens we'll be on the front line and you can say goodbye to all this."

"Nice." The complaint in Pious's eyes was difficult to avoid. "An'while you're upstairs sleeping I'll be down here, minding 'all this.'"

"Yeah, sorry." He inhaled deep, let it out. "Look, I think I need to be indoors. I'll come down when I feel a little better."

"Sure, take it easy, Markriss."

He was waved away without a glance, wondering if he'd caused offense, far too tired to care.

"You too, be careful."

Chileshe appeared beside him. "I'll come."

She didn't wait for acceptance, pressing the call button without another word. The doors shut. They rose like soda bubbles.

"What happened to you?"

She wrinkled her nose, pushing up glasses. "What d'you mean?"

"You never came to work."

"Oh! I took the day off, thought I should run off shots, right? Of the riot, you know. I wasn't going out there last night, so . . ."

She broke off into nothing, discarded speech whistling through teeth. He felt as though he was encased in something solid. Words had left him. His body still shook. He watched numbers ascend.

"Wanna see?" Chileshe angled her digicam toward him. "Go on."

She swiped through photos she'd taken with a finger. An old woman, lips caught midpurse, veiled by cigar smoke in the dusk beyond a doorway; kids playing in the relic of old buildings; young men looking into the camera with absorbent eyes: the usual. Chileshe explained the woman was Ila, a nation who offered their first morning smoke to God by blowing into it, thanking the Molder for raising them in health that day. He'd seen it all before, not wanting to look or imagine the lives of people he might have known a lifetime ago, outside. Chileshe swiped, passion making her unaware of his discomfort.

"You should see, Markriss, some houses have window frames so rotten the glass hangs by hinges while kids play beneath it! Can you believe that? There's no one taking care of the kids cos the parents work, you know, and they're rough of course, kids all the same. Funny thing is, I walked with my expensive camera all day and no one even looked! I mean, I didn't go as far as Outsider territory, but I was still in the Poor Quarter and I didn't get robbed, beaten, or raped. The place is a law unto itself, Markriss, it's alive! There's nowhere else in here like it!"

"So," he said, head tipped at the cam, "you gonna show your editor those?"

A teeny smile, hands wrung as she stared at the metal floor. He was reassured by her raised head, the subject changed without comment. Chileshe understood the futility of recording events in that place. The lift slowed; a second later the doors eased open.

Markriss felt a generation had been born, raised, and delivered back to earth in the time since he slammed his front door behind him that morning. He touched cold metal, a hand flat against the door. The pulse of his index finger beat steady affirmation. Chileshe said nothing, simply watching. Her thin, sincere face was ordinary and untended, bearing no makeup, someone with attention focused elsewhere, outside of herself, always on others.

"I hear what you say, but facts are facts," he told her. "We're lucky to be here, in this place. And we're certainly better off than the ones we left outside."

Her flinch spoke, even before she did. "Yeah, *we* are. What about them, down there? Are they?"

The answer lived in each other's eyes. They looked everywhere else, waiting for the moment to pass.

"I'm gonna go," he told her. "Shall I knock by you tomorrow?"

"If the building's still here!"

Her smile faltered when she saw his pained expression, eventually died. Markriss kissed the skin below her ear, avoided the look she gave him, and pushed his ID into the door until the indicator went green. Home. Metal snicked to a close. He switched on lights, crossing the room. Back at the ledge, he stared at the crisscross of roads and blocks, watching the streets for hours, from that place.

Later, inside the sleeper pit, a thin sheet tucked beneath his chin, Markriss listened to the shouts of Poor Quarter residents. Cackled laughter, calls of elation. The wailing cry of women. If night followed its usual pattern, he'd take three melatonin and attempt to find a few hours before the alarm. So he swallowed and waited, even as shouts grew loud and glass broke, showering brittle rain. He stared at the ceiling, trying not to hear or think, hoping for sleep.

8

Waking the next morning, ironhearted, he showered and approached his window to view what was fast becoming familiar. Empty, war-zone streets. Shops blinking the light of amusement arcades. Chest and shoulders shaking, he chuckled relief. Nothing had happened. A young mother and child crossed the street from the Poor Quarter, peering at battered storefronts with all the wonder of viewing relics from a long-forgotten time. She tugged the child as he dawdled. Groups of men boarded broken shop windows along Prospect Road, the routine thud of hammers reverberating until they were all.

He got dressed and ready for work. After collecting Chileshe from her allocation as planned, they rode the lift to the ground floor.

"Last night was a relief." He watched for her reaction, unable to help smiling.

"Yeah, I was thinking I wouldn't be able to sleep, and then *bam*, I was out like a Day-Lite. Must have needed it, all the walking I did." Animation lifted Chileshe's voice, her tiny face focused on the blank metal doors. Strange. She wouldn't even look at him.

He ignored her odd behavior, silence lending him voice, perhaps more than was needed. "I told you they'd be mad to try and attack the Corps. They'll only end up getting themselves killed, they must know that." Out before they could be retracted. Words, his words.

A wince flitted across her face, a bird in flight. "Yeah . . . But

106 ♪ A River Called Time

you saw my pictures. They *do* have a legitimate grievance, even though they're not voicing it right. You really should look. Some conditions down there are really bad—it's gotta be seen to be felt."

She faced him at last, only he didn't want to see. Her mouth a thin line, eyes blinking with concern from behind her glasses.

"I know that, Chileshe. I do know," Markriss said, exuberance gone.

"Course you do."

She turned back to the doors, Markriss resuming his worried vigil. Doors opening, Chileshe stepping through the lobby, him struggling in her wake. Though he promised he wouldn't let her strange air shake his cheer, the walk toward the reception desk was a test in good humor. Pious, a slide-screen held close to his face because he refused to wear glasses, was reading the morning edition of *Ark Light*. Closer, the headline became instantly recognizable—"Prospect Rioters Claim More Lives"—because his subeditor had penned it for his story. His first thought was pleasure. A front-page piece meant he'd be paid especially well.

He remembered the alleyway, his fear. Tried to convince himself the whispering man would realize the report was already written, though it grew difficult to convince himself, especially with Pious's glare.

"Hey, P, how did it go last night?" Feign normality. That was what he'd do—pretend everything was fine.

"Quiet." The guard eyed him with plain distrust. "Lots of noise, not much action. What's the deal with this?" He turned the slide toward him, its thin translucent screen minuscule between massive fingers.

Markriss shrugged. "What d'you mean?"

"This piece about the riots you wrote."

"Like what?"

Pious's glare was jagged and rough. "Like this bit saying many soldiers were injured in the fighting. The only soldiers down here were snipers! And this bit." Pious stabbed a finger at the words, finger thudding screen. "Talking about, 'Prospect rioters made a foolish yet desperate attempt to move their violence into Willington, but were held back by the efforts of our Corps . . .' And here! 'Unfortunately the Corps were forced to shoot and wound a handful of rioters.' That's rubbish! There are dozens of bodies all over the place with bullets in their heads! All those idiotic rioters did was smash up their own shops and streets and now they're dead! Why don't you report that?"

A number of residents entered the lobby, flinching at Pious's raised voice. A man exited the lift, looked into Markriss's eyes, and scuttled out of the building fast.

"Keep your voice down—"

"Why? Everyone knows this stuff ain't true . . ." Pious's knuckles, complete with a dark grassy outcrop of hair, grew white against the mini. "Things are difficult here; I thought you were different—"

Chileshe eased between them. "Okay, I think the block's heard enough. Pious, you know we all have jobs to do, right? Markriss," she said as she turned, "let's go. We're late."

He felt her tug his arm and opened his mouth, unable to think of anything to say. He stumbled backward, flailing.

"You're wrong. You know you're wrong . . ." he wheezed, Chile dragging harder.

Pious's face churned. He colored deep red. "I'm wrong? *I'm wrong*? You should be ashamed!" he bellowed. "People on the out would disown you if they knew what you were doing, you shit!"

An almighty tug. He only knew he was on the street when heat from the Lites warmed his cheek. He looked down. Chileshe's eyes swam.

"You shouldn't have said that."

"But he . . . You know what we have to do . . ."

She was close to weeping.

He felt the need to hug her, fully aware that in doing so, he'd be comforting himself. "That doesn't mean I'm proud. I might hide it. Don't *ever* think I'm proud . . ."

A teardrop, tracing a glittering path along her right cheek. Falling. He relented, embracing her like he had inside his flat when the fighting seemed enough to overwhelm them all.

"Let's get the L. Okay?"

He wiped Chileshe's lone tear, squeezing her shoulders with alert eyes, watching the streets. She nodded once, stiff, gulping back the remains of distress. They walked to the tram stop side by side.

His ruminations, coupled with Chileshe's outpouring, made for a somber parting as they entered 1322. She squeezed his hand after the security check, giving her wry grin.

"You know what my uncle used to say?"

Markriss shook his head.

"He'd tell me, 'If you want to know how significant you are, stamp your foot and see if anything changes.'"

"Thanks, Chileshe, that's real encouraging."

They managed a laugh. He touched her hand again and watched her trail down the corridor, unable to dispel the feeling he had somehow let her down.

"Hi!"

Keshni. Tiny smile, eyes glistening. A denim jacket over a pretty summer dress that made her look like a teenager.

"Hi . . . uh . . . how you doing?" He had to learn to be casual, otherwise fake it.

"Tired as usual. I feel like I'm always tired these days, you know? Like I could sleep at any time."

He laughed, envious. Her eyes and lips made almost exact circles as she remembered.

"Sorry, that was a little thoughtless."

"Don't worry. Shall we go in?"

They smiled together in a manner he'd recall for many hours; her looking up, head leaned to one side, him with hands in his pockets, taking in every detail. She was first to step away, through the swinging glass doors into the office. Markriss followed, thoughts of home, his mystery attacker, Pious, and the riots banished for a short while.

In the weeks that followed, something amazing happened. Not only did he and Keshni really hit it off, a minor miracle by any reckoning, he also managed to get her talking to Chileshe over the course of one lunch break. As dubious as he may have been leading up to their meeting, the women became instant friends. Even though he'd always suspected that Chileshe harbored unvoiced desire for him, he knew an introduction between the two was inevitable. Not long after that, they gathered on the roof garden for lunch. If there were any unrequited feelings, Chileshe handled them with great flair, teasing him like a favorite sister, inviting both to dinner at her allocation as though they were already an item. Keshni was equally amicable, witty, and clever, which made Markriss happy but also scared. He had no idea whether he was reading the signals right, or taking something for granted.

Somayina and the others couldn't understand what had happened. Shocked faces broadcast dismay. Although Chileshe was plain and skinny, she possessed a timid lightheartedness that meant a lot of the office guys found her attractive. Walking the corridors of 1322 with both women was enough to make him the talk of the building. Men he didn't know patted him on the back, giving him the thumbs-up when Chileshe and Keshni weren't looking. Others befriended him, while many wouldn't speak or look his way. Markriss didn't care. Those weeks were his happiest, for a while. He relaxed, feeling at home, and even began to look forward to work.

His only discontent concerned Pious.

On the evening of their heated argument over his report, he returned on the Y with Chile to find the guard missing. A younger, thinner man had replaced him, standing by the reception desk with an eager, nervous grin. Chileshe, still upset, demanded he tell them what happened to Pious. The young man was all eyes, suit a few sizes too large, as though his superiors had given him Pious's uniform along with the job.

"I dunno, nothin! I came to Inner City last week and I got transferred this morning!"

It was no use berating him, so Chileshe took to the lift. Markriss guessed he'd be blamed, although she said nothing. This was what he'd been trying to explain on that dark street faced with the shadow of a man. Truth was negligible power. His earlier doubts about what he'd written washed away in a torrent of relief at not being spirited off. He would never allow himself to end up like Pious, a troublesome memory. If he had to lie to protect himself and aid his continued survival, he would do it with no more qualms.

Chileshe felt the same evidently, for next morning she greeted the new guard with a smile, asking his name. Mannesh Kappaur. The youth seemed strained, though friendlier at her obvious change of heart. Soon, the three were swapping stories as though Pious and his shouted arguments had never existed.

The culmination of the proof that Markriss had been right was a reborn confidence, near impossible to hide. By the time he and Keshni stepped through the reception doors of 1322 and onto the P tram for their dinner "date," he was unable to stop talking about Pious, of Chileshe, even the man from the alley. He was still talking when they left the tram at Chaucer, the shopping and office district not far from their workplace. Pausing to decide which national menu they should sample—eventually opting for Italian—he continued in the same vein as they found a table and sat. He only came to his senses then, realizing there was a vague possibility that unchecked enthusiasm might bore his companion.

She seemed attentive enough, sipping a glass of wine while she ordered, nodding and saying "uh-huh" in the right places. Markriss took a token sip.

"So what d'you think, honestly? Of what I just told you, I mean."

She shrugged, sipping more wine, looking at the table. A bolt of fear. She might not share his views, might not understand . . .

"Well . . . you seem pretty sure of yourself. That's good . . ."

"But?"

"I can't help feeling you're not just asking for my opinion, you're asking for approval. I have the same job as you, Markriss, almost to the letter. Don't get me wrong. I know what you're talking about, but what else are we supposed to do? Write what we like? Journalism doesn't work that way. So do it anyway, get the sack and maybe get thrown out of here? Shouting the odds didn't get that friend of yours anywhere—"

"Exactly!"

Passionate relief, loud enough to make fellow diners look. He sank. Keshni smiled, an adult witnessing a display of childish pleasure.

"That's something else: you worry so much about other people's opinions! Your security friend clearly didn't know what he was dealing with, neither does that crazy guy who attacked you, though to be honest I'm not surprised someone came at you, living where you do. As for Chileshe, she's the only one who *does*, and how does she deal with it? She knuckles down and gets on. Like you should."

Sighing, he lifted his head from the cutlery with a half smile. "How did you get to be so pragmatic?"

"You have to know what you want, Markriss, believe in it with all your heart. I'm not sure you do."

The waiter arrived, thin and detached, expressing low-voiced concern about their failed neural connection. Markriss chose not to listen. Keshni was right. He was uncomfortable with the decision he'd made, to live by Ark rules, while she seemed to find leaving the outside world as natural as thinking. Only when he watched her chastise the waiter for approaching the table when she'd already ordered, restating her request with a hint of accent and impressing the stoic man into an appreciative comment about her mastery of his language, did he form any coherent thoughts about why. Of course she was at ease. Everything about her said she'd originated somewhere that knew nothing of Regent's Town. When he looked at the Ark from her angle, there was no time for remorseful feelings toward people he couldn't possibly save, had nothing in common with. He had to save himself.

He smiled at the waiter, pleased. Ordered food without an accent, ignoring the man's dissatisfaction, and felt good. When he left, Markriss hunched on his forearms.

"So, you've listened to me long enough. What about you? I still don't know anything, not even where you came from."

She flushed, making her sparkle—in his eyes, at least. "I'm not as good at telling stories as you."

"Yeah you are. I've read your articles. Just imagine you're writing a report on yourself."

"Okay . . ." Keshni sat back and closed her eyes, took a deep breath. Even though he didn't want to, it was impossible not to watch her, immersed. Fully. She opened her eyes. The flush was gone. She had a look of business, a look he was used to.

"First I'll tell you about my parents. Is that all right?"

"Sure, start wherever you like."

"It's crazy this story, really it is, and I don't tell it much," she began, looking happy at the prospect. "My mum was a lecturer at Dickens Literary College, you know, in South Marvey?"

He applauded himself, forcing jubilation down in an attempt to concentrate.

"Dad was some IT whiz who worked for a local firm, Globe Computers it was called. Well, Globe wasn't doing well. E-Lul more or less wiped out big competition, then started moving locally, shutting down firms. Before Dad knew what was going on, he was given a year's wages and made redundant. He ran around for a month spending money and tearing his hair out, and then had an idea. Why not launch an Internet dating agency? So, he put all of his redundancy pay into registering and setting up his company and went for it! Findamate.co.uk . . . Shitty name, right? But it was the nineties."

"Wow, that's pretty brave."

"Right? A few years pass, the site's successful, and Dad's doing well for himself. Mum, bless her heart, was struggling. Not financially as such, but she'd spent years studying and then got her job at Dickens straight out of university. Not much time for a social life, eh? She sees my dad's site in one of her women's magazines and thinks, *Why not?* She's nothing to lose. Mum fills in the application, gives her credit card details, and applies . . . Even though she gets confirmation via e-mail from Findamate, three weeks pass without a word. So she finds out the address where Dad works somehow, and drives down, determined to get an apology and her money back. You should see my mum when she's angry! It isn't pretty.

"Thing is, what she didn't realize is Dad knows all about her. From the moment her application came, he'd printed it out and carried it with him, looking at it when he was alone, wondering how he could ask her out on a date. With him. He reckoned the fact he didn't do that kind of stuff all the time made things difficult as opposed to easier. Dad was in his office with Mum's application in front of him, pondering what the hell to do, when guess who comes in with a screaming secretary behind her?"

"Your mum?" Markriss offered, unable to withstand the flow of the tale.

"Who else?" Keshni gave a tiny shrug of the shoulders. "So Mum forces her way into the office demanding to know what's happened to her application and money. Later, she tells me she was surprised to see what a handsome guy this Internet man was, even if she obviously wasn't letting him know that at the time."

"Figures."

"So she's going mad about consumer rights and all that, while Dad just lets her have a go. When she's done he gets rid of the secretary, finally gets my mum to sit down, and shows her the application. He tells her everything. How he didn't want anyone else to see her picture, so he never posted it. How he'd been thinking about her for the past four weeks, trying to pluck up courage. Apparently, Mum got really quiet, which *I* can't imagine for a minute. Out of all the things she thought she'd hear, she never imagined *that*. Dad asks her for a date, she says yes, they go out and like each other, he introduces her to me, we get on, blah blah blah . . ."

"*Whoa* . . ." He was frowning. "Did I miss something? You said he introduced her to you. Weren't you, like, not born yet?"

"Sorry, I forgot to say I'm adopted. Oh, here's our food!"

There was truth in her diversion; the waiter had indeed returned with two steaming plates on a metal tray. He placed them on the table, garnished the food with a sprinkling of ground pepper and Parmesan, tipped his head once, and left. Markriss watched her eat with new understanding, new context. Spearing morsels, Keshni had an amused glint in her eye.

"It's no biggie. Dad loved kids but was too busy with the site to settle down. When he made loads of money he thought what the hell, why not adopt? He could afford it. So he did. It certainly increased his bargaining power with Mum. She thought he was an angel from Ra."

"And how old were you?"

"About three, four."

"Did you have any brothers, sisters?"

"Nope." The forkful of pasta was shoveled inside. She chewed, swallowed. "Just me."

"How did you feel about being adopted? Wasn't it weird for you? Didn't you ever want to meet your real parents?"

"Not really. Dad always made sure I knew all about my natural mum, even though she was single, poor, and could barely look after herself when she had me. I was quite happy growing up with my new parents, so I never saw any reason to find her. We sent a few letters and photos back and forth, left it at that."

He was shaking his head in admiration. "You're so candid. About everything," he said, taking a first mouthful of his own food, widening his eyes. It was good. "And I mean that as a compliment."

"Uh-huh." Keshni concentrated on her plate, barely listening.

Across the table, Markriss looked out of the window in deep thought, slow confusion moving on his face. "But I still don't get what your parents had to do with you being here."

"Oh." Her fork waved, pasta with it. "They don't in a major way—I just love that whole story. It's so romantic! The irony is Dad has always been against E-Lul, especially after they closed down Globe. My mum hated E-Lul and the Ark too. You know, that whole thing about rich person's heaven, poor person's hell. She wrote long essays on the subject, sent petitions to Parliament, went on marches and sat on her arse in the middle of the street, got arrested, the lot. So when I decided to apply for the Excellence Awards they weren't best pleased. They thought it was my teenage way of rebelling. They even offered to pay for me to get in the usual rich way, though I refused. When I look back, I think I *was* rebelling . . . a little . . ." She trailed off, fork dangling by ear.

"Wanna talk about it?"

"Would you mind if I didn't?"

"No problem, no problem at all . . ."

Fog cleared. She was back, blinking. "Sorry. I haven't thought about outside since I got here."

"That's okay. The Ark has a way of making you forget. Believe me."

Keshni said nothing for a moment, moving food around her plate and into her mouth. "So . . . what about you?"

They stared over the table.

"How did *I* get here? I told you, didn't I?"

"No, not that. Your parents. How did they meet?"

Markriss paused, unsure how to tell her he didn't know, deciding to speak truth. He was surprised when she gave a shrug, clearing the last scraps of pasta from her plate.

"Are they still together?"

"No . . . uh . . . well, my dad's dead."

She tensed for a millisecond, relaxing when she saw he wasn't distraught. "I'm sorry to hear that." Head down, eyes on her empty plate.

"It's okay. It happened when I was really young. I suppose it ties in to why I'm here too, when I think about it. My mum was the opposite of your parents. I mean, she knew Inner City was supposed to be bad and all, but she still felt it was better than living outside in a place like Regent's. The Excellence Train used to go past the bottom of my house until people stopped coming and they closed the smaller Ark stations. While it was running, she used to watch with my dad and me too; this was just before my brother was born. I used to be out there with the two of them, resting my head against Mum's stomach so I could feel when the baby kicked."

He managed a grin. Keshni didn't crack a smile. She took his words in with what looked like every ounce of concentration.

"Mum used to go on at Dad about the train. 'It's our only way out,' she'd say. 'You're the only one capable of going. You've gotta get in there and send money back.' Dad tried his best. He wanted to do right by his family. He took supplementary night classes so he'd be ready for the exams and worked nights at a twenty-four-hour service station whenever he could." Markriss sighed. "He never passed. Took those exams three times, never passed once. Mum was encouraging though. She kept saying, 'You can do it, I know you can, you just have to study hard and believe.'

"After the last results came and he'd failed again, Dad got up and told Mum he wasn't worried. He'd try again next time. He gave me a big kiss and went off to work. A couple of hours later, Mum gets a call from the station. Dad put a hose in his exhaust. Two months later, my brother was born."

He stopped, unwilling to talk about Ninka. He stared at the

remainder of his meal, appetite a faint memory. Warm fingers wrapped around his.

"Markriss, that's terrible. I wish I'd never brought it up."

"No, it's okay. I told you, it happened ages ago. I'm over it. That's just another reminder of what I'm doing in here."

She caught sight of her watch. "Oh . . . We should go—if you've finished eating that is. I don't fancy catching the L from your side of town too late. No offense."

"Oh, yeah, sure . . ."

The break of mood was disappointing more than an insult. He hoped it didn't show in his tone. Insomnia was far from his concerns; he wanted to stay with her tiny hand in his until the Ark walls crumbled and the sky became visible once more.

"Do you live far?"

"A few blocks from here . . ." she said, dabbing her mouth with a napkin, left hand raised as the waiter returned. She pulled a face, realizing she was being rude. "The Wiltshire Buildings? Sorry, but we really should get going."

"Sure."

He knew the Wiltshire Buildings. Some of the richest on L1 lived in that neighborhood. South Marvey dwellers in the main, alongside other well-to-do Outer City regions. Writers, doctors, lawyers, and accountants rumored to grasp social mobility on occasion, moving up a level or two by various attainments, so office talk said. He and many of the others had never known anyone who lived there, and so never learned whether the stories were true. Markriss ingested the information, standing, putting on his jacket. No need to worry about leaving midconversation. Time stretched before them, constant as air.

9

Traffic was pretty good despite the time of day. They took the P to the corner of Reinhart Square, trying not to be distracted by screaming kids at the water fountains, then hopped on a Y to Prospect. The tram was jammed full of returning menials. Watching Keshni rush on through the queue to grab a double seat, Markriss could tell she rarely traveled by tram, if ever.

He settled down in the seat, trying not to notice how different passengers were on the Y. The P had been full of suited men and women watching the news on slides fished from their pockets, listening through wireless earpieces. Here, a hulking man in greased fatigues held the hand of a girl Markriss presumed was his daughter; he was possibly a minus-level temp worker, one of the unlucky few assigned to take care of the Ark sewage system, or run maintenance on the gateway. A shaking old man dressed in dark, flowing garments read the paper with difficulty as his head and hands shuddered in opposite directions. A large woman with tiny glasses squeezed herself onto a double seat, near enough drowning a red-haired skater dude beside her, the youth all skin and bones draped in black clothing.

Keshni asked something. He shook himself from his reverie, replaying words he'd heard and not taken in.

"Uh . . . what?"

"I asked if there was anywhere on the outside you wonder about. You've been here a lot longer than me."

He thought it over. "What happened to Burbank Park?"

Keshni winced as though pinched. "That shithole? That's the most memorable place you'd like to know about, in all of Dinium?"

Slighted, he couldn't keep emotion from his reply. "Yeah, why not? I liked the zoo animals when I was a kid, you know . . . the lions and ray birds . . ." Studying his ridged and lined palms, feeling stupid.

"Yeah . . . well, they've closed it since you've been inside. People kept breaking in and it cost too much to replace the animals, so they sent them back to Bulan, so they say. I reckon they shot them. More humane in the long run. Never would have acclimatized to being in the wild."

He looked up. Keshni peered out of her window at the wall of glass-fronted buildings running beside them, smiling, perhaps at the view.

"I liked Summerdale myself . . ." she said. "Dad took me there as a kid. The animals ran free until they enforced Climate Control . . ."

"I went there with my school once, when I was really young."

"Did you like it?" Her expression was controlled, forced neutrality that made him feel odd, and wary.

"Very much."

"I think it's better to let the animals roam. It makes them happy. No use seeing them mope in a cage, right?"

"Completely," he said, staring hard. Keshni turned back to the window. He couldn't stop watching her.

They stepped off the tram outside his building and he led her inside. Mannesh snapped to attention, eyebrows quivering in question. Markriss walked Keshni straight past, on toward the lifts. Upward, silent. In the corridor, still nothing. When he let her into the flat there was a moment where he wasn't sure what she might say; although plush by Regent's Town standards, he guessed it was pretty bottom rung compared to where she lived. He switched on a set on interior Lites so they were bathed in blue and the shadow of clouds. Keshni went straight to the living room window, the panorama of cleaned-up chaos.

"Nice view."

He joined her. Debris and human bodies had been moved from the street so trams could pass and packs of dogs would forage somewhere else. Now that glass was swept, all that remained were the darkened holes of burned-out shops dotted among the stores that had escaped, missing teeth in an otherwise clean mouth. Temple lights turned paving slabs bloodred. Fires, small and fitful, danced in the Poor Quarter.

"Would you like a cup of tea?"

Her eyes were cracked jade. She smiled again. "Thanks, that would be lovely."

After the kettle boiled and he filled two cups, they went into his podroom. Like most inside and out, Markriss used his pod for sleeping, although he'd long pushed an unused single bed into a corner of the room. Keshni approached the gray cocoon, running hands along the smooth surface, peering through the frosted lid. Uncomfortable, he stood back.

"A 12-series." Keshni hunkered down, knees cracking. "Did it come with the flat?"

"Yeah."

"Then it must have been brand new."

"I think so."

He crossed the room, sat on a chair. It squeaked reluctant acceptance. With her back to him, he imagined her frowning at the pod readout in confusion, wondering why it wouldn't do what she wanted. She emitted a soft grunt. Shifted on her feet to improve balance.

"These were top of the line a few years ago. Best design ever, or so E-Lul claimed. Enhanced visual clarity, greater feed comfort, faster crossover . . . the sports car of the range . . ."

"What do you have?"

"A 16-series. Easy to use, nowhere near as smooth. Do you know how much you can get for a secondhand 12?"

"No," he shrugged. She was too busy flipping panels and checking readouts to see him.

"I wouldn't sell though, not for anything. You keep this in good condition and it's like an antique clock. Work for years and bring in tics if you ever need them."

He left the bed to stand beside her, looking at his sleeper like an ancient relic unearthed. "You're really into these things, aren't you?"

"You're not?"

"I just sleep in the damn thing. Most of the time."

"Blame my dad." Monotone, eyes on what she did. "He was always stripping my pod down on a Sunday afternoon, rebuilding the thing. He loved to see what made them go."

She took a band from her pocket and tied back her hair, pressed a button that made the glass cover slide to one side, another revealing a panel of more buttons. The second panel was embedded on a corner of the machine, just beyond the space where his head lay. A display flashed. Keshni pressed a button repeatedly, scrolling through various displays.

"What are you doing?"

"Looking at past sleeps. Checking bodily functions, heart rate, respiration, REM time."

"What does it say?"

She frowned at the panel, punching buttons hard, display lights flashing on her face. "Bodily functions are fine. It's your sleeps that are the problem. This readout says they're being aborted."

He fell silent, drinking tea while Keshni worked, stabbing at the panel with an impatient finger, muttering. Rubbing her forehead, deepening her continuous frown. Markriss imagined her behind her desk, sweating over an article, juggling words between her lips. He could have watched her work forever.

"You've been offline ages. Did you have any problems with the internal feed when they cut power around here?"

"Uh, no." He fidgeted, warmed by shame.

"Then what?"

A look of uncertain query. Did she suspect he'd been messing with his pod?

"Uh, I dunno. I just don't connect. Neurally."

"Ever? So how do you control your allocation?"

Markriss cleared his throat, anticipating her response. "I, uh, I use manual." She was staring, so he continued. "I press switches. Lights, shower, cooker. Everything."

A pause, Keshni thinking. By accessing the astral bodies of their users, pods connected the elemental networks of ethereal bodies to a neural-kinetic system that removed the need for standard, voice-activated tech. This meant any tech in their immediate environment, from the nondescript to the exceptional, was accessed by mere thought. If the user wanted the lights switched on, or a convex heater to fire, they thought it into being and the job was done.

"So that was why the waiter took our verbal order?"

"Uh, yeah. I suppose."

An obscure moment of blankness passed across her face. A brief period of disbelief, or awareness he must be a crank, or perhaps was suffering from the beginnings of ITS. She chose to ignore him, lowering her head to readout level. Soft light bathed her forehead and cheeks.

"You know the story behind these, right?"

"No."

"You never heard how they were made?"

He shook his head.

"Some crazy professor alone in the sticks, a bungalow on Scotland's western peninsula, I think. He wanted to find a cure for his wife's cancer . . ."

Markriss tuned her out. He'd lied again, feeling fine doing so rather than making an attempt to elaborate and build even greater untruths. He'd covered the sleeper pods for a routine article on the latest model, way back when he'd arrived at the Ark. It had been a positive write-up, though some facts were difficult to skirt. Professor Harman Wallace was the country's greatest scientist and the biggest scandal to hit the academic community in centuries, possibly ever. Hired to codesign the Ark, his most infamous creation had been birthed some years before: the sleeper, a transmutation device used to induce unconscious nambula, said to promote emotional well-being through nothing more than the ability to provide pleasant dreams. Wallace originally built the machine for use inside the Ark to counter a proposed side effect of light deprivation, the inability to sleep. It stayed that way until a rich property magnate named Warren Rosenthal ordered a custom-made pod for himself. Since his work on the Ark and his wife's death, Wallace had turned into a recluse, shunning the scientific community and, if he gave interviews at all, publicly denouncing Inner City for its ethos of capitalist elitism.

For some reason Wallace made the sleeper for Rosenthal, perhaps because they'd attended university together and had even once been friends. Markriss saw pages of the scientist's notes on the machine, code-named Ausares, as part of his research, and read published extracts from the professor's diaries. Wallace hired a young scientist to help build his prototype, murdered her, and committed suicide in a prototype sleeper. He left behind his entire laboratory of equipment, research, blueprints, notes on that project and others, two sleepers, and detailed personal diaries. In a letter found on his laboratory desk, Wallace wrote: "I will share the secrets of my machine, how to build, use, and maintain it, so that every man, woman, and child can own one. Ausares will be my gift to humanity; may you use it wisely."

The professor got half of his wish. Within ten years of his death, E-Lul purchased the license to produce Ausares machines, successfully rebranding them and selling the product internationally until every household with a reasonable working income had at least one. The pods worked quite simply. The user entered, attached EEG electrodes, and went to sleep as normal. While they slept, the pod created a program that induced dreams of tranquil locations via crystalline energy: a lonely beach at sunrise; the view from the rim of a volcano; a lush, majestic rain forest cooled by a canopy of leaves. E-Lul called them "simulated projections," and the progams were endorsed by governments and religious leaders alike, no matter their political leanings or denomination. Human rights groups rallied against the pods, saying they were a government-sponsored, corporate-produced cosh. Despite petitions and appeals made by a number of protest groups, sleeper pods swiftly became an everyday part of modern life in a way no one could have predicted.

He picked up the tail end of Keshni's story when she started to ramble about the difference sleepers made to the fabric of society. How they had created peace in the world. It wasn't much of a topic, sounding like something memorized for rote performance rather than believed, and she soon ran out of steam, murmuring and punching at the panel beneath her breath. The lid closed. She stood, focused on the machine, watching the readout as though it might perform some trick while her back was turned. She stretched and yawned as Markriss watched.

"So?"

"Well, I know what's up."

He stood and joined her, looking down on the machine. "Gonna share the news?"

"Sure." Keshni smiled; his nerves fluttered. "Nothing. I've checked every program I can think of. There's not a damn thing wrong."

Colorless light cast from outside his window, the roof he never saw eliminating tranquility above. He always thought Ark Lites turned his flat into a football stadium, had cursed them beneath his breath, and now was grateful for them as he used the harsh light to read Keshni's thoughts, betrayed by her expression. They sat in the living room holding fresh mugs of tea, buried in chairs placed directly across from one another as though they'd argued. Keshni untied her hair band. Curled hair fell to her shoulders.

"Why am I not sleeping?"

She shook her head, sipped tea. "Who knows? These things, you know, the machines? They rarely go wrong. I heard something years ago, some story about a 4-series that fed the user negative dreams for like a year. Hell on earth, falling into an endless abyss, torture, that kind of thing . . . The paper said it turned the user mad . . ."

"Really?" Eyes wide in shock. He hadn't heard.

"That was years ago, and the pod was apparently looked after pretty badly. Mostly they just conk out rather than misfire."

"Yeah, but you'd hate to be the unlucky user."

"Yeah. Have you tried transmutation without your sleeper?"

"No."

"When did you last transmute?"

He looked away from her at the bookshelf. It was half empty, stacked with dusty volumes. His last meditation had been taken years ago, the night before he traveled the train into the Ark. To admit that he had used a pod after his brother's death, even to her, would be to admit it to himself.

"I can't remember."

"*You can't remember?*" Disbelief, resolve taking its place. "Try."

Markriss sighed. "I don't know . . . ten, twenty years?"

"When you were eight?"

He shrugged, watching steam rise from his tea. "No one ever believes me."

"That's cos everyone transmutes, Markriss. Everyone."

He threw back his head, knowing he looked exasperated, thinking he might cause offense, too late. "Not me."

"Wow."

She stared at him with new regard, fighting a smile that made her eyes gleam. Markriss was nervous, wary.

"So, what d'you think we should do now?"

"I think you should try."

Groaning, swiveling from her.

"Didn't your mum *ever* make you do it, or . . ." Keshni grimaced, gulping back the thought. "I really think you should. It would be good for you, honestly."

"I've always had trouble with those bloody machines," he said, getting to his feet slow. "What do I do?"

"Don't stand there like a scarecrow for Ra's sake, we have to go back to your podroom. So you can lie down, relax?"

"Okay . . ."

They wandered into the room as though he was being led to death, heads bowed in reverence. Markriss stopped and looked around at the few items he possessed. His neat and tidy home looked like a hotel room after the cleaner slammed the door rather than a place where one man lived out his life.

"Where do you want me?"

"Best lie in the pit. Get comfortable."

Her voice seemed toneless, businesslike. He did as she asked while she grabbed at a single wooden chair and dragged it beside the pod. Markriss lay with his arms by his sides, eyes closed.

"How d'you feel?" Keshni asked.

"Tired."

"Good." Hopeful. "Okay, so the first thing I want you to do is be very aware of your breathing. Actually feel the oxygen entering and leaving your body. See if you can feel the breath down in your solar plexus, be aware at all times and always have intent. Be clear."

She waited. He heard her light breathing, the rustle of clothes and the hum of the pod, a low-volume white noise. Outside, on the street, someone shouted. The honk of a tram. His fingers tingled. The sensation died.

"When you've got the rhythm, try slowing it down . . . So, breathe in . . . hold for a count of two . . . and breathe out. Breathe in . . . hold for two counts . . . and breathe out."

He sank, the fatigue of the last few weeks working like gravity, pushing him into the pit mattress. Her voice soothed.

"Now . . . see that dark space in front of your eyes?" Nodding once, eyes closed tight, hardly a twitch. "I want you to look into it. Focus your attention on the screen of your mind."

She paused again, the silence lasting almost a minute.

"Visualize a square, form it."

His fingers clenched.

"Got it?"

Another mute nod.

"Great. See how easy it is? Okay, now I want you to create what we call a 'command center,' a space that's of your own making you can go to whenever you need. Can you do that?"

"Yes."

Hands clenching tighter.

"Relax. Don't force it. Let the place come . . ."

Though he'd been skeptical and felt a little silly partaking in he didn't know what, the pillow against his head and the feel of slowing his breath was soothing enough to convince him that this transmutation business might be therapeutic in some strange, abstract way. His breathing was so light his chest barely moved. Dark encased him fully.

10

He strained to see. Tiny sparks appeared; few at first, and then everything seeped into view. Huge buildings towering so high he couldn't see rooftops, glittering from reflected light. A concrete walkway materialized under his feet, spreading fast as bacteria until he saw a seawall, a lookout point, and, many yards from him, the length of a pier. An expanse of water, vast and opaque. The River Azilé, running through the center of Dinium, although this was not the river he knew. This river was unfamiliar, untamed. He'd visualized the outside world.

Unsure what to do now that his vision was expanding and lengthening before him, he let himself move toward the lookout point. The night sky was brilliant as any his memory had constructed, populated by thousands of stars, a huge, clear full moon. He was touched, verging on tears. It had been so many years since he'd witnessed something so commonplace.

Beyond ink gloom, Markriss saw the lone figure of a man sitting at the bench. Bent, as though in pain.

He stood before the figure as though he'd jumped those few steps with his eyes closed. The occurrence didn't surprise him. It was a little disconcerting, as he wasn't used to such physics, yet somehow— in this transmuted state—it made sense. Now that he was closer to the figure, he could see more details. The man was small, thin, and dark-skinned, impossibly old, a hairless head reflecting white moonlight. He wore a suit that seemed to be made of a coarse brown cloth, rough as coconut husk, and a belt made of the same material. Attached to the belt were suede bags, also brown. Though Markriss tilted his head, it was difficult to see his face. The only other discerning feature was the knobbly stick the old man held in one hand.

Markriss opened his mouth to ask the figure who or what he might be. But the sound that emerged didn't come from his mouth and didn't enter his ears. There was no rumble in his chest, no vibration in his throat, movement of his tongue, or any *sound*. Instead he heard the voice in his head, as if he'd *thought* the words.

Hello?

Unsure how the man would respond, he waited.

The old man didn't answer, keeping his head bowed. Markriss was about to ask again when, millimeter by millimeter, the head began to rise. An age seemed to pass before he finally faced him— though *face* was not exactly the operative word. Although there were features—a nose, two eyes, lips that formed a mouth, cheeks—the face seemed blurred by a shadow as impenetrable as deepest night.

His fear rapidly intensified. He knew who he was looking at: his Prospect Road assailant.

Markriss was about to bolt, even though he didn't know where to, when an inky haze swirled around him, then cleared a little. The face came into view. Thin, the flesh of the cheeks falling to the floor like melting wax, as though sliding from his head. The dark eyes almost blue, yellow whites. A proud, broad nose.

What now?

That wasn't the question he had anticipated asking. He really wanted to find out where he was, but maybe this was what he needed to know. Before he'd worked out how he could rephrase his words, the man held up an arm and got to his feet. This seemed to prove difficult. Markriss had to stretch out a hand, help him up. The man was very short. Though his obvious physical discomfort—jerking pain, a hand pressed tight against his waist—would normally have distressed Markriss, he felt at ease. He was calm, ready to hear whatever the man had to impart.

As he took another look into the sallow, disgruntled face in front of him, Markriss understood who he was staring at. He'd seen the pictures while researching his early article for *Ark Light*, reading through notes and diaries: this was Professor Harman Wallace. The scientist, inventor, and murderer had somehow, without reason, been conjured into his nambula.

He took a step backward, recognition striking a moment before fear at his memories of what the man had done. A lethal dose of poison killed the young woman, injected while she lay in trans, testing a prototype sleeper. Though the murder had been committed over a century ago, Markriss couldn't help falling back. He didn't know what would have been worse: the professor, or the shadowed person from Prospect Road.

Wallace seemed not to notice. He stretched his arms wide, chin cast toward the night sky, his dark figure forming the silhouette of a cross. He seemed to ignore the younger man; then a reedy yet confident voice boomed deep within Markriss's mind.

Follow.

A flash of light. A second later the lookout lit up, followed in quick succession by the buildings, then the sky. Markriss craned his neck upward but gave up attempting to track the light. He looked down, and the brown suit lay in a heap by the empty bench. Thoughts of death by lethal injection emptied from his mind.

He looked up again. It was difficult to take in what he *thought* he saw at that moment—a stream of light that seemed to twirl and dance in the sky, changing colors as it moved. He tried to pinch himself and prove he was imagining this, only to find he couldn't: he had no fingers or hands.

The light stopped dead, hovering above the river. It shimmered, alternating between light green, a darker green, and vibrant blue, before the whole pattern repeated over and over. Markriss was intrigued as much by the colors as his intuitive discovery. He wanted to see them close up. Before he'd even thought as much, however, he'd left what had constituted the earth.

He had a conscious realization of the sky and the fact that he was floating. Stars were bright, close as family. He soared with a speed that caused exhilaration to beat in his chest. No walls to cage and keep him, only wind against his face and the ground far below. Gravity was a banished concept and it felt good, felt right. He looped a joyful loop, dropped low until he skimmed rooftops and rippling water, leaving the river behind in the blink of an eye, racing above the endless expanse of the Blin. Soon he moved so fast the bare earth was only a blur. His heart beat without pause. He pushed harder, harder again. He could fly forever.

The stream of light pulled up beside him with an almost embarrassing ease. Closer, its shimmer was electric, each color embedded with a white that shone like molten iron. In the depth of the light where the greens or blues were deepest, diamond sparks made it glitter like a precious bracelet laid flat.

It's beautiful, he thought.

So are you.

No neck muscles moved or eyes focused on what he could see. His perspective simply changed as though he were watching a film and the next scene had come into view. The light that was in effect his body had the same diamond sparks and shifting colors, his fiery red fading to a light pink and sometimes the dark purple of amethyst, which he observed with some shock and more than a little pride. They moved around what he could only loosely term his "body" in fluid motion. He felt laughter and looked over at Wallace.

Like what you see?

Sure.

Ready to see more?

He hesitated only a fraction of a second. *Why not?*

Wallace shot away. The next time Markriss looked, he was merely a blink of light on the horizon. Markriss willed himself to catch up and instantly found himself beside the stream, everything a blur beneath them once more. They moved at speed, in silence.

Good, he heard. *Now do this.*

Another burst of acceleration beside him—vertical this time. Markriss did his best to follow, and although he found his movements slow in comparison, after some thought he was able to speed up. Wallace and Markriss passed through thick cotton clouds that muted the stars like fog over flashlight beams before they thinned and dispersed into clear sky. Everything became darker, even as the sparks of light grew bigger and brighter, rounder and more defined. Wallace was a mere streak of rainbow ahead. That was all he could see until something burst in what would have formerly been his ears—a dull pop, no more. He glanced around.

He was in outer space. His rational mind refused such a discovery, even as another part, the part that believed what he was experiencing, said that he was meditating (or hallucinating—he wasn't sure which), wasn't he, so it was allowed, wasn't it? Didn't it make sense that Wallace had led him here—where his subconscious wanted to go—the ultimate freedom of limitless space? He didn't dare doubt the possibility of what he was seeing too hard in case it all disappeared and he returned to his podroom with the single mattress against his back, imprisoned within his physical body. Markriss wanted to believe. He wanted to see.

So many lights were around him he felt warmed by their presence. Some darted at full velocity, others meandered. Some saw him, or cruised past without taking note. So many luminescences, so many stars, so many colors, from orange to violet, peach to gray, swimming tropical fish in the vast sea of the solar system. The moon was a white ball in front of him; earth was the same behind, its sharp colors dazzling. He felt peace of a type he thought he'd never attain flow through him. He felt a part of something he'd never laid eyes on.

A light he took to be Wallace approached, glowing that familiar green and deep blue. Then, it began to transform. Out of light came a head, a male body that was tall, naked, and athletic. It was Wallace as a much younger man. Huge feathered wings made of the same glowing light grew from his back, unfolding until he resembled an angel. His face was stern. Although he wore no clothes, Wallace had no visible sexual organs. Markriss wasn't surprised. Why would a being that could create a head, arms, and legs at will need genitals? What for?

Wallace flared his wings, almost in greeting, before he was off and away. Without knowing why—only why *not*—Markriss followed.

They raced through cold space, streaking past the tableau of stars, some bright-yellow spots, others far and blue. Each seemed no more than a fingertip from them. Wallace moved with undeniable purpose. He saw where they were headed. The moon, that ancient desert, once a bright yet faraway glow, loomed on the horizon. Before he could take in the magnificent view, he was skimming the awe-inspiring craters and valleys that made up its pocked, plaster-of-paris surface.

Wallace didn't slow to give these wonders further attention. Flapping his wings harder, he forced Markriss to push faster still. In his enthusiasm, Markriss didn't notice the light fade behind him, or the darkened land, devoid of sunlight, they were racing toward. They moved with even more speed, over a limitless valley on the border of permanent night. The gash in the moon rock below him went on as if there was no end, as though giant hands had wrenched a huge tear in the land. Although Markriss blanched at the sight of such fathomless depths, he didn't slow. The wings ahead gave two almighty beats and dived into the darkness.

He tried to stop himself. Nothing happened. Though he mentally willed the opposite, he was heading for the chasm at full speed, without control. He tried to struggle against it, but that only seemed to add to his velocity. Night was everywhere.

11

C oming to, it took a while to draw his vision into focus; he did so by squinting, lifting his eyebrows and letting them fall, turning his head left to right in an attempt to jar sight into place. He felt numb, unable to move, arms and legs powerless, detached from his torso. Sharp light shot pain through the back of his head. Sight returned.

He was back in the doctor's surgery he'd dreamed on the tram. That same tiny room with paneled walls and the thin, bunk-like single bed covered in a dark-green sheet. This time the pod was directly in front of him, he on the opposite side of the room. He was standing with his back against what felt like a huge metal slab, arms and legs clamped as before. A smell of chemicals hung in the air. The computerized beep that accompanied his heart rate was strong and fast. He looked to his right. The drip in his arm remained, fueling him with that mysterious purple fluid. He looked to his left. A rack of doctor's tools and instruments—the customary scalpel, a curved and serrated knife, the doublehanded saw. Markriss felt his frown as he noticed a shining red fluid coating the edges of each blade. He looked down and saw the flesh of his chest peeled back like a ripe banana, a glistening wide hole at the center of his body. The meat of his insides was much the same as that of any other animal; jaundiced fat, the white of his gaping rib cage sparkling light. Blood everywhere, no pain. Nevertheless, the computerized beep gained speed, even as he noted three colored wires trailing from his chest cavity. Purple, green, and blue. Following the wires, Markriss saw a metal trolley on wheels just beyond and beneath his manacled legs.

The wires finished their journey at a point where each pierced a thick lump of meat placed on a coal-black machine. The meat was about the size and shape of a large pebble, jerking in time with the computerized beep. On the right-hand side of the trolley next to this strange muscled object was another machine, an identical twin to the first. On it lay a single large black feather, curled in an almost U shape, light enough to quiver with the slightest shift of air. The beeping grew faster still, the meat convulsing simultaneously as Markriss understood that the writhing fist of muscle alongside the LEDs flashing for attention on the twin machines was his own heart. Just when he recognized that he was dreaming, the machine bearing his organ blinked red, while the machine with the feather blinked green. A deafening Klaxon. He struggled and fought to wake himself, somehow couldn't raise a scream.

Then it was dark.

His eyes seemed closed, yet he was blinking: he could feel the muscles work, the faint touch as eyelids met, but when he tried to open them wider nothing changed. The black remained impenetrable. Then pressure on his chest, that same weight pushing stronger than ever before, stealing breath from his lungs. He knew what was happening, remembered his fight against this unseen force while his brother slept in the machine parallel to his. Even as he fought the crushing weight, he accepted that struggle never achieved success, inside or out of the Ark. Not knowing what else he could do, he let go.

Everything became distant, difficult to fathom. A croaking whisper formed just below his ear, words he couldn't understand yet caused a chill of fright, leading to a feeling he hadn't experienced since Burbank Park; the quick sensation of falling backward as though he'd sunk into the bed itself, falling with nothing to break his momentum.

Everything was clear.

Markriss saw his podroom as though suspended on high, marveling at the weightless sensation. An attempt to look himself over and check whether the doctor's surgery had been a dream produced that strange switch of viewpoint, the fluid flow of red, light pink, and amethyst he'd seen before. His arms, legs, and everything else he might term his "natural body" were there, only they were covered in a membrane thin as bubble skin, colors flowing on the surface in a never-ending cycle of motion.

It was mostly dark in his podroom, a pinch of faint light streaming from the window overlooking Prospect Road, casting shadows and bulky silhouettes. He caught a glimpse of his alarm clock; it was three a.m., though he didn't know how it had gotten that late. His focus was drawn to the center of the room. It was strange looking down from that angle, seeing his own self in the pod and Keshni next to him, studying him like text. He examined his prone body in great detail—the short and kinky dark hair, a pencil-thin nose leading to broad lips. The smooth skin, broad, bulky shoulders. A stern jaw shadowed with tiny hair. The dotted burn just below the thumb of his right hand and the mannequin pose he adopted with his eyes closed. Strange as the viewing was, he felt pleasure from his own appearance for the first time in years.

Keshni was more beautiful than he'd ever seen, an oval of green and purple flowing around her body, the perpetual shift a silent dance of energy for his eyes alone. His own sleeping form was also alive with what he now knew were "his colors." Their separate energy fields reached toward each other, absorbing and mixing, though no subsequent color came from the pairing. They merely churned together, as meeting oceans.

A shadow detached itself from its kneeling position beside his prone body. The young, nubile form was gone, replaced by the hesitant step of the old man, the hung skin of a dour face. Wallace. He lifted his arms upward, a gesture that reminded Markriss of a silent request for an embrace. They regarded each other.

What are you doing here?

Although he registered anger, Markriss was surprised to find his thoughts remained calm, serenity pervading. Strength coursed through his being, steeling his soul. Every nerve, every cell that made up his body, was alive.

I'm to lead you to the Way.

Snapping back, drifting closer to the ceiling, the colors around his sleeping body swirled in ever-faster revolutions.

The last time you led me somewhere, it was an abyss.

Wallace let his arms drop, bowing to appease him.

Forgive me. Though I made many attempts to communicate, fear kept you tethered to the physical plane. To bring you to this point you had to be freed from reliance on the gross body and all its senses. That's what I did.

I don't understand . . .

Markriss, all will be clear. There's little time for explanations that reveal nothing . . . Open the Way, and in turn you will know.

Wallace fell silent, allowing him to contemplate his position. He got the feeling he could say nothing for any length of time and the old man's emotionless stance would remain unchanged. This was a being of infinite patience. On the face of things, there was no way he could trust him; the professor didn't have the greatest track record for preserving human life, and following Wallace would mean putting himself at his mercy. It didn't necessarily tally that he had his best interests at heart just because he'd become an ancestor. And yet how long could he stay floating above his own body, watching energy fields join and dance?

Then what? A return to day-to-day living? His ordinary job? The physical plane Wallace spoke of?

All right. All right . . .

The dour face rose in his direction.

Good. The body you inhabit is a double of your physical form, a bridge between the formed and unformed world. As such, it is virtually impervious to danger, yet it can be damaged by traveling farther than your will has power to grant. You must go only where I take you, leave when I request.

Sure, he replied, grasping for meaning. *So this body double is my spirit, right?*

It is the ethereal form that houses your spirit and is known by many names. Bardo, chi, sunsum, prana . . . Every culture of the world knows a different name. In mine it is ka.

You're Kemetian?

Of course . . .

Markriss drifted back to floor level, lowering himself until he was floating centimeters from Wallace.

There are many more subjects I must explain, most of all my reason for communicating with you. It is of utmost importance that you see your true power without delay. Do you trust?

Yes.

Strength was powering through him, feeding his words with a confidence and certainty that matched his feelings. When he looked at his sleeping body, the colors were racing so fast they blurred. Keshni's jogged along at their former speed. They no longer seemed so compatible.

Look from your window . . .

He did as was asked. Beneath his tower block, the area that had previously been Prospect Road, the beginnings of the Poor Quarter, the shops and people that made the place he recognized, had disappeared. His tower seemed to be standing atop a sea of purple clouds in constant motion, their lazy roll making him dizzy. Puffs of vapor lashed against the brick walls of the building like waves against lighthouse rocks. Just beyond, a clash of electrical energy, two crackling horizontal lines ran parallel to one another. When they met, an explosion of light was created. When they separated, a bottomless hole was left in their wake, bright light occasionally erupting from within the depths. Markriss floated by the window, enthralled by the endless depth before him, devoid of thought.

You must dive into the light.

Wallace was by his side, illuminated by the intensity of elements.

I have to?

It is the only means of opening the Way.

He needed time to think. *What is this Way?*

You must dive.

He didn't know how to say he felt some vague notion of mistrust, and was scared of being hurt. His strength felt minuscule compared with the power he saw.

Set no boundaries that do not apply. You cannot fall and break your bones, for ka has none. You cannot spill blood, for blood exists

*only in the physical. Awaken your senses to the world in its entirety.
See beyond limits.*

Silence, deeper and longer than any Markriss had endured.

Okay . . . okay . . .

He moved to the window, visualizing the lifted latch, the frame
swinging outward as he'd asked, and felt no surprise when it occurred.
A noise like the roll and boom of thunder came from below, mixing
with the echo of chuckles inside his head.

*There's no need for windows and doors in this realm . . . Still, do
what you must . . .*

Ignoring the professor, Markriss drifted through the window,
cautious, alert for danger. On the other side, the thunder was louder,
overpowering any words he might have voiced. Wisps of purple leaped,
dissolved into nothing. He couldn't look down for fear he might be
swayed. Reminding himself how he'd gotten to that point, he abandoned resistance, letting what Wallace termed his "spiritual body"
fall.

Everything occurred in a blink. Racing downward, Markriss saw
crackling lines of electricity part to expose the pitch-black chasm he'd
been so afraid of. Nothingness was much worse the second time—a
place where even the all-powerful elements he'd witnessed couldn't
survive, a pit of unreachable depths. He was scared again. An instant
later the electricity returned, fusing into intense white light, eliminating any other. It was this light Markriss fell into, searing heat
burning him on the inside, torching all of his senses.

Markriss loitered on the corner of a busy intersection in the heart of
Chaucer. Trams rolled by, taxi horns beeped, and crowds of people
walked the streets at idle pace. Shop owners blared music through
open doors and windows, hoping to shock commerce from its
daydreams and into the tills. Wherever Markriss laid his eyes, an
illusion of prosperity and clean living could be seen . . . here, like
everywhere in the Ark, there was another story beneath the surface.
Beyond the walls, there was always another story.

Chaucer had long been notorious. Taxi drivers gathered by the
hundreds, vying for customers who came to town for consumer or

entertainment purposes. Sometimes, in their eagerness for fares, they would knock over a child, a young adult, sometimes a pensioner. The local community would petition and protest for better traffic lights, fewer taxis, slower speed limits. Rumors said that Governor Hanaigh E'lul fed those petitions through a paper shredder without a single glance. The Chaucer Crossing, as it had become known, kept its notoriety.

A brief once-over. Markriss felt relief to see his physical body, arms, legs, head, and chest, all solid as before. A second, more detailed inspection revealed a strange addition—a series of colored circles that spun at specific points. The circles varied in size, and were all over his body, the largest on his upper stomach, the smallest on his neck and lower stomach. A pulsing in his brow and somewhere farther on his head indicated that there might be more elsewhere. Turning his palms faceup, he found tiny dots at the center of each hand. Others on his shoulder blades, elbows, knees, ankles. Their glow emanated from deep within his body, changing his natural color into one he'd thought skin could not possess.

Your naardim. Energy that unites your physical form with your ka. Wallace spoke, facing traffic and the general public, standing next to Markriss.

When Markriss looked in the direction of Wallace's gaze, he finally noticed the circles running along the bodies of shoppers, parents and their children, young lovers, everyone. A woman and her teenage daughter each wore two circles he hadn't noticed, and now felt: one on their foreheads, another sending a mixture of light gushing from their crowns like water. The spray consisted of colors that mirrored his and made him feel at ease. The woman smiled. Nodding, he watched her go by, aware that the pulse in his head indicated the presence of his own extra naardim.

This is . . . This is something else. Something amazing . . .

He couldn't find words. Another roll of deep chuckling beside him.

You have done well not to be swayed by fear, yet your mind still clings to that which it knew. Why else would your first true step into this realm bring you here, to the subtle manifestation of a place you know?

He couldn't help feeling disgruntled with what Wallace was telling him.

What's my mind got to do with me being in Chaucer? Are you saying I asked to be here?

Not asked, demanded. Markriss, you are in control. You could not fall because you would not wish it. You cannot go where the Will does not permit. Bringing you here is the mind's way of making something strange feel familiar. That is why you see the Chaucer of the Way—the unformed Chaucer.

Right.

He was lost. Nothing made sense. He only believed because it was impossible to deny reality. The energy flow of his and Keshni's bodies, the naardim, Wallace himself.

Where are your naardim?

The most direct question he could ask, plucked from thousands.

I have none. I am not a physical being.

Back to square one, the list lengthened by at least a couple of hundred questions.

Let me show you this plane as it truly is. You may learn as we go.

Sure.

A flash, searing. Markriss floated in an expanse much like the depths of the chasm he'd dived into. He knew this because a vague light source came from somewhere above, illuminating Wallace a subtle candy-floss pink. Markriss turned toward the light. Here, wherever he was, his body returned to that formless band of light, colors swirling involuntarily in clockwise motion.

Where are we?

The professor said nothing, head moving up and down, left and right, as if to find his bearings. Markriss became aware of a steady chorus of humming along with a subtle tremor from all sides that brought a quiver to the tails of Wallace's suit. The chuckling returned.

Amazing. Though I chose to lift the veil from your eyes, control of how it is done remains in your mental domain. Remember, everything here is exactly how you would wish to see it. What you have done indicates your might. You surpassed the lower levels of existence and climbed to a higher realm known as Briah. Come.

Wallace rose and Markriss followed, confused again by words that stirred no understanding. The light grew brighter as they climbed, washing them a soft fairy-tale shade of pink, red, black at its darkest point. The polyphonic hum rose in volume, as the tremors did in strength. Sight and sound gained further momentum until its source was upon him. If Markriss hadn't left his physical body in the podroom with Keshni, he was sure disbelief would have made his jaw fall.

The Shechem, his guide said, with unmistakable relish. *The power behind all physical manifestation. Some would see the Fifty Oarsmen, or Fifty Skulls of the Kali Necklace. You have chosen to view the Fifty Gates of Binah.*

Markriss saw a procession of towering gateways that stood like oversize castle drawbridges, twice the height of the block he had leaped from, and made of what seemed nothing more than glowing beams of energy. Though none of what he witnessed was solid in the true sense of the word, the energy still resembled the huge bricks, concrete, and steel Markriss remembered so well from his journey into the Ark. Letters and words were inscribed all over the gates in a strange language. It was difficult to tell what was more fantastic—the sight of something that should have been solid and immovable swaying like a ghostly mirage, or the line of gateways standing rigid as parading soldiers, marching toward a horizon that never came, piercing the night with beauty.

When did you last see this?

Back when I rode the train into the Ark. We had to pass through a gateway to enter.

This is not the gateway you saw, exactly. The Gates of Binah are a visual representation of the Fifty Words of Power that aid your journey from physical to astral existence, via chants used during transmutation. Your memory fills in the blanks, presenting what you now see.

Then they're not real? Only a figment of my imagination?

Imagination or not is irrelevant: simultaneously, things exist and do not.

That he believed, more than anything the professor had said. A straightforward answer, even if the reasoning was ludicrous.

Now we leave, Wallace said. *You are not permitted here until you*

have reached a level of understanding far from your immediate grasp.
The results could cause harm.

Light came and went. They flew at speed above a charcoal desert, the cracked and barren land beneath them beaten flat. The tremendous humming was gone. They must have entered some kind of highway, as belts of light resembling Markriss's ka were all around, darting above and below in orderly streams of movement. Ahead, he could see a shadowed range of mountains growing steadily taller as he and Wallace drew close. Above the peaks, in what he could only loosely term as the sky, a sparkle of faraway stars appeared.

We have reached Asiah, Markriss heard, *the fifth and lowest level of the Phenomenal Plane. You may also hear it mentioned as the Taut, as like many other dimensions, Asiah bears many names. Some traditions know it as the Light.*

I've heard of that. A name he recognized. He felt relief.

Asiah is just a small step from the world you are familiar with. The lower half, where you will find your physical body, is Geb. This complementary structure follows the ruling adhered to by all creations of natural order: subtle and dense, antimatter and matter, formed and unformed, negative and positive. A union of opposites creates everything that exists in this plane or any other.

Okay. Okay, I think I understand that. My world and this are one and the same, right?

As are your ka and physical form.

In the midst of Wallace's explanation, Markriss failed to notice a belt of light loosen itself from high above, plummeting with lightning speed. When he heard its approach, a high-pitched whistle that lasted a mere second, it was too late. The ka slammed into him with the force of a cannonball, sending sensations through him that felt like pain, but as it went on the feeling was closer to unbearable pleasure, so severe there came a point where he couldn't take more. And yet the sensation went on. A screaming ecstasy pierced his hearing, the voice crying in harmony with his own. His vision became impaired to the point where colors were all he could see . . . A green-and-purple flashing sequence over and over, faster until they were one.

Then it was gone, the renegade ka off and racing into dimness, him reeling. Emotions leaped. He felt joy without knowing why, feared he might not experience anything like that again. Pain, not from collision but loss of connection. Ecstasy at its highest, most sustained level, and Markriss needed more. When he regained his senses the ka was a pinprick of light almost reaching the distant mountains. Before Wallace could say anything, Markriss gave chase.

He needn't have bothered. The ka was a darting, shimmering minnow in an everlasting ocean, hard enough to keep in sight, let alone catch. He accelerated enough to see its form in better detail until, over a hundred meters from it, the ka dropped pebble-like, disappearing before he realized what had happened. Markriss saw he'd almost reached the mountain range and slowed. Wallace appeared, floating toward him with effortless ease.

What was that?

Although you might not feel like it, your destiny has been blessed, Markriss. You experienced a meld. Your ka merged with another to form a bond that will manifest in the physical plane. You met your mate.

Then where did she go?

Assuming his mate was a woman could be presumptuous. The professor never paused to correct him.

The ka was traveling in the dream state, as most here do. Its disappearance is likely due to a reunion with the physical form, brought on by the meld. Put in simple terms, your soul mate either returned from transmutation, or woke.

He snapped to attention. Keshni . . .

Her name, before he could stop the thought—hearing it resound, he knew he was right. Why would he need more signs? The way she'd approached. The mixing of their ka and the instinct he possessed from the moment he saw her all pointed to the same thing.

Were the colors hers?

Yeah . . . Yeah, they were. Green and purple. I'd never forget.

Then it is inevitable. She's your mate.

Relief, impossible to fully express. Coupled with exhaustion, it bled former strength and left him limp, powerless to stop himself losing height, drifting toward the mountainside.

This way, Markriss. Just a little farther and you may rest.

They crept upward again, slower this time, crossing the mountaintop with great effort. And even while his head reeled at the prospect of finally having the relationship he'd hoped for, the view beyond the peaks was another spectacle that sent his senses into overload. Stars in the indigo sky burst into life like arctic meadows, dotting the heavens with varied sizes of white, blue, and red, leaving little room for anything else. Then, when his gaze could take no more, it was drawn to the backdrop of nebulae and galaxies—misted red-and-yellow clouds of dust representing the nearest, spirals of center-lit Catherine wheels in freeze-frame denoting those farther away. There was little time to see it all, the whole scene spinning and shifting to the east as he watched. From the west, he saw an inexhaustible pattern of more colored dust.

Wallace had brought him here to witness the land, Markriss guessed when he tore his gaze from the sky. The dry earth remained black on this side of the mountain, torn by fissures and valleys stretching farther than he could tell, though here the fissures were acres wide, the valleys open like a deadly gash, miles between opposing edges. Thousands of cracks and crevices formed smaller meandering trails between larger veins, islands of earth left in their wake. Luminous purple liquid flowed along these streams and rivers, carving bubbling paths that brought a flat glow to the persistent night. Markriss strained his vision, trying to see where the veins of liquid ended, relenting when he noted the lack of horizon.

I need to sit down . . .

You are in control, Markriss. If you wish to create a physical body for this realm, you must will it.

Okay. I think I got that now.

Sure enough, he thought and floated in a lightly glowing physical body much like his previous frame. Tendons, veins, muscles, arteries, and other internal workings were alarmingly visible, emitting iridescent light that seemed to surround everything. He watched his heart pump blood through his own chest, the muscle fleshy and stiff, until the sight made him nervous. He found a flat ledge among the rocks of the mountainside and let himself sit, loving the solidity. Professor

Wallace took up a similar position opposite, his brown suit, despite the lack of a body, falling in the faint suggestion of humanity.

Markriss breathed in, filling his lungs.

I need some explanations before my head explodes. First of all—are you really Professor Harman Wallace? And why are you showing me this?

The man bowed once again, this time in greeting.

Apologies, Markriss. Eagerness to open the Way causes etiquette to slip. You're right; I am Harman Wallace. Years ago, I was a Child of Geb like you. My people are from Tamana, a city built by ancient Kemetians in Northern Bulan, what you know as the Sahara. Our ancestors mastered Kemetic science, exploring and mapping these realms, passing the knowledge to those who came after, and so it became my field of expertise.

A *Child of Geb?* Markriss chewed that over, three steps behind, latching on to the name. *The physical plane?*

Correct. Trace a path from my lineage to yours, you'll find us related. I'm an ancestor, long resident of this plane.

Right. My parents are Nubian, and my mum always told me Kemetians originated from Kush, so that makes sense . . . Markriss looked at the guide with a great deal more respect. *So this is what I am when I die? Just . . . ka?*

Ka is what you were, are, and always shall be. It is your truest form.

So much information, an entire world he'd kept at bay, and Wallace had only provided a shortened version. On that black mountainside above the eternal flow of rivers and streams, Markriss wanted to hear the history of his descent, to know everything.

You're restless, Markriss. It's natural to have questions. It's the only way for the mind to grow. Yet I haven't answered your second question, and that's perhaps the most important, for it tells why you are here. Your will shall award you secrets of the realm, Kemetic science, and your ancestors. Do not hurry this knowledge or it will lead to danger.

Markriss bowed his head. Wallace was referring to his thoughtless pursuit of Keshni's ka.

I'm unsure whether your power comes as a gift, or if you were born blessed by chance. It happens only once in every while . . . A child of an era can be birthed with natural ability for the old ways as they can be born with blue eyes in a family of brown. There were key stages of your life when your power was at its peak, times when I called and attempted to make my presence felt. It was dangerous for you and those around you. Tapping into your spiritual energy affected your ka. The life force within you has the power to negatively influence weaker souls. There were . . . mishaps.

Nesta . . . and . . . my brother . . .

Yes.

Grief, weak at best. Years had sucked the tears dry, his sorrow focused on his ignorance rather than pain. Not knowing why it all happened, whether he was to blame. Wallace let him have a moment of staring at rocks, burying his head in his hands.

Go on.

Your gift is duality. The power to move between spiritual and physical states without the aid of sleepers. Your life force is stronger than many I witnessed. Sages, adepts, and masters transmute for a lifetime to reach your heights. Your Neter-given aptitude means that you are attuned to the indivisible dualities that encompass every aspect of every realm. There has not been the rarity known as "an Individual" for over five thousand years.

Events in the higher realms forced me to attempt contact well before your time of maturity. In my age your power would have been noticed, and you would have been trained in Kemetic science from birth; not so in yours. According to maat, a Child of Geb must make contact with the ancestors. Opposite attempts are not outlawed, though they are heavily frowned upon as the dangers are well documented. If, for some reason, an ancestor feels it's imperative to overlook the unspoken rule, there are also laws governing this. It must only be done in dream state, never during waking. The Child must be immersed in the Supreme Conscience before the ancestors make themselves known, so there are no doubts concerning the spiritual hierarchy. Most important, contact with an immature Child of Geb can only be made twice in a lifetime. Once as infant, once as teenager. If the ancestor fails to make contact, they must wait until maturity before they try again, sometime around the twenty-eighth year. That is the method I used.

Markriss nodded to show he followed, reluctant even to think in case he missed a point of vital importance.

So you've contacted me and showed all the things your law asks. Why?

In order to get help in a task that only you, with your powers of duality, may carry out. It is a simple task that I would perform myself, had I the gift. I do not, so it is left up to you.

Well, there had to be a payoff somewhere. I reckon you'll find that in one of your laws. Although part of him dreaded hearing the answer, Markriss had to know: *What is it I'm supposed to do?*

I have already told you how rare duality is. Rare, though not impossible, as your journey to Briah has shown. Unfortunately, duality also dictates that you are not the only bearer of this gift. There is another, a dark spirit, and that spirit is evil. He has used his knowledge of the upper realms to gain his own duality, and could destroy your physical world just by his existence; with that balance gone, everything you've seen will collapse.

Silence, taking that in.

So you want me to stop this spirit? Kill it?

As much as something like your "self" can be destroyed . . . Yes.

Elation dimmed into sorrow. A murderer asking him to murder. *I'm no killer.*

Markriss, you have no choice. You must do this or calamity will follow. It is the Law.

The vastness of the world he'd had opened up to him hit Markriss with an overwhelming desire to slip back into his physical form, back into his cubicle at work where he could write articles tailored to the paragraph, keep his head down and out of trouble.

Exactly what would happen if I refused? If I went back to my podroom and decided this whole thing was a dream?

He was looking deep into Wallace's eyes, hoping the professor couldn't read his own dismay at the weakness of his threat.

It is forbidden for myself or any other guide to tell when or how . . . But go back, and your physical body will be destroyed. This is the inevitable consequence of straying from the Laws of Maat.

He remained still, waiting for Wallace to say more. No way

forward, no way back. That was what he'd been told. An outpouring of emotion and injustice grew hot inside him until he forced it to recede. No place for it there.

They sat silently opposite each other, seemingly for an age, the enormity of what he had been told replacing Markriss's fear, growing in his mind until it caused a steady pound to begin where his neck met his head. Throbbing heartbeat, the pounding ever harder, until Markriss spoke simply as a means of taking his mind from the sensation. The calm he'd achieved, against everything, gave him strength.

Destroyed by who?

It's forbidden for myself or any other to tell when or how.

Markriss stared at the old man's sagging face, his infinite strop angled toward rocks. Remembered pictures he'd seen of the woman poisoned by Wallace, the voice of the man who'd threatened him. He tried to look into the professor's eyes, waiting for answers until it became evident he would give none. He wanted to know what reason Wallace had for murdering the young woman, unsure what response that would cause, or even if he'd be given the truth.

This spirit is in the physical world you said?

He is.

And if I don't go back to my flat, if I go back to destroy it instead, things will be better? I'll get to see Keshni and we'll be together, right?

Of course. She is your mate.

How?

The professor stretched his left arm out across the land, bringing the scene to Markriss's attention. From their high vantage point they could see the purple liquid escaping from underground pathways at the roots of the mountains, bubbling along smaller streams and diving via massive waterfalls into the crisscross valleys beyond. Markriss caught sight of movement in those depths. He stared into the rushing current, couldn't see.

River Time, Wallace said with authority. *Not an actual river as you know them, of course, like Chaucer Crossing, or even the Gates of Binah: your eyes and mind do most of the work. Nevertheless, be mindful that what you see does exist, if not in the form you view. This river is your means of getting back to Geb.*

But what about my control? Can't I will myself there, in my podroom and body where I started? Can't I stop myself being killed? I thought I had power!

More chuckling.

You have that power, yet also a way to go. You're not ready to circumvent events, even if you were experienced enough to return. And then, after you had accomplished that, it would still do us no good. In your time period the rogue spirit inhabits the Ark on a level far above your own. There are laws in your world too, Markriss, that would never allow the necessary access. You must use the river and travel to a time period where the Rogue operates on your level. That is why you are here.

Travel through time? To the past?

Not past or future, Markriss. This time lies parallel with yours.

Again, shock robbed him of thought, blurring vision. When he brought himself to look at Wallace, the ka was gone. He switched his gaze to the land. A blur of colors, too fast to trace. First, the blur was large, then the size of the stars, then no more than a pinprick. When it morphed into black Markriss leaned over the mountainside. Wallace had gone ahead.

Markriss! Markriss, come!

He directed his ka toward the guide, beside Wallace before the thought was formulated, floating above a body of liquid the width of a canal. The purple water was motionless, barely a ripple marking the surface. Other streams could be seen, other rivers, some waters bashing and roaring as though eager to flood, others quiet as their own. The movement he'd seen from the mountainside had been no optical illusion; there was further activity here, caused by creatures that swam in the clear depths like alien fish. Closer inspection caused him to lower his ka, floating nearer the surface.

A human head performed a slow spin, the eyes, when they reached him, open wide, teeth gritted. Markriss cried out, propelling to Wallace's side.

They are not real, the guide told him. *Merely thoughts, dreams, possible events seen through the lens of the river. It would take an eternity to explain the true concept of time. When you return to Geb, you must study these things.*

I will. You know I will.

Indeed. I can tell you this for now: There are many parallels to every existence. All eventual possibility can be found here. This is where the decisions you make are shunted into life experiences. Choose a path, stream, or river, and your predestined life will carry you to a destination. There are thousands of eventualities. Humankind has either lost her ability to explore them, or become too consumed by pod machines to know they can.

That was it. The final straw.

Please just tell me what you want me to do. If you tell me any more I'm not sure I'll be able to take it.

He wanted to express his helplessness and lack of knowledge, though it was impossible to tell if he had. Wallace's serious face was unchanged, his voice retained composure.

Dive into this point of the river. When you wake, it will be inside your normal physical form, though far from your original parallel. Don't be fooled by familiarity; there are subtle differences, some difficult to detect. The Ark and everything in it might resemble the place you recognize. Be aware it is not. Do not rely on people you knew to act as they once did, for although their forms are unchanged, their souls are strangers. Search for a man named Ayizan, leader of the Outsiders . . .

The Outsiders? They're mixed up with this rogue spirit?

The gift of duality is often used as a means to possess human bodies, forcing them to carry out destructive acts. The Rogue has done so with Ayizan. The results could mean great peril. He is the man you must banish.

Wallace held something to the light of the water: a thin band of gold on which sat a single carved snake, also of gold, poised upright as if to strike, midnight-blue stones embedded for each of its eyes. The band folded into three hinged sections. As Wallace opened these sections, Markriss saw the band was in fact a crown, the snake situated at its center. Wallace unfolded, then folded the crown back, and handed it to Markriss. He took the gift without a word.

It's more common for objects to possess duality than humankind. This is a uraeus, a weapon that uses your sixth and seventh naardim to harness psychic force. It works by breaking down the components of a spiritual body and redistributing that energy into other forms. Order it to banish the Rogue and it will.

So what happens to Ayizan when I banish him?

You've already seen there is more to spiritual life than meager physical existence. Ayizan will not die in the true sense of the word; he will simply be released into a freer mode of living. Exist as he was always meant to.

It was difficult for Markriss to keep track of the sense of anything Wallace had told him. He still wondered if the man Ayizan would be killed. Earlier, Wallace had asked him if he could "trust." He'd thought the guide meant did he trust the odd spirit of a murderer to take him places that he'd never been. Now he saw that it meant much more. He was being asked to throw everything he believed over his shoulder, learn a new language, laws, and methods of behavior. He wasn't entirely sure whether he could, or if he wanted to live up to Wallace's high expectations. His only lifeline, the only thing that made any sense, was Keshni. Being with her. His mate.

So I just have to let myself fall into the river?

Yes. Your will does the rest.

He moved down, halting just above the surface. Objects and people continually floated by, each on an eternal journey to future destiny if the guide was to be believed—a miniature allocation, a dog, a raging fire, and at one point even the hulking mass of the gateway. Markriss paid no mind. He was calm, in control. He was ready. Before he fell, he remembered what had been forgotten.

Wait, Wallace! After all that talking you didn't tell me what the Way is!

The guide's laughter came back. *The Way is everything you have seen, Markriss. Everything you have seen and are about to see.*

He broke the water, causing circular ripples to slide across the surface. Slow as he could, he let himself fall farther, creating more ripples. The liquid was cool, soothing. He was almost fully submerged.

Wallace! Will I see you again?

He was beneath the surface, purple glazing his vision, finding he could breathe. Markriss relaxed more, Wallace's ka fading as he began his descent to the deep with greater speed. Light dimmed. His guide was no more. He could see nothing beyond ethereal images of possibility and, above that, distant ripples of a chess-black sky. When the last star died there was no choice. He curled his body toward the depths, grasping uraeus tight, diving farther than he'd ever thought conceivable.

Part Two

The Book of the Ark

"In some way, which I cannot recall, I got the knowledge that I was dreaming and then experimented in
prolonging the dream."

—Oliver Fox, *Astral Projection*

23 November 2020

1

Bright, steady awakening. He lay in the soft-lit room, blinking at the ceiling, relishing cotton against his back. He didn't want to move or disrupt the feel of air through his lungs, the rumble of his heart, the pulse of blood flow, all signs of common existence. Every intricate working of his body's interaction with the outer world was experienced and understood with utter clarity.

He took deep breaths, inhaling the last until it became painful. Opened his eyes to the allocation. That low ceiling, those close walls. Light supplied by scattered candles, a dance of flames causing an illusion of rapid animation. He sat up, blanket falling into his lap along with something hard that rolled to his feet. He reached out, picking it up—the rough shard of a rose-quartz crystal, warmed by his clutch. He put it on the podside for safety. There was a window-like opening on his right, devoid of glass, a kitchenette beyond. He made out lumps and bumps of furniture, a solitary window that looked onto the barely decipherable street. A memory teetered on the edge of his consciousness, and he tensed as he tried to recall words he'd once been told. By whom? He couldn't remember.

He threw away the blanket. Cold raised his skin into minuscule bumps—he was naked. A pile of clothes on a chair. He stood and fell back into the sleeper, his foal-weak legs another surprise. It took several pain-racked attempts to stand upright, holding the wall to keep balance. Even when he let go, starting to walk as if attempting to find balance against a stilted, rocking tide, one hand remained outstretched in case he fell. Though it proved difficult, he straightened, still leaning against nearby objects. A simple pair of dark cotton trousers and a plain shirt lay folded on the chair. He slipped them on, feeling comfort, familiar warmth.

There was a wardrobe at the foot of the pod. He limped to it, opening doors to see jeans and jumpers, shirts and suits. A number of women's skirts and dresses, T-shirts, pairs of jeans. Markriss smiled, holding them to the candlelight, sniffing fabric in an attempt to catch a trace of her. Maybe he wasn't fooling himself. Maybe he *could* smell a whiff of perfume, a lingering echo. Pleased, he put them down.

Their podroom was too small for a podside cabinet. The pod itself had a cot-like frame on either side that ended halfway between the head and foot. The frame provided enough room for candles, a men's watch, a single metal key that brought a rush of nostalgia, his retracted knife, and a sprinkling of brown dust beside a random pyramid of tobacco. He picked up the key, holding it to his eye and turning it from end to end; he imagined the small box and smiled at the thought of its contents. Markriss fingered the dust. Hesitant, lifting fingers to his nostrils, savoring the smell. Piahro. The sleeping drug.

He'd smoked the narcotic since he was a teenager. As a man he used it far less, yet he still relished the intensity of its odor, perhaps above all others. "Piahro," the scientific name for a substance that apparently drove Poor Quarter residents to riot, soothed the pain of winos, vagrants, and madmen, and fueled protesters. Naturally grown, the plant was smoked, injected, or ingested. In concentrated form, a gelatin-based chemical derivative, it could enter the body via pores. Media sources claimed piahro abuse was rife in the Poor Quarter, though the truth was the drug healed more than it harmed. The media and the Authority hid its benefits, and, along with that, its actual uses.

Pleased to find at least ten grams, he limped deeper into the flat, patting pockets, feeling the empty sense of something lost, something he had carried. Something important. Again, he struggled with recall.

Without knowing what it was, he missed the object's weight. Distracted, Markriss pressed light switches. When the flat remained dark he raised his candle, looking around the tiny space with under-standing, nodding. Something remembered. The uprising, the lack of electricity. Power, the first thing to go when looting began.

In the kitchenette he lowered his candle, taking a glass from one of the cupboards. He peered into the fridge. Their obligatory bottled water was warm, which meant the uprising had been going for some time. He slammed the door shut, catching a flash of reflected light. Squatting, he narrowed his eyes. Photos mapped the smooth fridge surface, haphazard jigsaw pieces. He exchanged the bottle for his candle, raising the flame and crouching on his heels, gasping soft pain.

Pictures, memories. Ark tourist spots they'd visited in those early days of exploration and hope, those bright apple-cheeked smiles, heads pressed close, Chileshe beside him in every frame. Favored shots, gazing into each other's eyes with complete love, a unanimous proclamation. Together, they'd made a near-impossible journey. It was as if he looked at two people he hadn't seen in an age: the Chile in the photo was the woman he remembered when they first married, eyes glittering with expectation. She wore no glasses. Her face was rounder, her cheeks and thighs bearing more flesh, her skin bright as though lit from within. There was a quality in her eyes Markriss hadn't seen since they arrived in the Ark. Casual, almost sly knowl-edge, happiness the Chile he knew never expressed. Regret thumped, akin to his pounding skull. His legs screamed fire. He lowered the candle, deflated, poured the bottled water into his glass, and knocked it back greedily, only to spit the mouthful into the sink. The hot, iron taste was disgusting.

Claw-fingered worry raked his gut. Where was his wife? She should have been there. Slim panic began from nothing, surprising Markriss, building into a crescendo that drove him from the kitch-enette, shadows trembling as though in fear of his presence. The feeling of a bad occurrence on the horizon. A need to stop it from happening, if he could.

Returning to the podroom for the security of his knife, he lurched toward the door, reaching for the handle as candle flame exposed a large poster just above his head.

He stilled, chest raised, stood to attention, right hand placed across his heart.

Even in the vague light, he made out the green six-pointed star representing the fourth heart chakra, the gold capital *O* dead center and rusty orange background, still bright. At the foot of the poster, a phrase that reverberated throughout the Poor Quarter, the tenet of their belief, passed from parent to child like a nursery rhyme. Words that gave pride, simplicity in the extreme:

TODAY AS YESTERDAY, TOMORROW AS TODAY,
IS TRUTH!

He erupted from the one-room allocation, litter and dust circling before him, a swirl of movement. Candles and blue lamps lining the road stuttered in his presence, sending a domino wave of shadow along bricks and stone. On the other side of the road stood a lengthy row of one- and two-story terraced allocation flats.

Forehead burning, his mind filled with mosaic imagery, blurring actual vision. The deep blue of electric lamps became patches of mellow green, a gateway towering in the darkness, the features of people he knew and those he did not. Rolling, churning without end. His legs pumped. Nothing else, only the urge to run.

Poor Quarter residents backed away, staring owls. Infant children playing in the safety of front gardens stood open-mouthed, tugging garments for comfort. He ignored them, stumbling down the road, aware of the distance people kept from him, intense agony cramping his legs; driven by the urge to find her. His thighs and calf muscles twitched and twinged as though they hadn't been used, causing him to slow to a walk with a half-hunched gait, creating even greater alarm among the surrounding people. Cries of horror came with almost every step, coinciding with gritted winces of sympathetic pain; still he kept his eyes on the road. He didn't know where he was going, just that he had to find her. It was the only thought his confused brain would allow.

He staggered along glittering tarmac, almost falling, stretching fingers like a sprinter to maintain balance, pushing himself upright and into the path of schoolkids he recognized, expressions alarmed at the sight of him, bouncing Markriss toward a burly man strolling home for the evening. The man looked up, saw him coming. *Vyasa!* Maybe he could help. He'd been walking with his nose pointed at the pavement until he saw the body hurtling into his. Vyasa took a casual step to one side, holding out massive arms. Markriss tripped into the embrace.

"Hey, watch it . . ." He caught Markriss by the shoulders, at arm's length. "Markriss? You shouldn't be out here. Where's Ayizan, he should be making sure—"

"*Chile!*" Markriss screamed, loud enough to conjure surprised wails from those nearby. Head angled upward, facing the man full on, unfocused. "Where's Chile . . . ?"

Vyasa let him go, shocked; arms raised in surrender, mouth quivering. Markriss spun, sending people scattering for cover before he began to run hard, letting his feet land where they wished, pushing on despite the spasms of his legs. Lurching in all directions, he kept on. Temple. He needed to get to the Temple. Vyasa's cries grew distant and faint. He tripped, rolled with the tumble and rose again, not feeling the fresh bruises and cuts, sprinting past a group of stunned women and the outer rows of houses, into streets where blue lamplight thinned. Beyond, more buildings disappeared into dense shadow at a point where concrete night fell. And still he ran.

A hundred meters before that segregation of light and shade, Markriss saw the dusty building. Isolated from the terraces and shops on all four sides, a former school, its solitary spacing effectively creating a town square. The doors were shut, seemingly locked. Markriss pelted into them, fists banging against the wood, trying a sharp kick when he received no reply. His jaw dropped in a silent scream. Hands clasped his bare foot in pain. No shoes. He'd run out of the house with no shoes and hadn't noticed. He collapsed, running footsteps coming from every direction around him, echoing and bouncing from quiet streets.

They halted above his head.

"Kriss, what's going on, tell me what's wrong? How'd you get here with no shoes, you can hardly walk . . . What happened?"

Chile's face swam above him. He tried to speak.

"Wallace . . ."

His voice lacked strength. He had to save his breath. She lifted him to his feet with an ease that penetrated even his fog of confusion. So strong she was, so strong. He stumbled, scraped toes and strained muscles crying in protest at last, though she stood firm enough to break his fall. Righting them both, she gave him a long, clinical look, feeling his forehead and neck.

"Markriss . . . who's Wallace?"

He couldn't speak. There was nowhere for him to start, no explanation. He had no idea. "Ayizan . . . where's Ayizan?"

Her eyes hardly blinked. She stood before him, mouth forming an almost seamless line. "He's meditating, Markriss. In here. Don't you remember what time it is?"

She touched wood. The door was old, on the verge of rot. The only remaining paint flaked and curled. He looked up at the building, swaying as a wave of pressure swept his head. When it subsided enough for him to be able to pay attention to what he saw, Markriss noticed light from the upper floors. Nearer ground level, the building's windows were melanin dark. A prickle in his stomach when he looked up, a pull of energy. He understood what had brought him. He'd been called.

"I have to see him."

"He's in nambula, Markriss. I know you've woken, but there's no way we can stir him."

"I don't want to disturb him. I just want to see him, Chile. It's very important I see him."

Her full-moon eyes turned to the counterfeit ground beneath their feet. The moment stretched.

"Okay, Markriss. We go in, see Ayizan for *one minute*, then I'm putting you to pod and you're staying there, do you hear? You need rest too, you know."

"Yeah. Yeah, whatever you say . . ."

Chile produced a solitary key and opened the building door. At once, he smelled an odor of decay. She walked a little way from him, grabbing a lamp she'd left on the road, returning to lead him inside. Without the light they might have been blind; even with it, pitch black oozed about them, soaking every nook and crevice. Deeper inside, blue light began to reveal the building's interior: random graffiti, Outsider slogans and posters, messages to fellow members, childish cartoons. Markriss tried to work meaning out of the scrawls, but Chile didn't stop long, squeezing his arm, tugging whenever he slowed. They reached a duo of stairs. Right led up, left went down, both wreathed in shadows. She raised her lamp, filling the stairwell with blue flame. A low hum of electricity, just above perception. She inclined her head left, gave another tug, and moved into the bowels of the Temple.

For almost a minute they seemed to be doing nothing more than cleaving a pathway through the veil of black, going deeper beneath the ground. If it wasn't for the urge of energy tugging at him, growing more insistent with each step, Markriss might have believed he was being taken on a walk of infinite length. Flickering light appeared. Chile walked slower, allowing time for his pupils to shrink. They reached a thin corridor. There were at least a dozen doors in that confined space, maybe more. Lined up like schoolchildren, they resembled the classroom doors of Regent's and E-Lul Secondary, only much smaller. Six-pointed stars were painted and drawn in chalk everywhere. Further geometric shapes occupied space on walls and windows. Chile kept walking until she reached a point in the corridor where two doors were placed instead of one, denoting what he guessed was a larger room. Two words had been carved into the wood, one on each door—*Transmutation Chamber.*

She pushed a door. On the other side they found a modest hall. Eight male "sleepers" lay on their backs, eyes closed, arms laid by their sides. Scented oil sweetened musky air. A mixture of candle- and lamplight illuminated the room, exposing bookshelves and posters, crystals, plants, more geometric symbols. Chile put a finger to her lips, smiling. He knew why. The feel-good vibration of healing energy coursed through him, the muscles of his limbs finding strength.

"Where is he?" He felt a tinge of nausea, probably because it was extremely hot. He closed his eyes, swaying on his feet. Chile's smile faded. The almost seamless line separating her lips returned. Worry and confusion replaced cheer.

"He's right there."

Thin bile rose, bitter and stinging. He swallowed hard, trying to speak as normal. His voice was guttural, strange. "*Point* . . ." He cleared his throat. "Point him out . . ."

She pointed a finger in the direction of a tall man lying slightly apart from the others. He wore a faded green T-shirt and black jeans. Markriss moved closer. Ayizan was in nambula, although he was not prone. Every now and then a finger would jerk, or nostril twitch.

"Markriss, you mustn't disturb him. Come back, let him transmute." Her voice, somewhere behind Markriss, relegated to a place where he could pay it no mind.

"Just a minute . . ."

He reached the Outsider, looking on his corpse-like body. Handsome, the strong features of a man who could take charge, fearing no one. A natural leader. A difficult enemy.

Markriss crouched beside the body. Mouth moving, soft words. Loving recognition blurred his eyes, the passage of time and maturity. He smiled. The pulse in the base of his skull returned. He was filled with an immediate coldness he'd never known. His mind blanked, and he saw his fingers clasped around the unprotected neck, applying necessary pressure even as his conscience screamed against it. Pressing hard, squeezing demonic strength, the noise inside his head thunderous. The image so powerful, so instructive, he made to move, stirring and creeping toward his old friend.

A procession of stronger memories joined forces with his nausea — clasped hands, a harmony of laughter, dense silences — causing him to rise and step away, fitting epileptically. Naked feet made contact with the bare flesh of sleepers. Chile grabbed at him, unable to gain purchase. He heard her voice and couldn't make out what she was saying, or tell her what he'd seen.

Ayizan's eyes snapped open. Staring. Overloaded, his brain couldn't cope, pulling the plug and plunging him back into his subconscious. The world grew North Star distant, Markriss collapsing into a dead faint. Even as he slumped into Chile's embrace, that Outsider linchpin refused to let go, ideology following him into the depths. The knowledge. The truth.

A waking dream foretold that he would kill his oldest friend. Ayizan, whom he loved as a brother, and had known since childhood as Nesta.

2

Eyes opening, Markriss almost believed he'd been delivered into another, similar abyss and his time on the solid world of senses was over, perhaps forever. Maybe he'd simply moved from one empty space into another. Maybe a series of chambers filled with swirling absence like the bulbous, interlocking test tubes he imagined in high-tech chemistry labs as a child, linked by tunnellike sections of glass, creating areas of eternal space. Maybe a vast expansion without end. The enveloping dark was womb-like. He might have stayed forever had it not been for the pull. An urge, a forceful tug, except there was nothing to denote movement, or to cling to, only the knowledge it had occurred because he was physical and apparent inside the room. No solidity, no pain, no sensation or sense of direction. He wasn't, and was. Nothing into something. Dissolution became mass.

He knew this when awareness told him the darkness wasn't absolute. Tiny beacon pinpoints betrayed that he was back. Not starlight, not here. He recognized the jittering sway: candles. He placed his palms on either side of his body, the pads of his fingers registering contact and all his nerve endings firing at once. The scratch of clothing against his wrist, at his fingertips. One deep breath, a sweet aroma of melted wax. The almost-pain of sit bones when he pushed with his palms, rising until his back rested against the podside. The soft fall of sheets, the quiet rodent squeak of a chair. Movement, as bodies he hadn't noticed at the foot of his pod leaned forward, toward him, emerging from the gloomed depths of his allocation.

Their faces bore a wealth of history. Vyasa's broad, his cane-colored hair falling in all directions. Temujin's lean and pale, all thin, dark pits for eyes, mere essentials of nose, lips, eyebrows. Bible-dark hair melding with darkness, making her look bald.

He drifted, submerged in recollection. Bright-star Ark Lites, Vyasa staring at his outside clothing and numerous bags from across the street, eyes curious. Moving to greet him. A firm and thorough hand-shake, a gentle crack of bones. Days beyond that first meeting, Markriss ducking behind Vyasa's slab of a back to enter the dull light of another compact Poor Quarter allocation, identical in layout to his own. Temujin's eyes weighed down by the toothpick piahro splint in the corner of a mouth. Her shock at the face of a stranger, the unfamiliar hard ridges of her cheekbones.

"How do you feel?" Vyasa leaned closer, his tone measured, breath heavy.

"Good . . ." The word a spiked object scratching his throat. "Water?"

Temujin swiveled, saying something too muttered to hear, returning with a cup in her hand. Markriss leaned forward, gasping. Every move brought new pain. He drank. The water had the iced solidity of cold.

"Do you know what happened to you?"

Vyasa reached, indicating. Markriss passed the cup over, wincing at the discovery of yet another ache—his right forearm.

"I'm not sure. I can't remember much. I made the jump okay, found the plane, and then I think I met some being. I couldn't tell who. We spoke, and then after—"

"It wasn't Ninka?"

"I don't even know. Next thing I'm here, and I couldn't control my actions. I didn't know what I was doing, or saying . . ."

Temujin sat back, legs crossed. "Don't worry about all that. The spiritual realms are vast, even adepts get lost. It's just . . . obviously . . ."

"I know what you're saying. I'm fine to go back."

"But first you must recover." The voice emerged from the far end of the allocation. Ayizan. He stood at the foot of the pod between the others. There was something in his hand. Sea green, thin, and curling. Markriss's book of notes. "I'm glad you're awake and aware, but I'm worried, brother. That encounter wasn't good. I hardly knew who you were. If you could remember who or what it was, it would be worthwhile."

Markriss closed his eyes, feeling for darkness. Dreamlike, untraceable, it faded into dust. "I've never met anything like them."

"They might not be an enemy," Vyasa said.

"That doesn't mean we shouldn't be careful. They were strong, centuries old. I remember that."

"Not all ancestors are kind." Temujin's head fell between her knees. Vyasa's hand rested on the knob of bone at the back of her neck, stroking.

"I hear you," Markriss said. "And I think you're right. I'll stay here, meditate on how to go forward. In the meantime, I'll heal."

Ayizan placed the book of notes at the end of the pod, beyond the protruding lumps of his feet. "You'll need this. Something from your previous travels might tell us more about that being." He smiled. "I didn't read them."

"Thank you, brother."

Markriss kept his eyes on the blanket. Rage thumped in his chest, an alien emotion in conflict with everything he knew about Ayizan.

"Chile's gone for food," Vyasa said. "I'll wait until she gets back. I won't be in your way." He stood, looming over the others, pointing. "I'm over there. Shout if you need me."

The huge man kissed Temujin, enfolding her in his arms, and hugged Ayizan with a brisk touch of shoulders. He stepped aside so they could leave.

"Truth go with you, brother," they said in unison.

"Truth go with you all. Thank you."

Markriss closed his eyes, attempting not to expend unnecessary effort on consciousness. The opening door, Poor Quarter noise, louder for scant seconds. Kids' laughter, the wheeling sibilance of tires, the cries of a distressed child fading as the door closed. Silence, punctuated by Vyasa's heavy breathing. Ears humming monotone, persistent but low. Nerve endings tingled, causing mild static across every conceivable area of skin. Glands swollen with use, Markriss felt strange, unsettled in his body, as if upon his soul's reentry he'd found he didn't quite fit. Anything farther than the contained space outside his allocation seemed infinitely difficult to imagine, or place. A world away, rather than yards.

He slept until he heard the brisk clash of metal, smelled sharp onions, frying coconut oil. The allocation was hotter. Gossamer steam tendrils, a sizzle of contact, the mutter of one-sided conversation. A hum of vibration from walls that meant the generator had been repaired. Chileshe was home.

He stretched tired limbs to feel where the pain struck deepest. The muscles of his legs mostly, hamstrings, and the stiff tendons at the base of his neck. A slight, troublesome ache beneath his left rib cage. His temples ached, a random pulse at his epiphysis cerebri tapping like a fired nerve. All usual after a jump. The pulsing wasn't painful, just skittering at times, stopping for restful moments before it returned, soft and rhythmic above his eyes.

He waited, reaching for calm, and felt descent, that minor retraction. Immediately, a mental picture of hands clasped around bare skin. Knuckles taut with strain. Deep inside his own head, a grunt of exertion, his voice. He spasmed into consciousness, spine flat against the mattress, skull pushed into his pillow, the curved sides of the sleeper pit rising around him. The slow twirl of dust motes, sparking fireflies catching rare light. Breath came rapidly, feathery and quiet. He squeezed his eyes tight, the waking dream that flashed in the darkness conjured there too. His hands, Ayizan's neck. The future apparent.

He had no reason to dream anything like it, and future visions were always read with caution. Markriss often taught that assumption exposed astral seers to the negative influences of ego. Still, it was possible to probe images for useful information as long as the seer remained aware that readings were not to be taken at face value, and the spirits were exemplary manipulators of subterfuge. Ausares wasn't the only trickster in the pantheon, only the most reliably unreliable. Waking dreams hid meaning in every detail and action. It could be a coded reference of intent that concerned the reason for his ascension into the plane. The mission. His hands on Ayizan's neck might not be literal, perhaps not physical at all. Inherent in that potential reading was a further, riskier problem; the actual true meaning of his dream could lead to greater, hidden dangers. The spirit he encountered might have warned him of this. He'd meditate further to find guidance. Equally, as Temujin had insinuated, the Rogue might have implanted the vision to drive him mad by implying he should kill his own friend. Until the last moment, when the vision became reality, he wouldn't know.

He sat up, jaw rigid with yawning. A clang of finality, scraping cutlery. Chile's head appeared from the small opening above the sleeper, peering from the kitchenette.

"All right, you're up. Thought you might sleep all day."

"Could've. Still woozy."

"No wonder. It was a huge jump."

Earthenware pots sang, a light pad of footsteps and she was there, at the edge of the bed, holding two bowls. Five feet four and lithe, Chile always moved with the fluid steps of a dancer. Rarely tripping or dropping anything, her body's actions were expressed with a precision that suggested she knew exactly where she would go before each movement occurred, a flawless ballet of function and timing charged with beauty. Markriss feasted on the sight of her as he opened the sleeper door and she entered the pit. After that was simple magic. The door snicked shut behind her. Raising the bowls for balance, Chile allowed her knees to bend and her legs to collapse beneath her until she sat, limbs folded as neat as a toddler's stroller. She offered Markriss a steaming bowl.

"Might've grabbed this."

"Didn't look like you needed me to."

"Yeah, well, an offer is better than reality."

He gave a mock smile, which she returned. The bowl warmed his palms, playful heat tickling his chin. She was shoveling hers with a spoon, jaws champing. Markriss tried a mouthful. Thick chicken pieces, slippery greens, thick sweet sauce.

"Wow."

"Fancied a bit of Siam."

"It's lovely."

"Lots of green. Should build your strength."

They ate in silence, thinking of the void.

"It was almost two days, you know."

"Are you serious?"

Chile wrestled a particularly thick piece of pak choi with teeth and tongue. Nodded at the bowl, trying to cut it with the spoon. Successful, she ate, swallowed.

"What did I miss?"

"More uprisings." A pause to chew. "No one killed by *them*, six people injured. No kids, thank Ra. The Simms closed shop, but halfway down the high street, in that little yard with the bakery, Gonzalez is open mostly. We've got the veg we grew, some bread. Ayizan said we shouldn't touch those until we have to."

He nodded. A lot to have missed.

"Gen's repaired?"

"Couldn't wait. Vy fixed it not long after you came back."

"That's good."

The steady thud of a ball against a nearby wall. Akin to the intermittent pulse in the center of his forehead. Stopping, starting. He winced.

"So what happened? Any idea?"

"None."

"You've never done that before, right? Even outside?"

"Not as far as I know. I've never felt out of control before, I know that much. And my whole time in the plane's a blank. I can't remember anything."

He coughed, thumping his chest to loosen trapped substance. She watched until he stopped, spoon dipping and returning. The unseen ball thumped irregular time.

"Your count was forty-one hours and twenty minutes. Corps cut power after eighteen. Most people listened to your teachings and stayed offline, but shit, someone always doesn't, right?"

Fully aware that Chile was unconcerned whether he agreed or not, Markriss waited for her point.

"We lost Sylvan Mistry. From Oshun Way."

He rested his spoon against the bowl, watching for signs. She ate fast, spoon clinking quick time, catching fallen rice grains in her bowl without acknowledging whether they landed. A pause, a dip of cutlery toward her food, ending without contact. A hand raised to wipe the corner of one eye. The glistening knuckle of a finger, the mirror gleam of her eyes, and it was over, the moment fled. Her spoon clinked against the bowl, dinner eaten with even greater passion. She wouldn't look at what she consumed, the room, or anything else. He had no idea what she saw.

After, they walked Poor Quarter streets to let the community know he had woken. Day-Lites remained offline and cold, far above, unseen. Stuttered candlelight and blue e-lamps made front gardens difficult to view. Poor Quarter residences, uniform as soldiers, were mostly squat bungalows, flat-roofed and low. Some had multiple podrooms. Most were one-room studios like their own. The allocated homes were small and cramped in any case, walls easily dented or cracked, and, with very few windows, extremely hot in the summers that Inner City never saw, especially for the larger families, those with more children, cousins, or sisters. Many sat "out" in their gardens where it was a degree or so cooler, the feeling of being hemmed in less harmful. Despite the constant white noise of residents at all times of day and night giving the impression of a buzzing community, ITS was rife in the Poor Quarter, with little defense against the illness besides work and meditation. They tried to teach the people mental antidotes via spiritual practice, never quite managing to stem the steady tide of depression that had overcome 38 percent of the community in the last year alone. Suicide was on the rise: all manner of methods. A knife, a handful of pills, the local tram.

Their road team offered an alternative to the isolation of being trapped in homes that might warp the ability to reason logically, and to those who craved simple escape. To the air, the sky, or just a horizon, however built up or close. To hear the distant roar of an airplane. A bird singing to greet another morning. Their spiritual methods of living without interaction with the outside world was partially why the Outsiders had become the largest team in the zone.

Markriss and Chile walked arm in arm, bumping each other. He kept his head raised, alive to the feel of her against him, fingers clasping his on occasion, or caressing his knuckles, letting him know she was there. He breathed lightly, resigned to the taste of reconstituted air, which left a furry sensation on the tongue. Energetic calls of "Teacher!" came from many gardens. They raised their palms, unable to see faces. Cheers were heard, along with cries of "Àṣe!"

On some corners, outside terraced houses, residents were waiting spiders, poised ever watchful, hands in pockets, only eyes moving. Hanging piahro smoke formed tendrils in the air. Men and women let them pass, muttering through barely open lips. These were dippers, cutters, pimps, and dealers. People of the street. Their products and tools of various trades hidden inside the allocations they stood before, each home a somber, wrecked advertisement. Chile's arm tightened, body stiff.

Silence, then a thudding rhythm behind them, alien yet familiar. Markriss was unable to place the sound until he turned his chin over one shoulder, searching the dusk of quiet streets. Jeweled eyes, a stubby, glistening snout. Continual low growling. The dogs. One stepped into a patch of candlelight, harsh panting. He flinched at the tawny, emaciated body, huge despite its hollowed sides, its mouth open, revealing its ridged, meaty tongue. Red and gray-patched skin, fur tails resembling carpet frayed to the underlay. Another, then another appeared, similar in color, size, and breed, like siblings, each seemingly staring at Markriss. Begging to be fed perhaps. They were obviously starving. He dragged his feet, unsure what to do about such blatant want. Chile made harsh noises in her throat, and when that didn't work, began to hiss and bare her teeth. The dogs faded into darkness, steady as whales beneath waves. The couple moved on, neither admitting that the stilted tread of padding paws could still be heard on the edge of hearing, random, unattached to their physical forms.

The walk took them farther away from the high street, deep into the quarter and maze of terraced residences that mapped their territory, Charlton Estate. An Outsiders' zone, that was clear. Incense belched sandalwood ghosts. Gardens were filled with squat candles set in the form of their six-pointed star, the centered O. More difficult to see in low light were the spray-painted murals. Orishas, gods, deities, angels, and symbols adorned every surface: walls and fences, doors and windows, sidewalks. Prayer flags, symbolic representations of the chakras: crescent moons, triangles, upward swirls. Often no shapes or symbols, only merged formulations of colors. Seamless mosaics of red into orange, orange into yellow, yellow into green, green into purple. Markers of dedicated Outsider homes.

Passing deeper into those residences, a wave of movement turned candles into nocturnal coral-birthing polyp flames. Shadows formed and retracted in swelling motion. Doors opened and families came: Marstens, Amens, Wazzis, and Okoros. Trinitys, Mysses, Braithwaites, Maungs, Fajemisins. Surrounding Chile and Markriss, pressing deter-mined bodies against theirs, reaching for temples and foreheads with rough fingers, touching bare skin, offering greetings and gifts of food, foil-wrapped packages and bags of cloth. They wore dreadlocks and head wraps, hijabs and geles. A glitter of whisper-thin robes and saris, agbadas and lungis sweeping grimy streets and sidewalks with glints of starlight. People gave small, carved effigies. A cola-wood Ganesh, polished and embedded with circular, beige grain. A stone-gray Shango, pearl teeth gritted in anger, and handfuls of others, some beautiful, most simple. Markriss took them gratefully, otherwise Chile accepted on his behalf, concealing them in the hemp bag at her side. They would be given to the Temple, distributed among disciples. A rare few would make it to their allocation.

He talked with all who left their homes to meet him, reassuring he was well, untouched by Corps or uprising. He wasn't poisoned, neither had he succumbed to ITS. Teacher was in perfect health, alive. Questions came in muttered succession, each speaker knowing they should let them leave, eventually. Given time, they retreated, heads bowed, pulling moon-eyed children by reluctant fingers, back-ward like the rewound video of their childhoods until the doors closed and once more candlelight broke the silent darkness with its staccato, baritone language.

Markriss and Chileshe walked farther along the block, encountering more Outsider residents, who came and greeted the pair as their neighbors had. And onward to the next block and the next, until finally they arrived at a large two-story home adorned with white roses hung on the front door. The bouquet circled a sign made of simple white paper that bore the family name, visiting hours, and times of prayers in a careful, printed hand.

A lean, dark man smoked tobacco nearby. Markriss tried to remember his name. Chile, as ever, read his mind, standing on tiptoes, whispering into his ear.

The son, Parv, discarded his splint and came to them, clasping their hands. Reddened eyes, far-off, hardly resting on any one thing, a mind full of all the chores to perform inside the house perhaps, or in ether with the spirit of his loved one. Markriss recalled a similar unmooring after Ninka joined the ancestors. He wasn't even sure if he'd returned to the full consciousness of mortal existence, even after all the years since.

"Teacher . . . we're so sorry . . ."

Ah. Sylvan's misdeed, the source of Parv's discomfort.

"Don't be. It's done. We're sorrier to be here under these circumstances. We only hope your mother is at peace."

"Everyone tried to tell her, she never listened . . . She's obsessed by simulations . . ."

"Who can teach the old? Certainly not us," Chile said, voice made gentle with supplication.

Parv's smile cracked the tired lines of his face. "You must eat."

"We'll pray, though Teacher isn't 100 percent. We'll have to leave soon."

"Of course, of course . . ." Parv moved toward the house, crooked arm cradling space, pulling aura toward the door. "How are you, Teacher?"

"I'm getting there," he told him, and they were over the threshold.

Inside, a passage filled with people pressed against walls, gasping when they saw Markriss and Chile. Alert bodies, lowered eyes. A wave of bows, mutters, clasped hands raised and shaken in their direction. Word of his arrival traveled throughout the allocation. From a room he couldn't see, a rising, falling chant of bhajans led by the high, sonorous voices of the elderly, louder than all. Strong incense almost overpowered smells of cooking ghee, while raised voices came from farther in, the kitchen most likely. A small bell rang. Voices died into scattered Hindi, fragmented murmurs, before a new prayer began and they rose up, powerful again. Markriss closed his eyes. He couldn't help smiling. His eyes stung, and he was forced to wipe them. He bit back emotion, shook his head. Loss was a concentrated presence in the Mistry home.

Parv, eyes set with the glassed introspection of a doll, touched a shoulder to indicate they should move on. He led them, edging along the clogged passage, entering the first open doorway they came to.

A collected exhalation as the bhajan singers saw them. Prayers grew quiet until he raised a hand, gesturing that they continue. The carpet was covered with white sheets and mourners—close relatives of the Mistrys for the most part—sitting on the floor in every space and crevice, cross-legged, a plethora of combed and pinned gray heads. A short, rounded elder wearing a cardigan over her mourning blue-and-gold sari sat queenlike yet awkward on the sole wooden chair, clutching a prayer book so wrinkled it might have been covered with her own skin, turning pages with an orange-tinged finger. Muttering, she pushed sallow pages back and forth, searching for the right one. Acknowledging Markriss with a nod, she continued to lead as before. The pitch of her voice rang in his ears; relatives joined her, their harmonies splitting rainbow light. Chile and Markriss breathed light, motionless. When the energy of prayers flowed upward in familiar spirals, they nodded at one another, approaching the altar where a huge silver-framed photograph of Sylvan Mistry was placed beside an illustration of a leaping, dancing Shiva. Sylvan was smiling into the distance, against some unrecognizable background. It wasn't Outer City, the darkness behind her proved that. It was always dark in the Poor Quarter.

They stood before the twelve-inch steel deevo, stained rust orange and brown from overuse. Filled with translucent liquid, the pan alive with the tangerine flame of a burning wick. He inhaled melting ghee, closed his eyes. Pictured Sylvan fast-talking, and her precocious laughter, mischievous even at the end. The kind woman who cared for her community with grace and love, who cooked the most delicious vegetarian dishes in the Quarter. An invaluable Outsider presence, despite her sole vice of dreaming. Sylvan's warm ka entered him. Markriss felt sorrow, also peace. He opened his eyes. Caught heated air between his fingers, lifting it toward him, and touched his chest, eyes, and forehead. Whispering "Àṣẹ," he breathed deep, filling and expelling his lungs three successive times before he moved aside for Chile. While she gave her own tribute, he sat on the soft white sheet, enveloped by song and the close proximity of the Mistrys. Head bowed, he prayed.

3

The chair had woken sore points, each rigid slat uncomfortable and stubborn against the muscles of his back, rear, and shoulders. He shifted, trying for a more comfortable position. It was wooden, great for carvings, ornaments, and probably the old-style beds that existed long before sleepers, though he'd always thought the insistence on crafting trees into seating a grave mistake. He rocked side to side, trying not to be noticed. The chair creaked protest, so he stopped. It was always the same. He'd tried everything, from bringing his own cushions to sitting on the floor—which Ayizan disliked, probably because it wasn't official enough. He had been so caught up with their present troubles, he'd forgotten how much he hated the emaciated chairs they'd brought up from the dingy school basement. He muttered, stretched a leg, tried sitting upright, fell against the back of the chair, annoyed by the failure of his efforts, while Ayizan kept talking, pushing waterfall locks over one shoulder, casting glances between the pad on his knee and each adept in the Circle.

The others seemed able to cope. Vyasa and Temujin pushed their chairs together so they leaned against each other for support, although they never registered one another's presence, much less allowed their bodies to touch. Xander, at twenty-five the youngest and perhaps most agile of the Circle, sat cross-legged, back plinth-straight, a strand of twisted baby lock fallen across an eye, hands clasped in his lap, statuesque. Ayizan seemed relaxed, one leg thrown across the other, bouncing a knee, his voice calm and fluid. Chile would normally complete their Circle, but she taught regular home classes for families who couldn't attend temple due to childcare restrictions. Apologies were sent in her place.

He still hadn't recovered from almost two days' sustained meditation. As much as he and his fellow adepts exercised daily, being prone in a sleeper for that long was far from conducive to the body's well-being. That was the real problem, he told himself, over and above his long-standing issues with sitting for more than fifteen minutes in a wooden chair. It made listening to Ayizan much more difficult, though it was vital to learn everything he'd missed. Not having fully recuperated from his meditation meant everything felt off, not only in his body; his mind also felt bruised and sore with use. His temples ached, his third eye beat an irregular pulse, a gentle, random sensation, consistent as breathing. He ignored the louder creak of his chair as he leaned forward, attempting to squeeze greater concentration by making Ayizan his sole focus, trying to block pain. He pictured the image of an old washcloth held by a strong hand. Only when the fingers tightened into a fist, no water emerged.

He let the visualization go.

Their most urgent topic was the uprising, and their stalled dissent against the Authority. Going into transmutation just after the incident that prompted residents' fury had been risky, yet the Day-Lites had been online, protests were confined to main streets, and the Corps presence was minimal. There had been a football game, nothing major or of any real merit, Barnsley Zone versus Charlton FC, sworn enemies on the pitch at least, their long-standing rivalry birthed in a friendship going back to the glory days of the Ark inception, when the gateways first opened and everyone hoped. Willingly or otherwise, the matches reflected the very societal structures they represented, each game promoting fierce competition between rich and poor. A given, most believed, seeing as Barnsley housed a more affluent zone of tower blocks, Inner City workers, and families. Charlton was the official name of the Poor Quarter.

For decades, both teams refused to buy into the competitive fervor of fans, playing down animosities, posting online selfies of drinking and socializing after games no matter who won, trading players and managers alike. No one knew if they'd been forced to publicize their actions or decided to themselves, the Ark too small and intense for anything other than open camaraderie, despite the contrived nature of every promotional opportunity. They were often commended by the Chief of Corps, the brick-headed Chintana Wells, and the wider media praised their efforts with loud, celebratory, and overzealous headlines.

Pal Mullen, the famous 1980s striker and ex–Poor Quarter resident, nicknamed Sagarmatha due to his extreme size and build, had begun his career with Charlton. There he won the AA Cup and League three times in a row before he switched teams, accepting the mantle of Barnsley captain until he retired. Goalies married the sisters of defenders from the opposing team. Coaches became well-documented best friends, and the only aggression between sides came from the fans. There were fistfights in stands that spiraled into violent free-for-alls, attacks on stadium security and even Corps. Occasionally, on the streets, there were deaths. On match days the entire spread of L1 was put on high alert, and security drones were deployed. There were curfews. Matches had been canceled, sometimes hours before kickoff.

The present uprising wasn't born of a clash between sides. It came after a Poor Quarter resident, Enos Weston, a twenty-eight-year-old gateway worker and father of three, tried to exit the curfew zone to buy emergency supplies for his sick daughter. He wasn't a fan of either team. He didn't even like the beautiful game, preferring track and field, the 200-meter hurdles specifically. Weston's spouse, a pragmatic L1 nurse at Chaucer Cross, suspected their eight-year-old daughter had come down with measles and sent her husband to the mall for paracetamol, a pint of fresh orange juice, and a desktop humidifier. On a good day it was a simple journey, perhaps half an hour there and back. But Weston ventured out not long after the final whistle of that year's AA Cup quarterfinal. The home team won, trouncing Barnsley in a decisive 4–2 victory. Street parties blossomed on every block up until the Corps perimeter, the corner where Prospect met Willington. Well-seasoned meat smoked on roadside barbecues. Monolith speakers were erected on rickety sound systems. Corporation soldiers appeared, face-masked and armed.

Weston had only asked to leave his zone and return. When the soldiers refused, he grew frantic. His child was in the early stages of fever. If it worsened, the virus could infect his entire family, hospitalizing them with possible fatal results, maybe even affecting their zone. The last outbreak of measles in the Poor Quarter killed four children, as expensive vaccines were only available to the rich. Eyewitnesses said the Corps became agitated. They forced Weston to the floor, gun butts raised flags above their heads, threatening further violence. Weston refused to return to the Quarter without supplies. It was entirely feasible that he believed his daughter might die. The security forces tackled him into a choke hold and placed him under arrest, grappling him into submission. Enos Weston died, one cheek pressed against the cold speckled tarmac of the street, limbs convulsing robotically, in less than two minutes.

And the Poor Quarter took to the streets.

"As of last night, Bay Weston finally allowed us to intervene on her behalf," Ayizan said, scrolling the information on his slide. "I've sent e-mails and v-mail requests for meetings with Wells and E-Lul. No response, so I'll keep the pressure on. I may need to ask one of you to take over if this continues. They've ignored Bay's requests too. They won't even give her basic respect."

"They've got no intention, we know that." Without moving, Xander was alive with fierce, abrupt venom. Only darting eyes and the quick rhythm of his chest divulged emotion. "And then what next? We wait for raids? More killings?"

"It won't get to that point," Markriss said more quietly than he felt. A wave of nods traveled the circle. He fidgeted against wood. "We'll move first."

"Exactly." Markriss read grateful thanks as Ayizan caught his eye. "In the meantime we'll use official means of contact even though we know it's useless. Just to say we communicated in their language. It's the Bulan way."

"Fair enough." Xander blinked himself still. "She'll need food, tics, childcare."

"Tics we can cover with donations, but could you handle the rest?"

"I'll make it happen."

"Thank you, brother. Ready for the next item?"

"I am." Temujin's eyes flitted between appraising Markriss and checking the others with swift glances. "How do you feel, Kriss? Can we talk mission?"

"I'm actually good." Up until that moment there'd been little exploration of his aural response in the aftermath of his failed jump. The strength of his voice created a ripple in his element he wasn't sure his Circlemates picked up. "I've been reading my notes and taking small meditations up till this morning. I'm still not sure what happened, but the simple explanation is I got lost during the jump. It's strange. I met that rogue being, and didn't see any of you, even though you'd all mutated. But I'm ready for another transmutation."

"When do you think?" Vyasa picked at the heel of his shoe with desperate attention, aura brightening rose pink. An emotional flush, Markriss read. Possibly concern born of love. Or fear.

"The end of this week?"

Another nodding wave. Ayizan wrote in his response.

"It's not that big a jump. I've done bigger. It should be easy, barring clashes with that rogue."

"Quicker the better, I'd say. Let's talk more later," Ayizan said, looking at the notes, striking off the item. "Next. Medical attention for residents."

"I've contacted Dr. Amunda," Temujin said. "He'll be here by morning, the checkpoints are less busy."

"Good work." Ayizan scratched that in.

"What's the injury tally?" Markriss tried another position, finding it just as bad.

"One fracture, one suspected broken leg, four mild concussions, one confirmed broken finger, and Bay Weston's daughter with measles. Oh, and Syn Adebayo thinks she's pregnant again."

"Syn by name . . ." Xander cut in, getting a laugh.

"Yeah, I see how you look at her." Vyasa grinned, shoulders heaving. "Imagining sin."

The young man rolled his eyes, imitating serenity, losing. "Nothing wrong with admiring a bodily aura . . ."

"Mr. Adebayo will cut it off. Turn the other way." Ayizan chuckled with the room. "That everyone for injuries?"

Markriss raised a hand, caught himself, and let it drop. They hated the gesture, yet kept up the habit like trained pets.

"Can we put me and this bloody chair? It's killing—"

"Oh, here we go . . ." Vyasa sagged.

"All right, people, focus." Ayizan raised his own hand, pen waggling for attention, a command. "Nearly done. Next item, waste collection. Right, can I start? We have to keep on it, yeah? We won't have the confidence of our own team, let alone the residents, if we allow rubbish to build in our zone. We promised."

Xander winced. "It's not the team's fault, it's us—I mean, where do we put the f— Sorry . . . the stuff?"

"I thought we decided that," Temujin said, craning toward her husband at last. "We dump it in the next zone."

"No, we don't dump it in the next zone," Markriss interrupted. "We chuck it in the Lowers for Capra Paorach and the below-levelers to incinerate. I thought we knew that. Does Rick know that?"

"Rick does *not* know that," Temujin said, sitting back, arms folded, blue ink on pale skin a disrupted Celtic map of illustrations and half messages. "He thought it went in the next zone and refused to let his people take it. Said he didn't want anyone shot."

"Okay. Xander, tell him otherwise and leave it for him to sort. He asked to run waste disposal; it's his shout. We've done our bit. Right?"

"You're the boss."

"Thank you very *much* . . ." Ayizan sighed. "Onto the best part. Any other business?"

"Have we discussed the Quebanos' wasp nest?" Vyasa said, huge raised hand eclipsing the candles behind him.

"No, we haven't, it's taken care of. I did it myself, and it was a nightmare, thanks for asking. We don't need a meeting for that."

"Bloody well *did* need a meeting for that," Vyasa muttered beneath his breath. He was ignored.

"Anything else?"

Silence. Reluctantly Markriss raised his hand. Ayizan's smile became a wince.

"Kriss. Make it quick, I suspect these lot want to go home."

Him too, Markriss thought. Ayizan's eyes were rimmed black, tired. He took a deep breath. Waited.

"I'm not sure I have an answer, so I'll say it anyway. What do you propose we do about the media coverage down here while we wait? Uprising after uprising it's the same nonsense, and I don't know how you guys feel, but I'm tired of the crap. I heard some people talk about it on the way in, the usual stuff, you know. The protesters looted for no apparent reason, other than the urge to smash up their own zone; looting was capitalist in nature, more about clothes and tech rather than basic provisions like food, water, medicine. Lies about attacking and injuring Corps soldiers, no names, photos, or proof . . . And then, you know, they don't say nothing about what Bay Weston and her family's going through right now, nothing about people like Sylvan Mistry corpsing in their machines, or the injured, and everyone else left to rot. Like I said, I don't have answers; I just keep thinking about the media and the way they deal with us and I wondered if there was any way to lobby them so we highlight the misinformation, or change the narrative in some way . . ."

They watched him with an intensity he hadn't felt before, Markriss pulling his energy inward. Calm. He needed calm. He felt the rush of rapid breath, the chair squeaking with each movement, a chattering, excited animal. Ayizan faced him with forensic deliberation.

"Sorry about that, I just—"

Ayizan's bright palm, scored with dark pathways. The markers of future life, elders believed, although few left alive could read them.

"No need to be sorry. We feel what you say and agree, don't we?"

This wave of nods went all the way.

"The real question is whether it's possible to do more than we've already proposed. They're media. They have the backing of entities like Hanaigh E'lul, the Corps, and the Authority. We're a group of allies trying to help the community govern themselves. Rock versus sword."

"But surely there's—"

"Rock versus sword." Weighty, deliberate. "If you can come up with a method of disarmament, I'd like to hear it. But fighting the media's like trying to fight smoke. Until we can blow enough air in their direction, we should concentrate on what's manageable."

Markriss conceded, nodding as they had. The knife-sharp pain in his back returned, deepening. He stood in one quick movement, causing the chair to emit a wailing bark.

They stared of course. He was alone on his feet.

"Meeting closed," Ayizan said, palms held together like prayer, pad dormant on his knees.

The high street was desolate with abandoned buildings, the shop windows blank, cold glass. Broken doors and bent metal shutters lay smoke-blackened, prone as sculptures. The street was mostly empty, only residues of past life—husks of roasted plantain, cassava, and potato chip wrappers, tiny remnants of bone—to betray what had once been. The Lites were on, dimmed to sallow beige.

At the opposite end of the street, behind the closed barricade, was the Corps, suited for combat, staring down anyone who dared to venture out of the Quarter or Prospect Towers. Residents hurried past, heads dipped, shoulders hunched against silent threat, moving with the quick purpose of night creatures expecting the worst.

The men stood alone beneath the awning of Sarfatti's tech repair store. Window signs screamed SALE, beside scattered offers of discounts. A pale-blue e-lamp shone in one corner of the window, indicating that the store was open for business to residents who knew what the signal meant.

Fully masked, heavily armed Corporation soldiers formed a line of fifty or more. With supporting vehicles and machinery, they stood in row after impenetrable row, still as winter trees. Sharp-edged drones hovered above like evil thought, a horizontal buzz of motion and bluebottle whine. These autonomous machines were equipped with .22 bullets and HD digital recording equipment, no mics. A security precaution in case the Corps were recorded saying anything that could be hacked and transmitted out of the zone, perhaps even out of Inner City. How they enforced their will on camera was of no concern.

Ayizan prepared a tobacco splint, licking paper. He kept his sights on the Corps best as he could, even with his head ducked; one quick movement and he was up, returning their mechanical stare. It was wise to see what they did, or might do.

Hands in pockets, Markriss also watched.

"Brother, I'm with you," Ayizan continued, between lighting the splint and emitting smoke. Scented caramel rose. He blew the fiery tip. "News sites, VS, bloggers, news drones, even writers and poets. You saw the Hogan piece, right? Very few stand to support us. Most agree our lives are worthless, so I totally get what you're saying."

"Then why shut me down in the Circle?" He kept his voice light, at low volume, back resting against glass, muscles warmed by lamp glow. It was also wise to take precautions against being overheard, in case former protocols had been reformed overnight.

"When you get the plans, we also need to identify where the people who write those articles live and persuade them to stop. One way or another."

"I can do that." Markriss watched, alert for the next question.

"How long?"

Shrugging, toeing a stray chocolate wrapper. "Let me see. I'm not certain for sure; I'll know when I've made the jump."

"Good. Just let me know as soon as you can. And keep this between us, okay? Don't even tell Chile. They're all over the Quarter. I wouldn't even speak too much in temple until we find how many bugs we've got. I put Vy on it. He found eight or so in chambers, which means he probably missed even more."

"Got you."

Ayizan passed him the splint. It was hot, smoldering. Markriss put it to his lips, inhaling, eyes on the barricade. The masked Corps were like the corrupted auras of vengeful spirits—the most negative aspects of the plane, only more dangerous.

"What should we do about residents using sleepers and medis? Sylvan wasn't the only addict. It's rife."

"I know." Ayizan examined the end of one lock, let it fall. "We can't force them to stay offline. They're unable to keep disconnected, even when they see the consequences. Those machines have a greater hold than we thought."

"Yes, and they're stupid."

"Misguided, I'd say." Ayizan grinned, his boyish expression filled with genuine humor. "But you're always more honest than me."

A few quick puffs, before he passed the splint back. Ayizan's eyebrows raised in thanks.

"Let them. Either we'll win by example, or we won't. If we try to impose our beliefs, they could turn. We'll lose."

"Right."

Ayizan spat at his feet repeatedly. The Corps bristled, masks angled their way. Drones rose higher, the buzzing angrier, mini camera snouts pointed at them, whirring.

"What you doing?" Markriss asked.

"Bit of tobacco."

"Yeah, well, don't make your shit rolling get us killed."

They swapped glances, laughing.

"Oh, on that note, I've been thinking. We should be wary about giving residents unequivocal cross-pantheon support. Sending condolences is one thing. We must, of course, particularly when they're Outsiders. What you did, attending ceremonies, taking part in rituals . . ." Grumbling, a fitful shake of the head. "I'm not sure. Not sure at all."

"You just said we can't force people to choose our ways."

"We can't. But we shouldn't encourage them not to. It's double standard."

Markriss leaned his head back against the glass, warming his skull. It felt good. Without overthinking, he closed his eyes. Luxuriated in the freedom of not having to care for a moment, almost as good as the comforting vibration at the curve of his head.

"Double standard is telling people we're different from the Authority because we respect all forms of worship while we stifle the traditions of others. That's not right to me, or what I teach."

He waited out the silence, hearing a rustle of movement, guessing he was being regarded when he felt channeled focus, a new quality of warmth from that direction. In quiet streets, a continual buzz of drones, the bark of dogs, and labored hum of the e-lamp, the window sang a gentle vibration like mantra. Markriss sighed, hardly making a sound. Felt the motion of everything, organic to mechanical, Corps to fruit fly, at his nerve tips. Breathed them in.

"I hear you, brother. Don't entirely agree, but I hear you."

He opened his eyes. "I hear you too, brother. Truth."

They touched fists, held them in place. Slight pain, rubbing flesh and bone beneath. Solidity. Ayizan let go first, dropping his splint with a free hand, crushing tobacco-filled paper against sidewalk with a foot, exposing tarred guts. Drone engines lifted higher in pitch as three machines gained height on their sibling formation, swinging left to right as if from string until they maintained that new position, cameras trained on the men. So they faced them, knowing they'd lost that particular battle, expressions set in mute defiance. Their only resistance a singular, wordless protest, watching the watchers.

4

To the sea-green notebook, thin yet vast with potential. He twisted the small key to open his wooden safety box, retrieved the pages, and sat beneath the window on their worn sofa, using candles to reread his own words, squinting at untidy recollection, edging closer to light, humming snatches of ancient songs. A slight pause to think, muttering half-decipherable meanings as he listened for answers. There were other, more worn notebooks charting previous explorations, seven going back to his first Circle meetings, fresh with ideas of how they might help people like themselves. While important and vastly educational, only the notes he'd written over the last few months truly captured his advances, tracking the precise details of how he coupled his studies, teachings, and everyday practice into opening the internal sequences of his body. This revealed methods that could lead to actual change for the poorest Inner City residents, perhaps even those who came after.

Chile worked on the other side of the room, reading through a leaning pile of texts, writing her own notes. They'd undergone morning transmutations together, separating afterward to concentrate on their own efforts. Every so often, there was a hesitant knock on the door. She'd rise to greet a resident who'd come searching for advice, herbal remedies, or for general help. They would go "out" into the garden, Chile pulling the door to, whispering until they were far enough to speak normally, voices rising and falling beyond the window. Markriss barely listened. He read his own memories, drank tea, made further notes. On occasion he looked over at their sleeper, thinking of Harman Wallace, its creator. The scientist's name had been on his mind ever since he'd called it to Chile. Professor Wallace would have read many of the published texts and written on transcendental states. If he had produced any books besides his account of the events that led to his suicide, it would be wise to read them. He scratched the thought onto his page.

His own explorations—"Notes on Mental Transmutation"— consisted of thoughts on his intentions before every meditation, and journal entries made after, including a coded outline of each mission objective, heavy with jargon, abstract enough so they couldn't be deciphered if found. Over a year of entries were written in that particular journal, short and nondescript, nothing dramatic. They began to pick up six months ago, when he'd made his first real discovery, and it was his last four entries that held the most promise. Yet Markriss went back to the beginning, flipping worn, smudged pages, moving from notebook to textbooks and back, attempting to decipher patterns that might lead him to remember what happened during his most recent transmutation: why the only remnants of the journey, a waking dream, gave him the nightmare vision of killing a man he would probably trade his life for.

Mundane entries from those first pages, yellow and broken at the spine, made him smile. Often he was unable to remember writing the words, due to being in trance, he believed. An example:

> Is it possible to touch the physical body while in astral form? I don't think so. I've tried many times but the urge to reconnect with the physical body is too strong to resist, perhaps because of the close range. It feels like the tug of two magnets placed close together, a kind of undeniable, invisible force. Whenever I've tried, the tug gets stronger and next thing I know I'm looking at my own ceiling, annoyed with myself for making the attempt.

He had no recollection of having those thoughts, writing them down, or even making the attempt to touch his physical body while in astral form. And yet it made perfect sense that he would try. Textbooks taught that the ability to achieve higher planes of existence made all things possible, and to inhabit the astral body as an adept, someone who'd mastered higher energies, meant that the spirit being could live pretty much as their physical form. But to touch your own living body with yourself? He wasn't sure if the sensation would be satisfying, or if he would even remember the feeling if he had. Maybe it was something he'd achieved during his last transmutation. Did it account for his lack of memory? He wasn't even sure he'd want to know.

Another:

I just fell asleep and had an unconscious transmutation which led me to discover this: ascensions made on the stomach cause the senses to reverse—up becomes down, and down becomes up. Sight is the most reliable means of finding your true direction. So I should remember not to ascend with my eyes closed ☺

Smiling, he turned pages.

Those in the zone who'd practiced longest—"Circle Adepts," they called themselves, shortened to "the Circle" without discussion—believed that conscious meditation unaided by sleeper programs brought greater awareness of the upper planes. They encouraged Quarter residents to keep offline and meditate organically, to forego the restraints of enforced pod simulation. Without them, people were free to discover the realms of the unknown. Truths led to freedom, or, as Markriss often taught, "Truth is Freedom." Direct, on-the-ground revolution was useless. Physical battles with the Authority and Corps soldiers only caused bloodshed and death; the abundance of zone uprisings proved this. In their aftermath, the poorest resident still inhabited the Quarter, did low-paid menial jobs, and, barring a chosen few, remained poor. In the abandoned depths of the secondary school that was to become their temple, the original five members of the Circle—Ayizan, Chile, Markriss, Temujin, and Vyasa—agreed on a more covert form of resistance. Enlightenment would lead to emancipation, should they choose the Way. They would study mental transmutation and learn to divorce the spiritual from the actual on higher planes of existence, in order to teach what they discovered to the masses and effect momentous revolution on their physical plane.

He flipped further pages, finding grouped passages where his thoughts began moving toward more serious intent than simple, regular, daily practice allowed:

> It's interesting that, as well as ascending, I can stay on the level of Geb and explore the world of the physical plane. I see my own allocation, the streets outside. I can even visit the Temple of the astral plane. When I ask the others, they say they can't stop themselves rising. Whereas I seem able to rise, stay on the lower planes, and move at will? If I can explore the environment I see every day, could I perhaps go on to others I don't? The upper levels? Places my physical form wouldn't allow? And if I can do it, could I teach it? Exciting thoughts.

He read the passage three times at least, pen tapping against his upper lip. Scratched an asterisk in the margins. Visualized thoughts fused with intention should have meant their mission statement was easily achieved. There had been no problems before. And yet he'd missed something. A glitch. Perhaps due to the Rogue, maybe the machines.

He skipped ahead to the portion of the book inhabited by blank, empty pages. Wrote: "Maybe the machines???" But how was that possible when he'd been offline? Perhaps the presence of online users in the zone affected the ether. Although the sleeper ban was largely successful among Outsiders, in practice there were always those who slipped into old ways, informed by the habits of several past generations. The ability to go offline and transmute without the aid of pods was an isolated, relatively new phenomenon. Even Markriss had only begun the practice since his arrival in the Ark.

The trouble with encouraging people to disconnect on a regular basis wasn't confined to the disruption of sleep patterns. It amounted to a disruption of their daily lives. No household tech, much less environmental, worked neurally for users anywhere in Dinium without the conduit of sleepers. This was a greater part of what the Outsiders were up against in teaching machine abstinence. To go offline in the modern world meant having no access to online facilities of any kind. Offline homes ran manually if the user desired, but so did travel, work, recreation, or anything else the user might access in the cities, Outer or Inner. A large portion of technology was confined to the neural network. To use those services, you had to be online. Going offline wasn't against the law, although it was possible that residents who did were flagged up as people the Authority, and therefore the Corps, took greater interest in. While it was believed that the linking of offline residents with Outsider activity hadn't yet been made, most thought logic would be followed to its obvious conclusion soon enough.

Sleepers had always given Markriss a strange, intuitive fear, especially after his brother wested. His mother, unable to cope with the surplus duties that came with raising a son alone, trusted the machines implicitly, even after everything that happened. She'd insisted Markriss use his pod on a regular basis, especially during the day. He believed her obstinacy came from a desire to keep him out of her way, sedated by comfortable dreams. Willow's preferred method was drinking whole bottles of whiskey or rum, and so in the beginning it had been easy to feign online connection, pretend to be unconscious for a short while and slip out onto the streets of Outer City searching for Ayizan, called Nesta in those days, and his road team.

One morning of early pink sky, after a night spent burning pi, drinking, and hanging out on the estate with young women who would have horrified his mother had she met them, Markriss came home to find Willow awake, waiting. Entering his room, locks shifted all over the house, the clank of metal connecting an ever-repeating echo until every one was closed. Willow said nothing, staring at Markriss in silence, unwashed hair lank and matted. He smelled her musk from where he stood. Like clogged gutters, dry earth.

Willow left him, a sour look set in his direction, alone in growing light. That night and each following, window and door locks slammed to a close with metallic finality the very moment he arrived from school until the next morning, fully dressed in the shirt and tie of his uniform. With brute strength greater than her size, Willow wrestled him into the pod night after painful night, slamming the lid shut before he could escape, engaging the gamut of pod-simulation programs until the day Markriss was old and big enough to make his way and left home to find better purpose on the streets.

Over time, he formed his own theory as to why pods killed. Both Ninka's and Sylvan Mistry's bodies corpsed when the machines were turned offline in the midst of simulations. In Sylvan's case, this was caused by a power cut. In his brother's, Markriss didn't know; the systems just failed. He was only sure of this: when simulations were disrupted in the middle of a program, the astral body became lost in the higher planes, trapped and untethered, with their corporeal form stranded on Geb, left to become husks, objects of flesh and bone, no elemental substance to guide them. The human body could only function without the spirit for a short time. Any longer, and the organs keeping the body alive—heart, liver, kidneys, lungs—were starved of ethereal instruction, and broke down. Markriss, writing this in his early notes, gave the process a name: "corpsing." Yet he wasn't the term's originator. He'd been told it by his younger brother, encountered six months before on the higher planes.

Back a few pages to April 14, 2020. He lay back, arm resting against his forehead.

Good news. Brilliant news. I don't think I've been this happy since I was selected for the Ark. This is way, way better, and hopefully it has a much happier ending. Today's transmutation pretty much started off as standard. I readied myself with a grounding, which I allowed for a bit longer than usual, as it felt like the natural thing to do. I quickly fell into trance without incident. C was beside me; she had fallen into trance way sooner. On my ascendance, I found I entered a mirror plane perfectly matching my own. My double pod, my window sofa, my political posters. I was in my own room, C sleeping beside me, her ka nowhere to be seen. Where is her ka? I asked the empty room. Except it wasn't empty at all, I knew that. A presence made me tingle; my nerves could feel it.

I moved around the allocation, but couldn't find it until I went into the kitchenette. I'm not sure why he was there, but then he always did love food, so maybe that was just the most familiar place to turn to. There was a shifting substance there, invisible on the inside, its outline easy to see in the dark. A man, riffling through things he found in the fridge. He'd brought an apple out to examine the blush, the stem, I couldn't tell which, and he was looking at the thing as if he'd found gold. I didn't recognize him at first—how would I, he had no discernible features, and even if he did I had no recollection of how he'd look because he'd never grown old enough for me to see him as a man. Of course, we were on the astral plane, and on the plane connections with other beings work using the whole of your senses and neural mechanisms, not simply sight or memory. So I entered the kitchenette and looked at the man, and he looked at me, and we both began to smile, because we knew. We each knew who the other was.

He was Ninka. My brother, though not my brother of the physical realm at the time of his death. Not five years old, with baby teeth and arms like a magician's balloons. The Ninka of the age he would be if he'd lived. He'd grown taller than me, and he was thin rather than the pudgy little kid I knew. Yet the way his head was held when he looked at me was the same, like he took me as the older brother I always wanted to be.

Right then I made another discovery. On the plane you can cry, just like Geb.

He closed the notebook, rough-swiping his eyes. A quick look out of the window ensured Chile wasn't coming back for her notes, or herbs, or a bookmark. His brother's westing remained difficult to revisit, even after so many moons. The silence of a space that once contained thundering footsteps, pealing laughter. As he'd learned so often during spiritual practice, answers were never laid at your door. They occurred when you let them reach you.

He sat up, holding his head, breathing deeply. The physical pain, remembrance. He went into the kitchenette and removed fresh mint from a glass jar, boiled water for tea, and took his steaming mug into the front garden.

They'd made the paved "outdoor" area comfortable with a couple of wine-red easy chairs, folding metal seats in case of more company, and a three-seater by the wall marking the confines of their space. Potted plants sat beneath their window, mostly herbs Chile sold or transferred to the Outsiders' larger garden at the Temple, for wider consumption. A barbecue rack near the front wall was never used, as Chile had a potent dread of fire. ("If one of these cookouts goes up, the whole level will burn," she'd said so many times Markriss never bothered to argue.)

Chile lay back in the nearest easy chair, eyes closed, the pages of her book wide-open wings soaring on her lap. Markriss wasn't sure if she was sleeping. He perched on the arm of the chair, sipping carefully. The tea was very hot.

In time, he noticed the still figure in the next-door garden. An elderly man wearing a white robe so long it brushed against his bare toes, bright cloth contrasting with black-and-brown locks falling in equal cascade, hair almost touching the floor. Large black sunglasses. Lumped, rocky hands, one on top of the other, resting on a walking stick that resembled a wooden stalactite, and might have been as old. A classic visage of the ancients: wizened, hooked nose, thick eyebrows, and protruding chin jutting at the world with proud defiance, unabashed, set with time. Despite his stillness, the old man looked alert, ready to leap to his feet. The occasional insect—a bee, or fly—hovered about him, perhaps taking his robes for petals, yet they made no great difference. The elder kept his motionless countenance. They hovered, lost interest, moved on.

He maneuvered his body toward Markriss. Raised a hand.

Markriss called: "To be at peace, Sares!"

Reversing, Old Man Sares faced the road, stilled once more.

"Let me know if you need anything from the shops."

Markriss tried another sip of tea. Better, still not great. He eyed his next-door neighbor. The elder, formerly a menial worker, had at some time become a wandering prophet of sorts, walking the squared confines of Poor Quarter streets, a book of wisdom tucked beneath his arm, imparting knowledge of the spiritual planes on block corners in a shrill, powerful voice to anyone who might listen. Though Sares treated their Outsider faction with respect, accepting regular donations of food and clothing with humble gratitude, he always refused to join their ranks. Ayizan said that elders of this nature were "necessary," and Sares's impartiality was a natural consequence of zone democracy, imparted by their road team. As long as the old man taught the Kemetian ways, he would be tolerated.

"Kriss! Kriss!"

A high voice, pierced with excitement. He walked toward the sandy rumble of plastic wheels against grit and concrete.

"Hey, you, what you doing?"

"Riding," the little girl said, her expression bemused query, wondering if he was stupid or blind. "I'm racing myself."

"Oh. Who's winning?"

"It's a tie," she said, beaming like light.

"You're funny. Don't let anyone tell you different." Markriss balanced a leg on the wall.

"As if," she snorted, off around the front garden, creating a jerky, too-loud circle on her bee-striped trike.

Pharah Mengus, six-year-old daughter of Shola and Credan Mengus, had proclaimed Chileshe and Markriss her best friends since the first day she moved into the Ark. Cirrus-haired, lisping from an errant front tooth, sociable and chatty, Pharah was there to greet them most mornings before school, often afterward. Today, she was clearly too busy for small talk, her sights trained on the middle distance, pressing down on tricycle pedals, turning handlebars to maintain tight circling, the clatter of wheels a continuous blurred noise. He sipped tea, watching. Racing herself. Everyday signs might be found in child's play, Markriss often taught as guidance. He'd do well to heed his own lectures.

Strong fingers kneading his shoulder. He looked back, resting against her.

"How you doing?"

"Okay."

Pharah threw a wave, feet moving fast, faster. Chile grinned back.

"Hey, precious!"

"Hi, Chileshe!"

He always wondered what Chile thought when she watched Pharah. She loved children, although they'd agreed it was cruelty to bring them into a world like the Ark. They reiterated their decision every so often, yet whenever Chile's eyes drifted Markriss thought he saw intense sadness, rich with imaginings of possible futures.

"Such a cutie." Whispered low, sighing. "I should get back to work."

"Yeah, me too. Made you tea."

"Saw, thanks. I'll get more mint later, and some bits and pieces from the garden on order. Need anything?"

"Nothing I can think of."

"Okay." Kissing his temple. "Any progress?"

"Yeah, some. I need to connect with Ninka. I think he'll guide me."

"Of course he will." She rubbed his shoulder and went in.

Markriss laughed, shook his head. Wise was the adept gifted with patience enough to show where to look, not tell what to see. He sipped tea, readied himself.

First, he secured his aura by grounding. Markriss always took protection before a transmutation, deciding to spend more time on this, visualizing his back against rough tree bark that scratched against skin, his feet buried in long grass tickling his soles. Saw energy coursing from the sky and into the leaves, through the trunk, and into himself. Into green stems, into earth, into roots beneath. Allowed his breathing to slow to slight rhythm, almost nothing.

Let himself fall.

The expanse he remembered so well before and since, Burbank Park, that lush green. Bright sky, wheeling birds. His brother's silhouette, tall and watchful, walking with purpose toward him. The crush of flattened grass, his connection with organic life making Ninka's steps loud, a hundred decibels' multiplication. Powerful sunlight, expanding beams a halo beneath Ninka's head. The outline of his body and approximate features shifting heat haze; each time he caught a glimpse of something resembling a face or expression, it was gone, rippling into formless nothing. Seeing Ninka was similar to looking at sheer plastic immersed in pellucid water, a glimpse and uncertainty after. His brother came closer, reaching for his hand, and there was the anticipated contact with nerve endings, his fingers moving through Ninka's as though encountering a ghost. Brightness grew until it was painful and there was nothing else.

Light faded to reveal a building. Armed guards at twin doors, a multitude of tinted windows. The people inside saw out, the people outside only wondered. A microcosm. As above, so below. Separated by circumstance. Nondescript, dowdy even, the building one of many corporate blocks in the zones of commerce near the Ark center. The better off paid dues in those places, blind duty for an Authority that deemed them more worthy than others. Like gifted babies, loyal to the offering of positive inheritance, tethered to the only mother they knew.

Numbers imprinted the building, the only markings that differentiated it from any other. 1322.

And there was his brother, gliding upstairs and toward the doors then floating through them, past security guards—made double by the reflective gleam of marble floors—who looked into the distance. Equipment—blinking metal detectors, the feline purr of baggage-check machines—silent and immune inside the lobby. Ninka was through the next set of locked doors, disappearing. Markriss did the same, allowing his astral body to move past the security, through the locked doors, and into a cloud of sooty, fogged space gathered beyond. He couldn't see, couldn't hear, moving deeper inside the mass. A tug, like being yanked by unseen rope. The sensation of resistance in his lower spine. Acceptance flooded him as he allowed himself to be pulled back, toward his body and the realm of his own.

Purple into mauve. In the foreground, a three-dimensional pyramid of thin wrought gold shattered into pieces that tumbled outward in svelte fragments, slowed to a pause, then fell inward on themselves, where they came together as an eight-pointed star that turned in lazy, fixed rotation. Fading into nothing, consumed by black. When his eyes opened, Chile was watching from the opposite side of their pit, legs crossed, glasses removed. The calm blue aura shone around her, suggesting she'd not long finished descent.

Their dim, cool room. Candles extinguished, walls humming with the subdued power of their generator.

"Better?"

Markriss nodded, blinking at solidity.

"I looked but I still can't see your aura."

Reaching for water, Markriss smudging the condensation at the sides of his cup.

"It's a really odd realm," he said. "I'm not sure what being there means. Everything's like here, just with different rules. It must be similar to your own journeys, right?"

"I'm not sure. I'm trying, but buildings or objects just aren't my thing. Only people."

He sipped, wincing from cold. Alternate versions of the plane existed according to how receptive an individual's naardim were to spiritual dimensions; he had yet to discover, or be taught, the true meaning of those differences.

"I can see everything. People, buildings, machinery. But it's a blank, no sound or connection. I'm a ghost, like Ninka. I'm not even sure how he found it."

"He didn't communicate at all? Not even thought?"

Markriss placed the water back on the side of their pod. "No. He just showed it to me, and I was tugged back. I think I can get there by myself next time, without guidance. I'll try anyway."

"Okay." Chile took light sips of air, mouth barely open, limp hands resting on her knees. Without the distraction of glasses her eyes glowed in dim illumination. He watched them catch rare light.

"We should tell Capra. We're almost ready."

"Yes. I think Ayizan will want to come; you should too."

"We'll see." She caught him looking, smiling at the mattress. "What?"

"You seem very relaxed."

He slid to her side of the pod, rested on a shoulder, catching the sweet, tangy odor of shea and avocado butter. She often mixed the lotion in the kitchenette, filling their allocation with the smell. He nuzzled against the warmth of her neck.

"So you come to disturb me?"

He heard her smile, kissed her collarbone, once, twice, traveling down. The root of her neck. The curve where it met jawline, that faint road of bone leading to her chin, lips. Her soft lips. They kissed. Explored how it felt as though they never had.

Markriss returned to her collarbone, nipping, nibbling.

"Should I leave you alone?"

"Did I say that?" She jerked, leaning toward him. Giggling. "You're tickling."

"Good." They laughed. He put an arm around her waist, sighing. They'd been apart too long.

"I was letting you work. Don't you have work to do?"

"This is more important right now. Don't you think?"

She wrapped her arms around his neck. Content hummed deep inside her, he felt it. Traveling between them, yoking.

"You know what I think. Better grab a towel; I've got my cycle."

"Really?"

"You okay with that?"

"Course. I just couldn't tell."

He found a large towel in a drawer, bringing it back to spread across the pit. She uncrossed her legs, lying on their mattress, pulling him to join her. He lowered himself, testing weight. Rested against her body. She sighed, a gentle outpouring as he relaxed. Arms around his neck, wrist against the back of his skull. The soft and rapid pulse of flowing blood. Her breath solid as the fingers on his cheek, a moment before they tasted each other. Minutes savoring. Chile pausing to slide cotton over her head, him rubbing a cheek against the sheer material of her bra, lower, feeling tiny, almost invisible hairs, listening to her gasp, going farther down, lips drawing a damp line against the vague muscles of her stomach. Chile writhing, meeting. Kissing her belly button, playing the indentation with his tongue. Gentle exhalation, light hands placed on each hip, anticipating tremulous reaction.

White light flooded the sleeper. As it came, the consistent hum of the generator rattled before ceasing, replaced by seconds of tension, then the growing surge of online machinery booting up outside their window, a loud, collective whine, which had to mean it was taking place all over the zone. Audible gasps of wonder, cheers punctuated by explosive chatter. Poor Quarter residents caught outside their homes, engaged in rapid discussions about what this meant, conversations rumbling, avalanching. The pod lights blinked silent animation as its internal workings hummed into life. Chile's eyes widened, caught his. Quickly, she sat up, pushing him back, leaning one arm over the pod and thumping the control panel until start-up died, the wind-down a mechanical sigh of disappointment, a promise lost. Chile's shoulders relaxed, her body spilled liquid as she slipped back into the pod, her head propped where feet would usually rest. They waited, saying nothing, listening to Pharah Mengus scream at her parents to come out and see, the power was back.

"Well," she said, lifting her head to see him.

"Well." Markriss balanced on his hands, looking out of the window. "We've got a little bit longer."

Laughter erupted from her. "You're actually serious?"

"Come." He took Chile's fingers, drawing her to him. "I'll show you."

They lowered into the pit.

5

By the time they emerged from their allocation, Poor Quarter excitement had waned into something less than wonder, closer to the anticipatory spirit that came before a gathering. People strolled for no other reason but to look up at the gantry Day-Lites, amazed. Gardens were filled with families camped on deck chairs, drink tables, and picnic spreads. Many residents wore sunglasses. They lay on sun loungers, fanning themselves and talking of heat. It was a bitter disappointment for Markriss and Chile to see how overjoyed people were to be granted their most basic of human needs, that of light. Indignation burned him, matched with his understanding that they had forgotten who'd taken that right from them without considering what it might do to their psyches, or the community at large. Yet still, the terraces were content.

They took the streets that led to the Poor Quarter depths in slow disbelief, watching residents whoop, calling up at the mile-high ceiling with joy. A disheveled man in bright shirt-ripped tatters, trouser-torn flags, ran up to Chile, kissed her cheek, then sprinted away, blistered heels disappearing around a corner before she or Markriss could respond. The foul cloud around him took longer, though eventually left them. People were happy, it was undeniable, and they felt slight pleasure to see it, though each time he looked at Chile her lip was curled, and when they exchanged glances the set frown between her eyes echoed his own. Yes, it was a celebration. No, there was little evidence of even the faintest amount of righteous anger. Their steps became wooden, bodies turning robotically.

Fireworks crackled, trailing abrupt smoke. A glitter of burning lights arced upward, searching for ceiling. At their peak, exploding into a shower of flint sparks and dust, the Lites made them difficult to see against their glare. No one gave a damn, launching more regardless. The torched smell of burning sulfur brought Markriss comfort even as Chile recoiled, frown becoming shock, hunched with fear. He rubbed her shoulder to placate her. She was tense as stone, so he stopped where they were, hugging her to his chest. Kids screamed, playing chase and kicking footballs. No doubt they hadn't been allowed on the streets during the prolonged nights without power. On rooftops, shadowed parkour runners leaped from edges, their splayed limbs dark stars—though some ran for sport, others were drug dealers' mules. No one could tell the difference. Dogs loitered, skittish and afraid, eyeing people with bared teeth, low-gear growling. Markriss always tried to recognize them individually and found it impossible; one seemed as mangy and decrepit as the next. People squinted, shielding eyes. After days of darkness, "normal" light hurt. All over the Poor Quarter, streets became a desert blessed by rainfall, life, color, and humanity blooming where once there had been a barren, listless expanse, a dead zone.

Blocks from Ayizan's street, Markriss's left eye jumped, rapid twitching. A growing pressure spread across his brow, his eyes grew heavy. The ache became stronger as they passed a two-story allocation, a slab of broad, flat, lifeless brickwork, much as the others. Markriss slowed, turned, curious and unsure. Unlike the surrounding houses, which all seemed neat and well looked after, this one wore a dirt-blackened air of dereliction. Shadow blooms of dust suggested it had survived a long-ago blaze, yet there were no signs of fire in its past or more recently. Broken windows were boarded with wood, shark's-tooth shards of glass firm in every pane. The front garden was overgrown with tall weeds, bowed by the weight of successful growth. The upper windows were also boarded, red paint graffiti-sprayed even there, mostly incomprehensible scrawls. Markriss saw an Outsider insignia almost eclipsed by newer, less accomplished attempts. What little he could make out of the roof was patched with the scabbed wounds of holes. This was also strange. The house seemed older than the terraces on either side, which wasn't possible from what Markriss knew about their zone. Old-timers told stories that suggested all of the accommodation in their region had been designed and constructed simultaneously. And yet there the house stood, alone in discrepancy, the front door shut, the insides silent, lifeless.

He faced the allocation. Chile let go of his arm.

"What's wrong?"

"Nothing, just . . . Look at this."

"Yeah, what about it?"

He found himself by the crumbling front wall. No recollection of moving, or forming the thought. Over his shoulder, she craned her neck up and down the street, biting her lip. She scratched the rear of her calf with the toe of a shoe. The arc of her body made her look like a discarded kid's doll.

"Can't you feel it?"

"Yes. I don't particularly want to."

"It's not bad. I don't think, anyway."

She kissed her teeth at length, Markriss imagining her expression. Loose-lipped petulance.

"You're not exactly the best judge."

He laughed, swiveling. "I'll be two minutes."

"You're going in?"

"If I can."

Markriss tried ignoring the gravity of her sigh. Better to concentrate on what he was doing. The pinewood slats across the door were flaking, corners tinged with orange crescents at the screws. They spanned the upper and lower windows of the door. Between the two a handle. If it was locked, he'd have to give up, although the boarding was also strange. Vacant houses around the Quarter were normally made secure with metal panels and digitally locked doors, left to rot on the insides unless the zone ran low on accommodation, which hadn't happened in decades. He pulled the top slat toward him with both hands. It gave with a bounce, suggesting the screws were quite loose, most likely worn, so he kept pulling until the wood came off in his hands. He tried the next, and the others. After a time, six piled at his feet like firewood.

"That was easy," he threw over his shoulder. For reassurance, he supposed.

"Tell me again when you're an ancestor."

He feigned a smile, grabbing his sleeve and bringing it up over his fingers. He grasped the material in a fist and eased his arm through the broken glass, slow, as he'd done as a child playing that game with a hooped piece of metal and the buzz of electric wire. What was it called, something like—?

"Shit!"

"You okay?" Behind him, pitched with worry.

"Yeah, yeah, caught my sleeve. No blood."

"No common sense, you mean."

He chuckled, kept going. Pressed down on the door handle.

It opened.

"Coming in?"

She rested on the brick wall, smoking a roll-up, one leg thrown across another, foot bouncing. Veiled smoke blown sideways, toward the street. The scuffed white crescents of each toe.

"Nah. Stopped tramping round old houses when I was a kid."

Hands on his hips, he looked up, stung by unexpected brightness. Sharp light pierced his eyes. He looked down. He wanted to convince her, wouldn't allow himself to admit he needed company.

"I'll be five minutes. Promise."

"I'll be here."

More careful than usual, disturbed by Chile's reluctance—she was right about most things—Markriss grabbed the door, levering it open in stiff jerks, slower when he heard soft glass tinkle like emptied bins into a distant garbage truck. He shook his head. Always thinking of Outer City. He kicked the wooden slats aside with a heel, scraping them in squealing protest across the floor, pulling the door farther out until there was room enough to slide his body past the door's edge and stiff tongue, weapon-sharp. He looked over his shoulder. Chile studied her sneakers, lost in patterns of lacing and stitching. Of being entwined.

Whispering prayers, Markriss entered.

The homeliness surprised him, particularly since the house had clearly not been inhabited for some time. Smudged walls bore swarthy patches and there were holes in floorboards where carpets had once been laid, and yet picture frames remained even if the photos were long gone, pearls levered from chipped oysters. At the bottom of the stairs, a mahogany table was first-knuckle deep with dust. Above his head, a mock chandelier, with many glass baubles missing. Surely— and this was something that wouldn't stop nagging Markriss in the days and weeks to follow—he would have noticed an allocation this opulent before? He'd walked this route every day for eight years, and he'd never seen this place, he was certain. He ran a hand across wallpaper so old he could barely discern faded patterns: Bouquets of flowers? Bundles of wheat wrapped in fine blue and red ribbons? Who wallpapered houses anyway? Everyone painted, had done so for a generation at least. So how old was this?

He moved toward the rear of the house—though the tug of sensation was strongest up those stairs—needing to learn the personality of the space, perhaps glean something of its past and why it pressed on his spirit. A bare kitchen, with stone counters and gap-teeth slots, presumably where a cooker and white goods once lived. Cupboards, empty apart from one that contained the skeleton of what he presumed was a dead mouse. Dusty twinned living rooms, also bare, two imitation fireplaces left to mark the purpose they'd served. Markriss was surprised to see them intact. Not worth anything, he suspected—if they were, they would have been long stolen. It was odd they'd been fitted at all; within the Ark there was no need. He always assumed fireplaces were banned because of the obvious risk. Yet this allocation had two.

A downstairs bathroom, confined as a cubicle, then the upstairs podrooms where the presence he sensed lived. Upstairs, he found two doors separated by a small passage fenced by a half-broken banister, whole sections missing. He let his hand rest. Built from robust wood, the banister was rich with aura and smooth to the touch, yet wobbled like a milk tooth. He snatched his hand back quickly as it shook, narrowly avoiding a fall to the ground floor. The upper floor was dingy, little of the Lites seeping in. Wallpaper was sparing, paper strips peeling like fruit until they were bent double, figurative heads resting against bare wood, or the staircase. The air entering his mouth, windpipe, and lungs felt gritty, laced with chalk. Stuffy, difficult to breathe. He wished he'd brought water. Above, in what he presumed was the attic, he heard skittering clawed feet, hoping the animal was tiny and spooked enough to stay up there.

He poked a head around the open bathroom door, flicking the switch. No working lights. Rusted, stagnant water in the full belly of a rolltop bath, the remains of a collapsed half sink that looked bitten by giant teeth. He backed onto the landing. The presence was behind him. Coming from one of the white-painted podroom doors, most likely the right. The door was ajar, Markriss unable to see beyond. Faint brightness of Day-Lites spread from the room onto the landing, nothing more.

Houses in this state reminded him of being younger, when he'd escaped from home and the road team he'd chosen as family reached the point of the night when their need to sleep became paramount, and *where* became an ongoing mission. Sometimes they even called it that—"the Mission." They couldn't sleep on Outer City streets. As young adults, they understood potential dangers were so numerous it was never even voiced as a consideration. If their go-to safe houses were habitable, or empty, or hadn't been reclaimed by owners old or new, then the mission was short, and they slept relatively easy. If their chosen house was compromised, they were forced to walk hostile streets. Markriss and Nesta were together on occasion, although he often took missions with kids he barely knew, or a clutch of childhood friends like T'shari, Karis, and others, going from house to empty house, levering locks and slatted boards with broken tools. They called those mornings "Shallows." When sleep was at its thinnest, least restful. When the worst things you could imagine made themselves known and convinced you they were real. No one knew who'd coined the noun, yet it fit perfectly, and so remained.

If they were lucky and managed to gain entry without running into immediate danger, they would walk a passage or landing, feet treading the creaking floors as quiet as humanly possible, in hope a door they were about to open wouldn't contain animals, or men, or a security precaution that might cause them to lose their lives. Hearts pulsing at throats, weapons raised, eyes fixed.

He hated the fear that pricked his fingertips, drying his mouth so his tongue lay dead and foreign, and carried the emotion with him anyway.

Markriss pushed the closest white door with outstretched fingers, allowing it to swing farther open by its own weight. The room was well illuminated, empty of usual furnishings—bed, carpet, wardrobe—and open and spacious, nothing like he'd imagined on the landing, those vicious places of memory. Cracked walls and jagged floorboards. Fogged windows and stained, muddy curtains.

In the far-right corner, a steady sheen of light thrust from bare floorboards up to the matte-gray ceiling, where it erupted into a churning cascade, a shimmering river, a waterfall reversed.

Markriss watched the light until he noticed a presence.

Old Man Sares was poised and motionless in the opposite corner. Cross-legged, dressed in his usual white robes, a plethora of unwrapped locks falling over his knees like tendrils, thumb and first fingers touching. His eyes opened.

"Markriss."

Dark stare unfocused, set beyond him. The old man couldn't see, though he knew.

"Teacher." Bowing, a slight nod. "I thought you were an ancestor."

Old Sares offered no response. He chewed on something unseen, making bovine movements with his lower jaw, head set in Markriss's direction. Or so it seemed.

"You brought me here?"

The old man shrugged, shoulders relaxing. "I couldn't if I tried."

The voice was difficult to catch, low, tinged with the coarse burn of a thousand cigarettes, feet scraping across gravel, and the low mist of raised dust. Markriss never saw Old Sares light up, let alone take a drag of anything. Stories persisted of the old man and his assigned work in the Lowers, the warren of underground levels beneath Inner City. Something about machinery accidents leading to disfigurement, though no discernible scars etched Old Sares's body or face. Markriss never found courage enough to ask his neighbor if the zone gossip was true.

"So how did we find this place? I walk this street every day, I've never seen it."

"I don't have answers for you."

"Okay." Searching plain walls, trying another way. "So how did you get in?"

"I came to meditate. Just like you."

Markriss opened his mouth, closed it. Crossed the room to sit by his neighbor's side, leaving enough space for comfort. Nearer, the shimmer emitted a tuning-fork hum on the edge of his hearing. Subtle vibration purred against his thighs and buttocks, through floorboards. He laid his hands on the wood.

"Will Chileshe be joining us?"

"I don't think so. She's waiting outside. She's scared."

"She is wise."

Markriss smiled at his knees. Thought of her smoking another roll-up, possibly looking at blind windows, wondering how long he'd be. "What is it?" he asked.

The wait for an answer took so long the immersive rush of the shimmer, that gentle continuum, began to lull him into a sensation close to entrancement. He believed Old Sares had slipped into meditation, or had no answer, or didn't care for the question.

"A point where our normal understanding of physical time and the higher energies converge," the old man said into quiet, the timbre of his voice harmonized with the purr. "A place you couldn't see due to lack of vision. You've transcended. You've found a cross stream."

Listening with intent, trying to overstand, Markriss noticed the material of Old Sares's white robes flutter, a motion like the sigh of a breeze. Swelling, falling. If he closed his eyes, allowed it, Markriss felt something caressing the hairs of his arms and neck, cooling his skin.

"Chileshe's right to be cautious. These manifestations are dangerous."

"How so?"

Old Sares faced him. Eyes huge and dark, all pupils. Angular features seeming carved rather than birthed. Markriss was convinced his expression of confusion had been noted, possibly judged, even while he knew it wasn't possible. There were ways, of course. Multifarious ways.

"Learn, Markriss. Allow it."

The old man turned away, bowing his head. His breathing deepened and slowed. Markriss nodded, understanding. He lowered his chin, closing his eyes to begin grounding.

Chanting quiet mantra, he gave way.

The Lites had dimmed a few degrees. Counterfeit evening settled on the Poor Quarter as Markriss emerged, pushing the stiff door. The lengthening shadows of roofs and terraces, the sallow glow of streetlights, the shouts of children. Paired lovers, bodies pressed tight as they unified steps. Elders prone in gardens. The louder hum of varied mechanics, fifty-inch slide-screens making windows shine with stuttered glows up and down the block. A feel in the air he recalled from Outer City, one of good — gathering people, the promise of future, the buzz of a burgeoning summer, and all contained by the earth's position in proximity to its sun. There would be celebrations, parties, and outdoor food. The Poor Quarter would reconfigure, as always.

Chile dropped her roll-up, squashing it underfoot, standing. He took her hands and kissed her. Smoke lingered, an aura.

"Got what you came for?"

"Think so." He shook his head. "I'm not sure."

"Sares doesn't give things easy. He sets your path, the rest is yours."

Markriss squeezed her fingers lightly, appraising her with more care. Threading them with his, she pushed him backward and away.

"You've gotta stop doing that."

"Hey, I see people, remember?" Touching his cheek with a finger, her eyes misted over. Her elemental aura read blue, the color taken when a person was teaching, or engaged in action promoting sensitivity. "Ready to go?"

He blinked, unsure what she was referring to. A woman in shorts, sweatshirt, and flip-flops sauntered by, heels drumming a lazy rhythm of slap and slide, slap and slide. The pace of her walk echoed along the block.

"Yeah, sure."

Markriss took her hand.

Although they'd been friends since they met on either side of a grainy nursery school sandpit, the weak sun leaden and high above their matted heads, Markriss found much of Ayizan's ways as mysterious as a stranger's. He possessed the quality of a person who achieved blank spaces in their life without trying, moments and experiences no one, even those closest to him, could penetrate. Markriss called these events subconscious voids. Most of the time his old friend didn't know how he behaved, he was positive of that; the sheer epitome of being, he just *was*. If they walked, Ayizan would disappear without warning, only to reappear at their destination as if nothing had happened. Or if he arrived at a gathering, talking loud and fast with excitement, he'd bring someone with him he'd known for months, even though he'd never mentioned their name. He'd speak in depth on subjects he'd previously never shown interest in—trigonometry, or the omega nature of wolves—or even show adeptness in skills Markriss had never seen him practice or discuss. Over time, especially in the claustrophobic blocks of Inner City, others put the trait down to Ayizan's blessing as an old soul, something that Markriss had long considered to be true. And still, ever since childhood, he harbored a secret belief of his own: Ayizan was magic personified.

The most obvious manifestation of those black-hole spaces was his belongings. His allocation was a mirror double of Chile and Markriss's home, yet while theirs was untidy despite being relatively free of all but essentials, Ayizan's was packed to the ceiling with *things*. Every possible space was filled with some object or other, and still the impossible was made real—the allocation was tidy, almost like an Inner City show home. Chile would often comment on it when they left the flat, hunchbacked to avoid being overheard by neighborhood gossips, speaking in whispers that verged on jealousy. They didn't understand how he managed it. And it wasn't even that the things he obtained were shoved or squeezed into spaces where their inexact positions left them exposed, awkward, obscene. Wherever they'd been stood, laid, or hung, there was barely a sliver of room between the place he'd found for an item and the item beside it. Simply put, Ayizan's belongings always looked as though they belonged.

Perched on the sofa edge holding earthenware mugs of peppermint tea, starting at the sudden roar of Ayizan's generator booting online, Markriss pretended that he couldn't see Chile sitting beside him, head swiveling, eyes roaming the room in search of additional objects. He attempted not to follow her gaze. Ayizan constantly obtained new people and items. Markriss had no idea where he got them from, or even how, they materialized from nowhere in irregular bursts like teleportation. Lovers, work products, or pieces of art appeared in an eyeblink. Walls were filled with indigenous paintings, masks, and sculptures, composed of bright, astral colors and representing cultures from all over the world. Some depictions were traditional, more rural: the man fishing a calm lake, red sun falling behind him, or the step pyramids of Chichén Itzá bathed in tall green trees. A brown leather-bound *Kebra Nagast*. The narrow-eyed, contemplative stares of Bulan masks crafted from wood, metal, and even 3D Bakelite, hung beside Venetian cat's-eye masks, and another streaked black and white, possibly a badger. A varied forest of sculptures lined shelves and bookcases: a woman bent, drawing a calabash of water; a bare-chested man carrying his toddler son on broad, muscled shoulders; an Indian elephant adorned with its headdress, trunk raised; two Chinese symbols sculpted side by side, the Mandarin for "tranquility," Ayizan had once said. There were Kemetian ankhs; a cartouche with, from head to foot, a squiggled line, a feather, a bracelet with two beads placed in its center, a half-risen sun, and an eyeless bird. A metallic, eight-pointed "Lotus of the Soul," the inspiration for their Outsider logo, sat atop a bookshelf. Among them all were sketches of all manner of chakras and an unfinished canvas of a beautiful woman Markriss didn't know, and Ayizan never spoke of. Whenever he was asked, Ayizan would smile and say, "Beautiful spirit. Golden." He never mentioned her name. It drove Chile crazy.

Bookshelves were packed so tight Markriss wondered how he

freed the volumes to read. Shelves were somehow built into walls and placed around the room, which gave the confined allocation a smaller, darker feel, although the final evening beam of Lites managed to penetrate a lone, central window. The coffee table was stacked with a neat pile of board games: oware, chess, Chinese checkers, a slim and weathered dominoes box.

Balancing a too-full mug, pleased with a job well done, Ayizan entered the living area. In his other hand he carried a full plate of biscuits. He rested both on the coffee table beside the *Kebra Nagast*, huffed, surveyed their manner, smiled.

"Okay. Now we talk."

"If we can hear over that noise." Chile tipped her head toward the thudding generator.

"What would you rather, us go missing and end up in the Blin?" Ayizan grinned, motioning at the plate. "Have biscuits, eat."

"We're fine, thanks." Chile's palm rose to ward off argument.

"Made them myself? Honey and cinnamon." An eyebrow lift. "Sure?"

"You're a wicked man." Markriss lifted a biscuit and broke it in half to offer his wife, relishing the thin, pleasing snap. She pulled down the corners of her mouth, shrugging, took it. A hearty crunch. Chewing.

"No calories in mint tea, so you can afford to make them up elsewhere."

"I'll need parkour after this," Markriss said, taking a bite. Sweet not cloying, a cinnamon kick. "That's good."

"Well, you know." Ayizan's bashful expression set his face askew. "Practice, practice. I might as well do something useful with my time."

"No word from the Authority or Corps?"

A shrug, a sigh. "The usual. Their standard reply, a form letter from the Complaints Committee saying they'll launch an investigation and instigate a report. We know where that's going."

They listened to the clatter of a trolley or suitcase roll by on the street, looking at their hands.

"Family's doing well though," Ayizan said, straining for brightness. "I'm not sure I'd be as strong or composed. They're inspiring."

"Will there be a funeral?" Chile's voice low, noncommittal.

Ayizan thought a moment. "I don't know how they'll play this one. Honestly." Another sigh. "How was your walk?"

"Good." Chile leaned forward. She'd read Ayizan's true intention, to discuss what was happening in the Quarter. "The people are happy, of course."

"Of course."

"And they seem in easy spirits, better than I would've believed if you'd asked me before. Lots of barbecuing and lounging in gardens."

"Tons of kids," Markriss added.

"Yes, loads. You haven't been out?"

A seesaw motion of his hand.

"A little. Down the road mostly, though I spent the morning seeing members and writing e-mails back to the Authority. Got food for dinner, that was it."

"It seems calm," Chile said, considering Markriss. "Don't you think?"

"For now. People are happy the Lites are online. They're not thinking why, or who put us in this situation."

"They want things the way they were." Ayizan sipped tea.

"They've been placated," Chile said, keeping a neutral tone.

"True." Markriss sat back. "Can we work it to our advantage?"

"We must." Ayizan smiled again, weaker. "It's the only choice we have. How was your transmutation?"

"I found Ninka. He led me to the building, then my thread wouldn't let me in."

"You're not ready." A frown etched Ayizan's face, rough fingers rubbing his forehead. Captaincy had aged him. Spiderweb hairs threaded locks, cheekbones protruded.

"It's not that. I think I need to go by myself."

Chile edged forward even farther, until she perched on the edge of the sofa. "He's fine. The first jump was a setback, but I think we're ready to see Capra. We should go soon. Markriss found a cross stream."

Ayizan sat upright, his mug hitting the table with a sucker-punch thud. His stare traveled from one to the other.

"Yeah." Markriss held his eye. "A derelict two blocks away."

"There's no such place." Confident, testing.

"It's there. I'd never seen it either, until now. I went in and found Old Sares."

"Shit." Head lowered, fingers raking his beard. Markriss couldn't see his thoughts. He tried reading his aura but found it difficult. Some red, a little white. Anger, mixed with truth. Confusion.

"I never went inside and only saw the usual terraces, but I felt Sares. That much I know," Chile said.

"Okay." Back bent, fingers tapping the mug, body swaying with slight motion, a sign Markriss always took to mean he was thinking laterally. "What does it look like?"

"Beautiful. Like a stream of silver shooting from the floor."

Ayizan looked up. Markriss and he smiled without knowing.

"Right. Capra's waiting to supply the canisters on our word. He won't get them made until we're sure we need them, so the more last-minute the better, he said. It's dangerous to leave them lying around."

"How long will that take?" Chile asked.

"A few hours."

"Can't forensics trace the canisters to him?"

Again, Markriss tried to read their faces. It was impossible. Each was shielded by intent.

"He'll print them." Ayizan's eyes widened, seeing his reaction. "Don't worry, it's an unmarked machine. One of his people hooked it up. They're not silly down there."

"Can 'his people' be trusted?" Chile asked.

Bright grin, safer ground. "Chile, when I say 'people,' I mean his oldest daughter. Convinced?"

"Still," she pouted. "No prisons in the Ark, right?"

They sobered, backs stiff. Once an Outer City myth composed of shifting gossip between road teams and career criminals, the mantra "No prisons in the Ark" was truth to centuries of outside dwellers turned permanent Inner City residents. There actually were no prisons in the Ark. Conviction of a C- or D-category offense stripped residents of work assignations, or ejected them back to Outer Dinium. Convictions involving violence, rape, or murder meant people disappeared without warning. Families cried and begged, lovers cursed, still the convicted A-category criminal was banished from existence like the life they were accused of taking. Many believed the guilty were buried in unmarked graves all over the Blin. Whispered discussion sometimes centered on whether the guilty were actually guilty at all. Over time, "No prisons in the Ark" evolved from rumor to mantra. Be careful. The chosen path might lead in a singular direction.

"We'll hold a gathering to celebrate the Lites booting online," Ayizan said. "It's nearly winter anyway, it'll look odd if we don't. While that happens, we'll go down. That means you've got forty-eight hours until Sunday night. If you can't get in, we don't go."

"Okay." Chile bit her lip. Her eyes were scared. Markriss took her hand between his, rubbing. Though warm, they were also rough, scarred by the past. He kneaded flesh, in hope it might soften.

"Truth?"

Probing for definite signs. This time they matched his stare.

"Truth." In unison.

"Then it's done."

Ayizan cradled his mug, one thumb stroking ceramic. The unseen clock ticked seconds away.

Their missions were simplicity itself. Media, in the form of *Ark News*, *Ark Light*, and its various subsidiaries, were the chief propagators of news that demonized Poor Quarter residents in general and slandered the families of those who came into violent contact with Corps, whether criminals or everyday residents. They supported the oppressive policing tactics of the security forces, using advertising and subscription revenues to fund a large percentage of the Corps budget. After all, when the bottom line was observed, the Ark was no more than a single conglomerate company. Inside the city, there was no one to regulate exactly how business was done, or bring anyone to task for foul practice.

The Outsiders' initial function was to voice zone concerns, while giving those under their protection the opportunity to strengthen their spiritual psyches against daily assaults by the city-state and its propaganda machine. In time, stories like Enos Weston's had become commonplace. Residents were shot or choked, tased or bludgeoned; found guilty in locked-room courts and spirited away, allocations given to unknowing new residents, or left empty and metal-boarded. The Ark official Complaints Committee had logged over two thousand custody deaths in the last two decades, with no convictions or even employer dismissals. Corps and their agents became a feared reality, the evil that parents warned children against when they were old enough to venture onto zone streets alone, telling them to keep their eyes open, be compliant when spoken to, don't make any sudden movements, be afraid. And then there was the present, ongoing pressure of life as a Poor Quarter resident, humiliating menial work a perpetual reminder of how the Authority defined its residents— although far better than being assigned to the depths of the Ark foundations, existing forever belowground as "tunnel rats."

When they had found themselves ejected from various menial jobs for differing reasons (most centered on their inability to absorb verbal, physical, and quite often sexual threats), Ayizan, Chileshe, and Markriss—black-marked, unemployed—founded the Circle, in order to heal themselves in the beginning. As the years passed and their Circle widened to include Vyasa and Temujin, later Xander, they realized the scope of their spiritual practices. They called themselves the Outsiders, a name that meant they weren't confined by Inner City rules, or walls. They read and meditated until they were ready, only then going into the pocket world of the zone to spread teachings, recruit further. At the urging of Ayizan, those early days were a slow, quiet time of gentle building. They shrouded themselves, not only with their clothing but in their lives. Ayizan knew the problems knowledge of their works could bring. They knocked on doors, lectured in the square outside the long-derelict school building, stood outside shop doorways handing out leaflets. With each yearly revolution, the Authority's oppression bore weight on the zone's neck with even greater force. If they couldn't breathe, Ayizan had said at a Temple meeting almost twelve months before, it was their moral right to push back.

And so they implemented a two-objective mission. The first was for Markriss, most adept at anomalous cognition, to seek astral impressions of their unseen target, Building 1322, and locate its schematic plans. The second was for Vyasa and Temujin, in the guise of working their assigned jobs as Building 1322 security, to plant a number of gas-based explosives at positions identified through Markriss's remote view of the layout. During offline hours, when the building was uninhabited, they would detonate the explosives.

If successful, the blast would temporarily disable L1's ability to transmit media communication in or out of the Ark.

If unsuccessful, and caught, they would likely be killed.

Music pulsed beneath raised voices, echoing long-forgotten elation. He imagined Chile and himself as two untethered bodies adrift in the lower dimensions, twinned ghosts immune to the call of their names, waving hands, the clamor of miniature explosions that crackled over their heads as if the air was aflame. They walked back the way they had come, Chile's lips set straight, eyes as blind as Old Man Sares's. She also dreamed awake. He wanted to tell her of the tiny fists that squeezed his gut, the lightness in his chest and prickle of a difficult-to-swallow object in his throat chakra, his voice stolen or overused, he wasn't sure which. She pressed against him, cradling his elbow with a guiding hand, and he felt she either knew him or shared his perspective. Their feet scuffed road. Their bodies met and separated, finding acceptance, each momentary contact forcing them to press closer, in search of a notion that couldn't be found in the brick walls and narrow blocks of their environment.

Two allocations from their home, just beyond Old Man Sares's flat, a lone dog. Fur the yellow of sun-bleached corn. A rack of protruding ribs and tight stomach, scimitar canines. The animal faced their direction, breathing hard, coal-glowing eyes, dark centers bleeding red. Feet planted firm against the tarmac, body turned at an angle, otherwise still.

The poor animal would be shot at the barricade. Nobody dared to go near them for fear of being bitten. And so they scavenged, racked with hunger. Something should have been done, he'd long thought that, Markriss always outweighed by other pressing concerns. He turned his back, shamed as he fumbled for his key card. Touch

ID wouldn't allow access without neural pod connections either. The only way to open his door was manually.

"Isn't this weird?" he said, hardly listening to himself. "All this, what we're doing?"

"Not here," Chile said low, sounding as though her lips had barely moved.

He slipped the card in, waited for green, and pushed. A flash interrupted his thoughts, immediate memory followed by something else. Him pushing the white door, opening into a glittering shower of cross stream, the open door of long ago leading to the blank corridor, where he'd found . . .

Head whipping, a violent twist. He stopped, gasping. Chile was at his arm.

"All right?"

"Yeah." Moving to their yielding sofa, wincing, he sat with head between knees, fingers kneading his temples. "Migraine flash."

"You're pushing too hard," she said, and slammed the thin metal door, causing another shard of pain. Familiar dimness, cool air. He lay back. "Sorry. It's all well and good Ayizan saying we've got to move, he's not making the biggest jumps in the Quarter."

"You wanted me to jump."

"Not at the expense of your health." Sofa cushions sank under her weight. "And you know what else? Don't talk around those flipping dogs."

Rubbing sore spots with his fingertips, frowning. Neck and temple, the back of his skull.

"Are you for real?"

"Yes, I am. I can't read them."

"They're dogs. And they're barely alive."

"All living beings have auras, as you know. Theirs are thin as ozone. All I make out is gray."

"Oh, come on." Seeing her face, relenting. "Okay. I won't talk in front of the dogs."

"Promise."

"On my life."

Chile winced.

"Bad choice of words. Sorry."

"Put your head here, will you." Patting her thighs, she maneuvered to make room, knuckles cracking, head rolling.

He spun lengthways, laying his head on her lap. Her fingers pressed his temples in small circles. A groan emerged from him, aimed at the ceiling. Silence shrouded the room.

Beyond their single window, gatherings evolved from diminutive genesis. A lit match, a loosened cork, passionate hugs or joined hands that led feet to imitate mirrored dance moves, laughter thrown toward the unseen sky. Connections, benign or violent with intent. Isolated moments exposing glints, however momentary, of life in voluminous creation, rich combinations of beauty and danger. The giving and the taking. Receiving and acceptance. Being open to the best, or abject despair.

6

Nowhere in the zone had a greater connection with the past than the Temple. It seeped through walls and brickwork, sculpted wood, statues and portraits, out of cabinets and faded nameplates, the still and dusted air. From the moment the Original Five had broken open its heavy doors, blue lamplight and slide torches raised to better explore the multitude of long-emptied rooms, Markriss had felt the presence of those who went before them, curious and tender at their sides.

He had flinched at the clamor of hurried feet rushing behind, around, and past him to run headlong down unfathomable corridors, bouncing high into air, laughing as they disappeared. He'd poked his head inside former classrooms to hear the muffled lessons of teachers, barks of voices raised as disciplinary warning. In the wide expanse of a former gym hall, an ebbing tide of prayer songs and hymns came and went, the irregular thud of a ball keeping offbeat time in harmony with squeaking sneakers. The Temple, unaware of what it would become, was alive with the spirits of its previous incarnation; they all felt that. The intensity of former lives sat behind each warped desk, strode corridors in hope of making it before the ring of a discarded bell, made long-scrapped pots and metallic trays clang in the expanse of the canteen. On rare occasions they even smelled frying chips.

The former school building drew those first Outsiders to it in wonder. They hugged in celebration of their luck, none more elated than Markriss. The others had found home; he had found sanctuary.

Channeled and brought to light by meditation, transmutative nambula, and crystalline work, among further practices, the space became a focal point not only for the energies of the building's past, but also their own. Temple was a space where ancestors, individual and collective, were called into being as a means to provide empathy, knowledge, instruction. It was there, in the depths of a transmutation chamber, that Markriss first made contact with his brother. And it was there that he discovered his more recent abilities, harnessing the mirror-image realm for greater exploration.

He walked the building's corridors and cramped stairways, heavy toolbox painful in one hand, past rooms that throbbed with the living as they made preparations for the gathering. And yet the sounds and feel of past energies mingled, remained. His eyes narrowed against the thud of falling hammers, searing drills—his migraine very much alive, causing a pulsing ache around his frontal lobe. High-vibration excitement saturated the air. Tremors at windows, the crackle of unknown aura connecting with his naardim. He tried to still himself, though it was there, that sizzle of nerves.

"Kriss! Yo, Kriss!"

He stopped, murmuring beneath his breath, turning halfway. A short man, lean and shaven, eyebrows dotted with perspiration. Io.

"What do you need?"

"Crepe." A carpenter by assignation, Io took care of the Temple's handyman duties. Today, as with all gatherings, he'd been given the more creative role of dressing old classrooms in preparation for various uses. "I've got a bit, but it won't hang the whole space."

"Tried the stockroom?"

"My boy says none's left."

"Send him to the shops, keep the receipt." Shouting over his shoulder, moving. "Tell him to come straight back if he sees Corps!"

"Will do, cheers!"

Bounding down steps to the second floor sideways on, Markriss went back on himself along the corridor and into the hall, careful not to rock the slab of toolbox into his knees.

There, Outsiders worked in every meter of the expansive room. Esoteric symbols, bannered mantras, and flags of countries comprising the zone's many nations were being hung from high walls using A-frame ladders. A group of women laid the black, skeletal limb of a lighting array on the floor before them, fitting arc lamps with gels and wires. Men sewed beads and sequins onto elaborate costumes denoting a range of Kemetian ancestral spirits: Sheps, Sebek, Amen, Tehuti. At the head of the hall, on a raised stage, a larger mixed group connected turntables and speaker boxes with trails of colored wires and a soldering gun. Ever since the Outsiders had shunned pod connections, they had disregarded conventional neural processing in favor of analog systems of computers linked by wires and home-made equipment developed by zone menial workers, who made up 98 percent of all Quarter residents. Nothing was bought, even the smallest component. Everything had been built in temple. They tracked the necessary parts down on search engines, 3D printing them using long-forgotten schematics that had gone unaccessed for decades.

Markriss paused before Ayizan, Temujin, a young Outsider named Iris, and Xander, all circled around a squared, ragged section of missing floorboards. They looked into the cavity as if expecting something to emerge. No one noticed him.

"Got what you need."

He dropped the toolbox, the thump sending tremors through his forearm. Temujin barely glanced at him.

"Where was it?"

"Where I told you. Who'd you send to look? Xand? You know he's useless."

Xander swiveled on his rear, kicking out, just missing. Markriss backed off, returned, edging closer to the hole.

"What's down there?"

"You haven't seen it?" Temujin said, amused. "Thought you knew every inch of the place. That's our very own Lowers. Dunno how they done it, but there's a kind of crawl space under the whole hall. They probably used it for performances, dunno why. It's not like it's the opera or anything."

"Goes right up and under the stage," Ayizan said, indicating with his head. "Even got well-camouflaged escape points."

"I don't reckon it was used for performances," Xander ventured. "I think they hid kids from the Corps so they wouldn't be killed."

"Thanks, Xand. Bring down the tone," Iris muttered at her feet. Broad-shouldered and athletic, she looked as strong as the men. Markriss often wondered if she and Ayizan were seeing each other. He never wasted breath by asking.

"There's tunnels and false rooms all over the building, not just here."

Ayizan sat on his haunches, waiting.

"So what happened?" Iris asked. "Why did they need them?"

"Old Sares will know," Xander offered.

"But would he tell you?" Ayizan smiled at their laughter. "All right, folks, let's work. Who's up for hammering some floorboards down?"

A rush for the toolbox. Markriss got up, eyebrows raised in Ayizan's direction. Caution rode the air between them.

"See you lot in a bit."

They waved, distracted by work. Markriss left them to walk from the hall, back toward the brighter light of the narrow corridor.

The earliest gatherings had been a means of releasing tension bred from living under the yoke of the Authority without sun, sky, or elements. Those original celebrations, necessarily small, were held in resident allocations or front gardens under heavy Corps presence, and usually marked the change of outside seasons. Over time, people emerged onto the streets and circled home blocks in a procession of costumes, masks, dancing, and drums. Meats were cooked, vast plastic barrels of punch concocted. When the celebrations grew larger, the first response of security was to crush them to size, resulting in zone-wide violence and the deaths of two Poor Quarter residents, Osman Farhardi and his nine-year-old daughter, Tamina. When residents refused to give the practice up, emphasizing their resolve by holding the next gathering after the Farhardis' cremation rites that following day, the Corps cordoned the zone off from the invisible border with its neighbors. No official announcements were made, although residents' committees of the time believed the Poor Quarter had been left to police itself.

Modern gatherings were often impromptu, kindled by any small occurrence. A birthday or marriage, a football win or, in this case, the Lites' return online. Once a year an official autumn gathering was held throughout Inner City, solemnizing October 11, 1910, as an auspicious date; the day when the Ark first opened its gateways to the world. The celebrations were huge. As much as they despised the politics behind that particular gathering, the Outsiders' influence on it grew more visible every year. Temple became their focal point, where they opened chambers to all, offered a crèche for infants, sold food and meditation aids, provided books and workshops, but most of all threw the biggest party in the zone. Ayizan and the remaining Circle members had conflicting feelings about whether such overt displays of influence were the right direction for them, but their leadership role in street and allocation parties was never up for discussion. Gatherings were essential to the culture. It was difficult to imagine the Poor Quarter without them. The release it gave their pressure-cooker existence was plainly evident from the enthusiasm of zone residents' participation.

Aimless, Markriss wandered back down concrete steps to the ground floor, then outside Temple. There he sat on the sidewalk, his back against cool stone. Wisp-thin weeds grew in cracks between concrete squares. He touched one with a finger, admiring its tenacity. The Lites had reached their apex, a one-hour duration after which, although they appeared constant, the machines dimmed degree by degree until going offline. Markriss searched his jeans and jacket, digging, revealing. Rolling papers, a quarter of cigarette, a self-contained wrap of piahro dust. Combining ingredients, he licked and rolled a splint. Patted his pockets.

No lighter. He must have left it inside the building.

He tucked the splint behind one ear, zone-watching. When the right person came, he would ask. Twisting strands of hair between his fingers, he whistled a partial tune between his teeth. The square was empty apart from the odd weekend shopper or resident paying a visit to family or friends. Quiet, low-threaded music wove from some distant allocation. Many stayed indoors during these hours, believing the Lites kept autumn months too warm, and the Authority should bring down the temperature; such heat wasn't needed inside. Others argued that the changing seasons were a fundamental part of human life. Detractors countered that by saying there was no weather system, so why simulate the cycle of Geb around the sun?

Shouts, explosive feet. Running. He pushed himself upright, back rising against the wall, straining to see. Noises echoed from every direction, impossible to tell where they came from until the figures shot into view on his right, limbs flailing, clothes flapping mute around them. A sprinting boy. Skinny, dirt-caked, a street kid. Three residents followed close, calling and pointing, all men, well groomed at quick glance, expensive clothes and sneakers, jewelry and watches creating spectrum diamonds under the Lites. Though they seemed familiar, Markriss didn't know them. The man in the lead, wide and strong, aimed a kick at the skinny boy's feet and caught him. Skinny dipped low, arms straining for balance, a sprinter crossing the line. Panic drew his teeth into a grimace of desperate fear. He knew what it meant to obey gravity. What the cost of losing won. His feet, seemingly working alone, knew similar. They kicked up tarmac dust, hoping to find much-needed traction.

The second assailant drew level, throwing a punch at the boy's shoulder, and it was over: he was down, they were on him.

The whisper of sneakers scuffing powdered dirt and the bass of landing fists consumed Markriss, alive to the pitch of Skinny's voice, betraying the difference between bones connecting with flesh, and piercing metal with the same. Skinny cried out with every thrust, the knife blows producing a shrill whimper that chilled his heart, made him wince. As he approached, taking stock, Markriss became aware of residents hanging back in gardens and on block corners, the others who moved to his rear, dressed in the bright sneakers and designer shirts of hustlers, blocking his escape.

"Leave him," he said, arm crooked behind his back, fingers barely touching cold metal, the existence of the knife reawakened against his spine. "Let him up."

The first man kept pounding. The rest turned on their heels, heads craned over shoulders, casual as business.

"Fuck you."

Ignoring him, they continued.

Markriss took a two-step run, kicking the stabber in his ribs, sending him skittering across the pavement, an upended crab. The people watching cried out, mostly in shock, some anger. There was enough time to punt the second between his legs so he fell across Skinny, his weight causing the boy to roar pain. The crowd gave another cry. When the third leaped to his feet, Markriss flicked the knife and held the blade erect, circling on light feet so he looked each crowd member deep in the eye, keeping peripheral sight on the men.

Third's weapon was drawn, thin and rusted. He crouched, arms wide in an empty, awkward embrace.

Sensing what came next, the crowd gave room.

"This got nuttin to do with you! Man's tief. Check im pockets, im still ave it!" Third's teeth, unlike the rest of him, were broken, rot-caked.

"Give a shit, you're on Square! Square's Temple, round Temple this shit don't work! I told you, let him go, or take us on. You wanna take us on?"

"Us? Who the fuck's us?! I only see one dirty suttin! Is me and you!"

Rope tendons protruded from Third's neck, crying outrage, fists clenched, forearms striped with muscles. Second, hands grasping balls, continued rolling on his back, crooning as if to lull away pain. First limped to his angered friend's side, a hand on his ribs, the other resting on Third's shoulder.

"Take time, bruv," he said, a line of dirt on his bright red T-shirt to mark where he'd fallen. "Is a Outsider, bredrin."

"I don't give a fuck! I'll kill him! I'll fuckin kill him!"

"Hey," Markriss said, softening his voice and palming the knife, thumb across the hilt, hands raised. "Hey, this don't need to go no further. Yeah? We can stop right here, the kid can give back what he stole, and we call it done. All right?"

First's head rocked, a hint of gold emerging between parted lips, while Third crouched, feet shifting, disrupted mouth open, eyes darting over Markriss's shoulder. Markriss knew what would happen. He swiveled, pivoting out of the way, the punch from the fourth assailant still glancing against his chin, sparking bright fire, snapping his head around to see Third's charge, blade phallus-ready. A step backward gave Markriss room and time, moving him away from the line of attack. His counterpunch met the temple of Fourth, a thickset allocation man. Fourth stumbled, eyes rolling, feet scrabbling as he tumbled into the knees of Third, who was pushed away and back, both knocked to the floor.

Two left standing, Markriss and First. The crowd sighed, stepping back a few paces. Markriss's knife returned to his fist, offered in irregular directions as he watched each facial expression for signs.

First jittered with nerves, hands raised. "Teacher, man, I'm not even involved bless. Man's done."

"Get your things, get your bredrin, and get the fuck outta my area," Markriss spat, hating himself. He'd succumbed. "What'd he take?"

"A watch, my gold watch."

"Get it back, now. Take anything further it's round two."

"All right, Teach, cool yourself down . . ."

First riffled the boy's pockets, immune to his cries of pain, digging until he found the item, a limp and scratched thing, probably worth a lot less than he'd been told. He slipped it into a pocket, helped his fallen friends to their feet, and they limped away from the square, arms thrown across each other's shoulders like dance partners. Third threw glances over his shoulder, having sense enough to remain silent. As they turned a corner out of sight, the crowd's shoulders sagged and chatter began.

Markriss kneeled beside the boy. He bled from at least three places, stomach, ribs, and thigh, lips coated, fingers rigid, limbs shaking.

"What's your name?"

"Keyon." Spluttering with effort.

"Okay, Keyon, I'm gonna sit with you and ring for Dr. Amunda. Any medical people here?" he asked, turning around.

"How you gonna ring anyone, you man don't carry slides," Keyon said, spitting blood. Instead of landing on the pavement, it trickled down his cheek.

Markriss laughed. "Don't worry yourself about what we carry."

A woman, mannequin serious, came close. "I live on Square. You can bring him to mine."

"Why didn't you say?" Markriss yelled, seeing her flinch. He caught himself. He needed water. "Sorry."

"It's okay." The unsmiling woman touched his shoulder, turning to the crowd. "Can some of you man grab him and bring him over?"

"And call Dr. Amunda," Markriss said, modifying his tone. He needed to calm himself, his forehead was damp with sweat. Bodies crowded the skinny boy, shielding him. Maybe it was better that way.

"Don't worry, I've already called. I work with him sometimes."

"Thank you."

Markriss stood, scanning the area. A mess like this on Gathering Day wouldn't be good for the zone. Scattered groups littered the previously empty square. Talk buzzed around him. Faces pressed at Temple windows and allocations everywhere he turned. On the far end of the square, just by the road leading out of the zone to the high street, stood Io's son Renno. Taller than most men, wearing a pitzball strip and lean with teenage muscle, watching the scene with an expression Markriss found difficult to interpret. Part contemplation, perhaps disgust. He didn't know.

Markriss pivoted, walking into Temple, the retracted knife cupped and hidden in his palm.

Down into the basement, where the music of tools and yells of working residents lowered to faint whispers. A place of cool air and damp walls, blue lamplight, guttering candles, and a veil of incense smoke. The lengthy chimes of a distant gong. The vibration of invisible energies. For the duration of gatherings, most under-level meeting rooms, workshop spaces, and transmutation chambers remained as they were, quiet, free of music, and barely decorated, used for nothing other than studied contemplation.

Arriving onto the dim-lit floor, Markriss's heart receded from thumping urgency at his chest, violent residue seeping into darkness. He tucked the knife into the space between his back and waistband.

A resident emerged, small and loose-limbed, flushed with the aftermath of ascension. Hair tied back, clothing loose and casual, she bowed, expelling nervous energy.

"Teacher."

"Afternoon. Chileshe still there?"

"Finishing," she said, taking the steps upward until she went unseen.

He frowned, ear pressed against the shut door. Voices, though he couldn't tell if any were Chile's. He knocked twice, knuckles flaring pain, raising them to the nearest light. They were skinned, bruised dark.

Wincing, he twisted the doorknob and let himself in.

This chamber was without furnishing except for a group of chairs at the far end. Across from Markriss, a small table was covered with a sheet of purple cloth, scattered crystals of all colors and designs laid on the material. Walls were painted with mantras, prayer flags hung. It was unusually humid, the air lumpen and weary. Five women sat cross-legged on individual hemp mats before Chile, who sat at the near end of the room, head tilted toward the open door. The women were barefoot and wore loose clothing. Their eyes were closed, wilting hands on knees.

He crept inside, realizing his mistake, wishing he'd found an empty, private space.

"Keep focus . . . You've all met my husband," Chile said, rolling her eyes, frowning. "He knows he shouldn't be here."

Rippling chuckles. Markriss shrugged, gave a meek grin, pointing at the chairs where he'd be out of her way. Tiptoed over. Eased down, closing his eyes.

Chile continued to speak, reminding Markriss of listening to her sleep-talk, mumbling and low, a relaxed monotone.

"Try to feel your way into your body. Feel yourself enter your toes. Your ankles. Your calves. Your thighs. Your womb. Stay with your womb a moment. Give her love. Don't cling. Don't regret. Accept her. Reassure her. This is an essential naardim right now.

Treat her with compassion. And then, when you feel her open or close, whatever's best at this moment, let yourself move on. To the stomach . . . Intestines. Ribs, heart. Linger there a moment too. Embrace her. Forgive her. Moving into the lungs, your throat. Mouth . . . Nose . . . Eyes, all three. The mind, the brain. Settle into yourself. You're home. Make yourself whole.

"We try to lower ourselves gently, not rush or force. We needn't panic or cling to places we've been, the people we're connected with. You'll see them again, I'm sure. At this stage we practice acceptance, and acceptance comes with love. Love who they are. Love who you are. Love where they are. Love where *you* are. Does that sound weird, or difficult? Loving being in here—not Temple, I mean Inner City? Good. Well, it shouldn't. There are things about here you like, even inconsequential nothings. The blue of e-lamps. Your favorite crystal. Kids laughing when the Lites go down, the smell of your next-door neighbor's vape. The sound of trams. What do you like? What do you love? Find that thing and hold it. That's the key to ongoing maintenance in this place, finding and holding. It's the thing that will help you get out *there*, with strength and with clarity."

A pause.

"Now open your eyes. We're done."

Murmurs, women looking around half smiling, rubbing eyes with fists, drinking bottled water. Throwing back their heads and rolling necks, feeling for cracks.

"Questions?" Chile's eyes were bright and glassy. The door swung open. A creak and the small woman Markriss encountered came inside. "Joanie, how you doing?"

"Better," she said, sitting on her mat. The nearest woman pulled her close for a prolonged hug, stifling though not drowning her voice. "Had a good cry."

"Nothing wrong with that." Chile looked them over. "You're bang on time, we were just about to start sharing. Anybody?"

A hand rising, hesitant, the woman who'd hugged Joanie. She twisted, looking at the others on either side of her, brunette ponytail bobbing. From where he sat, Markriss couldn't see her face.

"I'll go if no one else wants to."

"Sure," Chile said.

"I just wanted to tell you all what a lovely experience I've had . . ."

A round of *ahs*, more hugs.

"I'm twenty-five years in. My kids are teenagers, almost grown, and I've never . . ." A choking gulp. "I mean I never believed in this before, this streaming stuff, I mean, obviously I believed the rest . . . Oh, what am I saying? What I'm saying *is*, it's been so long since I've seen Mum and Dad, my nan passed while I was here and I just . . . It was so lovely . . . I just wanted to say thank you to Chile, and thank you all so much, I've never felt so much *love* . . . It's my first stream, as you all know, you've heard me say it a billion times; you've all been lovely and I'll be sure to come back . . . That's it."

Lengthy applause, Markriss tapping his fingers against his palm. This was why he became an Outsider. This was reality.

"Anyone?"

Withheld breath, tension. Heads stiff, attentive.

"I know our cycles aren't synched as they were, but always remember it's very important to visit chamber. Don't let the Ark block out energies. Even if we can't stream together, we can come together, yeah?" A pause, Chile watching. "All right, get out of here. See you next month."

They rose, rolling and gathering mats beneath arms. There was gossip and more questions, even though they'd been asked to raise their queries earlier; it was exactly the same as whenever he took classes. He watched Chile's ease, their banter, the way she rubbed a shoulder and almost smiled up into their faces, as she was shorter than the other women. Even so, her aura rippled brighter, with greater clarity, far lovelier than anyone else.

Markriss smiled at his feet. So many uncomfortable feelings assailed him on this particular Gathering Day. As much as he knew the answer was to let them flow, the practice was difficult in times of high stress. He should not attach, judge, or act; emotion should drift and ebb away. Pride was dangerous, given his position in the zone. He shouldn't allow energy to fester and impregnate his ego, but maybe that was why he was there, to hear Chile speak. To learn. Take her advice and see what he felt for what it truly was. Love. Pure, simple love.

His tired body, frustrated at being ignored, fired questions through swollen knuckles and red, broken skin. Pain. He closed his fist, turning it left and right. What did he know about love, his flesh and muscles asked, when he was consumed with the desire to injure? To hate?

He lowered his head, hoping to see. Sank into himself, sunsum-drifting. After what felt like a mere moment, Markriss looked up. The room had emptied, Chile saying last goodbyes from the door. He blinked, back arched, stretching.

Every month his wife tutored Bloodstream Meditation classes, a practice she'd discovered by close reading of Kemetic annals in the top-floor Temple library. The books arrived by all means, loaned or given by residents, donated from charities, brought by members and lent for others to learn from. She discovered the ritual in a textbook written by the Kemetian high priestess Amanitore millennia ago, *Divining Neter*. The writings focused on methods women might use to channel their specific biological makeup to access higher realms. Two chapters in particular gave detailed analysis of an ancient ritual undergone at menstruation, to work with lower body energies, and bring them in line with the women's higher selves. This allowed them to traverse the astral realm and make contact with members of their bloodline, in or out of the Ark, on a monthly basis. It had taken over twelve cycles for Chile to mistress the rituals, modifying them enough to bring the practice into the chamber. Ever since, it had become a regular Temple class, difficult to hone and greatly beneficial to the growing number of attending women.

Chile eased the door closed, sagging against metal.

"Nosy."

"Not at all. I needed to see you."

She peered at him, her eyes hardening, coming closer. "What happened?"

"Some kid robbed a few guys—from Alpern, I reckon. They tried to get their things back and crossed the square."

"Let me see." Chile raised his hand, hissing as he gasped pain. She touched Markriss's jaw, turning his head left and right. "Who else got hurt?"

"Just the kid, pretty badly. The rest of us will be sore in the morning, that's it."

"You look sore now. You need to soak your hand in water."

"I know."

"Well, it's your choice. If it hurts enough, you will."

She let his hand fall. He kissed her cheek.

"I was really angry, Chile. I haven't felt like that in a long time. I needed to calm down."

"We were in trance."

"It won't happen again."

"Yeah, well. Luckily we'd finished."

"I knew that."

"Yeah, right." She took his hand again, inspecting fingers. "Do you think they've got worse on the blocks?"

"How so?"

"More riled up. Tense."

He stroked her knuckles, noting the deep-ridged lines, the knot of bone. Skin a shade darker than the surrounding flesh. "I don't think so. They're overexcited, heat gets to them. Out there drinking, smoking pi . . ."

"One of the women, Hamadra, the one who said how much she liked it here, said there's been increasing violence on her block, even before the Lites came on. Stabbings, a murder. She thought it would stop when we got online, only it hasn't. She asked me to speak to you."

"Sure. I mean there's nothing wrong with taking a look. The boys are patrolling, right?"

"When there's gatherings?" Spearing him over her glasses. "Are you serious?"

"Fair enough. Talk with Ayizan. I'm sure he'll agree."

"All right. I will."

He almost frowned at Chile's old-man strop, before she relaxed, leaning into him. Markriss followed her mood, letting go of what he'd seen, hugging her to him, engulfed in her scent. Eased by every breath.

7

As a younger, many years earlier, Markriss had fallen in love with photography. From that point onward all thought, waking or sleeping, concerned the need to commit every detail of his escaping moments to the tightly wound film in his camera, imprinting them forever on celluloid surfaces in a vain attempt at avoiding suspect recall. When he'd first discovered the form, way before Willow allowed him to use bottled chemicals to develop his photos, he used an instant camera, delighting in the slow transition from darkness to color, blurred form to solidity, ghostly forms or environments into people and places he knew. Flapping rigid photographic paper into the wind, poised for results. And so it was probably inevitable that his spiritual body—seesaw wavering between the earthly plane and the numerous others that existed on the astral, ever since he'd woken—took on the form of those seeping, half-formed images he'd captured with an eager childhood grin, depressing the camera button with a finger, breath withheld, hoping the moment was right.

Like those photos, the images invading his present were difficult to see. Unlike them, there was no development into anything even vaguely decipherable as reality. He couldn't tell if they were fragmented or belonged to some forgotten whole. In the last few days, the images had begun to strike with increasing regularity, and even while he knew why, Markriss worried about the lack of focus they gave him, especially now, when he needed to concentrate on his surroundings more than ever. Still they came, immersive as the immediate world, nebulous as nightmares. The shape of something that might have been a woman half veiled in shadow, swirling smoke or thick cotton. A rotating form he struggled to make more apparent, and might have been the tires of a bike, although he'd never ridden one. A thud of noise, possibly footfall or heavy machinery, or falling concrete, or the distant boom of artillery. He didn't know and couldn't tell, so they remained vague, eyes blind with cataract abstraction. It scared Markriss, though he wouldn't allow himself to admit it. Meaning could be gleaned from those fragments, had they not been masked and coded beyond understanding.

Practiced adepts were wary of spontaneous projections, calling them "jump-backs." Postascension, they were prone to flashes of past, present, and future, particularly after sustained or aborted jumps. Moments of quiet meditation — recalibrations — alleviated most lasting effects, something Markriss had omitted after the panic caused by his last journey. Confusion led to his skirting normal procedure, behaving like an initiate rather than the experienced teacher he was.

He knew what had happened. Or rather, what he was doing to himself. He'd run from the task, neck-deep in procrastination, walking to temple like a man who had nothing better on his mind than to perform random errands for friends. Avoiding his future self. Fighting strangers, playing with the notion of murder, theirs or his, the possibility of ascending to become an ancestor. It was all diversionary, and as he left the Temple doors a second time, emerging into low light, fueled with renewed purpose, he chided his base self for being so easily swayed. He was a teacher. One who gave guidance. And yet he'd failed to counsel himself, much less to notice the askew path of his journey. He'd allowed his body to detach from his mind, to become unfocused.

He didn't hurry. Hands in pockets, eyes on the street, ears attuned to all, even though his step was casual. It was dangerous in their zone, perhaps even more so after what he had done to break up the fight. The people around him had an alertness he hadn't seen since the beginning, when he and Ayizan first declared themselves to the

Poor Quarter. Back when they were men of road teams and night, conflict and weapons, before they'd found spirituality. Violence at their fingertips, willing to do whatever felt applicable, men whose gaze was avoided by most. And now the people acted as they had then, unsmiling, heads turned or viewing his back with cautious eyes, crossing the street before he reached them, whispering as he passed. Talk had been traded, new stories exchanged for old. They overlooked Teacher, recalling his past. Conversation died when he walked by their silent gardens, replaced with stiff nods, resuming when night folded and collapsed into the empty space he'd left behind. With his head raised and his step fluid, blue light made him an untethered shadow adrift through the Quarter, a specter of their enclosed space they could not avoid or escape, and so they silenced themselves in hope that he would continue without noting their existence.

He could admit that the Circle had known he was struggling, leaving him to do the task in his own time, make discoveries for himself. No one wondered aloud why he sat with them whiling time, or why he wasn't below in chambers, alone, attempting to rise. He recalled their body language, translating what he'd seen, evasion as nonverbal questions. Glances at him and each other. Eyes hidden, cast at their feet. Subtle communication much like the unspoken language Markriss found on the streets. In the silence of his response, they had kept theirs. Deep love surged for their willingness to stand with him despite his actions' potential to harm. They trusted him.

Even as deep thought misted his vision, his attention was captured by everything, from the wink of distant metal on high gantries, to brickwork crumbling like moist cake. His awakened senses were more acute than ever, with the strangeness of a newborn feeling that had pulsed through every millimeter of skin since he'd woken from the waking dream. Tingling nerves, longing for contact, alive to every sensation: oxygen swelling his rib cage; the electric insect whine of a tram, so many blocks away; chinking cutlery high on the air, possibly from the Ivory blocks to the west, those dark monoliths of sparking window light. The buzz of miles-away people, unheard conversations. A pad of dog paws over his shoulder, hardly noticeable, their hesitance as he slowed to dig into his empty pockets, before they regained pace.

The vibration of online generators, their tremor in his soles. Life. Everything.

He walked the path to his front door. The skeletal twist of metal chair belonging to Old Sares was empty, leaning to one side. Markriss hardly knew how the old man sat, let alone found comfort, the cushioning threadbare, vomiting bile-colored innards. The Menguses' home glowed citrus light. Raised voices came from within, a clash of meeting plates. Pharah's tricycle lay on one side in the concrete garden as if collapsed with exhaustion, asleep where it fell. Again, that felt like a memory long forgotten, on the edge of remembrance. A flash of something that had happened in the past or not happened at all. Déjà vu. He examined the fallen trike—hashtag scuffs, pink and silver handlebar ribbons, scabbed dents—trying for recollection. An inner glimpse of a spinning object, sparkling light. The constant tick of revolution, nothing more.

He slipped his key card into the door. A push, the lock clicked green. Stark silence. Dormant furnishings, the calm of home. He could have chosen the chamber, closed the door, and made sure it was locked. Laid a hemp mat on hard Temple concrete, cleared his mind, and begun. Only there, with his cheek pressed against Chile's, breathing in her scent, he'd felt a call for his allocation. Nothing overt, just another simple recurring image. The pod, cold and offline, the austerity of enclosure. His familiar mattress, pillows, the fluffed duvet. Full-circle repetition—where he started and failed. It made an odd type of sense, and so he allowed his feet to do the work, mind set on autopilot. And it was done. He was home.

Other than his environment, he needed few things. A pen and his thin notebook. His stick of rose-quartz crystal, the stone of love and cleansing, which he'd keep for the entire jump. A custom-built meditation visor given by Capra. The cool, sterile atmosphere of the pit, his mantras, a glass of water to drink following descent, and the spirit of his dead brother. All was in place.

He opened the pit door, stepped inside, and lowered himself onto his back, looking at the cracked ceiling. Water pipes sang continuous harmony behind the walls. The thud of a parkour runner on his roof made him start. A thudding succession of steps, the final decisive stamp, and they were away, beating time into distance. Far music, bumps and voices from the Menguses' flat. Markriss listened to his neighbors. Language, when heard through the muting barrier of walls, became nothing more than unfamiliar sounds and grunts, baritone and mezzo-soprano, soprano and contralto. Like hearing someone who had lost the power of speech, an undiscovered animal. He listened to the alien voices until his eyes were heavy, thoughts adrift. He clasped the solid heat of the crystal in his palms.

Markriss grounded himself, imagining his body afloat in a calm black sea. One arm outstretched above his head, drawing a line around his entire body. Phosphorus illumination glowed blue, trailing from the tip of his index finger. Once, twice, a third time, until luminescence held. He relaxed, floating on still water, the ovoid circle moving with him.

He sank into darkness.

And rose.

A broad, muscular block threw lengthened shadow over his head. Red flag, austere walls. Number 1322. He raised his eyes, couldn't see the roof. The Lites were offline, the building windows dark glasses. The normally busy high street was empty, no rolling, electric-horn beep of trams, no commuters or bright shop windows. The Inner City night was still as the ocean he'd left behind in his meditation.

He looked both ways before crossing the road, a habit. If traffic came, he wouldn't be hit—this was not a physical realm. Up and down the long main street, miles of buildings, no movement. A shift of an invisible form, a shimmering haze camouflaged against brown stone.

Ninka.

His brother surged up the steps, a rippling wave on open water, through doors, and inside the building. Markriss went with him, hesitant. He had to catch him, to let him know. It was his task. Beyond the security guards—a skinny, balding one asleep with feet on the desk, a bigger, red-eyed one hunched before a twenty-inch slide-screen that lit the entire foyer with its flickering glow—he reached for Ninka, fingers moving through empty space where he just made out what looked like a shoulder.

The rippling haze paused, colors and solid material behind it shifting sand.

Alone. I must go alone.

Emotion bled into his aura. Relaxation, a loosening. The haze rippled to one side, the space beyond taking on a look of normality. The cloud he encountered on his last jump was gone. He hadn't noticed it disappear, it was just like it had never existed.

He moved. A silent lift area, three gray sliding metal doors, all closed, orbs of security cameras fixed on the ceiling. A simpler swing door with a sign above indicated a fire exit. The place he needed was somewhere above. Markriss closed his eyes, chin raised, and pushed upward so his ethereal form moved through a mass of dark concrete, wood, and steel until he emerged a floor above the lobby, in a wide room of Ark-gray, open-plan desks. He pushed again until there was a floor of walled cubicles, then one of well-defined offices and blank featureless wood, then the penthouse level, light and singular, taking up a whole floor.

He slowed, orienting himself. He'd emerged into an expansive open-plan space that captured the surrounding light of neighboring buildings, even in offline darkness. No walls in any direction, only glass and metal lattice, a repeating pattern of hexagons. From the center, where he floated, he saw the media zone and all other zones for miles; squinting, in the far distance, there might have even been the girders, red lights, and checkpoint security of gateways, to the west and east. He turned in wonder to gaze at the squared sections of blocks. Reminded himself what he had to do.

The floor had an office area with a desk, bookshelves, and cabinets, unmoored and incongruous on one side of the room without walls to define them. Sofas were hulking, well-defined animals beside miniature towers of drink and snack machines. A visor console and mini slide were set up in what was clearly a relaxation area. Not far from those was a four-person luxury pod and Jacuzzi-sized bath. Markriss had never seen a sleeper that size. A slide-screen and 3D projector hung from the ceiling, positioned so the picture could be viewed from either pod or bath. A steel-blue bath mat shimmered like still water beside a rack of clothes and a hive-like cabinet filled with fluffed towels. The bulk of a steel fridge containing the shiny round bottoms of wine bottles murmured energy. There were giant potted plants, a pitzball hoop (he could just make out the wire bin filled with yellow sponge balls), the offline gray squares of a dance floor area, a family of gym equipment, and in one distant third of the space an ornate library; otherwise this football-pitch-sized level, one in which at least fifty Poor Quarter families could live without discomfort, was empty.

Markriss drifted from one section to another, trying not to be angered, to keep calm. Capra had hinted as much; still, this was beyond any stories he'd been told. To see it was to witness the soft grip of injustice, and yet he knew this wasn't the worst example of privilege the Ark had to offer.

He moved toward the office area and desk. Over his head, unobtrusive but there, Capra warned, were pencil-thin cameras. Markriss thought he couldn't be seen—they believed the tech hadn't been developed to record bodies on the astral plane—although, for people moneyed enough to own a penthouse suite in their place of work, he couldn't be entirely sure. This was all new territory. The mission was the Outsiders' trial, Markriss their lab rat.

He saw what he'd come for as he hovered above the sheer metal desk and array of personalized keepsakes—a desk-slide programmed with a selection of 3D family photos, a mini pitzball figure complete with hoop. Relieved, worry lifted. The 1322 schematics took pride of place on the desk, every level secured beneath a sheet of plate glass. Every desk, unit, and office on every floor accounted for. Just like Capra said.

Glancing at the desk-slide, a studio picture of three children became the trio on an indoor rock climb, arms thrown wide and beaming, dissipating into snowfall pixels and replaced by a close-up shot of a woman, her serious expression. She wore baggy jeans and an old T-shirt, was holding an oil-blackened wrench. An upended bicycle stood in the background. Her hands were smudged with oil; she was probably fixing the chain. The woman looked somewhere off camera. She seemed dreamlike, unaware the photo was being taken, lips parted, on the verge of speech. Markriss didn't know why he was drawn to her. She reminded him of someone he couldn't place, someone he'd met. The woman was arresting, that was true, yet this was something else. He knew her.

One slow pixel at a time, the woman dissolved into the lanky, suited figure of 1322 CEO Jex Myatt. Suit and tie, award held high above his head in midcongratulatory shout, blond fringe falling across one eye.

He calmed, put the woman from his mind. Lowered his astral form until it hovered centimeters from the tiled floor. Staring at the schematics, he allowed the image of each floor to fill his vision, each line and room, not pushing, eyes flitting from section to section, level to level. It might have taken twenty minutes of focus and concentration—he wasn't sure, time was difficult to track on the plane. Adepts were known to miscalculate, over- or undercompensating. He forced himself to wait, viewing each level until they had sunk in, closed his eyes and released his astral body, falling through the floors to leave the penthouse as still as it had been before his arrival.

The persistent tick of water pipes, a gentle tattoo. Sharp pain in his hands, as though they had been cut deep with his knife. He looked down on himself, chin pushed against collarbone, remembering he still gripped the rose crystal. Markriss let go, solid weight tumbling across his thighs onto the mattress. He sat up quick, scrabbling for the orange medi strip on the podside, threw a leg over the sleeper side, climbed out, and nearly tripped over his feet as he bounded over to their small desk cluttered with textbooks, notebooks, a loose collection of pens, and a potted aloe vera Chile had nurtured for months. He tried not to notice the dry earth—it would have to be watered another day. He had a few minutes at most before he "cleared" and the memory of the schematics was lost. He pushed aside the items on the desk to make space, laid a sheet of white paper flat, took up the nearest pen, and thrust the medi-visor across his face so the plastic strip covered his eyes. It snapped around his head with the sound of a breaking rubber band, tightening, each end clasping his temples. He turned the visor online. A loading start-up, the E-Lul logo, a whirl of percentages. The bass tone of completion.

He thought-scrolled through options, selecting "Synch View/ Playback." The screen grew bright.

A digitized version of the desk materialized in front of his eyes— the landscape rectangle of paper, his grasped pen—and merged with the visual of his jump. First his head moving in all directions on the street outside 1322, the glisten of black tarmac and reflective glass. Playback excluded audio, so the low buzz of dormant machinery was missing, yet the picture was clear and solid, just as on the plane. The latest incarnations of Mediswear, four gens and beyond, provided a range of simulated transmutations, tracked dreams, recorded, digitally stored, and replayed meditations, and, using synch mode, enabled users to manually recreate objects, people, or experiences they'd encountered during jumps.

He wound forward, past Ninka and the lift area, up through the succession of floors until he was at the penthouse level, hovering above the desk. Paused screen. Enhanced view.

And traced what he saw.

First Markriss headed to Temple, and when Ayizan couldn't be found among the rapid vibration of high-level activity, he crossed the Poor Quarter in case he'd returned to his allocation. The night buzzed energy, the zone alive with all manner of gatherings on every block. Smoke and sizzling meats combined with a thick vapor fog, dulling the strung glow of prayer lights and the monotone of block chatter. Blade tucked into the small of his back, Markriss strained to see into every dull corner and allocation doorway. When retribution came it would be swift, without sign. If there were enough attackers, or he was inattentive, he wouldn't survive.

The street was quiet, although the square had been too. Outside Ayizan's allocation door, Markriss scanned terrace roofs for movement before he rapped his knuckles against the metal three times, turning to the street. Parkour runners not only trained their bodies and ferried narcotics, some killed in service of zone road teams. Guns were heavily prohibited in the Ark, although with the right software they could be 3D'd, or much less commonly smuggled inside vaginas or rectums, even stomachs. Murders of that nature were costly in more ways than one. They were expensive, easy to track by Corps, normally ending with the prompt disappearance of the perpetrators. "Stormers," the cheaper alternative, worked with a knife or machete strapped to their backs. They swooped down to "storm" their target, deliver the blow, and were climbing walls and racing along roofs before victims even realized they'd been hit.

A restrained snick behind him, the opening door. He followed its casual sway, entering the cool room and pressing the door closed behind him.

Ayizan was eating at his small coffee table. Iris sat cross-legged in his sleeper, a bowl clasped between her hands, watching a movie he couldn't make out on the big slide-screen. Orchestral music and very few words. Pale moonlight washed her face. Markriss kept his expression neutral, taking a little longer to wipe his feet on the doormat, acting as if he'd met Iris in Ayizan's allocation every day for years.

"Yes, Teacher."

"Yes. Hey, Iris."

"Hi, Kriss," she called, eyes trapped on the screen.

The two men pressed the fleshy sides of their fists together, brisk nodding. He sat opposite his friend, sighed. Ayizan seemed more tired than usual, eyes heavy, body sagging at a disjointed angle. He lay on his right side, dragging his spoon around the bowl in search of the correctly sized portion.

"How's it going over Temple?"

"On track," Ayizan muttered around food. Markriss only just heard him over the chewing. "We'll be ready. Decorations mostly done, systems wired up. Just gotta do lights, food, get drinks . . ."

"Important stuff."

"Damn right. We got beer; but the shops are low, of course. They're accommodating us."

"So they should. All we do for them."

"Exactly. They're lucky they got stock at all. Zekey's gonna perform."

"Oh yeah? Nice."

"Yeah." Sleepy grin. "How about you?"

Markriss looked toward the podroom, hesitant.

"Don't mind her. Go ahead."

He waited until Ayizan nodded, impatient, and dug into a back pocket to produce a clutch of folded papers. Opened each, one by one. Smoothed the paper flat with a palm, looked them over, kept one back and pushed the rest over the table.

"That's everywhere, including the upper penthouse."

Ayizan moved his bowl aside to lean over the schematics, eyes flitting from sheet to sheet, jaw moving. He paused to pick something from his teeth before his concentrated gaze returned, jumping from one piece of paper to another.

"They're brilliant. Didn't expect them to be so good."

"I had a bit of a mental block with the last jump I think, or maybe it took more effort, but I'm clear now. Ascension was no problem, no issues with the tether. Nothing."

"You're a genius." Another offer of a raised fist, met by Markriss. "Stone-cold genius. We're blessed."

"Ah, come on. I'm blessed to be asked."

"What's that?" Ayizan pointed with the spoon. Markriss looked into his lap.

"Oh yeah. Someone I wanted to show you." He opened the last sheet, flattening it with his palm as he had the others, taking more time. The woman from the office photo stared at the allocation ceiling, unimpressed. One last look at red curling hair and the upheld wrench before Markriss passed it over the coffee table. "Know her?"

Ayizan studied the picture, rubbing a temple. His lips moved as if whispering. "This is a really, really good portrait."

Shrugging, Markriss sat back. "I just pressed 'merge-pause' and copied what I saw. Like tracing."

"Yeah, but the details. Freckles, eyes, the twist of her mouth. You don't know her? You sure?"

"Never seen her in my life."

"Hold up."

Ayizan got up and crossed the room. The orchestral music stopped, abrupt as rainfall. Markriss watched him slide his body into the crack of space between his pod and the kitchenette wall, the sheet high for Iris to see.

"Got a minute, babe?"

Babe. Unusual. He tried not to look surprised.

"Sure, what's up?"

"Know who this is?"

A tidal wave of sleep rolled over Markriss. He lay back, legs protruding, eyes closing. The entrancement of the plane and its aftermath were kicking in. He exhaled, tired breath rattling his throat.

"Isn't this that anchorwoman? Keshni Myatt?" Half heard, Iris's voice was gravelly with lack of use or piahro smoke. "Used to be Roberts before she married that *Ark News* CEO. Presents on Ark One."

"I wouldn't know."

"Yeah, I'm pretty sure. My mum likes her, thinks she's pretty."

"She ain't bad."

"Oh, please."

Bubbling laughter, the light smack of a kiss.

"Awesome. Thanks, babe."

"You're welcome."

String music began. Bumps and the shuffle of clothes as Ayizan crossed someplace else, performing actions Markriss couldn't fathom with his eyes shut. Lengths of silence. Mutters of "Where is it?" It took some time for Ayizan to come back and lower into the sofa with a husky sigh. Markriss lifted his eyelids.

His friend stared at him, motionless, a thick hardback laid on his lap, hands rested on the cover. He thought he recognized the book, it was difficult to tell. The title was shrouded by dim light.

"Good form. Thought you'd ascended."

"Nah, just recabbing."

"Very wise. Keep doing that, you won't have trouble next jump." Ayizan rubbed his chin with a cupped hand, the scratch of his beard loud over the music, regarding Markriss with a flat look that seeped inside him, triggering the oddest physical reaction. A need to purge it like the tickle of a cough. An irritation, something to be expelled. "Why didn't you tell me about the kid?"

Sitting up. "What kid?"

"The one who got knifed on the square."

Blinking twice. He honestly didn't know. Consumed with worries? Numbed by the life they led? The kid, the violence, the bleeding, all dismissed. What did that say about him?

"I didn't think you'd want to know. You've got a lot on your plate. The mission, the gathering . . ."

"He got pretty messed up. He'll survive, even though they almost killed him. Those guys were Mansions, brother. Course I'd want to know. That kid, the guys who attacked him. All of them."

Mansion Row. A few blocks east of central Quarter. The Mansion Man road team controlled that area. That was how he knew them.

"We can't have Mansions attacking us on the square, Kriss." He lit a stub of piahro splint, expelling dragonish smoke. "It's not on."

Light trapped in Ayizan's eyes produced a veiled gleam so vivid Markriss couldn't see his thoughts. Even his voice was pitched in a shiftless monotone, canceling any attempt to absorb emotional intent, guess what he meant. It was dangerous for someone. Markriss had no idea who. He twisted to catch an itch in his lower back, wriggling against the chair. The orchestra grew louder. Iris's bowl clinked and scraped into the silence.

"How'd you hear?"

"Dr. Amunda. The kid nearly didn't make it. If the neighbor never had a home theater he wouldn't have."

They had grown popular in the Poor Quarter, trained doctors and nurses pooling funds to buy used, reconfigured equipment, often lobbying community donations to turn back rooms into makeshift operating theaters—with a lesser degree of hygiene, of course. There had been deaths from infections, and side effects; still residents preferred to take the chance on home theaters rather than wait for ambulance services that rarely came, or tussles with the Authority when they did.

"That's why I got involved. They were bleeding the kid right on the square . . ."

"Yeah, yeah, you done good." A dismissive wave. "I wouldn't ask anything less."

"Sure?" Peering, searching for truth.

"Yeah, for sure." Ayizan tilted his head toward the podroom. "That name mean anything? Keshni Myatt? Jex's wife?"

Another switch of topic. Ayizan's conversational movements often resembled the flight of a housefly. Markriss always wondered if it was a strategy to glean a more honest response. He pulled his mouth down, shook his head. "No. I might have seen her on-screen, I can't remember. I stopped watching SS ages ago."

"Yeah, same as. If she works for *Ark News* we should try and find out more. That might be our person. Right?"

"I hear you."

The level expression, settlement. Ayizan nodded once, patting the hardback on his thighs. The pads of his fingers made soft thuds.

"Been reading this."

"*The Book?*" Stiff nod. "How come?"

Ayizan's left shoulder jerked, an abrupt shrug. "Seemed right. You get me?"

"I do."

Ayizan opened it. The book flopped, tired as its owner. Tough skin on the spine had cracked in places, exposing paper flesh. Ayizan removed a thin blue ribbon bookmark, draping it over the cover. It fell limp.

"Hear this:

Within these walls, we take few things. Clothes, personal belongings, photos of loved ones whether family, friends, or pets; precious books, maybe a volume like this; our favorite means of hearing music, digitized or analog. Our arts, our sports, our trinkets. Our personal effects, verifications of self. Remember this: nothing is more important than what we carry upright each day when we rise from our pods to greet the world. Ourselves.

Who are we? What do we believe? Who will we miss, what will we miss? How do we cope with the lack of things you've never thought of, or had reason to lack? The life we are about to lead is a privileged form of confinement, yet confinement nonetheless—be truthful to ourselves about that. A great many of us neglected to make peace with ourselves before we entered this so-called paradise. Even more thought we had, only to be proven crucially wrong. Gather moments. Cherish each one so we might relive them again, when needed. They may very well save our lives. Work on ourselves on a daily basis, know the best and worst of who we are . . ."

"'For that is the only means of surviving isolation within this most modern of modern cities . . .'" Markriss intoned with him.

They wallowed, thoughts entwined, the orchestra fading into lingering strings. Dialogue, a woman's voice-over.

"It's like a bedtime story."

"Willow read to you?"

"No . . ." Choked, abrupt laughter between them. "When I was little, maybe, before my dad came inside, before I remember. Later"—shaking his head—"not so much. I suppose I just imagined what it felt like."

"Felt good," Ayizan said, the gleam of his eyes more pronounced. "Anyway, that stuff is gold dust. Gold dust! To know yourself is to prepare for isolation, you understand? There's nothing else but that, in the end."

"Yeah."

"You should read it again. Still got your copy?"

"I have."

"Good. Cos I ain lending you mine."

He was up again, restless, the spine of the volume shining from the coffee table at a barely readable angle—*The Book of the Ark*. No author. Markriss picked it up. Ayizan spoke over one shoulder, heading for the kitchenette.

"You drinking yet? I've got Xaymacian rum? Golden?"

"Nah, I gotta get back."

"It's gathering tomorrow!" Iris raised her voice over the soundtrack. "You've gotta drink tomorrow!"

Markriss smiled. "Maybe. I'll see."

He smoothed his jeans down, listening. A cupboard door opened and shut. A heavy object thumped, probably Ayizan's rum bottle. Markriss was more aware than ever of all *The Book* instructed, relishing the simple act of being, unsure whether he'd experience anything like it beyond that night, bathed in fleeting time.

8

The woman's legs stretched gantry high, or so it seemed, the luster of a thousand sequins throwing starlight, her body shifting with the pound of drummers at her feet. Beams of light reflecting from the sequins moved left, right, bending like they might break or she could fall, raised energy making her audience scream exuberance. Conjure-woman, extracting spirits from the cage of sweating bodies, emerging dragonflies swimming and diving about the square, freed to roam. Wherever she stepped people matched her, pivoting and thrusting, abandon stamped into artificial ground, lifting dust and kicking litter, the dancers below her moving to give room.

The circle at her feet closed and opened, a dilating pupil. Flared trousers glittered peacock blue and purple, the deep red of her blazer shimmering as her arms shook, writhing as her open palms thrust upward, head thrown back in unheard laughter. Higher. Higher. Face painted black in the guise of long-dead ancestors, joined by an able partner, another impossibly tall, face-painted woman. They clasped hands, swaying. A foghorn blared, loud over clapping and whooping, dancers bouncing on balled feet and long-forgotten joy.

Stalls lined the outer rim of the dance area, mostly food and drink, also clothing and crystals. Vendors hawked, shimmying to the frantic beat, tending wares. High above the crowd, red-clothed Outsiders perched as silent threats on the Temple roof and the roofs of the allocations opposite, scanning the crowd for thieves and rival road teams. More lurked within the mass of dancers. No stepping, no cups or food in hand. Staring at all, unsmiling. It was unusual for the risk to be taken, though if it happened the Outsiders were there.

Chile passed Markriss something covered in tissue. A gift of pastry; he unwrapped it and bit off a corner. Minced meat, mashed potatoes, chickpeas. Wonderful.

"From Clios." She nodded at a large vendor with a red bandanna and bald head standing behind a stall, ladling more fried pastries into a large serving bowl, dripping oil. The waiting queue behind him was long, salivating. Markriss raised the pastry, free hand held over his heart. Clios shuffled to the drums, pointing a finger at Markriss, shoulders heaving laughter as he continued working.

Chile broke a chunk from her own pastry as she swayed. Popped it into her mouth, wide-eyed. "These drums! Fallernum's on fire!" Rubbing her hips against Markriss, moving. Chile stepped closer. A knee between her legs, they rocked in time. He placed his lips against her neck, perfume seeping into him. Chile doing the same. Inhaling each other.

Lifted heads, eye-gazing. Drums fell away, somewhere beyond the senses. Movement slowed into almost nothing. She pressed her forehead against his, rubbing noses. Markriss thought he heard her say she loved him, even if her lips hadn't moved. He only felt it, his core trembling vibration. It settled, lingered. He sent it back and then there was a descent. Markriss tried to resist, due to the danger of having his guard down in that place and time, only he couldn't stop, he needed to see. He plunged.

The closed, locked gateway. Voices he couldn't recognize, not screams, a relaxed call, a sung choir. Prolonged, resigned pain. Dark helmets and visors gleaming, coming closer, possibly Corps, he couldn't tell. And the gateway again, this time the once-open doors swinging to a close, and he could see a glimpse of the wide and mighty Blin before they shut with an all-enveloping, ear-shattering noise of a powerful wave meeting the ocean, crashing with its full weight, then black submersion, and then . . .

The woman. Red hair, pale-green eyes. Keshni Myatt. Staring at Markriss with confusion, lips parting to speak . . .

He was back in the square, surrounded by deep night, Chile frowning. He nodded at her unspoken question, brisk, close-mouthed. Yes. He'd spontaneously projected. Her expression crumpled, body coming to a halt. She kissed him, soft where her perfume was strong, tracing his cheekbones with her fingers.

Hugging her to his chest, desperate to feel her. "I love you more than life. Remember."

Chile smiled, sad and lonely, whispering into his ear, "We should go."

She took his hand. They squeezed through the people, crossing the square to the opposite end, where the huge Temple doors stood open. Here there was space between vendors' stalls, although it was blocked by a knot of watching people, arms folded, nodding time, a number of children bored or tired, slumped against adults. Chile and Markriss passed through the group into Temple.

It was more crowded inside. The darkened shuffle of unseen heads, muttered conversation. Piahro smoke, heavy and stagnant. Movement was slow, though people gave way when they saw whom they stood beside. The music pulsing life from deep within the building was fast and intense, electronica fused with live instrumentation, harmonic chords and vocals floating about them. Chile pressed through a gap, hand warm and damp, toward steps down to the lower basement chambers, where muted sounds became a tunnel of vibrations and cool earth, submerged energy, dim coloration, the humid breath of passing bodies and the murmur of collective voices pressed close.

They found each other in the dark confines of the steps. Outsiders and their like, together in place. As one they breathed in, out. Stone temple walls, once material of the earth, collected life force in their pores to give as energy once the Lites dimmed into nothing, the music found completion, and the mass of humming bodies dispersed until the next time they came.

She pushed farther down the steps to the transmutation chambers. Here the atmosphere was softer, a floating void of musical abstraction filling the space, minimal to the point of absence, more harmonic. Dim red light made the contours of drifting faces partially apparent, expressions unreadable. The heavy thud of transcendental from the main hall became distant, walled vibrations merging with the music below, soft humming.

Markriss always believed the lower-level chambers were a subtle representation of the base chakras. Unblocked and open, they could be channeled to powerful effect. That night's gathering felt more potent than ever. He shuddered in brief, quiet acceptance.

A hand on his shoulder. The outline of Vyasa's towering form could be just made out in dimness. People stepped around him, muttering, "To be at peace."

"Hey, brother. Ayizan wants you to come."

He touched Vyasa's elbow in acquiescence. Following the broad expanse of his back past the run of doorways, they reached another set of steps at the corridor end. Above, arched brickwork created a semitunnel two meters in length, another door. Beyond that were Outsider antechambers of study and meditation spaces for the Original Five.

"What's going on?" He moved toward Chile, unable to see. The squeeze of her soft hand felt warmer and damper, though she said nothing. "Vy?"

They ignored him.

Vyasa placed his right forefinger on the reader. The indicator turned green, the door sighed open. Standing back to let them enter, he ducked inside after, scanning the busy corridor before the door closed.

"What's going on, guys?"

Vyasa's eyes were oval, empty pits. "You need to come."

When Markriss searched for Chile, she'd lowered her head. Her entwined hair flowed in plaited rows, a series of straight lines from the rear of her neck to amass at the top of her head in a whirlpool bun, its center raised above her crown. She walked away, toward the final door in the set of five. Ayizan's antechamber. Vyasa went with her, and there was something in the straightened poise of her back, the certainty of her walk, the way she refused to look behind her even though she knew he was confused. A shard of intuition. He knew what he would see.

She knocked on the door. The answer went unheard beneath muffled beats and distant revelers, until it opened, Chile nodding at whoever had received her. Only then did she look back.

"We should go inside."

He walked past Vyasa, staring at her. This time she met his eyes, held them. He went inside Ayizan's contemplation space. To his left, Xander stood dressed in red, a blind gaze focused on close brick walls.

Markriss nodded, curt.

"Brother."

"Brother."

The tiny space was similar to his own contemplation room, simple and unusually spare. A desk pushed against a far wall bearing notebooks and pens. Ayizan's slide, propped at an angle by a desk stand. A comfortable chair. Sparse shelves of books, only the most important titles, obligatory crystals, a puffed and worn easy chair for guests. A simple woven rug on brick floor. Scribbled graffiti crawling the walls, phrases, symbols, hypotheses perhaps — they were too illegible to read. Xander shut the door.

Markriss moved to the far end of the room. A second door, a dented brass knob, round and scuffed with age. He turned and pushed, entering the Chamber of Heretics.

This room was more expansive than Ayizan's. Eight by four, large enough to contain a reasonable number of people, small enough to feel enclosed. Damp, even more airless, and flooded with white light.

A single rectangular lamp was affixed in the left-hand corner. Three large men kneeled in the center of the room, hands and feet tied, bowed, sweaty foreheads touching a dark sheet beneath them, rear ends upended as if communing with their gods. Markriss knew the beings they worshipped took material forms of narcotic substances, bartered in trade and commerce and any conceivable reward that came with them. Even without seeing faces, he recognized the Mansion House team he'd fought on the square.

In front of and behind the men stood Ayizan and Temujin.

Machetes grinned in their limp hands. Webbed blood patterned each blade, saturating the white sheet laid on the stone floor, the men's bright clothing. Their victims shivered, weeping with pain.

Ayizan's head rose. "You came. Good."

"How long have they been down here?"

Temujin's expression was sour. "Not long enough."

"And you all knew this was happening?"

Behind him, when he swung to include her, Chile stood resolute. "Yes."

He stared at the trembling bodies. One, the man who'd backed off during their first encounter, had a deep wound in the region of his neck or collarbone. Leaking blood in a regular patter, the wound kept time like the bass thud above their heads. His breath jagged, panting. He whimpered on occasion. The man knew they were about to die.

Markriss tried to relax his jaw and stop his teeth from clenching. "Why?"

"I told you why."

"But it was over."

"You never said that."

"I thought it was obvious. We don't need them."

"Kriss." Ayizan's voice fallen weight dropped from great height, the power of the wave Markriss imagined one level above. "We don't turn our cheeks. We're not Christians."

A pause. The inelegant, random pants of frightened men.

"So what then?"

"You know what we have to do." Temujin's face was set inflexibly as Chile's, sculpted lips barely moving. She looked hewed rather than born. "Are you in?"

"Does it matter if I am?"

Searching Ayizan for confirmation. The machete was lowered, his hair untied so it fell past his waist, physically manifesting uncoiled energy. Like Temujin he seemed untroubled by the blood, the tears of the men, the piercing smell that struck Markriss along with faltering sounds of urination.

Ayizan shook his head. No.

Markriss approached him, raised a hand, footsteps muffled as if he walked in fog. Ayizan watched him carefully, turning the blade handle first, passing it to him. The leather was hot with emotion. He grasped it in both hands, lifting the handle to his forehead. One Mansion House victim, the man who'd attacked Markriss, he guessed from the rasp of his voice, began to wail loudly, a wordless lament that sent a feeling of such loss and dread through Markriss's entire body, he almost dropped the blade. He gripped tighter, whispering prayers for guidance, fortitude. The others whispered with him. Low, their combined voices remained strong, even below the pleas. The muttering, the unity. The westing prayer.

When the mantra was over, he lowered the blade, opening his eyes. Kneeled on haunches before the wailing man. The man's eyes were bloodshot, mouth smeared with dried tears and caked mucus. It looked like mud, or the parched earth of some isolated desert. An open knife wound split his left cheek like fallen fruit. Crystallized blood caked his lips. His right eye closed purple, vulva plump, the bloodied face in contrast with the sharp lines of his razor-close hair and beard, a fresh barbershop cut. One day fresh at most, possibly two. Markriss knocked the tip of the machete against the stone floor three times.

"Hey. Hey."

Another wail of injury.

"Stop, stop, stop. Give him water, someone, will you?"

Shuffling, Xander beside him, metal cup in one hand. The young man pushed it roughly against the lips of the older, who butted to the left like a goat. Water splashed, mostly on himself. Droplets caressed Markriss's face. Cool. Welcoming.

Xander roared anger. He slapped the man twice with all his strength, the contact echoing from walls. Blood leaped from his torn cheek like fruit flies. Xander raised his palm for a third.

"All right, Xan. Leave him please."

He paused, right arm high, the man attempting to close his mouth, stop whimpering. On both sides, his companions tried doing the same. Xander stepped back.

"So you don't wanna drink." Shifting weight for comfort. "What's your name?"

More blubbering. Markriss wiped a trace of water from his eyes and cheeks. Flicked it onto stone.

"C'mon, man, it's okay. Tell me."

Big gulp, lips moving, vague air emerged.

"Elliot."

"Elliot, yeah? Good, strong name. I like that." Another shift. "You know me, Elliot?"

Frantic, kneeling so his head touched the dark sheet again. Markriss watched, feeling cold, so cold.

"Nah, get up, Elliot. Get up."

He leaned back on his knees, bottom resting against heels. Eyes closed, head back, mouth wide. Crying from his heart. Like he meant it. Markriss was reminded of a nursery school child who had no understanding of his misdeeds. Lacking responsibility, acting from basic want.

"*You* did this. Understand? You."

"*No* . . ." Elliot crooned low, energy spent. He'd given up on a fair hearing. He was lost, falling. "No."

"It isn't my fault," Markriss said, and brought the machete down across Elliot's exposed neck.

The red line on pale skin was thin, barely noticeable before the flesh separated, exposing white and pink and red meat that belonged to a butcher's shop window rather than within the fragile body of a man. Markriss couldn't watch, choking on instantaneous bile. He swallowed, clearing his throat, standing with no recollection of opening his palm to let the weapon drop, only that it met stone and clattered, shrill, fast, over. Then it came. The reaction of fellow Outsiders, an exhalation of tension, releasing violent energy. A gasped "*Uh.*"

The unhinged cries of Elliot's road mates began from some shallow, disbelieving place, evolving through a series of vocal pitches, each higher than the last, exploding into frantic, never-ending screams. Shuffling, kicking legs as they writhed away from their friend's venting body, seeking escape. The forceful slap against his cheek, hot and pressing, reminded him of Xander's violence, before he realized this was too consistent, this was liquid. This was blood. A whistled hiss of high-pressure exit, fine and precise. Bubbling gargles like Elliot's had been pushed underwater, and he was trying to cry out, protest, do anything to express what was happening. The deadweight thud of crunching bone as his body fell, face hitting stone and floor meeting the dying man's nose, broken one final time.

They yelled out, jumping back from fanned blood spray. Temujin grabbed the remaining men by the hair, jerking heads back and sliding her machete right, twice in succession. Repeated noise, further blood. Markriss looked into the faces of his team, Chile especially. There was nothing, only a reminder of past moments and previous heretics, in this chamber and beyond: that iron odor, cries of loss, the rise in temperature, most of all that distant expression on every living face, their bodies devoid of soul for those long minutes, much like the physical death they had brought into the room.

He pushed beyond Ayizan, moving out of the chamber and into his office space. He intended to go to his own small room, when his legs gave. He collapsed into the softness of the easy chair, gasping breath. His head swam. Heart pounded. Pressure forced its way from the depths of his stomach, rising, and Markriss thought he might vomit, noisy and uncontrolled, into the room. He closed his eyes and hung his head between his legs, panting like a stray Quarter dog.

Nothing until the chamber door opened, closed. Her perfume, her aura. She watched him, simply breathing.

"Nobody wanted to."

He forced his head to rise, even that was too much. Another surge. He gave up, pushing his head between his knees again.

"They would have come for you first, you know that. You're lucky you hadn't been stormed already."

Another attempt. Gasping, trying to look. To see her.

"What's . . . gonna stop them now?"

She focused on the light installation, bit her lip. No answer.

"You took Circle without me. You didn't have to. I was already outvoted."

Finding him. Eyes glittering, beautiful. Back in her body, the woman he knew.

"Kriss, I'm sorry. We thought—"

The chamber door swung open, a gaping mouth. Chatter and movement on the other side. Ayizan. He paused just beyond the threshold, shut it gently. Inhaled quiet.

"We'll get the chamber cleaned up and go. Neither of you has to do a thing. We'll take care of it."

Footsteps. Silence. A hand lay on Markriss's bare exposed neck. Kneading. Even to him, the tendons felt stiff, immobile beneath the welcome pressure of Ayizan's fingers. His eyes prickled, flooding. He swallowed harder, blinking everything back.

"Okay? You done good, brother. I know what that took out of you, but you stepped up. It's done."

"I'll be fine. Just queasy."

"That's totally normal. I threw up, I can't lie. We mustn't get used to this shit. Don't let that happen to us."

"No." Shaking his head, panting once more.

"I'll be back. You've done well, brother."

The touch was gone. He heard the door again. Muted drums. The buzz of people over their heads. Chile's silence, he felt her eyes, her breath distinctive as words.

"I should have told you. You're right."

Deeper inhalation, a frantic gasp. The heavy wave crashed into him, startling, thrusting Markriss downward, separating him from himself, physical body left hunched, hyperventilating on the soft chair, elemental body descending, flat as an Outer City kite, peregrine graceful. Oozing black, warm comfort. Immediately a face emerged from the depths. Curling red hair, stark green eyes. Somber contemplation, he wasn't worthy. Closer, floating beside him with greater scrutiny, turning slow orbit.

Keshni Myatt.

She came closer. What did her appearance mean? He didn't know what she wanted. Was that judgment in her eyes, causing his panic? How would his soul journey after that night? Sinking lower, he tried calling out to ask whether the act he'd performed was righteous. Had he chosen the correct path, or was the place he was traveling to one of moral discontent, forgoing any chance of return? Keshni became more distant with every falling second, farther and farther above until she was a twinkling, solitary planet, cold and alone.

Markriss floated lower, and lower, disappearing.

9

He looked down at his clean, loose shirt and pants; they had
dressed him. Rough fingers entwined his. Chile's perfume
beside him, the familiar soft and firmness of her. A linger
of an echo, a recollection of the sound that had gripped him from
the depths, pulling upward. The slamming door. Looking behind to
see the white wooden rectangle, the black reader-panel on its right
edge. Temujin, blank-eyed a few steps beyond. He'd been lifted,
returned to Geb by the swift finality of the closing tunnel entrance.
Reality seeped in. The maintenance tunnel. They were descending
into the Lowers.

Sound reduced to bubbled silence. Ayizan, ahead as always,
reached the tunnel end, a blank wall of moss-green stone glimmering
with reflected lamplight. He kneeled and balanced on his heels,
opening a small panel on the stone between his feet, revealing a
simple brass padlock and hasp. Jangling keys were produced from
his jeans. He opened the padlock and placed it into a pocket, pulling
back the hinge with a faint tink of metal on rock. Chile and Temujin
moved to help him. Together, they lifted the heavy metal trapdoor
to its peak, then let it fall. All three had bulging packs on their
shoulders.

"You okay to do this?" Ayizan's tired eyes squinted. "If you feel
yourself jump back, try and let us know before it sets in."

He said nothing, his silence mute compliance. Beneath their feet, a long shaft, a metal ladder. More electric lights led downward. Temujin went first, wordless and grim. Then Chile and Markriss, finally Ayizan, stopping for a long moment to close the trapdoor, reattach the padlock, and make his way after them.

The ladder went down eleven meters. A confined space, a meter square, and if he slipped that would possibly be the end. They'd only done this twice, each time Markriss wishing he'd never been asked, nerves sparking at the thought of what might happen if he fell, or was caught by Corps. On this attempt he was strangely detached, a product of astral projection and the shock of his actions not half an hour ago, yet his absence of nerves wasn't reassuring; it worried him. He stopped, gripping metal. Chill seeped into his flesh and he shivered. Ayizan grunted over his head and so he kept on, trying to secure his feet on the rungs.

A fragmented memory of spurting blood, of hissing exit. He gagged. Stopped again, head hung.

"You can do it," Chile called.

"Nearly there." Ayizan's voice a repeating echo.

He pushed himself to keep moving. Something was happening to him that he had never experienced before. Blood had never bothered him. If he was honest, neither had killing. Both were a natural part of Outer City life and the Ark. There was no reason for his body to react as it did, and yet he remained cold, as if the chill of the metal he clutched spread through his fingers into his heart, and was transported by the network of veins around his whole body. He shook his head. That wasn't it. Cold had been inside him even before they descended, when he'd entered the chamber to see Elliot and his team alive with intense mortality. They had gone too far.

The sound of feet meeting rungs ceased below him. He closed his eyes again for the last few meters, knowing the risk. It felt better. He became conscious of ambient noises. Raised voices, metal clanging, an odor of hot vapor laced with various oils. Another backward motion, his feet met solid ground. A second step, he was standing. Markriss opened his eyes.

A shark-metal gantry, secured from above with broad cables intertwined like rope, or Chile's braids. Steel walls enclosed them on either side. The gantry flooring was latticed, though it was difficult to see how far down the actual ground was, or if, in fact, there was any. Shouting voices were closer, unseen. The air contained a mixture of damp earth, cooking food, and that rich aroma of fossil oil. Chile and Temujin talked low by the far wall. His wife saw him watching and took a few steps until she was at his side. Temujin's lips tugged in a ghostly smile, Markriss following suit as Ayizan stepped from the ladder to close their circle. Chile wouldn't meet his eye. Their arms touched.

"Capra said Paul would wait at the end of this landing."

"After you."

Searching his face, nodding, she took the lead.

They emerged from the passage confines. On their left, the sparse wall continued, flat and matte. To their right, a cavernous universe of e-lights, machinery, a series of squared landings mirroring theirs. Too many to count, they descended miles into the earth, each formed by a maze of gantries in a warren of crisscrossing pathways, some designed to create open space in which gargantuan machines were housed, others forming a square or rectangle where monitors, lathes, processing materials, computer banks, and robotic pincer arms were installed. Pipes ran along walls, beneath the lattice gantries, into machines and floor vents. Fine precipitation hung, steam erupting nearby on occasion, or far beneath. Men and women in overalls of various colors, with names and the level number "–1" on their backs, walked everywhere. Basic automatons rolled at their feet, round or square, speaking that strange, unfamiliar tongue, colored lights blinking. The area had an unyielding, military atmosphere.

Despite their urgency, they were unable to ignore the sensory overload that was the Lowers. Everyone knew the Ark foundations contained a proletarian class dedicated to making sure Inner City worked as it must. Yet it was a place few of the levels above saw, or even believed existed.

Markriss ducked his head from the dive of a drone—at ten centimeters, much smaller than he was used to. The tiny machine pivoted, blades whirring, clawlike mechanical legs exposed. Ayizan laughed, Temujin leaping to the gantry banister, pointing at the drone, which hovered further to get away. Filming, no doubt. Chile returned to hold his hand. He stiffened, not pulling away. When Temujin pushed herself from the banister, she paused to rub his shoulder before moving on. Markriss's aura filled with earlier days, past moments. By the time they reached the man sitting on the landing steps with his back to them, they'd formed a tight group with Markriss at their center.

Paul rose and turned, brushing foundation dust from his overalls. He was lean and over six and a half feet tall, head shaped like a lozenge or the dim e-lights surrounding them. His teeth were yellow, wide-spaced. Skin pale and overalls particularly oiled, full of lacy holes at the elbows and knees. Temujin stepped forward, stiff hand raised in greeting, which Paul clasped and shook. They hugged.

Temujin and Paul spoke in their language as the others waited, half listening in an attempt to interpret hand movements, or words they'd heard her use before in conversation with Vyasa. In the past she'd told Markriss the language her mother taught her was a former, interesting mix of proto-European Dutch, Norse, and French, subverted by ancient Germanic and Latin, the origins of both forgotten centuries before. Although there was vague scholarly interest in the dialect, no one in the country had spoken English since the Romans constructed Londinium in 43 AD. And yet somehow the language had survived in broken form to become the Lowers' dominant tongue. Only the most educated, or those with dual heritage, spoke Nubian, Meroitic, Swahili, Arabic, or any of the above-level Bulan languages dispersed throughout Inner and Outer City, besides the thousands of others from all over the globe.

Temujin indicated the group and Paul bowed. As one, the three clasped right hands over their hearts. The Lower turned, leading them down the steps to a small lift area, its mechanics evident and skeletal. They waited, Ayizan swinging his right arm, clutching the shoulder, wincing pain.

"These are original constructions," he whispered. "Some as old as the Ark."

"Let's hope they still work." Chile gave the lift doors a critical glare as Paul broke into a beam, leaning to speak with Temujin.

"He says they replace the lifts every ten years or so. These are about five years old."

Chile's eyes rolled. "So much for gossip."

"He understands Meroitic?" Surprise lifted Ayizan's voice.

"A little, but he can't speak it."

Swapped looks. Noted.

Gears rattled, unoiled guidelines squealing as the lift arrived, doors rumbling open. They stepped inside, their collective weight causing the lift to rock. Paul laid a palm on the reader, keying an unmarked pad, and the doors snapped closed, the lift plunging at great speed, rattling side to side in an unsteady gait. Metal whined as they fell. The fossil-oil smell grew stronger. They all moved to lean against the dirt-streaked walls except Paul, who stood, legs wide in the center of the lift, eyes closed, head thrown back.

The lift slowed as if tugged from above, jerking one last time until the surrounding noise ceased, the doors prizing apart with reluctance. Beyond: smoke, noise, music, people. Paul moved to one side, motioning them to go first. Markriss took Chile's hand. They stepped from the lift onto a black tarmac path, churned earth on either side. Immediately before them, a collective of metal storage units stretched into the near distance.

"Nobody call anyone 'country' down here." Temujin's expression barely shifted. "It won't end well."

"You guys hear that?"

Ayizan eyed each of them in turn, as Paul beamed even wider, heavy boots splashing miniature puddles, bounding past them to lead onward, talking over his shoulder in fast, explosive speech.

"He says we shouldn't hang around. These people have never seen Levelers, he can't vouch for their actions."

Bodies twisted in their direction as they followed Paul, and mouths hung open. Small children cried out, pointing, jade snot poised above upper lips, sore mouths crusted. To one side, piquant smoke caused Markriss's eyes to water. The origin, a sizzling black hot plate laden with various creatures of the earth—fattened beetles and worms, the delimbed carcasses of what he assumed were spiders, ruby-colored ants, all popping, crackling. The hefty woman behind the plate saw his shock and glared. A clutch of men in Lower overalls pursed greased mouths, spitting chewed insect shells into lumped mud. Past the stall, a dirt-caked woman sat on the edge of the path, hair disheveled and matted, left foot swollen three times its natural size as though filled to bursting point with water. Howling upward, it was difficult to tell if she was in pain or simply distraught beyond repair.

Paul looked over his shoulder, gesturing with clear meaning. He turned left at a small crossroads, deeper into the units. They turned with him.

In his attempt not to look on either side of the path, it dawned on Markriss that the storage units could be the Lowers' version of allocations, and their original function had been subverted, perhaps due to overpopulation. Glancing beyond the occasional open metal door, they could see glimpses of lives: a bare space, lined with empty sleeping bags; the hazy apparition of an elderly woman shrouded in cigar smoke, blowing, making fumes swirl; a group of children jumping with glee on a sagging double bed, no adults to supervise them; teenagers smoking pi and dealing cards around a crippled table, an unseen person closing the flimsy door as Paul walked by, trailing his visitors.

Eventually, he slowed down, relaxing. Ayizan appeared at his shoulder.

"How far down are we?"

Angling his head at Temujin, telling.

"A quarter mile," she translated. "The foundations go down five miles in all."

Ayizan whistled. Chile gaped amazement.

"Five miles of *this*?"

Paul twisted farther, finding her. A flattened blin Markriss hadn't noticed, smooth and winding, tracked from his cheek to chin, white, hair-free. Paul nodded. Indicated the nearest enclosure with an open palm and turned sideways, away from them.

A number of large men in dark-blue overalls stood before the tatty enclosure, a writhing plume of steam emerging from its roof. Paul whistled between his teeth, thin and low. The men looked back as one, parting. Just beyond an open door, solid legs spread wide, piahro splint chuffing between his teeth, sat Capra Paorach. Everything about him was huge. Feet, thighs, jaws. Though similar in height to Paul, Paorach's shoulders were unnaturally wide, his bald head shining autumn brown within the illumination of his lavender aura, solid as flesh. His body sheathed in an awkward glow, as if placed somewhere he didn't actually belong. Markriss only knew one person anywhere near Capra's size and that was Vyasa, which made complete sense, as the men were second cousins.

"People!" Capra removed the splint to lift in their direction, white teeth glistening. "I thought thou'd never arrive!"

"Gathering, family," Temujin said, slapping his palm, taking the splint to place in her own mouth. A deep drag, passing left to Ayizan.

"I can tell. We hear thee pounding down here!"

Laughter from the men, Capra's shoulders heaving. The Outsiders laughed with him. Markriss almost forgot the pressure of blood, the whine of exiting spray, hoarse, bubbling gurgles. A momentary smile rose and fell.

"I'm so glad you're all here." Searching faces, locking onto his, or so he felt. "Are you well?"

Heads lowered, nods.

"Are you sure?!"

Capra's boom pushed from his chest to vibrate in theirs, a rush of air and sound and vitality wrapped in life force.

"We're sure," Chile said, splint at her lips. "It's been a long few weeks."

"Of course." He studied them. "'As above, so below.'"

"'Only more,'" Markriss returned.

The Lower's smile faded. Blue eyes dimmed.

"Yes it is. It is."

Capra rose, gasping with his own weight. Fingers bumped Markriss's, splint heat warming his knuckles. For the first time he saw that Capra held a number of slim cards in his large fist. Brown one side, yellow the other. He began to distribute them among the surrounding men, each grunting thanks, secreting them in various pockets.

"Here, here, here," Paul spoke up. "I have to deal with our guests, but think of me when your belly's warm and your wives are loving you." The men erupted with laughter so loud Markriss's ears rang.

"Yes, not too much!" Capra shouted after them. "Don't get them jealous over tha's charms."

The men began to walk the narrow path, waving as they departed, disappearing in all directions. The Lower captain watched them go, smile lessening to become tight scrutiny. "Let's go in. We'll talk."

They followed him into the unit, Capra ducking his head. Close walls, low ceiling. The rich aroma of broth emitting from a large pot on a flimsy slab of a two-hob gas stove. To their right, jagged space where a door had been cut into the wall, Markriss realizing that two units were joined to make one.

In the corner, Maolisa, a slim, pale woman in strange wire glasses that looked homemade, sat on a threadbare seat eating from a dull brass plate. She smiled, her pinched face creasing.

"Ah!" Maolisa placed the bowl at her feet, making to stand.

"Please don't get up, we've disturbed you enough." Ayizan pushed downward with both palms. "Apologies for our intrusion. Eat, eat."

"A gentleman!" Capra roared at no one. "And here we were thinking thee religious thugs and agents of mayhem! Where's the champagne? Milk sweets! You'll eat with us, won't you?"

Another flurry of glances. A heavy thud, Capra thumping his heart. More booming laughter, the loudest yet.

"Oh, the fear! The anxiety! 'Will we survive? Can we stomach bugs and insects? We'll have to decline, surely?' Don't be afraid, our higher selves. We eat farmyard animals and food of the soil in this allocation, as do thee. But surely thou know that!"

"We didn't mean to offend." Temujin wore a rare smile.

"Me, family? No. How? I wouldn't eat the shite they serve out there if it were the body of Christ incarnate."

Chile caught Markriss's attention, rolling her eyes. He fidgeted, searching the confined space. Capra was digging in a small trunk, emerging with a pile of cushions and folded rugs.

"Ladies get the padding, men the expanse. As in life, some say."

"Can you spare our guests your filthy mind?" Maolisa's eyes crinkled, tired by her attempt to match her husband's energy. She reached for her plate, lifting it to her knees to continue eating, pausing to watch every so often.

Capra passed around his offerings, which the four arranged beneath them, trying not to look at each other. The flooring was dimpled metal much like the unit walls, the cold of sodden mud still transmitted through the material of the rug. Capra was at the gas stove. Bowl by bowl, the Lower produced steaming food and passed it over, women first, then men. It smelled glorious, steamed rice and gravy pungent with spices, a sweet hint of heady wine. While he refilled Maolisa's plate and piled a large bowl high, no doubt his own, Ayizan, Chile, and Temujin emptied their packs onto the floor about themselves.

Slabs of shrink-wrapped meat, smaller packages wrapped in tissue paper. Metallic components and tools that looked lifted from Ayizan's allocation shelves. Bottled condiments, perfume boxes, packs of incense. Markriss inspected the items his friends laid on the floor without making his attention obvious, lifting his spoon, tasting the food hesitantly. Chile raised a questioning eyebrow. He nodded, eating with more enthusiasm. The others were less keen, but hunger soon overtook their qualms. Capra came among them, sitting cross-legged. He placed the bowl at his feet, surveying the items.

"Good, good. Thou has the exact same quality merchandise as those useless wooden-top Corps. Maybe better."

"We get them from the same source, only they don't hate us," Temujin said, her expression featureless as the metal walls.

Capra laughed so hard he almost choked. "A very pertinent point." Retrieving his bowl and spoon. "I thank you for your kindness and apologize. I can't offer you water, as our inferior plumbing might possibly kill you. I have only beer, and the worst of Inner City wine."

"We'll pass," Ayizan said. "You've looked after us enough."

"My pleasure! Thank your stars I'm not doling you food tokens, like those poor bastards you saw outside. They'll be eating from the vendors, I'm afraid."

"We appreciate you, Capra, certainly."

"*Mmm-hmm*, you'd better. Good stew, right? Yes?"

"Lovely," Chile muttered, full-mouthed.

"It should be, the rats grow fat and healthy down here . . ."

Spoons stopped. Ayizan's face turned green midswallow. Capra rocked with intense mirth, even as Maolisa jumped from her seat.

"*Capra!* Don't listen to this fool! I have the packet! Look!"

A crackle of chattering plastic passed hand to hand. When it came to him, Markriss saw a styrofoam tray, a label, an artist's image of a plump hen. His stomach rolled relief. He passed the empty wrapping back to Maolisa's waiting hand, resting his spoon in the bowl.

"Bought it from Corps and cooked it himself this afternoon, he did, waiting for you lot!"

"My wife, the spoilsport! But your faces! Your poor, dear faces!"

Capra slapped his thigh, thundercrack loud. No one smiled, not even Temujin this time.

"Vy said you used to drive him crazy growing up. I see why."

"He can talk! Biggest prankster in Felano, that man was, don't be fooled! How is the old mule anyway?"

"A lot wiser it would seem."

"Oh! In my eagerness, I forgot—we must pray. Do you mind?"

"Not at all," Markriss said. "Especially if this might be our last supper."

"Ha! Funny! I like this one!" Capra closed his eyes, lowering his head and beginning to recite words Markriss knew into his chest. "Our Father, who art in Aaru, hallowed be thy name; thy kingdom come; thy will be done, on Geb as it is in Aaru. Give us our lives, each day we breathe, and forgive our transgressions, as we forgive those who transgress against us. And lead us not into want; but deliver us from fallacy. For thine is the kingdom, the power, and the glory, always and forever. Amen."

Maolisa's voice reached him, monotone in prayer. He whispered with them, all the words he remembered, Capra's lake-water eyes rising to watch him throughout. The prayer seemed strangely apt, sitting on a chilled metal floor, the heat of food cooling on his lap. Circumstance had power to compress the emotions. He couldn't imagine the strength of mind it took to live in the darkness of the city beneath theirs, tasked with the captaincy of many. Markriss thought of all the things the Lower must have seen as captain of the underworld. He was unable to fathom how Capra had kept his sanity.

Silence as they shoveled, spoons raking bowls. Despite the teasing it tasted good, Capra eating with an intensity that encouraged them to match him. Done, he leaned back, exhausted.

"Better. Now tell your news."

Ayizan spoke of their continued appeals on behalf of the Weston family, the reluctance of the Authority to even reply, let alone take proper responsibility for the murder. The block politics of road teams, some of whom Capra was familiar with, and the younger teams that had sprung up since the years he'd been inside. Westings, so many during the blackout, perhaps more after. The gathering, a moment's restoration of faith. The downtrodden feel of the zone as a whole, complacent despite their continual work with residents. Here, gravel scraped Ayizan's voice. Head hanging, body arched. In those moments he seemed too tired by far, on the verge of ruin. Markriss didn't know what to make of that, although he'd felt it too, fatigue at the intransigence of their lives, the inevitability of westing without bringing peace to the souls of others like themselves. Those musings kept Ayizan awake at night, Markriss knew, as he had been years before he found the spiritual sciences. For his friend, things were harder. Something else had gripped him during that time.

Surprising Markriss, his old friend began to talk of the confrontation with the Mansion road team. All three stiffened, acute, watching Capra's response.

He cleared his throat, releasing their gaze for the first time. Chile's head fell as though she slept.

"Bandyo's team?"

"He's captained for the last two years or so, yeah," Ayizan said without emotion.

"Which of you retaliated first?"

"Us."

Lips pursed, Capra found Markriss. "How'd you feel about that?"

Awareness of his aching fingers, the solid feel of the machete in his palm. "Not good. I understand it's necessary, but not good."

"It's unfortunate for sure, but there's little you could have done.

They put you in a place you couldn't win, robbing on your square. You never know, Bandyo might see it that way."

"Do you think we could've parlayed?"

A bestial snort. "Not with him."

Chile shifted on her rear, eyeing floor patterns. Capra followed Markriss's eyes. Sighed.

"Okay, well. We should get down to business, shouldn't we."

They collected bowls, getting up unsteadily. Maolisa took everything, waving away their protests. They loitered, unsure until Capra led them to the next-door unit.

"Come, come, this way."

Waiting until they were all through, Capra pulled a length of rugged gray-and-brown-speckled cloth over the door in violent jerks. On the other side, a small double bed, plain and sagged. A slim, pale woman sat near biscuit-flat pillows, eyes gleaming as they caught sight of her. Hair short, limp, and blond, she resembled Maolisa and wore a thin black trench coat made of contrasting materials sewn together. Leather, cloth, corduroy. Bird-wing coattails spread behind her.

"You don't use sleepers?" Chile said, looking around the room. "I haven't seen one since we got down here."

"No, we don't use them." Capra seemed wary. "I thought you all would approve."

"We do, we do. It's just strange not to see them at all. Only these things."

She toed a bed leg. To Markriss, she seemed fearful.

"They're not good for you, family. You know that already, but the full extent?" Capra tutted, shook his head. "Those things don't just control and record your astral pathways, that would be bad enough. They're collectors of kinetic energy. It's a greater percentage of how the Ark is powered, along with the solar panels on L4. Up there at least."

"Are you serious?" Ayizan said. All four stared at the Lower.

"Oh, deadly. Take the Day-Lites, for instance. The kinetic electricity gleaned from pods—at least 1.5 million of them, mind—go into these huge generators we have in the gantries which power mirrored plates set within a series of shafts built into the roof of every level. When the mirrors turn, they catch outside sunlight and bounce it from one to another, down the shafts, until it reaches the relevant level. All of those are powered by the kinetic energy of sleepers. It's a bit creepy to think of them siphoning from humans that way, and the main reason we don't use them down here."

"Ra." Markriss was cemetery quiet for a moment. "We didn't know. Right?"

Capra examined their expressions of shock. He cleared his throat. "Anyway, I've got stories that'll straighten your hair if you gave me enough time, which of course we don't have. You've met Aife, my daughter? I forget these things sometimes."

They exchanged muted grunts.

"Hotep." Aife's voice was deep, the word clumsy on her tongue. She looked at her boots, cheeks reddening.

"We can talk freely. Paul's waiting outside, so he'll let us know of any surprises."

Opposite Aife, beside a small metal cabinet, stood a row of four humped canisters. Dull, squat, nondescript. Gray verging on blue, scratched and dented. They reminded Markriss of tiny fire extinguishers, or scuba tanks.

"Aife rigged these up. I mean, I helped a bit, but this is her design and she did all the heavy lifting, literally. Each of those bottles is equipped with methane compound, a PE-4 block, and a wireless trigger with a five-mile radius. It's an old mobile transistor device, ancient tech. We've set it up to work from the Ark's cell site. Theoretically it's untraceable. That switch blows the lot, mind; you can't set them off separately, more's the pity. We tried to work on that, but neither of us got it. Next time, maybe. Each bottle has a range of 5 to 15 percent and 1.4 to 7.6 percent gas to air. That's the upper and lower flammability limits. Make sure none of your team tamper with them, dent them, release the gas, or anything else. Leave them alone, best as you can. You don't, and one of two things will happen: you blow your whole zone or the trigger blows the bottles and nothing else. Got it?"

"We do, I think. It's quite straightforward," Chile said. "Thanks, Aife."

The young woman smiled at the walls, revealing oddly straight teeth and twin dimples.

"You've got a blast range of about five hundred meters, I reckon," Capra continued, "so make sure they're spaced out. No closer than two floors apart. You want to take down the landing, not the whole building. If you put 'em too close together, there's a risk of the combined explosion fire-balling and razing the place. Bring that bastard down on us, and I won't be popular."

"We understand." Ayizan's sight was focused on the bottles. "It's an incredible risk you're taking. We appreciate it more than anything."

"Oh, well, we appreciate the gold, amongst more important things, like real meat. But listen, the only way I could sell this to the council was in the long term. You purge the Authority, we rise. It's all that matters down here. You see how things are."

"That's the plan, family."

"Good. But take time. This is just the first step. Be careful. Revolution doesn't happen in a day."

"We hear you, brother," Temujin said, bowing her head.

"We wouldn't be speaking if that wasn't true."

So many years had passed living as one family, they'd long learned to read each other's minds. Chile, Temujin, and Ayizan approached the canisters, beginning to lift them gently into their open packs, muttering at each other. Markriss put a hand on his wife's shoulder; as he'd guessed, she carried an extra pack for his use. Chile passed it behind her. He separated the black glossy material, unzipping the inner pocket until it gaped, a toothy mouth. Sliding a hand under the nearest bottle, he raised it as carefully as a sick animal, metal chilling his fingers. Against his own logic, Markriss listened for evidence of its contents; hearing none, he cradled the bottle in the crook of his arm, easing it into the pack. He zipped it up, carefully lifting the weight with one strap, sneaking his arm inside the other until the pack was high on both shoulders. Tightening both, he stood.

Aife Paorach watched them all from the sagging bed, hunched on lean knees, wiping tears dry with bruised hands, nose red, shoulders hitching. Capra enclosed his daughter in the overwhelming embrace of thick arms, effectively shielding Aife from her work. Her sobbing grew louder, making the others stare. Turned from the sight, she pushed deeper into his chest, immersed in the flesh that made her, aching to recall the child she had once been.

10

Beneath the tangerine glow of fading Day-Lites, he sat among wildflowers, thickened crop stems, and cultivated shrubs. Every few moments his eyes fooled his brain into believing they swayed with the breath of a low, untraceable breeze. Though occasionally air did move within the Ark, it was never enough to goad vegetation from immobility. For the Outsiders of the Poor Quarter, even those not part of their faction, the attraction of the garden wasn't lessened by lack of fresh air. Residents came to sit on benches in quiet meditation, couples strolled the winding pathway, whispering secrets. Outsiders watered and tended rosebushes, picking various herbs to place in cloth satchels, digging root vegetables to distribute among the most poverty-stricken, or cook in that night's soup kitchen and the following morning's breakfast club, each open to all.

The Temple garden had been a five-hundred-meter square forest of overgrown weeds when they'd first encountered the space. Nobody knew why the school building was abandoned, and no one alive remembered its previous grandeur. Chile saw the garden's potential as soon as she stepped through the back doors, vines and bushes forming a canopy over her head. She lifted her nose, inhaling, a broad smile rounding her cheeks. Enlisting the help of Vyasa, Markriss, Ayizan, and a number of young people from around the Quarter, she spent weeks marshaling the backbreaking job of chopping and shifting weeds, clearing the space, before going among residents on the hunt for seeds and plant cuttings. It surprised Markriss to learn how many people grew window-box plants, or turned concrete front yards into flower gardens and vegetable patches, forgoing what little space they had to bring the outside into the Ark. Miniature Edens grew everywhere. Many local horticulturists believed a large-scale garden couldn't be grown without direct sunlight. Chile not only proved them wrong, but showed that their hothouse environment in fact stimulated more abundant, healthier growth. Now that he knew the truth about the Day-Lites, it made sense. Over time, the Temple garden, started with humble thyme and mint flowers, began to bloom, take color, releasing odors of jasmine and rose. Potatoes, carrots, and zucchini were cultivated. Figs and apple trees lined the farthest end, bearing heavy fruit.

Markriss didn't consider himself a herbalist, yet something about the garden drew him, wherever he was in the zone. Away from the space, he smelled mint or felt microscopic green hairs tickle his fingers. He recalled the auric patterns he saw when he bent his head to petals, heard the *om* monotone of insects. Though he often forgot to visit, caught up with day-to-day functions of life, the garden often came to mind, and when he opened the back doors to step into that space, something—weight, pressure, perhaps even his spirit—lifted from his neck and shoulders. He was calmed, at one with the living beings around him. There was a sense of communication between him and the plant world he'd entered, away from technology and the counterfeit nature of the Ark. There, in the center of the garden, on his favorite bench, the one with a plaque dedicated to his brother's memory, the stillness of the plants made perfect sense. It was withheld breath, the forward motion of humanity on pause. The closest to the spiritual realm made actual.

Hands on knees, Markriss breathed silently. Focused by extending webs of connection, their aura and his. His center shifted from the lower chakras, rising to the upper where it filled his throat, heart. He drifted, relaxing, waiting for it to fill his head and third eye.

Nothing. Eyes stung, his left wrist itched. He allowed the sensations to continue, build in intensity. Outsiders walked by, heads turned toward the surrounding plants, leaving him be. Markriss stared through them. Did they know what happened in the basement?

Pure thought. He needed pure thought.

He uncapped a metal water bottle that reminded him of the gas canisters they'd brought to L1 and tipped his head back, sipping.

"Àṣẹ," Markriss said under his breath.

Solid chill slipped down his throat. Leaning forward, he poured another mouthful into soil.

"I am because we are; and since we are, therefore I am; Markriss, son of Vendriss, who is son of Idriss, who is son of Mantiss, who is son of Shemiss, who is son of Armiss, who is son of Nepthys, and all our ancestors who precede us. I have taken life. I humbly ask for your wisdom and forgiveness. Àṣẹ."

Another outpouring, errant droplets splashing his feet, darkening shoes.

"Ninka, my brother: I beg your guidance and forgiveness. May the souls of the departed and their kin find peace, in this realm and the next. Àṣẹ."

He sank into the silence, grateful for the life that surrounded him on all sides, an unseen presence pulling at him, leaden weight. Somewhere close, not ahead, over his shoulder from the direction of the Temple doors. He wanted to remain in meditation and ignore it, hoping they might leave. Instead it vibrated faster, heart rate rising, tense as a clenched fist. Watching. Aura probing, questioning. Young, inexperienced, very little control. Lower energy reaching for his. Sexual? He frowned, relaxing deeper.

No. Clear red anger. Markriss drew air into his pelvic floor, exhaling, lips rattling a sigh.

Ah. Renno, son of Io.

He allowed his shoulder muscles to loosen, stretching his back straight. Opened his eyes. The closest shrub, a coleus chocolate-covered cherry planted on the opposite side of the path, had been chosen especially by Chile in honor of his brother. The outer edges of the leaf were green fire, the inner section dark maroon, while on the inside a pink spectral form arose, like arms spread wide. The plant always intrigued Markriss, the energy of its coloring inspired him. It brought to mind his own physical and spiritual essence; green, the ethereal aura swirling about his body; maroon, his material flesh and bone; pink, the eternal soul housed within his physical form, the center of being. Colors of healing, moving into one's task, love. In viewing simple leaves, Markriss became aware that he bore witness to the microcosm in emulation of the macro. He was a vessel on behalf of the universe, pondering its larger existence. Aware of the present in acknowledgment of infinite realities. Chakras spun, shifted. His ka rose, pineal awakened.

Connected, Markriss let go.

He was ready.

He turned to face the Temple doors. Renno's gaze fixed on him. The garden had emptied, plants held breath.

"You would like to speak?"

Renno, impossibly lean and tall, approached the bench, where he lingered.

"You can sit."

"Give thanks, Teacher."

He sat, bony knees protruding, thighs extending from the farthest wooden slat, as far on the edge of the bench as he could go. His cheeks were lined with pimples, dark skin dry, uncreamed. A fresh haircut only made him look younger. The snake emblem on the chest of his pitzball shirt caught Markriss's eye. Coiled, hood extended, in striking distance. He blinked, staring for so long Renno cleared his throat to regain Markriss's attention.

He sat up, looking Renno in the eye. "It feels as though . . . Correct me if I'm wrong, but I sense an obstruction in you. I wondered if you'd like to talk about it. You can speak your mind."

The boy spun, examining the space over both shoulders, one after another.

"No one's here, and if there were it wouldn't matter. Please."

Mouth open, a frown etched Renno's forehead. He tipped forward once more. A knee bounced. His hands trembled, even as he tried to stop them. Below his throat, Markriss recognized an ache. Breath shortening, his ka retracted to his collarbone, where it settled.

Guilt. Renno feared him.

"Please." Softening, much as he could.

"I can't." Renno pushed upright, taking two steps. Turned, eyes glinting ice. "You told us you were men of peace. You said that."

He walked the path, disappearing around a corner.

Markriss contemplated the space he'd left.

Plants imbibed elements, reaching for light.

Time bent, folding on familiar streets. He needed to be careful, that was true. Awareness might have been his savior, although he needed to retain the intensity of the connections he'd forged in the garden—they were good, and true, and would lead him on the right path. It was possible he might find the western lands on the horizon of this particular journey, though he was strangely at peace with that notion, unafraid. When he tore himself from the present enough to ponder the eventuality, he knew that part of the reason he wasn't fearful was because he actually didn't believe it was his time. Whether simple arrogance or blind faith, Markriss was uncertain. Instinct told him something else belonged in the hazed mists of his future, so he raised his head, refusing to look at people, dogs, or allocations, to think of his friends, wife, or ancestors. He only walked.

Loitering outside that peculiar, broken-down house, he was surprised, despite himself, to find it still there. He trod the broken stone path to the front door, freed of wooden boards, stepping over the slats he'd ripped away like tree bark that remained stacked on the floor. He pressed his palm flat. Bent over, forehead touching flaked paint. Cross-stream energy thrumming, noiseless above his head, burning fire vibrating beneath his fingers, tiny hairs on the edge of his ears standing on end. Searching for traces of vague contact within his own memories, recalling himself as a child, immersed in the bushes and fragrant plants of his mother's garden, tiny fingers enclosed in the toughened flesh of a rough hand. That feeling of content, belonging. Being lifted into the air and lowered so he could be embraced by ambient masculinity. He pressed his forehead harder against wood. Needing to remember more of the presence he'd pushed away for such a long time.

Markriss stayed that way, respiring slowly.

He fell into waking dream, materializing at the Ark Station.

Faraway voices reaching beyond molasses darkness. Spun-cotton wisps, distant. Mind made up, walking broken glass and wood, careful, into the solid length of night. Nothing besides the mythical sense of physicality, knowledge of his existence arriving only from the brush of Nesta's body against his, their joined harsh breath. Heart beating, hot blood. The corridor, damp, old. A taste of odor, gritted sherbet. Covering his mouth, stumbling on unseen material. The floor thick with dust. Stubbing his toe on what he guessed were heavy blocks of concrete, more than once.

His sneaker landing on something soft, the give of flesh. An inkling of what came next. His friends, jaws static, screaming. Metallic banging, heels smashing against the mesh metal window. The thrust and pound of his feet kicking among the others. A scared-eyed kid looking up into his face, the moment he'd caught the boy's fear. Strange laughter.

A shadow rising, hands closing around his neck, pads of rough fingers tightening on his throat; realizing he couldn't breathe, falling onto his knees, the sharp and true pain of bone striking concrete, a swimming light-headed feeling he later knew as ebbing consciousness. Cold seeping into his body, fluid death.

Then everywhere was roaring, echoing from unseen walls. Being pushed, the sound of a heavy object connecting with something sodden yet hard, until fingers released him, and he breathed again, a huge, gasped intake. Sounds even more terrifying when his hearing returned, hands on knees, coughs tearing his throat. Traded harsh pants, growled combative forces, discernibly young and old. Bodies crashing into walls with dusty, tired thuds, cried pain. Nesta's infantile sobs. Clattering, the loud fall of bodies. Wheezed breath, screams of pain. The roar of an unseen man using every ounce of his greater strength to end a life, or so it seemed in the moment.

The click of Markriss's extended knife heard even over their screams. Crawling, pain slicing his hands, to the place where his friend's breath gurgled like boiling coffee, climbing on top of the stinking hulk of man, pulling stringed hair tight around his fingers, plunging the knife somewhere beneath him with his free hand repeatedly, screams merged in the darkness until only his and Nesta's survived. Falling, hands sticky, onto his back, unable to see anything, himself, his friend, or the person that was once human, now mere object. Halting tears beneath the frantic shouts of Karis and T'shari, finding them.

Head resting firm against the door, Markriss waited. In the months after the vagrant's westing, the first by his hand, he'd dreamed the sickened man was his father. Similar dreams returned in spells for many years after. Intriguingly, whenever he meditated, or rose into the upper planes, Markriss never encountered Vendriss. His father had gone into the Ark when he was very young, and Markriss still believed he would recognize something of him, if not his face, then his material essence. Yet it never happened. While that didn't mean Vendriss was alive, it had given him hope. He pondered how old his father would be. Thinking back on what he himself had done to survive and become the person he was today, he wondered: Would Vendriss be proud? The question went unvoiced and unanswered. He tried not to think it often, though in that moment when he did, Markriss imagined his father's withheld distress might well resemble Renno's.

Shuffling behind him caused feathery nerves to lighten his lower guts. The perfect time for Bandyo to strike. He backed from the door, anticipating a blow, turning when none came.

Old Man Sares. White robes, white staff. Silver ankh hanging from his neck. Locks untied, loosened to meet his ankles.

His elderly neighbor opened his arms, abrupt and wide, staff clutched high in the fist of his right hand. Blind eyes directed upward at the allocation. Seeing the elderly figure of a man, someone close to his estranged father's age, a physical sense of something broke inside him, his emotions venting with an almost discernible snap. He was a child again, vulnerable, unsure. Assailed by the realization of all he'd lost—a home, friends, father, mother. The caress of air against his cheek, river brine, the call of a gull. That weightless, secure feeling a moment before drifting into sleep, calm night beyond misted windows. He stumbled the few steps it took to reach Sares, buried his head against the old man's shoulder. Material scratched skin. Eyes dry, no tears. Too far gone to weep. And he was embraced, clutching meager shoulders in turn, energies coursing from elder to younger as auras communicated, and their spirits made peace.

He returned to his allocation, head low. When the door closed, he found Chile in the center of the room, legs crossed, head lank, burned sage clouding the air. He lowered himself on the sofa opposite her, watching.

Markriss waited for an extended period of time before Chile's head rose. A wisp of smile at the corner of her mouth.

"Hey there."

"Hi. Good journey?"

"Lovely. Almost didn't come back."

They chuckled.

"How were the gardens?"

"Good. Really good."

"That's nice."

Sighing content.

"I was thinking of vegetable soup for tonight."

"You dug up sweet potato?"

"No, they gave me a handful from the kitchen. Shall I?"

"Yes, please. I don't know why, I'm craving them all of a sudden."

"Probably need the carbs. I got young leaves too, I can chop those up and throw them in?"

"Can't wait."

In the kitchenette, he switched on lights, harvesting utensils while Chile played transcendental from the front room. Swirling strings, the harmony of an unknown singer's voice penetrating flesh and bones, exactly what he needed. He diced, collecting ingredients, eyes heavy, hands nimble, until several brightly colored piles were before him, water bubbling and gasping on the hob, and he was pleased. He dropped everything into the pot, pausing to thrust his nose into steam and smell the changeable quality of vapor.

Chile's presence, breathing at his spine, the pressure of her nose, lips and forehead pressed against his back. Arms wrapped around him.

"Okay?" he asked.

"I am. You?"

Movement against his clothing. He smiled.

"Want to get in pod? I'll give you a massage."

Paused surprise. Comprehension.

"Of course."

"Go on. I'll just do this and be over."

"Thank you, Kriss."

After he submerged ingredients, added spices, removed and poured excess foam into the sink, and lowered the heat, Markriss entered the sleeper. Chile was undressed, a russet blanket covering her waist and legs, humming to the song resounding through the speakers. Head between crooked arms, chin turned to one side, the window misty with condensation, the air sweet. A rhythm of bubbling soup blended with the singer's ambience. He removed his clothes, placing them on the podside, slid next to her, and inhaled her scent. Ran a finger in a straight line from her shoulder blade to hip. He pushed gentle pressure with his fingertips, making small circles.

"That's really sore."

"There's tension in your lower back."

"Are you surprised?"

He smiled, pausing to open a squat bottle of peppermint oil, pouring into his hand. Liquid made a flat circle, set like amber. Palm flat, he pushed from one side of her hip to the other, her skin a rippling tide. She gasped, finding a better position, head rested against her forearms. Markriss pulled back, repeating the movement with the same amount of pressure, sat on his heels, pushed again, this time with both hands. Attending to the lower back, feeling for the beginning and end of individual muscles one after next, hands rising like kundalini energy to her midsection, down the narrow incline of her spine and up the other side, one hand over the other in an idle, steady flow, bathed in music and the odor of developing soup, one ingredient fused with the next, and the next, and so on. Everything entwined, the sibilance of hands against flesh, the connection between limbs, the sharpened tang of oil and material of the sheets that covered the mattress beneath them, the push and pull of energy between bodies. Markriss finding a rhythm that lulled them both, swept by low current on the edge of the other world beyond theirs, that boundary of infinite wonder, the land of ancestors. Sometimes he forgot where he began and ended, feeling as though he inhabited that place fully, in life as it was in westing, and later he had no recollection of what he had done with his fingertips, only a vague notion of how the movements made him feel, a dream forgotten as he'd woken, a fading tendril of steam, dissipating yet present in its quantum, unseen form.

Three taps, sharp and precise, on their window. Markriss's hands slowed, and he rose toward the drawn blinds. Chile barely moved.

"I'll put clothes on."

He grunted, kneeling to find his. They dressed without speaking, grumbling at inside-out material, trapped limbs. When they were ready, Chile kissed his mouth, held him. They nuzzled, rubbing noses, lips touching and parting. Whoever knocked didn't again.

He crossed the room to the door and opened it. Ayizan's head was bent low. The machete firm in his fist. Beyond him, streetlights trailed farther than Markriss could see. He stepped back, let Ayizan enter.

A single dog positioned itself on the empty street. Ribs expanding and contracting, yellow-eyed. Its legs seemed thin and hollow, pocked by glittering red sores. Not knowing what else to do, he closed the door.

"Water, orange juice?" Chile gave Ayizan a light hug, already turning to the kitchenette.

"I'll take a juice, please."

Markriss sat beside him. They avoided each other. Saying nothing until the generator's heavy rumble started, settling into a familiar thrum of regularity.

"They're in. They'll plant the drop at the end of their shift, on last rounds."

Markriss rubbed his hands together, looking at the worn, moth-bitten carpet. How hadn't he noticed it was that bad? Chile returned with a plastic glass. Ayizan smiled.

"Give thanks. If we don't hear anything from them or the Corps, we've got away with it. If they come down on us like the vengeance of God, we're fucked."

"So that's it? No further contact until we instigate?" Chile looked from one to the other.

"Makes sense," Markriss said, bending to pick carpet tufts. "To be safe."

"I've thought about that." Ayizan was frowning. "And I talked it over with the others. There may be some merit in acting normally. Not doing anything different."

"What did they say?"

"They seemed to think it was a good idea."

"Shouldn't we stick to the plan?" Chile's knee bounced nervous electricity that Markriss felt from across the room. "It's been like this for months."

"I'm happy to go with whatever you think, Chile, I'm not going to argue if it doesn't feel right. I said I'd meet them at their allocation if we changed our minds, and bring them to my place where we'll instigate. If I'm not there when they get home, we meet at Temple like we said."

"Okay." Playing with a loose braid between slim fingers. "I think we stick with plan A. We'll be safer in the Lowers."

"All right then. Markriss?"

"I'm with you. Whatever Chile thinks." A pause. "On that note, she did mention being cautious about the dogs. There's one on the street right now. Or there was."

"Really?" Ayizan got up, turning to separate blinds with two fingers. He pushed his face against wood. "Nothing's there."

"I don't trust them. They're always following us."

"They want food."

"That could be what they want us to think."

Ayizan sat down. Back hunched, chin cupped in a hand. "I don't know what we can do about that, besides act like we aren't suspicious."

"I've already told Markriss: we don't do anything incriminating around them."

Both men nodded in unison.

"Well, I mean we can't not do what we're doing tonight, but I see your point. Good. Very good." Ayizan threw his head back, downing juice. "All right, I'm gone. All being well, we'll instigate at a quarter of midnight. Once I know they're back and safe, you'll hear it."

"Okay then."

They stood, hugging for a long time, Markriss's heart pounding against his rib cage. Sudden, real. They pressed their heads together, ignorant of pain.

"All right, see you at Temple."

Chile saw him to the door. Once closed, she climbed the sofa on her knees, splitting the blind as Ayizan had. She pulled back as if scalded.

"Kriss."

Waiting, almost knowing.

"Yeah?"

"It's there."

He crawled the sofa to join her, tense and careful, eyes pressed against the letter-box gap. Ayizan was far out of sight, the dog padding slowly in the direction their friend always took to his allocation, nose pointing, half lifted, sniffing air. Pausing, foreleg bent midstep, surveying the block with swift, robotic jerks of the head.

It snapped to the right, glaring through their allocation window, deep-set eyes and open mouth, wet tongue hanging, curved teeth on display.

Chile released the slat. They dropped into an impromptu huddle, backs thudding against the sofa like fists into a tired, heavy bag.

"Shit." Her voice a solid object dragged across gravel. "Shit."

They reached for each other, necks bent low, fearing the slightest movement.

After a time, the dog left. When they next looked through the slats, it had disappeared. Even for Chile, it was difficult to express exactly why they were so shaken by a stray looking into their window. Dogs roamed throughout their zone and had done so since they'd entered Inner City, trotting alongside everyone, tipping over bins, attempting to steal food from shopping bags on occasion, scaring red-faced, tiny children entombed in strollers. Dogs were and had always been as much a part of the landscape as e-lights, or brickwork. Fresh in their zone as a newly married couple, Chile and Markriss even fed them leftover scraps from cupped hands, wincing against moist sandpaper tongues, back when they were hopeful, young.

And yet. And yet.

Swinging between irrational thought and the solidified, cold logic of known reality—what they had seen, what it might mean—they did what they could to forget their pulsing hearts and shivers wriggling a chilled path across skin. First they kept to the sofa, arms tightened around each other. After long minutes in that position, Markriss pulled back into his knowing, thinking self and rose, blinking and yawning, stretched upward until his fingers touched the low ceiling. He walked over to his fragment of bookshelf, half listening to Chile moving, mostly concentrating on the titles before him. Placed a finger on his find, tipping it toward him.

At the desk he whipped pages, frowning into his hands, blind as Old Sares. He was unsure of what he searched for, feeling his way through indecision, alive to the woody scent of paper, dust that leaped and tickled from sharp turns, the heft against his palm, the volume cradled in his hands. It had been so long since he cherished that weight. Had he been avoiding it? He wasn't sure of that either.

Who was this person who didn't read the books he once cherished? Who recoiled in fear at dogs that had roamed outside his door for as long as he'd lived in the zone? Why did he repeatedly think of his father when he hadn't for so long? Where did this new fear and mistrust come from? The vision of killing Ayizan, just as a sickened vagrant once attempted to kill him as a boy, was real, gaudy. He could admit he often saw it when he closed his eyes, biophoton patterns of color forming human shapes and imagery. He still had no idea why it persisted.

Nothing felt like him anymore.

He flattened a page smooth with a palm, settling in the seat. The letters were small and hard to read in the dim light:

In our quest to become accustomed to this new way of being,
we must remake ourselves anew. We work toward this diligently
as the caterpillar works toward becoming butterfly, ever in the

knowledge that our wings are not material, or physical. None
shall be witnessed with mortal eyes. We will not feel their beat,
or the air stirred by others. We must eat daily, in fact we must
gorge ourselves, again not meaning the physical; thus our work
should go unnoticed, invisible on this plane. Imbibe what is
good for us, reject adversity. Learn what does us harm and
avoid those occurrences, as best as can be, practice acceptance
when we cannot. There are many distractions to living a full
and formless life, yet they are only true distractions if we make
them so. It is in our power to give them power over our beings.
We are landlords of this residence our soul is housed within.
Anything that takes place is in our control.

For this, we must strive to become what our ancestors call
"Nun," primeval or formless water. As even the smallest child
knows, Nun, parent of Sun God Ra, deserves everlasting thanks
for our creation. They are boundless, dark and turbulent. On
the physical plane, they are essential to our being. We cannot
live without water, it permeates every mode of existence. And
yet it can be shaped and molded, whether in word or in deed.
It responds both to our actions and the things we might say,
always remains unchanged. It takes on any form, exists in any
confines, yet given even the smallest opportunity it is free. Water
does not battle, nor fight among itself. Water moves collectively
to achieve its aims.

He lowered the pages. When he'd first reached Inner City, *The Book of the Ark* served as mantra. Passed from resident to resident, heavily bound or home-printed and stapled, held together with plastic binds, or taped repeatedly at its farthest edges for poorer readers, the book had become the Poor Quarter Bible, lender of hope, adviser of all. There wasn't a bookshelf in the zone where it couldn't be found, even in allocations where families did not read. It was digitally recorded and duplicated. In temple, teachings were extracted regularly and rendered as plays, children taught its ways during interfaith services. There was a suggestion that a decline in younger readers led to the rise of road teams for generations to follow. Markriss wasn't certain that was true. Notwithstanding this, all that the Outsiders believed stemmed from those cherished pages.

No one knew the author. The book appeared like a sapling, no one to witness the seed. No name on the title page, or any others. No mention of gender, country of origin, class. Where it was first circulated further deepened the mystery, several zones laying claim to being the original readers and disseminators of *The Book*. There was no publishing lineage, or initial print run, on the inside pages. Although scholars claimed the book had existed for hundreds of years, it was never cited in relevant texts of earlier times, only latterly.

Markriss turned the weight over in his hands. Hardbound, leather dark, surface ridged and tactile. Embossed gold font and Kemetic symbol beneath, three circles placed inside each other, a triangle within all. He was barely aware of his fingers skimming the cover like a caress, weight tumbling from one hand to the other, lips moving without words, thoughts and images behaving similarly, one end over another until he seeped into the present moment, ink on white paper. He leaned farther back. A mug of mint tea he hadn't noticed emitted steam beside him. Chile had returned to meditation, her own mug resting by her side.

He read more, meditated further. They returned to the pod, undressing without hurry, making love much the same. Held each other with possession, in hope they might retain the feeling of skin brushing against one another, the sharpness of sweat and rough scratch of pubic hair across bare thighs, soft flesh of breasts against the gristle of nose cartilage, lips against pelvic bone, fingers enclosed around the recoil of glutes. All the while knowing nothing would survive beyond the scant, transient notion of the present.

And in deepest night, while they lay submerged in each other, dark void a material substance around them, a dense force rippled through the walls, floor, and windows. Shuddering, rocking. Like the vibration of wind, but stronger and hotter. Solid became fluid, their pod shifting with the power of it all. And then came the blast, a sound that followed seconds after, outside streets forming corridors for misplaced air to rush, nothing to stop it, window frames and glass vibrating. Voices heard through the allocation walls on either side, then on the street.

They dressed in the clothes scattered around the pod, emerging to see. First, there were mere tendrils, wisps. Soon after, coarse black smoke began to fall, making breathing difficult, limiting vision. The bombs had done their work. They wandered from person to person, checking if everyone on the block was accounted for, touching elbows, hugging neighbors, guiding children back to their families. Parents screaming into muck, dust, and paper, bumping shoulders with other people, coughing as they filled the street. Old Man Sares squinting, hand raised to his eyes, leaning against his allocation wall. The Mengus family pushing Pharah back toward their front door, scarves tight over mouths. Residents clutching each other, eyes streaming, fear lining their faces. Dogs running the block, barking at the unseen. Young people forming packs of stiff threat, machete-armed, jostling.

Chileshe threaded an arm through his, leaned against his shoulder to watch 1322 burn, with the others. Staring into distant flames, high enough to bear witness, far enough to convince themselves they might survive what they had done.

11

They knew the Corps would find them. Their only surprise was how long it took before they came.

He laid his jacket on the sofa and sat beside it. Chile paced the room, tiny fists clenched, halfway to the podroom, back toward him, a lapping tide. She gave off an impatient, tense energy he often imagined as part of her makeup since she was a child; in those moments he saw her as a toddler, teenager, a young woman with that same buzzing aura, static fizzing in the immediate air about her. They refused to look at each other, in fear of being made aware of their own doubt, the inevitable a warm body, alive in the room. His stomach tightened as though he'd leaped from great height without thought.

Pounding at the front door. They caught each other, wide-eyed in panic. Chile rushed across the allocation, threw it open.

"They're here!" Vyasa roared, unseen by Markriss. "Let's go, *now!*"

Barely time to think before he snatched his jacket up and took *The Book* from their desk, running to the door. Not a moment to worry about everything he left behind. The notebook, the medi, his long-dead and underused slide. Trinkets and offerings of Outsider brethren that lined his shelves. He ran onto the murky street, Chile too, close beside Temujin, Vyasa stutter-stepping by the brick wall, bellowing, urging them to move faster, and right away he heard it. Buzzing overhead, accompanied by pinprick red lights blinking through misted dusk, all he could see of them. Drones. A tiny whistle past his left ear, brickwork exploding fireworks in miniature. They were shooting.

He put his head down, sprinting.

They ran in one sure direction, not looking up or to either side. Footfalls of Outsiders began to mass and join them, and there was more firing, Markriss grateful for the cover of smoke. He wanted to catch Chile and Temujin, only they were faster and fitter, a distance ahead, and soon they were veiled by clouds of billowing smog. He heard Vyasa breathing hard, thuds of heavy feet matching his. He gritted his teeth, wishing he could move quicker. His thighs already burned, knees ached. He lifted higher, with more power; it hurt. His time in the sleeper had weakened his muscles. He tried to relax, hoping it would help his body move with more ease, panic driving his adrenaline, hindering motion. Somewhere at his rear, dogs barked. Drifting smoke flattened distant sound. The clatter of metal gear and stomping boots, the whine of something he recognized though couldn't place, which almost made him stop, swivel, frown into hazy air to catch it.

A vehicle. The revving engine, the guttural voice of low gears.

Knowing the danger, he couldn't help looking back. The snub-nosed armored transport was a glistening beetle crawling from the smog, almost as wide as the street. Cautious, it slowed further, the stubbed bonnet pointing accusation.

A masked Corps solider leaned out of the side window, took aim.

Markriss yelled out, veered left, ducked.

Nothing came.

He risked another look. Both vehicle and soldier were being swarmed by machete-wielding residents. The crowd took up the whole street, banging windows with knife handles, climbing onto the roof. The soldier fired. Someone fell, and the next resident pushed the body aside, wrenching the gun from the soldier's hands, pulling him from the window. They were beating his limp body when Markriss turned away and kept running.

A drone flew close, a whining mosquito. He covered his head, flinching, saw it fly past, toward the vehicle. Shots pinged the transport hull like popcorn on a lidded pot, throwing dust and metal flecks. More drones emerged from gloom, engaging in battle with the first, swooping and pivoting, tiny orange flames glinting from undersides. The first drone exploded into flames, dropping.

Markriss didn't look anymore. He ran harder.

From roof-level fog, bloodred beams of light emerged, touching the undersides of two whirling, darting Corps drones. Engines shuddered, stilled. The machines fell to the ground, bouncing, metal legs exposed like dying insects. They didn't move again.

He couldn't see. Smoke too thick, people too close. More shots, bodies hitting the floor, causing him to trip, fall. Chin meeting concrete. Iron-mouthed, spitting blood. He crawled, the sound of gunfire louder, screams of pain echoing. He got up from his hands and knees, starting to run harder, lungs burning from flames and his own harsh breathing. Muscles aching with pain. Emerging from the row of blocks onto Temple Square.

The large doors were propped open halfway. Chile and Temujin's mouths wide, gesticulating. He heard nothing. On the opposite side of the square, the short, rounded figure of a man was surrounded by a pack of strays, six or more at a hurried glance. He wore dark glasses, bright hustler clothes, T-shirt and jeans swollen with muscle. The machete in his hand gleamed, a fallen crescent moon. He raised it at Markriss, teeth bared. The dogs leaped, began to run.

It was Bandyo.

Markriss forced a last push for the door. Feet pounding on pavement, he focused on Chile. Her arm outstretched, fingers reaching. Sweat smeared across her forehead, hair wild. Her eyes said he wouldn't make it. Reddened from smoke and welling tears, indistinct fear. Her head shook. Mouth opened. She saw what was coming behind him, and it shook Markriss to the center of his being. Her lips pulled back in a grimace that ripped his heart. He reached for her, the distance too large. The growling pack louder, more prominent. He had to leap.

Thudding connection. Whimpered canine pain. The clawed skitter of fumbling claws. Markriss took his chance, jumping for the door to land just beyond the dark interior, pulling himself over the threshold with the last of his strength. Shouting voices. High-pitched shrieks. He rolled onto his back, frowning. Temujin. Markriss sat up, the last thing he saw before the door closed a spinning, whirling Vyasa, gouging flesh with his machete in quick twists of his body, dogs hanging from his shoulders, legs, chest, blood streaming like spilled paint, the huge man swinging in wild circles to displace them, Bandyo running close, blade high, bringing it down in an arc destined to meet Vyasa's head . . . and the door was shut, it was dark, the noise overpowering on either side.

"Go, go!" Xander cried, his pitch chilling Markriss's heart. Temujin threw herself at the heavy doors, thumping and kicking, fighting men off in her attempt to open them again. Three went down in a series of sharp connecting blows. More came, pulling her aside, locks turning regardless. Strong hands pushed Markriss toward the steps. He reached for Chile, reassured when her fingers closed around his. Raw emotion soaked his face, racked with pain.

They took the steps down sideways on, fast as they could manage without falling, releasing each other to push against cold walls, running along the corridor, past chamber doors. Temujin's wails rebounded from confined space, though she was with them, and he was glad of it. Through the fingerprint security reader. Along the squat corridor, those blank six doors. Past another reader at the far end, on through that heavier iron door into the longer dead-end maintenance tunnel where Ayizan waited, the open panel beneath his widespread feet, glaring fire.

"Come on, come on, let's go!"

Above, unseen conflict. The tunnel shook, metal framework creaking, dust shimmering fireflies in e-light, swirling about their heads. One after another, they descended. Chile, Temujin, Xander, and Markriss, who paused, head poised, level with the upturned panel. He watched Ayizan bound over to the reader, key a succession of numbers, and sprint back to the ladder. The control board beeped three times, red-blinking, set to kill code. If the door was forced, the mechanism would explode. Markriss quickly took the ladder steps, no time to think of falling death, only to wonder if Ayizan would secure the panel above them before they were found, noting the rising volume of explosions and gunfire at ground level. And then Ayizan slammed and locked the panel shutter, the digital reader was set, the primed red light blinking, feet rattled the ladder, and they plunged into the city depths, gasping, afraid.

Though no one expected him, they found Paul in his usual spot, holding the lift doors open, anxiety deepening the lines of his weather-beaten face. They ran inside its confines as he hit the button, releasing pent-up breath while doors slammed together, showering fine earth. Temujin collapsed. She wept loudly, unrestrained, bleeding knuckles pressed to her temples, chin tilted toward the ceiling. Tendons of her neck red and straining. Lips pulled back, a wailing child. The men shuffled, unsure. Chile sneered at them all, sitting on the mud-strewn floor with her friend, rocking her limp body, wiping eyes with a sleeve while the lift fell like a rock thrown over a mountainside, rattling in its chassis. Unspooling metal pulleys filled their ears, the agonized whine of metal against metal that almost drowned Temujin's grief for the long, unbearable minutes of descent. No one spoke. The men kept away from each other. Just leaned against the lift sides to catch their breath. There wouldn't be another rest stop for a while.

They remained a still tableau, ever falling. Darkness ebbed through hairline cracks in the metal like gaseous substance, until it grew difficult to see themselves or the person beside them, even when the ceiling lights brightened, or seemed to, exposing particles of earth and darting dust around them that had probably survived since the lift was first brought online. Shudders intensified, becoming fitful, and the rocking threw them against the walls. There was nothing else to do but join Temujin on the dirt-spattered floor and listen to her mournful sobs. Lights flickered, bringing Markriss back to the recollection of standing at the end of his mother's garden, watching the train take Excellence Award recipients into the Ark, the repetitive gleam of windows bathing his upturned face. That clatter of relentless wheels, squealing metal. Hot iron burning his nostrils, matching the liquid that filled his mouth years later, inside the crazed, shaking lift. Ninka's wild, ecstatic laughter thrown heavenward, a grin stretching his own cheeks until the area beneath his eyes hurt like toothache.

It was difficult to know what Markriss cried for—Vyasa, Temujin, his brother or himself, his lost past or the present he'd fought so hard to win—as they plunged deeper into the flesh of Dinium than many Inner City residents ever traveled, into the very bowels of the Ark.

The floor pushed resistance. Markriss wished he'd held someone; nausea rushed, threatening. He retched. When he looked at Chile, her rounded cheeks were tear-soaked, arms wrapped around Temujin's neck, the Celt doing likewise, both squeezing their eyes shut tight as if every waking experience was pain.

And then it was over. The lift silent a moment, before the doors split apart so easily, an invitation. A heady smell of brine rode the darkness beyond. Paul fussed with a metal plate beneath the array of buttons and controls that opened on a hinge. He buried his head into the hole, emerging with a number of flashlights, which he passed to the Outsiders one after another. Each was long, silver, marked with age. When Markriss flicked his on and off it worked, the emerging beam a solid object in its own right. Paul shut the panel, kneeling before Temujin. He placed a hand on her wrist. His voice calm and gentle, he looked into her eyes and spoke for long minutes.

Temujin wiped her face, inclining her head to show she understood.

"He says we've come lower than we originally planned, but it's our only chance of getting away. It's a long walk and will probably take the night. Capra's waiting a little farther on. He'll have supplies and he knows the way. It's dangerous, Paul says. That's mostly good, cos they won't believe we'd come this far down, but . . ." She huffed, gave up, rose. "Ready?"

Quiet. Ayizan crossed the lift, kneeling to embrace her. Her body shook and kept trembling. For a time it seemed she couldn't find a way to stop it, as all four came to her, arms clasped around the next shoulder, sharing life and energy until it subsided. They wept together, in near silence.

Paul's weighty hand appeared on Markriss's shoulder.

"We know, we know. Thank you."

They let go, stepping into the cold expanse beyond the lift door, switching flashlights on, beams roaming in every direction. To their left, a small orange flag attached to a metal pole. Markriss placed a hand on the smooth plastic material, stroking for luck. It was difficult to tell exactly what kind of place they had come to. Above, concrete pillars and girders of steel formed a complex latticework that reminded Markriss of an Outer City motorway overpass, if it wasn't for the pipes and cables and computer networks that covered every centimeter. Beneath their feet, sodden mud and water covered their shoes, making it tough to take the smallest step. He lifted his foot; mud sucked, grasping hold, his shoe browned to the curved smile at his ankle. Markriss looked up. Doubt transformed Ayizan's face. The boyish charm had gone. Markriss had never seen him look so lost, so uncertain. Xander too had the scared eyes of a boy told to go to his room without the lights on. He bit his lip and the flashlight beam shook.

"What d'you think?"

"There's nothing *to* think," Ayizan snapped, jaw clenched, further thought bitten back.

"Let's go," Chile said, moving off arm in arm with Temujin. She reached her free hand toward Markriss, fingers wriggling. Refusing to look back.

He tried to walk faster so they might make good time, though it soon became apparent that was the quick way to end up sprawled in mud. Paul touched his elbow, held up a finger. *Wait*. This, he told Temujin, was the foundation. He spoke of the dangers that came from mud-dampened clothes stuck to skin, lowering body temperature, causing a sickness of the lungs known as "the Lower chills," and of toxins in soil, deadly if licked or swallowed.

Paul took his time, picking the best spots to place his feet, which was difficult without being able to properly see where those spots were. They frequently lifted their flashlights into the distance to see what they were walking into, the view ahead always the same: an ocean of mud in static low-tide waves, flashlight beams disappearing into a starlit galaxy of dust motes, the gray canvas of concrete about their heads, glittering and plain. As above, everywhere. Minerals danced and shone in every direction. Mud sucked feet, legs faltered, they stumbled. Every three hundred yards, the robotic spasms of their lights caught more small orange flags on metal poles, tilted by sunken ground, emerging from mud like emaciated, dwarfed trees. A means of guiding their way, Markriss assumed. Paul said there weren't too many placed, as more likely than not there was some advantage to people being lost.

Markriss didn't answer. He held Chile's fingers. They stroked each other's knuckles with thumbs, kept silent. No one spoke except for Paul. Sometimes he'd stop to tell them about the surrounding area, where they were in relation to L1, or would pause, passing his flashlight over mud and concrete until he spotted a marker, obvious or not, then continued. His serious, unworried air remained, steadying their nerves.

A short time into their journey, Markriss smelled fire. Thin smoke in the distance, barely visible against the blackened atmosphere. As they went on it grew thicker, developing into smog. Paul instructed them to wrap their clothing over mouths and noses, to join hands in a chain. He would take the lead. They made confident progress that way, deeper into clouds of ash, eyes stinging, closed for most of the way, almost falling. And then slowly, like waking from a dream, the cloud thinned, became nothing, and they emerged into the gloom of steady night and soft earth. No one commented. Paul kept the pace, head straight, beam held beyond their group, moving forward.

After an hour of walking, Paul suddenly slowed to a halt and gestured for the others to hang back. He rubbed his chin, pressing the toe of his boot into damp soil. Kneeled, pushing his fingers into earth, watching the response. Markriss couldn't see anything beyond murky water filling holes where Paul's fingers had been. The Lower shook his head and made a right turn. He muttered something to Temujin, who faced the rest of the group.

"There's some kind of bog," she said in a monotone. "Where they couldn't dam the river, or it leaked around it, and the earth turned into quicksand. Half a mile wide. Shallow Lake, he calls it. If we walk that way it'll take the lot of us down in under a minute. Lots of bodies, he says. Quite a few kids. He'll take us around."

Markriss didn't ask more.

As they walked, noises—amplified by wide expanse—squelched and clattered around them. Once or twice the nerve endings of Markriss's cold feet awakened to the sensation of tingling toes and

ankles, at times his calves. First he believed it nothing more than
blood returning to flesh; later, he began to recognize the probing
contact of small animals—rodents, most likely—sniffing at the group,
skirting them, hoping for sustenance. Dropped food, or bodies.
Promising either way for starving creatures. When he tried to catch
sight of them with his flashlight, they were too quick.

He was hungry, chilled. There was little feeling in his fingers,
despite the warmth of Chile's. Air hurt his chest, his lungs beginning
to rattle. He wasn't certain if that was due to smoke inhalation, or
the polluted atmosphere of the underground level itself. A pain in
his side had given birth to throbbing below his ribs. He tried to push
it from his mind, to keep moving forward. The farther they went, the
worse it ached. He had to push himself or cease functioning at all,
worrying that it might mean he could collapse at any point, and the
same was undoubtedly true for the others. Temujin looked hollowed
by creeping grief, the flesh of her cheeks tightened around the
contours of her face. Ayizan gasped, wincing, with every step, one
arm around Xander, who was attempting to hold him up, only the
strain was too much. Markriss saw glassy-eyed fear reflected each time
he craned his neck to check on them. He dropped back, ducking
beneath Ayizan's free arm. His friend was a deadweight. When he
asked what the problem was, Ayizan shook his head, lips pressed
together, concentrating on each limping step.

Paul grunted, gesturing with a hand. Forward, forward. The details
of his meaning lost due to their reluctance to press for information—
Forward how long? They trusted him, walked. Saved the effort of
asking for the energy it took to go onward.

After another hour, they saw an electric-blue e-lamp. Flashlights
struck the concrete structure arching overhead, falling to run into
black distance on either side. A hulked form leaned in the shadows
by a door covered in faded graffiti.

Capra.

He brought them each to his huge chest, held them. Temujin
longest, the Lower stroking her hair in an absent manner, eyes red
sunset, unfocused. When he released her, Temujin's back had straightened. She looked more like the warrior spirit of her Celtic lineage,

her normal, tense expression returned. Capra bent over a small crate, unlocked the lid, then paused, hands on each side, quick breath hitching in his throat. Markriss realized he was sobbing. Capra contained himself, reached inside, and passed around a bundle of three-quarter-length jackets, padded with hoods. A selection of heavy boots followed. Jeans and thick sweatshirts, T-shirts.

"My wife guessed your sizes, so if they don't fit blame her."

Though he tried for his usual good cheer, something in Capra's voice was lost. They strained lips upward in attempts at smiles, all failures. Markriss removed what he wore, slipping with grateful acceptance into fresh clothing made of dry hemp. A sweet odor of washing powder made him wish for his allocation, the habitual entrapment of clean podsheets. The boots were heavy though didn't fit badly, a bit more room at the heel than his flat shoes perhaps, and plenty of protection from dank soil.

Around him, the others brightened a little in their dry, borrowed clothes. Markriss placed a testing hand on his side. Pain flared. He winced, allowing another look to make sure his friends were preoccupied. Stood taller.

Chile's arms wound about his waist and she kissed his cheek. He moved slightly so she didn't press his wound, guiding her hands to a safer place. They rested their heads against each other, looking into the other's eyes, holding arms by the elbows.

All dressed, the crate filled with their unwanted clothes, Capra placed a hand on Paul's shoulder.

"Put everything in the furnace. The whole lot."

Paul took the crate by its extended handle, bowing to the Outsiders.

"We thank you. And we'll never forget. Go well," Ayizan said.

The lean man held a flattened palm over his heart. He pushed a code into the door reader and entered the building, leaving them on the mud, the door closing behind him with a click.

"We should leave, in case he's caught," Capra muttered, sending a shiver coursing through Markriss despite the comfort of his new jacket. He ducked his head in agreement. They regrouped and set out again, more sure-footed in their new boots.

Capra had a backpack that he swung open as they moved. Inside, he'd packed paper-wrapped sandwiches, pasties, baked sweets. Only a single water bottle to share, though Capra said it didn't matter, because if they walked strong enough, they'd reach the eastern city before Day-Lite. They ate as they walked, swapping sandwich fillings they didn't like.

Although they hadn't long begun, Ayizan was already meters behind, clutching his right thigh, a dark spot on his jeans clear and visible. He swayed when Xander left him to approach Markriss and the others, looking as if he might not stay upright without support.

"Look, he's been hit," Xander whispered. "I'm not sure how badly, but it's his thigh. He doesn't want to slow us down."

Capra swore through gritted teeth, hands on hips, spitting at his feet. "Always say!" he shouted to the air. "Don't put your westing on our conscience!" Another, heavier spit. "Come on, then! Who else?"

Markriss sighed, raised a hand. Ignoring Chile's slap to his forearm, glaring at him.

"Flip me," Capra hissed at mud. "Come here, you fools, let Uncle Capra take care of it."

That raised a grim chuckle. They gathered around him in a circle, pushing soil with their steel-toed feet, straining ears to listen for movement. The pressure of silence was like the full weight of Inner City on their heads. Markriss felt as though his ears might pop. Chile continued to glare; her expression said there would be problems when they were alone. From the backpack, Capra produced a roll of brown surgical tape, a small medicine bottle, scissors, and a carton filled with bandage roll.

"Good thing I listen to the wife, eh? Kriss first, lift up."

He bent closer to Markriss, who'd already given Xander his jacket, raising the borrowed sweatshirt just below his chest. Capra dabbed the bullet wound with neem antiseptic, making him wince and swear, then plugged the bleed with a strip of bandage cut from his roll, wrapping it tight around Markriss's torso with the tape. After taking a look at Ayizan's thigh, he repeated the treatment, one leg extracted from the Outsider's jeans, held aloft by Xander and Markriss. The neem made him growl aloud, mouth wide open. After Ayizan had been bandaged, everything was put back into the backpack, the zip wrenched closed. Capra stepped back, rubbing his temple.

"You've bullets in you, silly bastards. Know what that means, right?"

"We have to move faster." Chile's eyes swam behind her glasses.

"We do. Markriss, yours is pretty deep, and the bullet sliced the skin. As long as you treat it and keep it away from the mud you'll be all right. But mister over here, I'll have to carry the rest of the way. Any objections?"

A round of shaken heads.

"Who told me to send the crate on wheels back with Paul?" Capra groaned, crouching as the men lifted Ayizan onto his back. "*Shit*. Thought you lot were into fasting, you heavy sod!"

They laughed, this time moving into darkness.

As the Lower hoped, the group walked with greater purpose after their enforced break. The pace was more consistent and, according to Capra's watch, they journeyed well. Yet it was a struggle for him. Xander and Markriss offered help, only he wouldn't allow it. He removed his thick jacket, which Temujin carried over her arm, and his chest and neck became bathed with sweat, not solely due to the Outsider's weight, but also the slippery mud underfoot. Sometimes he would sigh, put Ayizan down for a few minutes, and the Outsider would stand heavily on one foot, guilt in his eyes. Though for the last hour, Capra refused to stop. "We've lost 'em," he said. "But I don't take no chances." Apart from this, the group kept silent for the journey, Capra grunting with every awkward step, each of them panting hard, mud sucking and popping at their feet like living organisms.

Just when it seemed to Markriss his body might give in, another arching wall appeared, more circular blue light. This time the figure beneath it was slim, their patchwork overcoat casting a dim reflection of collected flashlight beams.

Capra whistled a two-tone greeting, trying not to stumble. Aife returned the same, kicking from the wall to face them with outstretched arms, a rectangular cloth bag hung from one shoulder.

"Failt," she said, eyes on empty space behind them. The smooth leather of her jacket was a strange contrast to the scratch of wool that was her sweatshirt, rough against Markriss's cheek as she hugged him and each Outsider in her distant, noncommittal way. They stood, chests heaving.

"She says welcome," Temujin breathed.

"A real pleasure to hear you keep your father's Manx as well as English, even though you muck about with this lot." Capra smiled, kissing his daughter's cheek. "You'd all better leave. It's dark up there, but won't be for long. Aife will take you to your level, give you the help we promised, and then you'll part ways. You know where to go from there, right?"

"We do." Ayizan clapped Capra's palm and shook, then threw himself at the Lower, hands clasped around his body, head pressed close.

"Come on, come on, enough emotional stuff. I know you Outsiders, you're not turning me into butter!"

Capra looked behind their captain, swiping his eyes. They gave thanks, one after another. Markriss shook his large hand with both of his, staring Capra in the eye; no words could express what he had done for them.

Aife was already at the door, keying in code. They followed her, entering a confined white passage, chalk-dust walls, a faint oil smell. The closed outer doors of an elevator shaft, black windows. Aife pressed the call button, smiling, a little awkward without her father. After an uncomfortably long wait, thunder grew above them until the outer windows brightened and the lift doors crept open.

The rattle of mechanics seemed to ebb then grow louder in concert with Markriss's heart, the pulse at the back of his neck and center of his forehead, his breath. They found separate places to sit cross-legged on the dimpled floor in varied states of meditation, eyes closed, centering. Markriss decelerated everything within him, his brethren doing the same, reaching out to see their bodies glint purple and yellow against the dark of his eyelids.

Better. He was better.

The lift finally ceased shuddering. He opened his eyes to Aife sitting as they were, legs crossed, hands on knees. Skin flushed, she blinked as though she'd returned to her body, as they had. They exchanged glances, rising as the door opened on another concrete shaft.

Maneuvering with more urgency, treading light on their feet, they followed Aife along more nondescript white corridors, until Markriss had no idea which direction they might be going. Ayizan limped between Markriss and Xander best as he could. Aife didn't say much until they reached another ladder, hung flat against a wall. She muttered in Manx, one hand on metal.

"This'll take us onto the street, she says," Temujin translated. "A small alleyway, I think that's the word she used. But it's outside, between two buildings. She'll go first to make sure no one's there. After that, we're on our own."

Aife looked into their eyes, waiting for Temujin to finish. Then the Lower genuflected, sighing, and lifted herself onto the ladder, climbing a few steps before she looked down.

"Come."

They each in turn grabbed the cold bars of the ladder, following Aife. It was difficult for Ayizan. Going up was tougher than walking and his wound began to bleed again. He grunted, teeth bared, Xander holding his hips with both hands, pushing him up. Progress was noisier than it should have been, filled with pained shouts and yelled curses, Markriss fearful of what they might have summoned when they reached the shaft entrance. One Corps was all it took. One security guard, one conscientious member of the public. He imagined the cold, empty wasteland of the Blin, wind lapping his face and ears, tried to forget the image. They would not end that way. He squeezed his eyes tight, attempting to block Ayizan's cries of agony, Temujin stopping above him; he almost bumped the wedged heels of her muddy boots with his forehead. He couldn't see more than the ants' trail of stitching on leather, hearing buttons depressed, clanking. They held onto the rungs, mouths open, still, every waiting moment a searing ache. Light fell across his face. Familiar scent, fresh air. They rose, the last push, Ayizan screaming behind closed lips, sweat pouring from his head, glossing his skin.

Finally, they collapsed onto the L1 surface. Aife had been right.

On either side, brick buildings stretched high, a two-meter distance between walls. The ambient noise of the sleeping city played in Markriss's ears. Blue streetlights were soft water. He lifted his head, bathed.

"All right, let's do it."

Chile at his side again, gratitude for her presence swelling his heart. He dropped his head, taking in the sight of his friends. They looked terrible, beaten and disheveled, dressed as they were in too-large jackets, clunky boots, eyes rimmed black, tired. Defeat settled on their shoulders like the ash they'd stumbled through, weighted by grief. Xander hoisted the strap of a rectangular cloth bag Aife had given him, lifting it over his head, arranging it at his hip. Markriss swallowed, turned away. No way they'd pull this off.

At their feet, Aife sank back into the ground like a being of legend or fable, one hand grasping the panel, which she pulled to a close over her head, welling eyes disappearing as she gestured a farewell. The illusion could not hold. They had been there, had seen. Walking Inner City streets would never be the same now that they knew what lay beneath them. Enormity clutched Markriss's heart, gripping until he hardly breathed. They'd sought to liberate themselves and their allies. If the consequences meant the place below their feet continued to exist for many more lifetimes, he would never forgive himself.

They left the narrow stretch of alleyway to enter the awakening main street, striving for normality. The Lites above phased through the preset beginnings of the rotation, a spectrum that came with the arrival of early dawn, first deep purples, then the growing flush of red, a saturation of yellow. They kept their hoods raised, heads low, staying close to each other, moving aside only to let others past, avoiding faces, speaking to, or glancing at each other. Markriss found that, contrary to his earlier trepidations about how they might stand out in this affluent zone, Ayizan's planning had been wise. Early-morning Inner City was the dominion of menial workers: engineers, cleaners, those who fixed the plumbing, or baled garbage into trucks, or took the children of others on school runs; those who fetched, hefted, scrubbed, delivered, served. As such, the Outsiders were camouflaged. They looked exactly like those they walked among. Even Ayizan's limp was commonplace for those hailing from the poorest zones. Injuries and disabilities were everywhere they looked.

Menials dressed in oversize, oil-patched jackets that often hid the person they protected. All-in-one jumpsuits. Old and battered shoes were gaping maws, the boots much like theirs. Women in threadbare cardigans, thin hooded coats. Paper masks across the lower portion of faces. Among them, the homeless, the drug-addled, those who'd hardly slept a full hour. All waking to greet the day.

And so they walked, tired and stumbling, much like those at their sides, unsure what the hours stretching before them might carry, not daring to wish for anything more than sleep at the end of their day, that restful peace of oblivion.

12

They arrived as Day-Lites bled yellow, allocation windows became illuminated, and familial noise seeped onto the empty street. Chatter, clinking utensils. The odd burst of laughter, squealed delight. It felt more conspicuous to walk the sidewalks of a zone in this quarter, where the builds were not terraced but detached, with gardens of grass, children's climbing frames, sometimes central fountains bearing winged cherubs spitting water. One of the gardens was dominated by the outspread branches of a cherry blossom, causing Chile to slow in wonder, tugged by sweet petals and perfume until she remembered all that had occurred. Her eyes narrowed, furrows etched across her brow.

There was no one on the street at that hour, a blessing. They opened the waist-high gate, taking the stone pathway that led to a two-story allocation, giving thanks for the height of a carefully pruned hedge enclosing the doctor's garden, hiding them from view. Ayizan gave a furtive knock at the door, with a discernible wince. Markriss pressed the tape around his sides with tentative fingers. They waited, heads low. A dog's bark caused them to jump, searching the vicinity before they realized it had come from inside the allocation.

The door opened a slim crack. One half of a gaunt face, the other blocked. Dr. Amunda's mouth fell open in surprise.

"Ah!" A pause, no one sure what to do. "You must come in. Yes, come!"

He allowed the door to swing farther open, blindly reaching for the dog at his ankles, which bounded toward them with unrestrained glee. Quickly, they filed inside one after another. The hound was staring up at them, tongue dangling, slim and quick, black, short fur, bright-brown eyes, flopping ears, an inquisitive damp nose probing each crotch that passed. It jumped, trying to taste sweat on their skin, Amunda pulling it by the collar and closing the door behind the last to enter, Xander. At Amunda's instruction, difficult to hear over the frenzied barking of the dog and the doctor's shouts for quiet, they moved through the passage, past a flight of stairs to their right, a gleaming modern kitchen, then to the left into a modest back room where Markriss imagined the doctor might receive patients.

Ayizan, Temujin and Chile took the only available seats, Ayizan groaning, nursing his leg. Xander and Markriss rested their backs against the wall. The room was a neutral brown, three paintings hung, one of flowers and the others generic Outer City landscapes. Markriss swallowed hard, observing his scuffed boots. The barks grew mute, didn't cease.

They watched the doctor limp to his desk, shallow panting with every step. He was short, bowlegged. Pale-green Eurasian shirt, earth-brown corduroy trousers. He turned to sit behind the desk, his white beard trimmed close to cheeks and chin, the edges of silver glasses catching window light. Bending, he opened an unseen desk drawer, pulling out a plump bag of piahro dust, tobacco, rolling papers, which he placed on the desktop, gnarled hands on either side.

"Smoke, anyone?"

They looked at each other. Markriss approached the desk, taking everything in one hand, shamed by crusts of dirt smeared on the heel of his palm and trapped beneath his nails like henna.

"Take what you like, I have more."

Markriss thumbed a sheet, cupped it in his hand, and rolled. The crackling paper reminded him of distant fires, of holding Chile's hand in the center of their street, burned substance filling his nostrils. Vyasa's screams.

"Apologies for Apnu," the doctor said. "I hope you don't mind her. She's quite friendly, and I need her around these days."

Silence. Amunda cleared his throat.

"It's terrible what's happening in your quarter. I only knew you weren't dead because the Corps kept on killing. It lasted the whole night. They probably haven't stopped, it's just got quieter."

"What do you know?" Ayizan's eyes were brilliant in the murk that encircled them.

"Just what they say. You can imagine what that's worth. They claim your bombs destroyed the top three levels of 1322. Combined concussive force or something like that. None of the security guards were harmed, though they say there was one casualty. A janitor."

Quick glances between them. The promise had always been that there would be no menial casualties. For all, that was the only way the mission could go ahead. They wanted the zone on their side, not against them. Markriss tried to see misgiving in Ayizan's expression. He remained solid as ever, unfaltering, a captain to the last.

"And what about the Quarter?"

Even his voice was steady, Markriss noted, although Xander avoided looking at him, the younger man focused on the tufted carpet floor, jaw working.

"They've cordoned off the zone, nothing in or out. I heard people tried sending bots out to record what was happening, but they were destroyed miles from here. You could hear it sometimes. The drones, assault vehicles, the killing." Amunda's fists clenched; the doctor hadn't realized his physical response. "What on Geb were you thinking? What did you hope to achieve?"

Ayizan held his eyes. Amunda's ticking watch filled emptiness.

Markriss lit his splint, glaring at the elder. "He's been shot, doctor. We need to get the bullet out."

"So have you," Chile reminded. Pain surged, the swollen ache returned.

"Okay. I'll look you both over, get you situated, and then you'll tell me what you're going to do. You're welcome to stay as long as you need. That okay?"

"Sure."

"I'll just set up the room. You'll have to wait a moment."

Markriss listened to the old man shuffle past to the door, exhaling smoke toward the ceiling. He passed Ayizan the splint.

The doctor saw Ayizan first, while the others waited in the medium-sized room. They were gone for a frustrating length of time, and as the others milled, fighting impatience, light from the window grew broader, the ambient noise of the local community increasing. Slamming doors, calls goodbye. The patter of children's feet making their way to school. Brief moments of stillness in their wake, until the next family left, and the next. Collective departures peaking as the last scooter grumbled by, a parent shouted at their child to stop at the curb, the final diminishing thuds of a pitzball, the chatter of teenage friends becoming as distant as the space between those inside that room and the community beyond.

Temujin's eyes drifted, body statuesque. She had slipped into a place no one could go; if they spoke, she ignored the speaker, or stared through them. Chile's arm rested around her shoulder, gaze fixed on the fluffed gray carpet. Bored, Xander took a spot by the doctor's desk, opening the cloth bag given by Aife. He picked at the contents one after the other, turning the objects this way and that with his fingers, holding them to the light, putting them back on the desk, and shuffling them like a dealer immersed in a game of Find the Lady.

The items were five slim plastic cards, white fading into overcast gray, portrait photos of each of them in the upper-right corners, six-digit numbers stamped across the centers followed by three capitalized letters, the first of their surnames. The laser tag was a series of raised bumps in the lower left, carrying all the resident's personal details.

Markriss walked over to Xander, blocking the view of their cards from the women, and bringing measure to his voice, speaking low. "What are you doing?"

The young man seemed confused. Markriss touched the center card in the pile. Vyasa. Xander drew in sharp breath.

"*Shit.*" He glanced over his shoulder, palming the card and sliding it into his bag, a trickster in reverse. "Kriss, man, I'm sorry . . ."

"I know this is hard, you've still got to think, Xan. All the time. We don't get days off."

"I get it, I totally get it. I'm really sorry."

"Put them away. All of them. And don't get them out again until I tell you."

He returned to the only available seat, collapsing. Chile searched his face and he shook his head quickly, shut his eyes. Imagined reaching for Vyasa instead of priming his body to leap.

He hadn't known. Truthfully, he hadn't known.

He wriggled on the wooden seat, irritated and itching almost at once. Sat on the farthest edge, eventually the floor.

After half an hour more, Ayizan came into the waiting room. Pale, favoring his good leg. The bullet was out, he said. Dr. Amunda had stitched him up and warned there'd be a scar. As long as he rested and kept the wound clean, he'd be fine.

"Your turn," he told Markriss, unsmiling.

In the confines of Amunda's makeshift clinic—formerly a podroom, from what little he could tell—Markriss lay on the large bed, naked from the waist up, eyeing the blank white ceiling. A radio played gentle kora. The room glowed with reflected light, the sole window covered by white canvas. Amunda seemed to have lost the urge for conversation, apart from mutters as he surveyed and chose instruments, busying himself between a metal rack and the injury itself. He produced a large-barreled needle, raised it to his eye.

"You'll get this for the pain and then I'll clean and stitch. Shouldn't take a minute. Okay with needles?"

"No," Markriss replied as it pierced his flesh. He sucked inward, chill fluid entering the vein.

When it was done, they returned to the waiting room. The atmosphere had altered. It was clear Temujin had been crying, and perhaps the others too. Eyes red, no one could look at him.

Amunda positioned himself behind the desk, false smiling at Xander, who perched on the opposite corner, hands in his pockets, one leg raised on the mahogany surface, the other steady on carpet. Markriss leaned against the wall, tension clenching his jaw. The aftereffect of fatigue and the injection made his head swim. His stomach clenched, rolled.

"So what now?" Amunda said, after time passed.

"We stick with the plan." Chile looked resolute, fierce.

"The plan will get you killed."

"We stay here too long and they'll kill you too. You don't know how many neighbors saw us walk this block and come to your allocation."

The doctor leaned back in the chair, fingers entwined. "Let me worry about that, it was always going to be the risk. I'd rather that than have you all dance into their party like fools."

"We appreciate what you're saying," Markriss said, "though we don't have a great deal of choice. We've had a great job done on IDs and clearance. As long as we keep our heads we'll get through."

Taking stock, all of them thinking.

"Might I see one?"

Markriss inclined his head at Xander. The young man took a card from the bag and passed it over.

Amunda raised the ID to the light, squinting. Brought the plastic close to his nose, even sniffed it. He ran his fingers over the surface, ducked beneath his desk, and rose with a portable reader, squat and blue, then let the ID rest at the base of the machine, peering at the readout.

Markriss raised his eyebrows, waiting. He was light-headed, hollow. The first test.

"Where were these done?"

Markriss shifted, eyeing the ceiling.

"Remarkable job. I halfway believe it."

"L3, here we come." Ayizan's good cheer made a partial return. No one laughed.

Amunda gave the card back. Laid his palms on the desk. "From your mouth to Ra's ears," he said. "I think we should eat."

Hours after Day-Lites faded, the street outside was silent as the Blin. Zipped inside a sleeping bag on Dr. Amunda's living room floor, Markriss and Chile forced their bodies against each other, lips and hands gliding hot flesh, roaming every inch. Xander and Ayizan had taken a guest podroom upstairs. Temujin had retired to the waiting room floor not long after they'd eaten. Amunda worried about leaving her alone, although Temujin had insisted, promising she would allow the doctor to administer a strong herbal sedative for the night. The medicine was brewed from hot water and honey, piahro mixed with unknown plants Amunda wouldn't disclose. Within the hour, when Chile entered the room to check on her, she was sleeping.

Tracing bone and muscle, desperate for the other, they removed what little clothing was left—his underwear, her glasses—shifting their bodies until he climbed onto her, and she slid open to allow him. Grasping, gazing into each other's eyes, lips pushed against mouths with frantic violence, or against the skin of each shoulder, neck, collarbone, Chile doing what she could to avoid his wound. Nipping skin, tasting soap and sweat, jaws tight, straining to remain quiet, grinding teeth when they found the right place, forgetting their avowed silence, letting go. Listening to the room tick as they returned to their bodies, reason seeping into consciousness, alive, aware.

He rolled to one side, the pounding beneath his rib cage suddenly prominent. With the flash of pain came those foreign images: hands clasped around the unyielding neck, fingers depressing flesh into small craters, the opening gateway. Veiled sunlight, a droplet of blood. Shuddering in the darkness, a film of sweat contracted into dry goose bumps on Markriss's skin.

Chile pushed herself beneath an arm, nose buried in his chest. "Man stink," she whispered. Chuckling.

"I showered, you saw."

"Need to again."

Head shaking, he smiled a little. Beneath the closed living room door, a gap no bigger than ten millimeters from where they lay, came a spurt of breath, snuffling, a patter of claws. Chile tensed, holding her breath until it was gone.

"Can't believe he's got a dog."

He placed a hand over his eyes, appreciating the full darkness it afforded. "Chileshe . . ."

"He better get rid of it. You better tell him."

He took his hand away from his face. "Don't say that."

"I'm not taking anymore chances. Tell him to send it away or I will."

Markriss pulled Chileshe to him and kissed her temple, lips caressing baby hairs. Wishing it all away.

They stayed with Amunda three more days before Ayizan said it was time. By then, Markriss was struck by how accustomed they had become to being around the doctor, grateful for his calm manner and home-cooked food, his steady hospitality, the warmth of his home.

There wasn't much they could do with their time except help to keep the house tidy. Chop vegetables for dinner, offer to brew tea. Xander had taken to doing repairs, fixing a bolt on a broken kitchen cupboard door, restarting the ventilation unit in the bathroom, unblocking the pedestal sink. As instructed, Ayizan rested his leg with his foot raised on a spare seat, and was often to be found in the living room, face hidden by a hardback text borrowed from Amunda's extensive library, or the battered pages of Markriss's *Book of the Ark*. He slept for many hours, waking to brood without interruption, even when someone entered the room. Markriss worried about his state of mind; he hardly ate, his cheekbones protruded, and his locks had become grayed, old rope. On the second morning he came downstairs, hair cut to the scalp, locks hefted in a swollen carrier bag, asking if the doctor could bury them in the garden when they left. It was shocking to see him that way. Though they knew his intention was to match the photo ID, and the shave had been planned from the beginning, Markriss was still disoriented by their removal.

Temujin found her place by the kitchen windows, staring into the garden at colorful flower beds, barely saying a word to anyone apart from the doctor. They solidified a friendship of trust, having both lost partners—Amunda his wife from spinal cancer years before, only a few months after he entered the Ark. As he dropped potato chunks into hot water and seasoned meat to marinate until it was needed later, they spoke in low murmurs about their memories of beaches they had visited, beers drunk, people they had known. Steam grew on windows, and Temujin would fall into silence, her length of black hair veiling her face. Amunda continued to slice, pouring himself a glass of prosecco, dancing swayed steps to a song on the radio. If Temujin came back to the present, conversation would flow as before. Quite often, she remained silent.

Early the third morning, Markriss woke to firm weight on his bladder. Unzipping the sleeping bag, he rolled to his feet and began to tread softly across the carpet. At the door, Apnu growled at his scent, eager to play. Markriss rolled his eyes. Last thing he needed. Cautiously, he stepped into the passage, one hand wrapped around the door, hoping to pull it softly without waking the others. He looked down the passage into the kitchen. It seemed the dog wasn't desperate to greet him, and instead was scratching at the bottom of the closed waiting room door. Rump high, tail wagging. The door cracked open. Dr. Amunda emerged, stopping at the sight of Apnu at his feet, taking a moment to adjust his dressing gown, kneeling to stroke her. Markriss heard Temujin's whisper, knew her laughter. Though it had been only days, years seemed to have passed since she laughed. Mouth open in concentration, he slipped back into the comparative warmth of the living room, pushing the door closed, braced for the anticipated squeak of untended hinges, shoulders hunched once it ceased, forehead resting against cool wall. Long moments passed until the soft pressure of slippered feet took the stairs upward, dying somewhere above. Markriss gasped withheld breath. Resolved to keep what he had seen from the others, for everyone's sake.

Chileshe had become insular. Wandering the allocation with ghosts in her pockets, avoiding Dr. Amunda's pet. She hated everything about it. The smell, the hairs it left behind. The sibilant brush of its wagging tail on walls, the moon-eyed, soppy way it looked at her. The name Amunda gave it, a portent in her eyes. Worse still, the dog actually liked Chile, as though sensing what she planned for it, determined to win her over with purest love. When she entered the room it would always thrust a snout between Chile's legs, paws climbing her thighs. Amunda, mindful of Chile's discomfort and even more so the reasoning behind it, began to fear her naked reticence whenever Apnu was there. He'd drag her out by the collar, the animal's high-pitched, pitiful whine an insertion of discomfort in the otherwise casual atmosphere. Only simple proximity saved Apnu's life. There was no way for Chile to do what she threatened without the entire house knowing, hearing. Though the others barely gave a damn, Chile wasn't yet coldhearted enough to kill Apnu within earshot of her owner. And so a reluctant impasse formed, Markriss keeping half an eye on his wife, the doctor minding his animal. If Apnu got too close, or wandered to a place where Chile had the ability to keep her promise, each steered one or the other away.

The day Ayizan gave the order, they sat around the kitchen table among breakfast leftovers, flaked croissants and empty cereal bowls, half-drunk mugs of tea. He dragged a hand across his face, stroked his bare chin.

"We're making the push this evening. Thoughts?"

Amunda paused, round-bellied teapot in hand. He'd only just refilled it with kettle-hot water. "You're not serious."

"Oh, come on, not this."

"Yes, this. You're barely able to walk, let alone anything more. If I was practicing I'd give you four weeks' recovery time, most likely six."

"Well, you're not, and we all know why."

Amunda's mouth snapped closed, he sat. Poured from the teapot, avoiding Temujin's eyes.

"Listen, I'm sorry. I didn't mean that. But the longer we're here the more danger we bring you, and I don't want another . . ." Huge sigh. "It's not gonna happen again. Do you hear me? It won't."

Unable to speak or raise his head, the doctor moved the pot around the table, filling each cup.

"We've lost our weapons, so everyone needs to gather what you can. Kitchen knives, garden tools, medical stuff. Whatever's here—that okay, Doc?" A pause, eyes searching over steam. Acknowledging. "Thank you. Nothing big, all right? It needs to be small, inconspicuous. Easily bagged. We'll drop them before the scanners, if we get that far."

"We'll need to separate," Markriss said.

"Okay, go in pairs, one tool each. I'll go alone."

"Now you're really being stupid," Chile sneered.

"I said. I'll go. Alone. Okay?"

Lips twisting, expression bitter, Chile turned on her stool, away from them.

They discussed the remaining details. They'd travel to the gateway together, at which point they'd pair up, wait for the last minute to drop their tools before they entered, or give them up to the security forces, hoping the ID Capra and his team worked up got them through the checkpoint. If successful, they'd travel to L3, at which point they'd part company and journey alone to the rendezvous point, the doctor's former medical center, west L3. That was when Amunda suggested they borrow clothes from his wardrobe in order to maintain their pretense of hailing from a middle-class L3 community. He'd kept particular items of clothing that had once been his wife's. Although musty, he admitted, they had aged well. Ayizan agreed.

Following that, the doctor raised a further proposal. Since they were posing as health specialists, and he was the only trained medic, it made perfect sense for him and Apnu to go with them.

The suggestion caused an instant rift, voices raised over the table. Chile, Ayizan, and Xander against, Markriss and Temujin for. Chile blazed anger, flailing hands almost knocking mugs over, spilling hot tea. From the moment the argument began, he and Temujin had lost. Three against two would not be undermined. Markriss sensed Chile was upset about his siding against her, given his knowledge of how she felt about dogs. Ayizan and Xander thought him mad, telling him so. He wasn't sure why he'd raised his voice to counteract theirs in the first place; it may have been to protect Temujin in some way, although beneath the assertion was instinct, raw, itching. The truth was he didn't know, and actually believed his gut might be wrong. As they made wild gestures, shouting in each other's faces, pointing and spitting without realizing what they did, Markriss watched Temujin gaze outside, locked in her own thoughts, alone. He followed her sight line into the garden. Wondered if there was anything to see. Did a rose nod, a leaf sway? Probably not.

It was solid night among the hushed blocks of Lixus allocations as they readied to depart. All wore calf-length weatherproof jackets, woolen coats, and sensible pants, belts that clung, restrictive, scratching at their hips. The men wore cheap, soft-soled sneakers. Chile was given gym shoes, while Temujin had kept her boots, unable to find a pair in the house that fit her. They squared their shoulders, an attempt at looking privileged, heads high and backs straight as the doctor instructed. Their clicking heels and the squeak of old shoes played on Markriss's nerves, his fists clenched in coat pockets.

The doctor's expression had wrenched Markriss's heart when they stood on the path outside his door, pain aging his stricken face. Loss, always loss where Amunda was concerned. First his wife, then self-control. Conscious thought, medical training, the ability to reason without the injection of drugs into his veins, and then finally, the lost vocation that brought him into the Ark. Now the unkind possibilities of love, however fragile, transitory.

As they had packed away what little of Amunda's belongings they'd use, Markriss tightening a sleeping bag into a rolled nylon tube, Ayizan entered, returning to the subject of the doctor's proposal to join them. He thought Amunda might be bereft without the job of medically assisting Outsiders and their followers throughout the Quarter. Although many residents needed his support after the Corps raid on the zone, it was too dangerous for the doctor to return, especially if Bandyo worked for the Authority. The Mansion captain would gladly have his head, even if he'd killed Vyasa as an act of simple revenge for the murder of his own men, not part of the retaliation attack of Corps soldiers.

Markriss pushed his feet into Amunda's old, worn sneakers, one after another, listening. For the bubbling lilt of Temujin's laughter, Amunda's soft tread on carpet stairs. The void that followed after.

Had their 1322 strike been worth it? Though the others might think it too early to say, he doubted. The road shimmered blue with elevated e-lamps. Seven miles west, at the opposite end of the Ark, fires raged as before. He had lived flames and stinging heat. They had changed nothing more than their tenuous grip on mortality. Ascension was their future; its promise wriggled beneath his skin, tingling at his throat. Of that belief he was certain. Though they didn't speak about it, he refused to accept that any of his companions were fooled. No one had the intention of making it to L3. A plan

formulated to contend with their best-case scenario had been implemented for the worst. It was suicide. And they knew.

Nevertheless, they walked from the comfort of shadow, unspoken
thoughts, and familiar bodies, away from the immersion of a zone
that could easily have been theirs if they had been other people, who
lived other lives. Past the quiet blocks of wealthy allocation homes
and onto a high street lined with bright shops and restaurants, window
displays of elegant clothes, consumer technology, and the darkened
interior of banks, moving toward the harsh glow of light that was the
false promise of the Eastern Gateway. And while it was impossible
to see beyond fierce illumination, a stark white that brought to mind
the fury of the sun embedded in a blanket of cloud, they heard the
whir of electric rotors joined as one, the rise in volume as they
approached. Shouting, amplified by loudspeaker, echoing everywhere,
too loud to make out what was said. They stopped. There was nowhere
to go, no place to run. Fingers touched his. Ayizan. He reached left,
finding Chile's. All five, hands joined like paper dolls.

Inching from blinding floodlight, bristled rifles pointing staunch
at their bodies, the Corps soldiers emerged, advancing.

Markriss faced left. A glass-fronted building block, a collection
of square computer banks with screens set up outside the windows,
each resembling office filing cabinets, antennae fixed to their apex.
The logo on equipment sides, *Ark News*. Incredibly, that face. Curled
hair, unyielding features. Eyes like broken glass. Keshni Myatt watched
him, a microphone poised at her lips, the woman beside her lifting
a miniature digicam to her eye. Others pointed, mouths forming
shapes, emitting words he couldn't hear.

Ayizan squeezed Markriss's fingers. His attention whipped forward.

"You all run. I'll distract them. On three."

Spoken through unmoving lips.

"Are you stupid, we should—"

"One, two, *three*."

Ayizan let go, limping at the line of soldiers. Markriss felt the
brush of clothes, Chile's hand leave his palm. He wanted to scream,
stop them, only it was done. He spun back the way they'd come,
forcing his legs to move, and saw Chile run two steps, stutter, arms

flying high, fingers tensed, patches of dark red blossoming on her back and shoulders, and he roared her name so loudly the words dragged at his throat, a rock against bare skin. Whistles sped past his ears. He was punched, legs, arms, back, the force making him fall, skinning limbs on concrete, unable to see anything beyond cracks that seemed like deep valleys, he was so close. So close.

And he rose. Seeing all, his prone body, the dribble of blood leaking from his mouth. The advancement of soldiers, that decelerating surge, the bodies of his friends and beloved laid out in various positions, the spectacular ascendance of their elemental forms, colorful wisps of being. Residents transfixed by murder. Keshni Myatt barking into the microphone. He tried to call their spiritual bodies as they elevated, finding the trauma of hurried disconnection too great, they were caught by the splendor of stinging light above their heads, blindness in their eyes. And yet somehow, he stayed low to the ground. He was free.

He wanted to go with them. Couldn't move. Everything was there to be viewed, his ethereal form swirling, and he saw Dr. Amunda paused at the far end of the block, tears streaming behind the old man's glasses and down his cheeks, loose fists holding Apnu's leash, the dog straining, red material made taut.

He stared into the yellow eyes of the animal. Bright amber, refusing to leave. It kept him, compelling him. Apnu pulled the leash farther, powerful neck reaching for something, and then she broke into a galloping, determined run, not toward Markriss, but a sure diagonal line, leash dragging behind her. Amunda screamed as Apnu ran toward the glass-fronted buildings. Gazing into the building, Markriss saw what the dog had.

Something shifted in him; he took the chance. Tugging his ethereal body in the direction of the running animal as his physical body placed both hands flat on concrete. Pushing, it stood once more.

Cameras flashed lightning. Spectators roared fear. Amunda had stiffened, voice caught midshout, taking a faltering backward step, mouth alive with horror. The body began to run behind the dog, arms positioned at his sides, stumbling, jerking knees lifting, tethered to the ethereal form darting like a silverfish before it. A thunder of shots. Buzzing drones swooping close, Markriss pushed with quick bursts of energy toward the crowd of media spectators, following the lithe, bounding form of the dog, his physical body close behind.

Keshni Myatt and her colleagues registered dumbfounded, quizzical gaping, before settling on the idea that it was real, the dog and the dead body were coming at them with equal speed. They dived to one side to avoid Apnu sprinting past, leaping into the shop window. It shattered from the impact of her skull and the rounds of bullets that followed, webbed glass fragmenting sheet ice. Markriss flew his ethereal body through the falling shards, bringing his physical body with him. The carcass jumping the heads of the living, fingers splayed, impatient for his destination. Beneath him, fear, disbelief, wonder, a digicam following his spasmodic, clumsy leap in a ninety-degree arc.

He landed on the other side. Fell to his knees. A crack, the ethereal body saw white pain. Blood rained from multiple wounds, bullets gouging chunks of muscle and flesh from his back, neck, thighs, sending him to the polished floor. Among the dull interior, a restaurant devoid of customers, no lights, tables and chairs bare as empty fields, meals half eaten, herbal teas steaming, the warmth of radiators congealing air.

Apnu crawled on front legs and back, beetle-like, fur matted in knots of blood, sliding across the polished floor, staccato in motion. The ethereal form heaved at its tether, pulling his body to the dog's side. A glint of camera. The reflection of soldiers' helmets collecting below the broken teeth of the window frame. Markriss took no notice, seeing.

In a corner of the room, gushing silver erupted from floor tiles, creating a roiling churn of energy where it met the ceiling.

Apnu touched her wet nose against the rush of light, falling limp. Her elemental body emerged, oyster pink, thrusting upward. Climbing to the ceiling, drawn by great power, dispersing.

Markriss made himself crawl farther, until he was beside the dog's prone body. Thundering shots rang violence, peppering his shoulders and legs. The base of his head. He clutched back at his spine, sharp with pain. Air whistled in his throat. He reached out an arm, fingers stretched. Brushed Apnu's fur.

His jaw opened. Lips moving.

"Good dog. Good dog."

Grasping for the cross stream, fingertips pierced by a thousand tiny knives. Agony. Swift, earing light. He was lifted.

13

Emergence. The subtle weight of liquid dripping from his forehead, ears, and shoulders as he broke the surface to be freed, appraising the sore, cracked landscape, taking a gasped mouthful of something. Not air, surely, not here. He wasn't quite sure what it was. He paddled his arms and legs in an effort to tread water until he remembered. It was possible to rise farther, if he willed it. Arms at his sides, concentrating, body shedding river water as he rose.

Black-shadow mountains, the trail of purple liquid scything through dark earth like veins. Wheeling spirals of galaxies over his head, improbable in their number. He had reallocated somehow, farther up or down the River of Time. He couldn't tell which. Still, the everlasting land was recognizable, he knew this plane. Asiah. The Taut. The Light.

He rose until barren desert was far below his feet. He thought it, and was immediately sat on a high outcrop over the riverbank, watching ghosts of faces, landscapes, animals, even whole cities go by. He panted, hyperventilating, trying to catch breath. Frantic eyes darted, trying to find the others. There was no one. He was alone.

Head bowed, Markriss wept. Grief amplified into enforced pressure in his chest that made it difficult to breathe. For brief moments he couldn't, forced to cough the pretense of life back into his lungs, inhale more rapidly to make them expand and fall as he was used to. He couldn't die in this place, yet mortality remained lodged in every action. He existed as he was accustomed to, unfamiliar with the ways of the ancestors who called this plane home.

Astral forms whipped through the sky in dozens, moving as comets, fiery and swift. Chileshe? Ayizan? Too numerous to tell apart, too rapid, the universe they inhabited too vast to even think of giving chase. He'd made that mistake before. How many had existed since humankind's first death? How long would it take to find the people he loved?

A scratch of movement, fallen earth.

Harman Wallace beside him.

The old man peered, frowning, curiosity etched into every wrinkle. Perhaps Markriss reminded him of a long-ago experiment he'd once made. They said nothing for a time.

Why did you take me there?

The professor considered. Looked toward water and probed the rocky earth with his stick.

I think you'll find you took yourself.

Anger lit his fifth major chakra. He was aware of his aura, flushed with emotion.

What's that supposed to mean? I didn't ask for any of it! I was a murderer. I lost my wife! I loved them all. We were killed!

And yet here you are.

Open-palmed, the stick held nimbly in his right thumb. Markriss was caught by the fact that the professor's hands had no crease lines. No prints or wrinkles. They were perfectly smooth.

His throat chakra wheeled faster, he could feel it. He looked into the dark hood.

You know how it feels to die?! Have bullets take chunks out of your skin, to see someone you love get shot to death? Have you seen anything like that before?

The hood motionless, the face still within it.

Death of the earthly body is inevitable. You know that. But the awareness something greater exists should cause you to embrace that truth, not fear it. That your wife exists on other planes is all you need to know.

He accepted the tension of clenched fists, opening his hands.

What about the uraeus? I never saw it.

If you needed the weapon, it would have been there.

And Ayizan? You know he was my friend, right? I've known him all my life. On my parallel he's like the Rogue you describe; on that one he was entirely different. Why was I meant to kill him? He was a good man.

Was he?

Markriss paused on the verge of speaking.

Okay. I see what's going on.

Do you?

This is a test. You're testing me.

Harman pushed a small rock with his stick, shrugging.

I haven't the power, Markriss. I'm nothing more than a guide. My instructions are to show you the Way. I make suggestions only. Any experience that follows is entirely yours.

Head low, Markriss contemplated trickling water meters beyond his feet. Dappled life adrift on soft currents. The chuckle of liquid traversing rock.

I loved her with everything I had.

Pressure. A hand on his. Harman was close again, staring into his eyes. Light blue, glistening. Mirror reflective. The lack of feeling was disconcerting, he was so alone.

Does that change how you feel? Now? About Keshni?

Everything, he said, eyes filling.

Harman bowed his head. Thought for many seconds, stick tapping, toeing rocks.

There are other places where your spirits converge. Where you could find her again, and the others you knew. The river has many. Please don't expect me to guarantee the outcomes, or that your life with Keshni as you wished for originally doesn't reoccur. That's impossible.

Yes. I hear you.

I should have told you in the beginning.

Markriss heaved a sigh.

It's not like I have a choice.

Harman considered him further. Absence of light made it difficult to see if he was pleased, or otherwise.

Come. The place isn't far.

They ascended, traveling at once without thought. Onyx earth ran beneath them, glittering starlight. The river widened, contracted into almost nothing, grew again until the banks of either side were wide apart, and the waters thrashed and churned. He wanted to ask the professor what place in the time line it was, only the elder's ka was far ahead, and try as he might there were no means to catch him. As much as Markriss learned, Wallace remained the elder. He was zamani of the Swahili tradition, an ancestral spirit of infinite past, a spiritual being who knew and could do so much more than he. It was a useful reminder, and yet, despite his acceptance of humility, he was also filled with an ease that came from repetition, the calm of the man he had been on his former physical plane. Teacher. Swollen with knowledge. His better self, perhaps. Racked with pain, complicated though fulfilled by life and the people he had known. Immersed in the pleasure that came from multiple connections, a strengthened web of being.

Where the land became bulky with rock formations, and the river was a slim creek, a pebbled bed visible beneath water, they slowed, came to a stop. Wallace lowered onto the bank. Markriss hovered above the water.

Good. Well done, Markriss. You've learned a lot.

I'm not sure how, I just know.

You have grown. It's beautiful to see.

I feel it. I have you to thank.

Mauve water burst with ethereal life. Illuminated against the darkness around them. Inviting, so different from the first time.

You have no mission, no uraeus. In truth, the Rogue left the parallel you'd been sent to not long after you arrived. It vacated the body of your friend to rejoin the astral. When it makes itself known, I'll find you. Or you can return by stream. They exist on every parallel, you'll see them.

Cold lapped the soles of his feet. His aura vibrated black velvet, denoting the entrance of a portal, eyes closed. He was ready. He allowed himself to fall.

You won't remember! Wallace shouted, barely heard over rising

bubbles that frothed and burst at his chest. *Only when we next meet!*
I understand, Markriss said, river water covering everything.
He sank into the welcome twilight beneath him.

Part Three

Awakening and Liberation
(*Ānava Samāveśa*)

"The creation waits in eager expectation for the children of God to be revealed."

—Romans 8:19

21 November 2019

1

Vibrations sang through his body, immersive pressure traveling a charged and stimulated atmosphere, vitalizing numerous layers of flesh, sending infinitesimal tremors through veins, tendons, arteries, the beating pulse of organs. He sighed, rich energy washing through him, a rippling wave that saturated his epithelium, every hair rising to attention, the subtle atoms formerly at rest above his mortal body awakened, chakras spinning, primed to make a superfluity of connections. In the moment, Markriss saw a geometric shape formed in darkness, like something primordial. Needle-thin beams of fluorescent green spun from the depths, tumbling straight lines that arrived from every direction, top, bottom, left, right, as if by attraction, joining to become a three-dimensional pyramid, skeletal and diaphanous, rotating slow in its completed form.

He wondered at what he was seeing, half aware. Vibrations rushed through him with greater volume, and then he heard it properly, a steady rotation bringing circular motion to every part of his body, mostly his vision, and he spiraled into himself, a sensation he'd never experienced before. The pyramid remained steady, spinning on its base with slightly more force, something like dust emerging from the angles between those straight lines, smears of green like chem-trails, slight, apparent. More smears appeared from other corners, beginning to spiral into a gentle vortex that resembled the movements he imagined his body had made. And it was the strangest sensation. Him swirling, the pyramid swirling, trailing clouds at each corner, all swirling. Emotion flooded him, peace and warmth. Like he was alive to the temperature of blood coursing through him, feeling the rush of its travel and every one of its 99.5 degrees. He heard himself laugh, loud and uproarious, and somehow that brought him back, so when he opened his eyes he lay on the bed, blinking.

The last fading note lingered, though Keshni had long stopped moving the striker. Bitter smoke hung from the bunched white sage she'd insisted on lighting until the leaves puffed, smoked, and then were waved around every room of the flat, high, low, everywhere, before their session began. She was perched on a small cushion at the foot of the yoga mat she'd laid for him, copper hair tied back, half smiling, leaning forward, eyes clinical and small. Her light-green dress fell around her, sheer and translucent. In her left arm she cradled the bell, hugging it against her lower stomach, while her right held the striker poised, as though she might continue to play.

Their flat was snug, cluttered. A small living room section where he lay, a dining room area with a square table, and an open-plan kitchenette in a corner. Away from those cramped spaces, twinned bedrooms he'd never seen, a bathroom. One bedroom served as their study. Markriss knew because he'd been told.

"Okay?"

He licked his lips, nodded, struggling to sit up. His mouth was very dry.

"Don't get up too quickly, take your time. You're gonna need a moment. Would you like water?"

"Yes, please."

Waiting for her to pass the cup, smiling as he took it. He gulped the contents down until it was empty. Placed it on the floor.

"Thank you."

"You're very welcome." Keshni beamed, watching close. "How d'you feel?"

"Odd. Like I had a massive nap. How long was I out?"

She shrugged. "Twenty minutes or so. Not long. I wasn't keeping track."

"Oh man. Feels like days."

"You snored a bit. And you were giggling," she said, laughing herself, fingers covering her lips. It was cute and made him smile.

"That's a powerful instrument. You wouldn't think so to look at it." He rolled his neck, swinging his feet until they rested on chilled wooden floor, rubbed his eyes. His socks were blue, dotted with the heads of little dalmatians. He hadn't noticed when he'd pulled them on and left the flat. He'd been late.

"Yeah, it's pretty capable. They used to say they're from Tibet, then when I got into playing more I found there's no record of them in Tibetan musical history. I mean they sing, and use clanging in healing practices, not bells."

"Bells?"

"I mean bowls. These things. Bells are what they actually call them, bowls are what they're known as. Or gongs, or sometimes cups. They're Chinese. Date back to the Shang dynasty, sixteenth century BC, I read."

"Oh," Markriss said. He was hungry, wondering what to eat. Chinese would be nice.

"So what did you see?"

"Nothing much really. Just darkness. It felt nice though," he said quickly, as her shoulders slumped. "I might have seen a pyramid. It was tough to make out."

"That would have been cool. You respond so easily, I think it can really help with what you're going through. Get your energies up, realign your chakras. You might even want to try Reiki. I love it, actually. See how you feel in a few days."

"Sure." He got up, pushing his feet into twinned Chuck Taylors. "You know how I am about this stuff."

"I know, I know, you said. Wanna hold it?"

He didn't, though worried about causing offense. Opening his hands, he waited for Keshni to place the bell between them.

It was heavier than he'd expected, a weight that belied its size. Warmed by Keshni's lap, it was the color of bronze and a darker tone reminiscent of mahogany, with a continuous run of patterns or writing around the outer belly that brought to mind runes. Inside the bell, three layers of circular illustrations were carved. What looked like leaves in the uppermost section nearest the rim, a series of overlaid petals in the center, and at the very bottom an unfurled lotus flower. Raising the bowl to the light, each design gave the illusion of moving in clockwise and counterclockwise directions, like the spiraling motion he'd experienced when Keshni made it sing.

"That's pretty trippy." He gave it back.

"Yeah, I wouldn't take acid and play these things. You might not ever come down."

They laughed as though they'd signed a mutual contract promising hilarity, awkward once finished. She was looking at him in that peculiar way she had, head inclined, without guile or restraint. It was one of the things he liked most about her, her openness, a mature innocence he'd never encountered in anyone he'd met. She took his hands with both of hers, held them. Markriss felt a little embarrassed, didn't let go.

"I'm glad you gave it a try."

"So am I. And I liked it, definitely. I'm just not sure it—"

"Wait." She smiled wider, chuckling. "Let it settle. See how you feel."

"Okay," he said, and they laughed more. He couldn't help smiling. It pushed at his cheeks, made them ache. "What are you doing this evening?"

"Dinner, maybe a film. I'm dying to see the new *Charlie's Angels*. Depends if we catch a screening."

"You should do. It's early," he said, letting his fingers slide from hers. He searched for his puffer jacket, avoiding the eyes of photos arranged in various places around the flat, found it laid across the sofa, slipped it on. Zipped up. Familiar snugness enclosed him.

"What about you?"

"Ah, not sure. I might link up with a friend if he's free. He's probably not."

"That'll be nice."

There wasn't much left to say beyond that, evidenced by the fact that she wasn't really listening. He wandered to the flat door, Keshni following. Markriss reached for the latch, looking back.

"Thanks again, Kesh. I really appreciate you taking time for me, especially after all the fuss I caused."

"No problem at all! Let me know if you fancy another session." He opened the front door, stepping outside, struck by cold, damp air. Shivered. Keshni touched his shoulder. "Oh, by the way, don't tell those lot at work about this, yeah? I try to keep this and that separate, if you know what I mean?"

"I understand," he said. They leaned forward for the obligatory kiss on both cheeks, "European style" as Nesta called it. "See you."

"Bye, Riss," she said, closing the door.

He waited in the basement a few moments, hands deep in pockets, thinking about what they had done. The reverberations of the bowl echoed in his head. His fingertips buzzed stimulation. The pulse at his throat was steady, obvious. He had felt something, he could admit, though it was strange to. Like some hippy cultist. It was as though his mind had been invaded. He needed to go somewhere and live the experience by himself, let his feet wander wherever they wanted to take him, be alone. He climbed the steps, emerging onto the street, where night enveloped him, all the noise and odor of burning gas from a nearby exhaust, the orange lights, the light blue of approaching dusk.

The idea of finding his own space in the busy city excited him. His own bubble. He'd filed copy that afternoon, and so he was free for the evening. Head tucked into his chest against the chill, Markriss walked back toward the station, skirting parents clutching strollers, colorfully dressed tourists wandering, stopping, looking around and down at maps, a gaggle of bodies moving as one unit, coming to a halt at the indecision of their leader. The slim man with the tiny dog, the legs of the animal close to the ground for some reason reminding Markriss of a millipede. Though it was cold enough to see his own breath, still damp from an earlier downpour, he was invigorated by the early-evening air. Perhaps it was the glaring contrast between the noisy streets and Keshni's calm home. Notwithstanding all of his trepidations, his fears for the future and the weight of shared pasts, he loved the city maddeningly, an inexplicable joy that climbed from the mist of blurred green traffic lights, the roar of vehicles as he turned onto the main road, the amber glow of pubs and shops, and the sweet rose of a passing vape.

Then came the first, most important question. Bus or tube? Or maybe he should walk? The river was only a few hundred yards from where he stood, after all. How long would he take to get by any route? It was only then that he was aware he'd chosen his destination subconsciously, almost from the moment he'd stepped into the cold. The southern bank of the river, certainly. Where else for isolated contemplation? What better place? He prized his phone from a pocket, typing into Google Maps: forty-one minutes to walk the river, twenty-two by C10 or 507, and thirteen by the Victoria Line, with a change at Green Park for the Jubilee, where there was a reduced service. The tube had it. He put away his phone.

Still, there was the nearby allure of Tate Britain. He carried a membership card in his Oyster wallet, although there were the tourists and enthusiasts, most of all the art. He needed a blank canvas, not the ideas of others. He needed space, the continual run of his own thoughts. Markriss walked down the inclined slope and into the light of the thrumming station, pleased with what he'd decided. There was the river, perhaps bottled beer, maybe even ramen; not Chinese at all, close enough.

He descended into the lower reaches of the city. Once there, he ran for the train, making it just before doors rumbled to a close, feeling vaguely embarrassed by attempts to ignore the spectacle he'd made. Searching for the nearest available seat, middle carriage left, one with space beside it, thank God—surprising, given the time of day. He sat hunched into the feathered expanse of his jacket before he realized he was growing warm. Straightened his spine, unzipped his puffer, tried to relax.

No one looked at anyone, as was the etiquette, so he focused on the blank reflection of the window, the tunnel and colored cables racing beyond. Metal wheels screamed conflict against the tracks, and he heard again the chime of the bell, or bowl, whatever she called it, an everlasting note he only discovered when he was underground, away from the light and noise and surplus stimulation. He marveled at how it had stayed with him, grew louder in volume; lights flickered above him, and the shriek of train wheels became a screeching demon, Markriss entranced by the reflection of half-formed images in the window.

Without notice, the dark background of the tunnel became rust brown, everyone around him disappearing, and he was truly alone. The rattle of the train became stronger, painful to the ears, sounding as though it had shaken itself from the tracks—only when Markriss blinked, he was the sole passenger in a huge empty goods elevator instead of a train. He felt himself plunge, nothing to stop or catch him. A clogging physical presence of loss balled in his chest like the immovable product of a cold. He hacked and coughed, alive to pain. Mouth crying silence. Hands crushing armrests.

Then he was back in the train car, glancing up and down at the blank faces of other commuters, oblivious to what he'd seen. The overhead advertisement said, *The Future Isn't What It Used to Be.* An office worker in slim black gloves and ankle heels gripped an *Evening Standard* bearing the headline "Hoffa Missing." That threw him, until he saw the black-and-white picture of Pacino's face, realizing it was another ad for the new Scorsese movie. The real headline above: "No Anti-Semitism Apology from Corbyn." The seat beside him remained empty, even though they'd stopped at a busy station before that, and the remainder of seats were full and people were standing. He sighed, rubbing his chin. He needed a shave. The well-spoken, automated woman's voice told their car the next stop was his. Doors opened. Time to leave.

His second tube journey was mercifully without unbidden hallucinations. He rode the escalator upward, rising into the stark vestibule, bright as waking daylight, where orange-jacketed TfL staff loitered, a man and a woman wearing expressions of slight annoyance, stiff barriers opening in welcome or to allow commuters to exit. Outside, light was failing. He might just make it. Head ducked, he fast-walked to the subway tunnels that ran beneath the roundabout and advertising lighthouse of the IMAX, a venue he'd never been to despite his deep love of cinema. Too commercial perhaps. Too overflowing with popcorn bags and difficult-to-negotiate hot dog buns. He surfaced on the opposite side of the road, among lanky teenaged parkour trainees who tested their skills against stubbed walls, bike riders in glowing reflective wear preparing for the rush of madness that was evening traffic. And still, even as he walked northward, the eternal call of the bell rang like a thousand voices humming in both ears. Not loud, or overpowering, only present like the sound of his breath, or the swish of clothing in response to hurried movements. Though it was strange, he imagined the sensation was common for people who'd taken what Keshni had called a "gong bath." He didn't wish the noise to end; if anything, Markriss found it a calming and pleasant addition to his walk.

He passed between the white sheen of the BFI and smooth-hewed bulk of the National Theatre, avoiding oncoming pedestrians, trying to make his legs move faster, though they felt heavy. A notification pinged his phone; he ignored it. The shouts of people sitting on metal benches and the polished stone of crescent installations, eating sandwiches and talking on phones, made him turn left at the edge of the cinema, breathing out. He slackened his pace, panic over. He maneuvered himself among bunched figures perusing trestle tables stacked with books, scanning with half an eye, the other kept on the movements of others, careful not to bump anyone.

The Southbank Centre Book Market had long been his respite. He wasn't sure why, it was just as bustling as any place in the city, with the teeming BFI bar and restaurant opposite, crowds walking doggedly along the river path between the theater and Tate Modern. Each crammed table was always heavily occupied and, on many occasions, his hand would reach for the same volume as another's. Yet there was an air of quiet stillness about the place, of focus and commonality. Of studied contemplation by way of titles and authors he knew, just knew, could be found beneath the rain-cloud overhang of Waterloo Bridge. Perhaps it was the pacing walk up and down trestle pathways, a miniature labyrinth of literary accomplishment. Perhaps it was simply the sight of all those covers and names. Over the years he'd found a treasured Beryl Gilroy *Black Teacher*, a couple of decent Baldwins, a copy of *Nineteen Eighty-Four* he'd bought as a birthday present for an ex-girlfriend—though most of the time he didn't visit to purchase anything, just to be surrounded by fading light and words. He came after work on weekdays, or sometimes arrived on a Sunday evening to find the tables crowded by booklovers, all moving in remote silence. Twilight was his favorite hour. He liked to flick through pages in subdued winter light, never quite sure what purpose it served.

And then, parallel to the book market, the river. Much as he loved the odor and feel of secondhand pages, he was drawn to the indifferent lap of tide, and he'd prolong his back-and-forth walk along stacks, moving closer to the water and then farther, ebbing, awaiting that final moment of release: the moment he relented, called time, and replaced the last poetry collection or yellowed, brittle comic where it belonged, blind-stepping from the confines of tables, crossing sidewalks until he was there, by the cold wood railing, looking out at the embankment on the northern side.

There were times when he would smile, as he did then. Struck by the frosted brilliance of Christmas lights on either bank and convivial radiance of street-food stalls, the river a glimmering universe, dark matter rippling with constant motion. The distant red light of cars, sluggish, moving in one direction. The riverboat transporting commuters to various destinations across the city, drawing to a stop at Embankment Pier, picking up and depositing office workers.

On a summer day six years previously, Markriss had walked this route and strayed farther west, keeping close to the wood-topped railing until he noted an abstract vision poised on the very edge of Queen Elizabeth Hall. A life-size boat, sitting proud on the roof, stranded like Noah atop Mount Ararat. His first sighting of it produced stunned laughter. He paced up and down, immune to the clatter and low-level roar of skateboarders, avoiding people, trying to see it from better angles. It was quite huge, the bow jutting into empty space as though it might tip at any minute, the hull made of wood and dim metal under the waterline. The boat was such an incongruous sight, Markriss couldn't get it out of his mind. Though he balked at going inside the building to inquire why it had been constructed, his curiosity was tickled, and he began to talk of it with friends, a few of his colleagues at work.

It was only during a lunch conversation with Chileshe and a group of fellow workmates that he learned the inspiration behind the boat. Part architectural project, part art installation, its tertiary purpose was to provide a one-room hotel-slash–creative space for artists of all disciplines. Up to two people at a time could pay to spend a night or more above the river, looking down on a vista usually witnessed only by the homeless, and then from a reduced, ground-level viewpoint. The South Bank and its environs in fixed night, when every tourist, worker, commuter, artist, and skateboard enthusiast left for home.

They talked about whether they would choose to stay there or not, who their companions might be if they did. Markriss, going through another of his regular single bouts, said he'd like to have the experience alone. Someone, he couldn't remember who, pointed out the designers modeled their installation on the riverboat Joseph Conrad captained during his time in the Congo, fictionalized later in *Heart of Darkness*. The information had floored most of his colleagues.

He'd first read the novel at university. While he engaged with the work as an artistic feat of great significance and prowess—particularly its end, which moved him so much its gravity remained with him for weeks—he'd been troubled by the book's inability to escape the very racism it claimed to refute. Africans were kept on the periphery, reduced to inhabiting a darkness drawn from the author's unjustified misunderstandings, Marlow exhibiting little or no understanding of their truth. Then there was the false, stark equivalence of the rivers Thames and Congo, created by Conrad, in the words of Chinua Achebe, to posit the waters as binary opposites, "one good, one bad." More than anything for Markriss and his fallow reading mind was the pervasiveness of naked cruelty toward the continent and people of his heritage, the inability of the protagonist to adequately challenge his own prejudice, or even accept it as a simple epiphany gained. Maybe that had been the novel's true aim, the charting of a racist mind changed by experience. He was never sure.

Still it unsettled him, and when he returned to the novel after a time—and again, when discussions for and against the merits of the book raged—those feelings intensified. The unabashed hatred of the central protagonist and the world he came from was Markriss's daily reality, an echo that assailed him each time he stepped from his home onto London streets. To read those words again, especially in recent times, the product of such violent thought and deeds, brought a pressure to his heart he could not ignore.

Whenever he came to the South Bank after that first sighting of the boat, Markriss had taken to looking up and left, unable to stop himself, immersed in the soundtrack of rolling skateboard wheels, that tense absent pause, the powerless thunder of safe landings. He would glance up at the boat and register pain caught in his body; it was like being tugged from inside. One summer night, after years had passed, following an evening at the cinema on a date with someone he later wouldn't remember—and at that moment knew wouldn't last beyond the night—he'd turned in that direction to find the Conrad boat gone. A hollow feeling settled in his gut as he stared into empty space. He wasn't certain how he felt. A conversation had occurred. Concluded by others, moved on. The sky seemed even larger behind the solid block of the hall. The voices around him too loud, the skateboarders' radio too obtrusive for him to fold inside himself, to decipher the flavor and consistency of his emotions. His date tugged at his elbow, fast-talking up the merits of YO! Sushi tempura rolls. He allowed himself to be led, and never forgot.

Night rushed through his door as he turned the key and pushed inside his flat. Under Chuck Taylors, a welcome mat of spindling autumn leaves and glossy campaign leaflets. One red, one yellow. No blue.

He dumped his paper bag of leftover ramen in the small fridge. The one-bedroom was a Notting Hill Housing Association flat he'd rented since his midtwenties; he'd probably never have the money to buy. Cozy as Keshni and Chileshe's home, even if a little more compact, he kept the place minimal, secretly proud of his achievement. A sofa beneath the sole window near the front door, another against the right-hand wall, and on the left his music system and bookshelf. Behind him, a robust headmaster's desk he'd bought from a Portobello Road antique store, on which he kept his laptop. In an alcove beyond that wall, the kitchenette. Beside that lurked the bedroom, though it was actually more of a semienclosed space with just enough room for his double bed. The bathroom hid at the rear of the flat, an afterthought.

When he first moved in, Markriss hooked up his stereo and cleansed the space by playing J Hus loudly to help him unpack. On his second day, the front door knocked. He opened it to see a tall, aging Rastafarian, white locks emerging from his skull like tree roots, reaching his ankles. He squinted into the flat, which was a little intimidating. Months later, Markriss came to realize the elder was partially blind.

"Me nuh love that bangarang music yuh play," he told him, dark eyes settling. "Yuh must vex me spirit wid all the noise?"

Markriss apologized and said he'd turn it down. The Rasta frowned. It was as though he'd been expecting more of a fight. He raised a clenched fist, held toward Markriss.

"Give tanks," he said. "Call I Sirus."

From then on, he and Sirus became good neighbors. The old man invited Markriss to his upstairs flat for a rum and smoke on many occasions. After a time, no further invites were needed.

Markriss collapsed onto his bed, lights off. Felt his way around the mattress until he found the remote. Switched on the TV. Took idle glances at his phone: Twitter, Facebook, Instagram. In his eagerness to visit the South Bank, he'd forgotten to text Nesta. He rolled onto his belly, sending a message about hooking up after his lectures the following day. Nothing came back, although he expected that. Nesta was always busy with something or other. Unlike himself.

He flicked through channels for something to watch, settling on *Fight Club*. It was his first time seeing the movie, and he'd always harbored a vague interest, especially since it employed actors he loved in the leads. Though the story was compelling and the performances entranced him, by the halfway mark, residues of his insomnia began to kick in. His eyelids fell, beginning to burn, even though he wouldn't actually sleep later. He was wired, and supposed he should take his melatonin, yet if he was honest the tablets hadn't worked for a while. By the movie's conclusion, Brad Pitt standing at a panoramic window as buildings went up in flames around him, Markriss couldn't help wondering what would have happened if it had featured Black male protagonists, rather than Norton and Pitt. That week's news was swamped with the furor over *Blue Story*, a film about young gang members' involvement with postcode wars that had been pulled from a number of major cinemas after reports of gang violence up and down the country. Although the film was eventually reinstated, Markriss guessed he had his answer. Back in 2012, when a Colorado premiere of *The Dark Knight Rises* was stormed by a gunman in tactical clothing, killing twelve and injuring seventy others, no one had dared suggest a movie about a masked vigilante at war with a homicidal maniac was even slightly to blame.

Credits rolled. Markriss lay in darkness staring at the white ceiling, unable to think of much else. The rumble of a passing night bus shuddered beneath the continuous tone of Keshni's bell reverberating, on the very edge of hearing, like a sound from a distant past.

2

Insomnia woke him just after four a.m. He decided that, instead of staring into nothingness or curling into a ball in hope of returning to sleep, he might as well get up and work on the project. Two slices of buttered hard-dough toast and a cup of milky tea later, Markriss was ready for the morning. He flipped the switch on his desk lamp. Outside his lone window, night was viscous and murky. He opened up his laptop, typed his password, and while he waited for the document to load, he turned to his small wooden box.

He opened it with a key kept in his desk drawer, retrieved his fake black Moleskine—bought as a pack of three from Ryman—and laid it flat, caressing the soft cover. Something about its smooth surface always beguiled him, although he treasured the rough corners and broken, exposed spine equally. Others, if they'd noticed its disheveled state, might have seen the notebook as a type of condemnation, a confession of work unfinished. The eight years he'd spent filling its pages were totally worthwhile, every day and every sentence he'd written, every character he created and spirited thought he'd had. A year after buying the notebook, he'd had a small tattoo inked into his upper arm at Camden Market: *TboTA, 25.8.11—The Book of the Ark,* and the date he'd started the novel. A space for the finishing date left vacant.

He'd formed the idea for the novel during his time at Brunel, though his degree had been in journalism. He refused to take creative writing because what were the odds of being an author versus the odds of finding work at a mainstream paper? Exactly. Even so, stories and characters flooded him, and while they never steered him toward writing the book itself, he always gave them space, made them welcome. Markriss began separating notebooks, one for articles and nonfiction, the other for poetry and prose. When he learned he was inept at poetry, he concentrated further on fiction. He would write anything that came to mind, from one-line ideas to fully formed outlines. He'd cut pictures and quotes from magazines, pressing them tight against lined paper with Pritt Stick, smoothing down bumps.

As his studies went on, however, his imaginative bent lessened. And then around that time, stemming from nothing more than an uncomfortable bout of sleep paralysis, where he woke feeling that he couldn't breathe, couldn't move his body, couldn't even scream for help even though no one was there to hear him, he'd felt the odd sensation of being lifted from his body so he could view himself from above. It first happened in a tiny hostel room he'd managed to worm his way into on the recommendation of an ex-girlfriend, Raymeda. Although she'd kicked him out of her own hostel room after they split, she'd taken him to her housing project and had him put on their books. Markriss could never thank her enough, though it was years since they'd last spoken. His hostel had a single bed, a narrow white wardrobe, a chest of drawers at the foot of the bed, one chair, and that was it. In that first episode of paralysis, from his ceiling-high vantage point, he'd seen a figure perched on the chair edge, leaning over the bed as if whispering into his ear. Hooded from head to ankles, he couldn't make out their face. The figure spoke in a clogged, guttural language that sounded like choking.

His vision frightened the paralysis from him, and he awoke.

Markriss didn't believe what he'd dreamed was real, and yet the image remained in his memory. He'd torn the plastic cover from a fresh notebook and wrote the experience down before he had fully woken up. For the following seven years, he was visited by regular dream fragments and episodes of a story that unfortunately never quite formulated into a whole. The oddest thing about it was—unlike

when he normally wrote—he didn't really care if he finished the
novel or not. It was the enjoyment of his self-imagined world that
was the pleasure, not the idea of writing, or even completing a serious
work. When the time was right, he told himself, the book would
come. And so he wrote his visions as they arrived, whenever that
was—an alternate world, a city composed of a building that housed
a population of millions within its walls. Gateways and terraces, the
poor and rich separated by clearly defined zones, his characters'
names stolen from actual people he knew. It was gratifying, a means
of easing the tension in his shoulders, and he wrote for hours at a
time, as he had that morning, head down, teeth biting lower lip,
striving to put images that danced beyond mental reach onto the
page. He searched the Net for stimuli, Blu-Tacked findings onto the
wall above his desk. Schwimbeck's *My Dream, My Bad Dream* was
most prominent, although he couldn't let his eyes rest on the painting
often, as it was too close a representation of what he'd experienced,
and he avoided it as much as he could.

This morning, Markriss felt compelled to write the outline of a
scene he'd dreamed, set outside the barriers of a huge gateway to his
imaginary world. Where it went, he didn't know. Markriss hadn't
imagined that far. He only saw five friends, hands joined, all facing
down an armed militia. He wrote of a black dog, struggling with a
maddening sense of déjà vu that made him unable to separate whether
the animal had haunted his dreams, or existed in a reality that had
taken place at some earlier point of his life. By the time he finished
his notes, Markriss felt good about what he'd done. It was six a.m.
He needed a shower. Within the hour, he would leave for work.

He had been granted fourteen days' leave from the *Warrington
Ark* after his last big piece, an exposé of a community-based youth
center funded by local government, which his investigations proved
had misappropriated funds. The center owner and selected staff
members had given themselves lavish salaries and an abundance of
material perks: cars, mortgage payments, holidays abroad. Grants
meant for the center's use had been diverted into a number of personal
bank accounts. No fortunes were made, though people lived much
better than the average worker of their status. That story resulted in

further articles being commissioned on the topic, as well as a handful of anonymous people making contact with Markriss, threatening to kill him. Though he didn't take the threats seriously, his senior editor, mindful of Markriss's ongoing mental health and well-being, advised he take a fortnight's leave to get back up to speed, after a three-month run of late shifts and weekenders. While Markriss appreciated her care and attention, the truth was that after a few days he missed the office. He suggested a compromise, which she agreed to: though he could work from home, Markriss would attend their daily meetings when he wished.

He traveled to Holborn by bus and tube early enough to avoid rush hour, and spent the journey scrolling between Twitter, Facebook, Insta, even Myspace, making notes on his phone, double-tapping between windows. Labour leader Jeremy Corbyn claimed to have produced a sheaf of documents proving the current government intended to sell off the NHS following Brexit. Nationally it was no wetter than normal, although Watnall, Sheffield, and Scampton were on course for their wettest November ever. The Conservatives were embroiled in a row with Channel 4 after the PM hadn't turned up for a live debate on climate change attended by all four leaders of the major political parties, causing the broadcaster to televise an empty seat. A study found young people became panicked if denied their mobile phones.

When Markriss arrived at the office, a cheery, tired-eyed receptionist waived his bag check, giving him a nod and smile. He took the stairs rather than the lift, as he needed the exercise, although he was puffing and overheated when he reached their floor. The office was an open-plan, low-level maze of gray desks, black phones, and glistening Macs. When he looked into the office of the building directly opposite, it was the mirror image. Markriss had no idea what they did.

He waved hellos at his coworkers, who wandered the floor with glazed demeanors, whether starting their shift or about to leave. Markriss flopped into his regular desk space. He was well known enough for his usual desk to be left free, mostly; as they hot-desked, there were occasions when he arrived to find a warm body and back of neck on show, typing with stubborn fury. Somayina, his next-door colleague, who'd been frowning at his screen, looked up.

"Oi, oi."

"Morning, brother." They slapped hands. "Ready and set?"

"I am. Not sure why you're in though."

"Just thought I'd pop by, is all," Markriss said, booting up the Mac.

Somayina blinked once, staring. "You got to be kidding me."

"What?"

"If you're here because of why I think you are—when you've got nothing on deadline, nothing to produce come nine—I'm seriously worried about you, mate. Seriously."

"Carry on, yeah?" Markriss said, swiveling toward his screen. A long silence followed. Then the static clatter of keys from Somayina's desk, building up velocity, white noise so loud it penetrated thought, drowning self-accusation along with conscious knowledge. If he heard work, he would think work, surely.

Their daily news meeting took place at nine a.m. to the second, as usual. Somayina had been right: Markriss had nothing to bring to attention, therefore no actual reason to be there, especially as he was technically on leave. His phone double-buzzed as people began to arrive for the meeting, turning chairs around from nearby desk spaces, or grabbing at empty ones, pushing them closer to form a rough circle, so he managed to avoid the quizzical glances and swapped looks between colleagues by focusing on his screen.

Nesta: Finish @ UCL around 4. Wanna link?

He typed a quick thumbs-up, pushing his phone into a pocket. When he looked up, a cluster of faces stared into his. Somayina, who'd spun his custom, red-woven office chair to face the rest of the news team. His senior editor, Maxine. Nadine, Teresa, Robert, Ed, Frankie, Roger, Keshni.

Chileshe had found a place to look over his shoulder, somewhere out of the expansive windows, even though he tried smiling at her. Glasses perched on her forehead, eyes narrow, she squinted past him.

"Riss," Maxine said, level-voiced despite her obvious surprise, cradling a wafer slab of iPad. A short-cropped, elfin brunette with high cheekbones, she wore a loose-fitting, navy-striped jumpsuit. Straight-talking, lighthearted, everyone on staff loved her. "We didn't expect you this morning."

"Hey, Maxine. Everyone all right?"

He waved a noncommittal hand. Maxine looked at him for a few more seconds, clearly wondering if he was going to give a reason for being in. Markriss had the feel of cold air against skin, the subtle despair of rising goose bumps.

"Okay, let's see what you've got," she said, turning to the others.

They went around the circle, pitching stories. Keshni wanted to run a general piece on the royals, a follow-up on the aftermath of the Epstein scandal. Maxine didn't seem too keen, urging her to think about the legal ramifications; she didn't want to go there. Keshni nodding, writing quickly, took the note. Somayina had found another Grenfell fire story in which a man had pretended to be a squatter in the tower block, when he actually lived in Cheshire. Maxine knew the story; it had been picked up by the BBC. She gave it a green light. Roger pitched an international piece on a former US journalist and his wife running a gay porn empire. That prompted laughter, and ten minutes' chat. The story also got a go. Markriss gave a half-hearted, strung-together pitch about racism in football, including a summary of verbally abused players and their matches alongside the testimonies of a handful of Black supporters, how they felt about attending games where abuse was rife. Surprisingly, the story piqued Maxine's interest. He received the nod to write it up, a one p.m. deadline.

He couldn't help a look at Chileshe, pleased. Work had won out, even if he did have to wing it. He'd been hoping that, as senior video producer, she'd be assigned to film content that would help bolster his story, only to see her farmed out to Robert, who'd pitched an office workers' poll for the general election that involved digitally recorded lunch-hour street interviews. As the meeting drew to a close, Markriss sat back, aware of an undeniable sting, looking down at his clasped hands, opening phrases and concluding paragraphs for his article swimming before his eyes. Chatter rose about him. He remained seated, resisting the urge to join in. Work, it would have to be.

As Nesta had moved south not long after finishing university, Markriss agreed to travel into Brixton a few hours after he filed copy. That meant tackling the rush-hour commute, which he normally avoided and actually thought he had, until he remembered Thursday was the new Friday, and the big squeeze on buses and tubes began two hours early. At Oxford Circus, he waited for a train among a crowd so dense two southbound trains passed before he could board, locating a position just inside the single carriage door, back against glass, fellow travelers pressed around him. At the following station, Green Park, a man on the platform began to shout as soon as the doors opened.

"Budge up, you lot, make room!"

There wasn't space to turn and see him. A push of bodies rippled toward him as the speaker edged inside, over his shoulder.

"Come on, mate, move up a bit."

Close in his ear, spitting.

"There isn't room to."

It was true. A woman in a camel coat and hijab was so near, he saw his breath ruffle strands of cotton on her arm. Behind him, the man kept pushing. Someone stumbled, gasped.

"Yeah there is, go on."

Markriss squeezed his eyes closed. When he heard doors shut and the train start to move, he opened them. The commuter who had been in front of him had edged farther down the carriage, and a reasonably tall man, square-cropped hair, thin unshaven face, and translucent glasses covering pale-blue eyes, had taken their place, glaring.

"See, told you. If you'd moved your arse there would've been room, wouldn't there?"

He held the man's eye, saying nothing.

"What? What?"

Markriss turned the other way, looking down the carriage as they rocked like bobbing ducks. A brunette woman beneath the pusher's armpit set her gaze in that direction. He couldn't tell if they were together, or she was just unfortunate enough to be standing next to him.

"Thank you," she said, voice low.

"You're welcome," Markriss replied.

Pusher colored, became jittery, bit his lip. Silence, until their destination.

Brixton, alive with crisp air and brilliant lights, drums and the smell of good cooking, was its expected sensory explosion when he trotted up the steps and into evening. He weaved along the busy main thoroughfare, as always filled with people and buses arriving or leaving, families shopping and men playing steel pan outside Iceland, others selling incense and oils. He walked south and crossed at the lights to arrive at the relatively still oasis that was Windrush Square, scattered with people, composed of an entirely separate atmosphere to the street two lanes of traffic and yards away.

Across the square was the aqua-green bust of Sir Henry Tate, the philanthropist who had gifted the Tate Library to Lambeth, a building that later became Brixton Library. Tate's business of refined sugar had been built on the trade of human beings kidnapped from Africa and brought forcibly to the "New World." Although Tate was only fourteen when the Slavery Abolition Act passed, and his business partner Abram Lyle only twelve, the raw sugar imported by their company originated from estates established on the enslavement of Markriss's ancestors. At the time of Tate & Lyle's dominance, those same sugar plantations were worked by impoverished wage laborers and indentured labor across the Caribbean islands. Many works of art in Tate's galleries were given by or associated with benefactors who were owners of the enslaved, or had made their wealth from the trade. Markriss had written an opinion piece on the subject years before, attempting to track injustices of the past to inequalities of the present day. It received such a negative response from the general public, the comments section was shut down within the hour.

He angled for the bloodred light of the Ritzy Cinema. He leaned his shoulder against heavy doors, saw a raised hand of greeting, and there was Nesta, waving from a corner table.

"How you doing?" he said, standing to greet Markriss. His friend was dressed halfway between smart and casual: blue jeans, black loafers, a crisp white shirt and beige corduroy blazer. Locks tied back with an assortment of multicolored rubber bands, he looked postteen rather than his actual late twenties. "I set you up already."

Following his gesture, Markriss saw a weeping green bottle. "Cheers, man. You been home, or come straight from work?"

"From work. Had to, classes all day. Fucking nightmare."

"Tell me about it. The tube's murder at this time."

"Ah, yeah, course. Sorry about that. I walked from Gower Street to Russell Square and took the bus. It's slower, much more sedate."

"I could take that."

They grinned, Markriss thumbing the menu. The bar area was brightly lit, every spare inch filled with tables, nearly all full. Predictably, soft-volume reggae played above their heads, Sizzla's *Black Woman & Child*. The obligatory laptop owners bashed away in hunched frenzies, faces pale with screen light, phones and brown-rimmed coffee cups at their elbows. A family of mum, dad, and two school-age boys finished up their dinner, sipping tall glasses of hot chocolate. A few well-put-together, well-matched couples dotted around the room seemed on Tinder dates. They barely spoke, and spent a lot of time checking their phones, scrolling with an offhand finger. Markriss had had a few like that. Two beautiful young women, early twenties, sat near the red swing doors side by side, all pouts, figure-fitting clothes and glowing weaves, taking selfies.

"What are we like, eh? As a human race?"

Nesta followed his sight line, laughing. "There is something about their focus I can admire."

"If only that could be harnessed to find the cure for cancer."

"If only. You eating?"

"Yeah. I'll order in a bit." He laid his hands on imitation wood, sighed. "So. What's going on?"

Shrugging, scanning the room. "Not much. Busy, busy. I'm missing Corbyn's interview with Andrew Neil for you, I'll have you know."

"Oh shit, totally forgot."

"You, my friend, should never forget that."

"I know, I know. I actually think I'm trying to avoid the whole thing. Stupid, yes, seeing as I don't have a snowball's chance. If we get Johnson—"

"C'mon, man, why say that?"

"I say that cos Black people are voting for him. People of color are voting for him, so they say."

"Don't remind me."

"I'll leave the flipping country if they win, I swear. My job, I can do it anyplace. I'll rent out my flat on the sly and go back home. Drink rum and work remotely."

"The dream."

Nesta raised his short glass. Dark liquid and ice sloshed. Rum drinking had already started for his friend, from what Markriss could tell.

"To the dream."

They toasted, glass clinked.

"Can you imagine? Four more years?"

Markriss put two fingers to his temple, made a trigger of his thumb.

"Anyway. Think cheery thoughts. How are things with you-know-who?" Nesta beamed, untying his locks.

"Ah, come on. That's unfair."

"How so? Telling me there's been no developments? Or you don't want to talk about it?"

"Amen to both," Markriss said.

"You can't be serious. The whole reason I'm here instead of home marking essays and getting set to watch Corbyn versus Neil, is you, Chile, the whole love-triangle thing."

"No way. I definitely do *not* want to talk about that."

"Wow, bro. You really got it bad."

"I'm gonna go order. What d'you want?" He stood.

Nesta patted his pockets, belly-laughing. "All right, all right. Get me a grilled mackerel, yeah?"

"Safe, don't worry yourself, I'll get it. In a bit."

Leaving Nesta chuckling, Markriss joined the queue beneath a sign that stated the obvious: *BAR*. He raised his chin, fidgeting, spinning a debit card between his thumb and first finger. He did not want to think about the feel of her hip beneath his fingers. The soft tickle of hair against his chin.

He exhaled, resigned, and when it was his turn to order, mumbled for a chicken-and-avocado burger, Nesta's mackerel with fries, and two more drinks without making eye contact with the bar staff. Sometimes it was better that way. After receiving his drinks and table number, he tapped his contactless and went back to the table.

Nesta rolled the short glass between his hands, gazing at them. Markriss turned sideways to avoid a customer heading for the bar, and set the fresh rum before him.

"Save us getting up again."

"Ah, nice one."

"No problem, bro."

He sat. Nesta half looked up, a mischievous gleam in his eye. The volume of the bar area had risen a good few decibels. A film had ended, its audience flooding the space; Markriss wondered if *Joker* was still showing.

"All right, so we won't talk about Chileshe. Wanna hear what I lectured today instead?"

"Sure. Go for it."

"You'll be proud of me, I swear. So I was teaching my students the theory of inflation. That's the idea that space isn't just bigger than what we see, which is obvious I suppose. But it's actually infinite, right?"

"Yeah, that's what I thought."

"Exactly. It's what everyone thinks they know. Now try to imagine the implications of that a moment—space and time is so huge, basic probability suggests there are infinite alternative versions of this country, this city, that exist in other universal bubbles, solar systems, and planets. Which means there could also be infinite versions of ourselves."

"Okay. So, like, parallel universes?"

"Yes, that's it."

Markriss blocked a smile by putting his bottle to his lips, drinking.

"Don't make that face. And don't make me start on eternal inflation."

"I would never."

"Good. Cos it would fry your brain, which is why I never inflict it on my poor, addled undergrads. We talk about the microcosmos and theories of quantum mechanics instead."

"Lucky old me."

"Our theory of the microcosmos works on the principle that multiple particles can exist in the same place, at the same time. We know this to be true, because we've run tests where it's happened. As long as we have machines to check the results, it's all good. The only thing that changes the experiment is us, looking at them. That's when the particles sort themselves out and we only see one, in one place. Physicists get excited about that experiment because for some of us it means the possibility exists, theoretically of course, that humans can also exist in simultaneous spaces, or overlapping realities, at the same time. I can be here, or on a beach in Negril, or at my grand-mother's house in Brooklyn, or at work—"

"Or at home watching Corbyn versus Neil . . ."

"Precisely. Quantum mechanics posits that we can be in all those places and millions more at once. Wild, right?"

"And reassuring. For multiple baby fathers at least."

"You're winding me up, I appreciate that. But you can't. This is too good for that. Here's the thing, and then I'll shut up about it, I promise. We create these parallel worlds by observation. When we see a particle, we choose whether it exists on the left or right. Or maybe it chooses us, I don't know. Anyway, even though we're certain both realities exist at once because we've run the tests that prove it, it's our sole perspective that makes a choice about which viewpoint is dominant. So the remaining particle is there, somewhere, even if we can't see it. It exists. We just don't know where *there* is."

Markriss slumped, head resting on his hand, for a good long minute. The noise of cinemagoers had faded. Many had left, while others sat, quietly discussing what they'd seen.

"This is why we never talk about your work. Didn't we make a pact or something?" He paused, took another swig of beer. "What do your students think?"

Nesta placed two fingers at his temple, pulled the thumb trigger. They laughed.

"It's the same whenever I lecture on this. That's when I show them this BBC documentary I dredged up, which happens to be the easiest way to explain it I know. You'll like it too, being a writer and all. It says: think of a story in a book, or an article, maybe one of yours. There are many copies of that book, or article. How many stories?"

"One," Markriss said. He smiled again, different this time. "Okay, I like that. And I kind of think I get it. But your original point is?"

Nesta made an expression of acute dissatisfaction. "Don't teach astrophysics, obviously."

Bellowed laughter. "Oh, come on!"

"All right, as you insist. I haven't one really, more's the pity. Other than the fact you can rest assured, if you believe a word of what I've said, that somewhere in the multiverse, Labour's won, the trains are empty, and you've got where you wanted ever since the-one-we-shall-not-name first started at your work. Out there, infinite probability allows that at least one version of us is living the life we want, in the here and now."

Nesta held up both hands to prove he was indeed finished, shrugged, and sat back. A slim waitress arrived at the table cradling white plates, singsonging their food orders.

When they'd eaten Nesta wanted a smoke, so they went out into the cold, letting red doors slam in their wake. The beautiful young women were still taking snapshots of themselves with their phones, striking poses, ignoring each other. On the square, the pavement was furred with evening frost. The bulk of a leafless plane tree loomed above the surrounding buildings like the skeleton of a giant placed among autumnal darkness and light. Local old boys and young hustlers sat on chairs and the stone-gray semicircle outside Brixton Library, weed smoke emanating from their fevered conversations. A block to the south, the delicate lights of the BCA spread warmth onto the grass and pathways before it.

Nesta fired up his vape, took a deep drag, blew skyward. "Gotta stop."

"Keep telling yourself that."

"Truthfully. These people at work are bad influences."

"I hear that."

An erupting siren. The police vehicle maneuvering around traffic, finding a clear path, powering up Brixton Hill.

Nesta puffed, considering Markriss. "How you doing anyway?"

He shrugged, studying his feet.

"You looked at those people I told you about?"

"No." Markriss kicked at nothing. "I'm not sure I'm ready."

"You should talk to someone, Riss. A qualified someone, I mean. I'm here for you, man, whenever you need, but I don't have those tools. I'm worried about you, if I'm honest."

"I appreciate that."

"Seriously."

Before he was aware of the fact, Nesta had turned, was hugging him. His chin bumped his friend's shoulder. Corduroy rubbed his cheek, he smelled the remnants of morning aftershave, musky and Eastern, mixed with the familiar mango flavoring of vape smoke. Nesta rubbed his back with a solid hand, whispering sentences he could barely hear. Pressed so tight it verged on hurt. He wasn't sure what to make of it all. He was slightly embarrassed, that was true, though heartened by the knowledge Nesta wasn't. He realized how long it had been since he'd been hugged in any way that wasn't perfunctory, meaningless, or fraught with consequence. Loneliness struck him, icicle-clear and precise.

They let go. Nesta held his elbow, looked into his eyes. A double buzz in Markriss's pocket. He ignored it.

"Whatever you need. Okay?"

"Thanks, Ness. That means a lot, swear down."

Nesta placed a hand on his own heart, staring at him. The serious expression he adopted almost made Markriss laugh. He stiffened his jaw and kept his composure. Mango smoke drifted into his face.

He heard snuffling, felt a soft object tickle his ankles, Nesta chuckling miniature clouds of smoke. When Markriss looked down a dog was sniffing his feet, tail wagging, head whipping left to right, frantic and panting. At that moment it stood on hind legs, half bounding up his thighs to greet him. Short gloss-black fur reflecting sodium lights. Due to its uncommon length and fox-like features, he was unsure of the breed, the type of dog he usually just called "dog." He backed a step away, only partially reassured by the red lead at its collar and the sight of the dog's owner, a bespectacled, graying African man in a large, disheveled Nike jacket, tracksuit bottoms, and too-huge sneakers.

"Whoa . . . Hey there . . ."

"I'm so sorry," the owner said. He was well spoken, a voice entirely at odds with his appearance. "She's a bit hyper, super friendly though. Anu! Anu! Leave him alone!"

"Lovely dog. Beautiful color," Nesta said.

"Yeah. She's lovely," Markriss added through clenched teeth.

The man burst into laughter. "Anu's not like this with everyone, truthfully. She's obviously taken a shine. Anu! Anu, stop!"

"It's okay. I'm fine with dogs. Good girl. Good girl." He kneeled, ruffling her back, pushing long, firm strokes from neck to hindquarters. Anu tried to lick his face. Markriss wasn't having that. Hot breath caressed his cheeks. "No, no, no. That's a nice name, where's it come from?"

"It's Greek. Short for Anubis, Egyptian god of the afterlife. She reminded me of it, somehow."

"Very cool." Markriss got to his feet, offering a hand. "Markriss. Most people shorten it to Riss."

"Ra," the older man said, shaking his hand and turning at once to Nesta, who shook too. Beneath them Anu whimpered, a high-pitched keening.

"Egyptian too, right? Your name?"

"Yes, it is. My family are from Aswan, they were into that type of thing. Ancient myths, whatnot." He paused, peering at both men. "Can I ask you something? Have I met you gentlemen before?"

"Shouldn't think so." Markriss looked at Nesta.

"I live round here, so you might've seen me in the Village, or drinking in the Effra," Nesta said.

"No, no, no. It's not that." Ra shook his head, pulling at the lead. "Strangest thing. Never mind. You both have a good evening, hear?"

"You too!" they chimed, watching the dog. It strained the lead taut as tightrope, seemingly trying to get back to Markriss all the way past the library, adjacent to the stone semicircle, not even giving up when Ra turned the first corner onto Rushcroft Road. They disappeared.

"Odd bloke," Nesta said, finding a pocket for his vape.

"Proper odd," Markriss agreed.

They reached for the doors and went inside.

3

It turned out the buzz in his pocket was a message from Keshni that Markriss didn't see until he reached home. He sat on his bed with a mug of peppermint tea and brown-eyed disks of chocolate biscuits on a side plate, reading with no lights, even though it gave him headaches.

> **Keshni Roberts:** *Hey u, hope u feeling better after your gong treatment? It was really nice having u over. Me and C wondered if you'd like to pop to ours for dinner and drinks Friday 29th. Let us know if u free . . . Kxx*

He reread the message for the next few minutes, unsure how to respond. He wasn't certain if he wanted that, or whether it would be good for him, given his current state of vulnerability. If he could stand a night of looking into Chileshe's eyes and seeing hurt. Raw, open flesh sprung to mind, vivid and sore. Still, the fear of what might happen between them if he didn't accept was as crippling as the discomfort he'd most likely undergo if he did. He continued to read the message over, trying to look beyond words in an attempt to glean deeper meaning and decipher what they wanted, until his eyes hurt, his forehead throbbed. He leaned over, switching on the bedside light. Typed "Sure Rx." Lay on his back, trying not to convince himself he'd made a bigger mistake than the first, which had started it all.

He'd done his best to make sure it hadn't happened that way. When Chileshe first joined their news team he'd played it very casual, even though he didn't feel like that inside. She'd been crossing the office floor to talk with Somayina about an interview they were assigned, and when he saw her there was a feeling of lift, a moment where he became aware of a noticeable leap from his chest to his throat. While she walked not two feet away, not even seeing him, his mouth hung open and his eyes would not stop trying to take her all in.

He listened to her talk. Everything about her seemed to light his nerves. The way she formed vowels, mouth and depressed tongue emphasizing sounds. The faint smell he picked up, not perfume or detergent lingering on clothes, rather the scent of her. Flowery, powdered stuff, like incense. Her confident, slightly nerdy laughter, her braids, thick sweatshirts, and crappy jeans, her dark-rimmed glasses. He bent his head lower, trying to concentrate on what he typed while his heart thumped loud in his ears. He tutted to himself, whispering under his breath that he should get a grip, even while he was unable to follow his own order. When Chileshe left Somayina's desk and passed by his, she looked down at him, said hi. Markriss only just managed to raise a hand in reply. She smiled; he felt her pity. Like a woman overly familiar with the emotion she roused in others. She walked away.

"Eh-eh," Somayina grinned. "Put your tongue away, bro! Cleaners ain't gonna sweep the floor till late shift."

"Joker," Markriss shot back, knowing he'd been truly caught when Somayina wouldn't stop laughing. He hadn't known he was that obvious.

Over the next few months he tried to rein himself in, and found it no good. It was blatant. Everybody knew. When he talked to Chileshe, fire burned under his skin and the thump in his chest was like house-music drums or something, as if he were raving or the rave was inside him. The whole office saw, and that made him feel worse. He'd never considered himself someone who didn't know how to hold a conversation; they normally happened naturally, especially with women. He didn't need chat-up lines, one-liners, or jokes. He'd just talk and everything fell into place naturally—the next thing he knew, he would be dating. With Chileshe it was different. She had some inner core that made him stutter whenever they fell into conversation, and he couldn't look her in the eye. Perhaps it was her spiritual beliefs, the time she spent learning meditation, yoga, African cosmology, and all. She rarely spoke of it, though he saw her commitment from the red, gold, and green wooden bracelets and pendants she wore, the heavily wrought silver earrings. One day she came to the office wearing a black-and-white T-shirt bearing the slogan "Roots Before Branches." She wasn't a hotep, that was for sure, though she was woke.

Given time, they were thrown together for assignments, and as he got to know her Markriss discovered how cool Chileshe really was. First, she was brilliant at her job. Her videos were competent, her photos like forgotten dreams. She brought the best out of portraits, her subjects rendered in precise detail with a spectacular eye for their inner beauty. Her landscapes were stunning and epic, all wonderfully composed, even when she simply pointed the camera and shot. Markriss never understood how she managed to find that right moment, and click. It wasn't simple luck; it happened too often for that. And when he began to talk about her work, Internet-stalked her site, then came back to her in awe at what she'd created, they talked about her inspirations, the artists she loved and films she'd seen. He mentioned the names of his favorite films, so they decided to see a movie together, then hung in the foyer talking for almost an hour, and finally, despite his nerves, everything fell into place organically, like normal. They became friends.

They'd go to literary and visual-arts launches. Hang out on Sundays at the South Bank. Trawl Portobello Market, Chile wandering stalls in search of the best secondhand clothes, Markriss guessing the origin of her dated 501s. She'd crash out on his sofa, wake halfway through the night, and leave in a sleepy hurry for the night 52. Before she woke, he'd watch her curled up and know that that time would come, hating himself: he was in fucking love. Much as he tried to stem that awful thing, to be the person she wanted from him, a good and loyal friend, it was there. A cancer lodged within his deepest flesh.

Because, of course, there was Keshni. Everybody knew that too, had from the very start. Even him. He'd known and pretended not to. Office gossip was office gossip, he supposed, and so it was no secret that Keshni and Chileshe were in a relationship. Partners. Living together. Married. Yes, he could admit that. It was the reason Chileshe left her old job and joined the paper, to spend more time with her woman. And he had unflinching love and respect for Keshni too. She was beautiful, giving, one of the most ideologically distinct people he'd ever known. They'd worked together for three years and she was the journalist he respected most out of everyone he'd met, at any paper. She would be a major writer one day, Markriss knew that. Novels, stories, nonfiction, film, plays, poetry, Keshni did it all. She was an open soul, a latent genius. What's more, she didn't ever seem to mind how close he and Chileshe were. She actively encouraged them to spend more time, joining them on occasion, most often not. Keshni was from a big, wealthy family. She had an ample amount of friends, was always busy. People loved her; it was as if she was not so much distracted as fully able to lead her own life. Markriss found it refreshing to see two people so in love who managed their separate lives so well.

And yet he couldn't stop emotion from gaining force inside him, drawing his lower body to earth.

They'd gone to watch *The Last Tree* at Picturehouse Central almost a month previous, leaving the auditorium busy with sparking thoughts and perspectives. In the first-floor bar, they'd talked it over. Markriss got the drinks, bottled cider for her, beer for him. It was Saturday night, quite late. The music was loud, the clientele boisterous. Keshni was in France, in a farmhouse just outside Avignon for a poetry retreat, and Chileshe had no need to hurry back to the flat. He'd waited at the counter for his drink order, flushed with good feeling about what they'd seen, of being in the company of someone who understood the significance of it, a general feel of rightness in his bones. If he'd been paying more attention he would have known attraction played a major part. Yet he wanted to be centered without the need to question or analyze. If struck by any inkling or urge to examine his emotions, he pushed it away.

He'd brought back their drinks, dumping them on the table. Chileshe was already leaned forward, speaking before he even settled.

"I feel seen!" she beamed, arms thrown wide. They laughed so loudly, propping each other up, rowdy drinkers looked over.

"I've not gone through anything near what Femi had, but I know what you mean," Markriss said.

"No, me neither, it's just to see ourselves well lit—"

"Hear our voices—"

"See our streets, places we know—"

"It's a mood, right? I hadn't realized how much I missed it, till it was there."

She beamed. "Tell me about it."

They talked more about the film and its commonalities with their lives, before digressing into personal sharing, things rarely said, well-buried instances. Markriss told of the time he'd witnessed a racist attack as a child that resulted in a man being murdered, although he hadn't known it then. It was a road-rage incident between a group of men in a van and a lone driver in the town he'd grown up in, Uxbridge, on the western outskirts of London. They'd pulled him out of the vehicle and beaten him in the middle of the road. Markriss was eight. Chileshe spoke of the night she'd been abused by a family member. She wouldn't say who, though from what she told him, Markriss guessed it was an older cousin. He'd been staying in their house over the weekend, came into her bedroom, and held her down while she slept. They talked about the frequency of those bitter life experiences in others they had met. The depiction of trauma in art, whether it was necessary for the work, or if it was possible to create without it. They hugged, Markriss feeling damp against his temple. He swallowed his emotion, many times. He wasn't sure what he could do to help either of them, and perversely, he wanted to remain in the cinema forever.

At Piccadilly Circus, lit by the brilliant allure of the underground rotunda, they hugged again, for a long while. Markriss heard a thousand footsteps about him. Breathed traffic and her scent. The roar of a bus and the mix of unrecognizable languages swelled inside him. They rubbed cheeks against each other. Nuzzled. The cider of her exhale. The irritation of her cotton scarf. A soft corner of a mouth, a beginning. Their lips touched. Parted. They accepted each other, using all the time they needed, Chile allowing a knee to slip between his. Hands firm on his waist. Markriss swore the building above them and the circus beyond fell away, became cardboard, until they were standing on a street of yellow-brick terraced houses, flat-roofed, square blocks replicating themselves forever. Obscure light bathed them blue. His eyes were closed, and so later he wasn't sure how he'd seen anything at all. Nothing around him, apart from Chileshe, was recognizable.

She pulled away. He was returned among pedestrians and smog.

It was wrong, both were aware of that mundane truth when their eyes opened. Not that it felt wrong, it hadn't. It was almost too good, everything lost but the feeling they'd created. Her head was low, though she reached for him, caressing the place beside his ear, trailing down his lower jaw. Stayed. He put his hand over hers, rubbing her knuckles.

"It's okay," he said. "Don't worry about it, or me. Please don't."

She nodded, held his eye, couldn't keep it. Dropped her gaze once again. Dropped her hand. "I better go."

"Text me when you get in."

"Will do."

Chileshe pushed a smile over her shoulder. Even though he knew he should savor the moment as much as he'd tried to keep the sensation of their kiss, she was gone.

He walked toward the crossing and pushed the silver button, waiting for traffic to pause.

Days after he'd met with Nesta, Markriss lay on a sofa, scrolling Twitter and Insta feeds, when the notification came through. "Breaking: Police are responding to an incident on London Bridge after reports of shots being fired."

He jumped to a sitting position. Made a swift check of his laptop;

wire copy had chimed an alert, yet it'd somehow eluded him. Switched his television from a blink of light into a full screen. From what he could tell, there'd been a terrorist attack on London Bridge. A number of people had been stabbed. It wasn't yet discernible if there were any deaths. The attacker had been tackled by members of the public and eventually shot by armed police.

He logged on to PA Media to view what little video footage of the attack there was. His phone beeped with messages from work colleagues, Chileshe and Keshni individually, Willow. His mother sounded frantic. He called to reassure her while simultaneously texting the women to say he still planned to come for dinner, so he probably wasn't paying the greatest attention. *Yes, he was fine, no, he'd been in all day. No, he hadn't been sleeping.* The breaking-news reporter filed copy as he spoke, Markriss reading their boiler-plate with the phone pressed between shoulder and ear. He touched "End" on the phone's screen and grabbed a shower. He spent a further two hours watching news channels, drinking coffee, and checking the breaker before he put on clothes to brave the preweekend rush.

It actually wasn't that bad, and he reached Pimlico about ten minutes later than usual. Keshni let him in. She wore one of her usual flowing, formless dresses, a low-neck, deep-purple tie-dye that fell to her slim ankles. Her light-red hair was tied in a bandanna of the same color and material—she could've just stepped off a beach in Petit Carenage. They hugged, or rather she hugged him, Markriss awkward, hands full with a bottle of Tesco prosecco in one hand, own-brand apple crumble in the other. She pressed her cheek against his for what felt like forever. Kissed both sides. He couldn't help feeling weird.

And then he was met by the solid warmth of central heating, trying not to look for Chileshe, even though it was impossible. She was poised before the oven, wearing oversize gloves like mittens, peering into the living room at their slim TV, tuned to BBC 24, the London Bridge incident. He saw the images he'd watched in his own home: suited men and women, the dark bulk of armed police, a fire extinguisher, an improbable narwhal tusk. Chileshe, in the process of extracting small tinfoil parcels set in neat formation on a baking tray, used their equally full hands as reason not to give her usual embrace and twin European kisses. She wore her faded jeans, a nondescript yet sparkly blue-and-purple sweatshirt. They kept meters apart, seeming hardly to register the other's presence. Markriss settled for finding the American fridge, putting his offerings where there was space, trying to stay upbeat. He'd changed everything. It was entirely his fault.

"Another, for God's sake! The selfsame place, I'm telling you!" Keshni said loud, placing cutlery in pairs along the table.

"Yeah, well, I'm worried about all the brothers out there labeled 'terror suspects' who're just going corner shop for a pint of milk!" Chileshe slammed a baking tray onto the oven top and removed her gloves. "*This* is a dangerous precedent. Watch the Tories now."

Keshni angled herself toward Markriss, eyes full and waiting.

"I'm surprised they didn't call you to go down there," he told Chileshe, feeling his lack of vocal power, standing. She ignored him.

"They did." Keshni shrugged. "She turned it down. It'd be too late, be done before she even got there."

"Oh. They didn't call me."

"They wouldn't—surely you're too senior?"

He said no more, noticing that Keshni saw his discomfort from clear across the room.

"Hey, you know what? Have you seen the McQueen exhibition?" Keshni asked.

Chileshe stiffened, bug-eyed with shock; she looked pale, a marionette in Levi's and box braids. It stunned him, making him unsure what to say next.

"No, I haven't actually," he said, aiming his reply at Chileshe.

"*Oh*, we should go, it's only over the road. Dinner can wait. It won't take half an hour, what d'you reckon?"

Markriss shrugged at the table. "Sure."

Outside, the women walked arm in arm. By keeping level with both, Markriss almost convinced himself they were all just work friends, out for a simple evening stroll. They crossed the busy Vauxhall

Bridge Road, so many cars and buses the traffic was slow-moving sheet ice, pedestrians weaving through vehicles, mindful of the odd motorcyclist, bike courier, or scooter. A walk between tawny pub windows and a sleepy Thai massage/beauty boutique onto quieter roads, around corners, hurrying to escape the cold, and there it was: the hulking mass of Tate Britain.

The gallery was a bustle of jostling bodies, many more than he'd imagined on a Friday evening. A wealth of languages he couldn't place, swollen North Face jackets and woolen hats, pushy kids. Hi-vis-clad, nervy security guards, rapid-moving Tate staff. They made for the Duveen Galleries, Markriss already isolated, the women resting their heads against each other, talking low. So close there was barely space between them. They swerved, straightening, hardly conscious of their surroundings.

The exhibition comprised 3,128 photos of every Year 3 class in London, from pupil-referral units to state schools, a means of capturing that pivotal moment in their development, the children's eighth year. Class portraits of over 76,000 children were combined into a single gallery installation, and exhibited on advertising hoardings in thirty-three boroughs across the city. Markriss had noticed a few on his daily commute. They always made him smile, thinking of his past.

Entering the space, his initial response was gasped shock. Duveen was a narrow cathedral-like hall with beige marble pillars and white arches, its walls lined with the class portraits, an echo chamber of teachers, teaching assistants, and the proud faces of their charges creating the effect of stained-glass windows for the entire length of the gallery. He peeled off to make his way alone, struck by the unconscious expressions of hope on unblemished faces. Greater than innocence, or new beginnings. Unfathomable, apparent. To see them all—new beings on the verge of the person they would become, forever captured, looming and cinematic—made him blink, eyes smarting.

Vision blurred, he saw a carousel of lustrous movement in place of gallery walls and class photos, light and dark traded in equal measure. The strange sensation of falling he'd felt on the tube returned, only stronger. He couldn't shake a familiar noise, heard from somewhere distant he couldn't place. A whirring bike chain, shushing tires on tarmac. A steady clank of metal rubbing against metal in lazy, circular rhythm.

He came to.

When he turned to one side, there were the women, gazing at images. He swallowed, dry throat clicking, walking to join them. Markriss just about made out Chileshe's expression on her partner's left. Contemplative, searching the immediacy of glossed paper. Keshni's smile was tiny and knowing, a secret. Unnerved by his brief hallucination, unwilling to break their solitude, Markriss stayed to her right.

A class of three rows, wearing uniforms of undeviating navy blue, one teacher in their midst, another to their left. The backdrop, Jesus Christ seated midair, his robe sky-blue, winged archangels afloat on either side.

"So beautiful," Keshni whispered.

"Yeah." He didn't know what else to add.

"I love their little faces. So much going on. Not just happiness, something else . . ." Chileshe broke off, shook her head.

"That's what I thought."

"They're glad to be alive." Keshni's shoulders were hunched. "I remember feeling that way. I'd jump out of my dorm room, raring to grab the day."

"Do you? I don't," Chileshe said. "I hated school."

"I know, babe." Kissing her forehead. "Poor you."

"Might as well gone boarding school, the way it was."

"No way, you would've hated it. I didn't, but it wasn't anything like people make out. *You* were better off where you were."

"Yeah, right."

Another kiss, a squeeze of shoulders. Markriss pushed both fists into his jeans pockets. Spotted a photograph he hadn't yet seen, wandered over.

He'd dragged himself through a fair amount of bad nights out in the past, yet dinner that night with Chileshe and Keshni still ranked close to the worst. Compounded by the fact that it should have been a great evening with two close friends, his mood was a push and pull between elation and, if he was honest, complete misery, which made him wonder why he hadn't called Nesta, or gone to his mother's, anything other than hang out with them. Had he been mad? Had he not fully understood what would happen when he stood before Chileshe and the feelings she caused did not go away? Surrounded by the evidence of their lives together in photos—bad enough—matched with the actual lived realities of their partnership? Ornaments she had bought while out with Markriss that now inhabited the flat, secure as though they'd always been there. Keshni and Chileshe's moments of fleeting touch, whispered jokes, elbowing each other, exchanging sly grins. Over and above those stabs of jealousy, the fact of his affinity: moments when he forgot that night at Piccadilly Circus, the heady sensation of their bodies crushed together, and fell into easy conversation and quick-fire jokes until he felt self-conscious and caught himself between laughter, staring at her, remembering. Unnoticed by her wife. He had wondered if Chileshe thought it too, and was certain she must: for she fell into awkward silences at times, snatching unconscious looks at Keshni.

"*Oh*, tune! Tune, telling you!"

One finger pointed at low white ceiling, hips a rocking wave, Keshni swayed, sure-footed, free. Markriss and Chileshe, pretending not to notice. Yazmin Lacey, singing of remedy.

Sandalwood oil, a bubbling lava atop a metal burner. Cold white wine, mouthfuls of heaven in saltfish fritters. Rotis and thin gifts of tinfoil parcels opened to reveal baked, seasoned white fish. Pink rice and peas, steamed vegetables, sunset sweet potatoes, chickpeas, and the gentle melting ice of a sorrel glass. The resting bell in a corner of the room, tilted on a sky-blue cushion. Experiencing that low vibration as he registered its presence from his place at the dining room table, enveloped in the foods he loved, the music he appreci-ated, and the people he felt close to, even after everything.

They talked work and cultural politics, the general election and art. Music, film, theater. Lively, honest discussion, their converged alignment making things even more difficult. He forgot himself, until he noticed Chileshe receding as the evening went on; she was mostly quiet and he was the cause. She complained of a headache, still he knew. He knew. Perhaps he had been selfish not to think of the after. In his fleeting mind's eye, they worked out some way of seeing things through and no one getting hurt, and yet here, looking across the table, Markriss saw that was ludicrous. They would both be, were this to continue. He had no intention of that. They were too special, not just to him but also the world, to warrant that. If their lives changed for the worse due to his actions, he wouldn't forgive himself.

Chileshe slumped in her chair, eyes red-tinged, half closing. The corners of her mouth turned down. He was struck by an unbidden memory of her sweetness.

"This'll go down as the weirdest election we've ever had, everyone knows it," Keshni said, pouring more sparkling wine from a curvaceous green bottle. When Chileshe held a palm over her glass, she simply removed it, tipping until the contents fizzed.

"Most shambolic, worst for people of color . . ." Chileshe murmured, eyes shut.

"You saw that car-crash interview, right? Corbyn on Neil?"

"At least he had the courage to go on, unlike the PM."

"Is it any wonder things are this bad? With the Scourge of the West in office over the pond, Brexit madness over here?" Markriss sipped from his glass, savoring bubbles.

"It's like some kind of epidemic!"

"Fuck that, they just pulled back the curtains and exposed the wizard's arse," Chileshe sneered, seeming to revive. "Surprise! Racism over here too!"

Bitter laughter, leaned over the table. Slapping palms against the surface, plates and cutlery rattling.

"You lot see the new Burger King ad on the buses?" Keshni open-mouthed, eager. "Picture the King of Burgers. Juicy, succulent, even for us veggies. Caption: *Another Whopper on the side of a bus. Must be an election.*"

Even louder laughter. Keshni wiped at her eyes, shoulders trembling from a giggling fit.

"I mean, whoever does their campaigns is genius."

"Or certifiable," Markriss added, to further chuckles.

"Seriously, though, there's never been a better strategy of divide and rule played on voters, when we should really be coming together against the issues. Anti-Muslim, anti-Sikh, anti-Hindu, anti-Semitic, anti-Black, anti–working class, anti-women, anti-LGBTQI. Anti-disability, anti-NHS. Has there ever been so much shit flying? And we know where it all came from."

"It's always been there, babe."

"Yeah, it's always been there, but don't you think it's stoked up even more of late?"

"It has." Anger tightened Markriss's brow. "And I really think we're too busy looking at each other sideways to see what's happening in our face. It's people like us that's mostly to blame."

"That's what I'm saying. We're to blame because we refuse to take a step back and think, to see how much we're being used."

"Yes, us, us, but also *us*." Using a finger to draw an invisible circle around them all. "The whole media. Papers, television, radio. This race stuff's out there, it already exists, but most misinformation on the subject comes from people with our jobs reporting lies, omitting truths. If those are the voices heard over people like us, the journalists committed to telling real stories, it's no wonder the public don't know what's going on . . ." He shrugged. "You know Britain's ranked thirty-third in the World Press Freedom Index? Says a lot, right?"

They sobered, staring at the table. Markriss waited, refusing to look around, hollow inside. Another black hole he'd created into which conversation fell. Another void, another silence.

"This discussion calls for dessert," Keshni declared, beaming unexpected radiance. "But if we're gonna avoid post-sugar slump getting in the way of what we've really got to say, I think we'll have to wait until we're done."

He frowned, noticing, across the table, Chileshe's rigid countenance return. Her knee bounced fitfully until she saw Markriss watching. She sat up, tried to smile. Couldn't.

"Crumble's in the oven, I set the timer."

"Thanks, babe." Keshni winced. "God, where's the old Dutch courage, eh?" Letting the prosecco bottle roam glasses a second time, hovering, to lift again.

"What's going on?" Markriss asked. "Are you guys okay?"

"Yeah, fine," Chileshe said, only it was certain she wasn't. Her gaze was set beneath the table. Hands clasped, legs still, nervousness expressed by the occasional, fitful twitch of a knee. Keshni leaned over the table, grasping one of Markriss's hands. A million fluttering nerves took flight inside him.

"Riss. You know how much you mean to us, Chi and me both. You're a brilliant friend. You're kind, talented, funny, generous, such a loving spirit. I don't know how we would have managed to cope if you didn't work in the office with us. Every day I come through the door, I'm grateful you're there."

"Oh, man." Swift glances. "This feels like a breakup chat. Is this a breakup chat?"

"Don't be silly! Let me finish, will you, it's tough enough to say as it is."

"Okay." He focused on her fingernails. Slim, gloss-painted. Oyster-shell glazed.

"The reason we're telling you this is because we need you to know how dearly we think of you, Riss. We're so lucky to have you as a friend."

"I'm lucky too," he said, panicking, before he remembered: no talking.

"That's sweet, but you don't have to say it. You don't have to say anything. Now . . ." She cleared her throat. "I don't know if Chi said anything to you before; for the past half a year or so we've been looking into having children of our own."

Stricken, watching her lips move. Feeling Chileshe's eyes.

"And it's a really crazy process, whichever way you look at it, whether you go artificial or natural. Foster or adopt. We had a good talk, and a bit of a discussion this week, and we agreed natural's best for both of us. The other ways . . . Let's just say, it all felt a bit too artificial for me. Us. So, we agreed on that, then we were stuck with another dilemma, and that was who the natural donor would be, if we went that way. Neither of us want some faceless guy from a clinic in Sweden, or Trumpville, USA. We wanted it to be with someone who felt organic to our lives, and hopefully, over time, theirs. Someone who could be around—not to raise them or anything, we'd do all that. But as a presence when they needed it."

His head moved to show he understood, mind racing. He swallowed wine, too much, almost choked. Dry coughed.

"You all right? Okay, good. *So* . . . we were wondering if that person . . . possibly . . . could be you, Riss. You can say no, or tell us if that's really weird," she said quickly. "But if it doesn't freak you out too much, and if you wouldn't mind doing us this honor, we'd love you to be the father of our child. Children. Perhaps."

Keshni took a huge gulp from her glass. She was pale. She looked as though she might be sick. Markriss's heart pounded, a live, writhing entity. He was hot.

"Wow, I, uh . . ."

"You don't have to answer right now."

"No, I want to say something. It's an honor to be asked. I appreciate it massively."

The oven timer went off, making them start. Chileshe jumped to her feet, racing for the kitchenette. She hadn't met his eye once.

"I'm glad you think so," Keshni said. "We're not trying to use you as some mindless donor, I hope that comes across. We'd want our child to be born into love like any other. And I think, what with the relationship we have between us, how much we respect and care about each other, that would be the case."

"Yes. Yes, I understand." He looked down at his own hands. Bowls and cutlery sang from the opposite side of the flat. "Wow."

"I'm sorry to spring this on you. It's a bit much. We couldn't think of any other way."

Chileshe emerged with steaming crumble, spoons, a blue tub of single cream, a larger bowl of microwaved custard. She dished them out on the table, eyes low. "Help yourselves, take as much as you want."

"Thanks, Chileshe." He tried to find her, glancing up as he took a bowl and spooned crumble into shallow depths. She wouldn't let him. "Look, I'm really pleased to be asked. And, uh, I don't wanna keep you waiting, I know how stressful that would be, but uh . . . I really need time to think."

"Of course you do. That's totally normal."

"I've never really thought about having kids." He chuckled. "I'm a bit irresponsible to be honest."

"Would you like me to tell you a bit more about how it all works?" Keshni's eyes shone.

"Sure, yeah."

It was all quite simple. Keshni and Chileshe had decided between them that the natural method meant what it implied. There would be no artificial insemination. For this they'd chosen to alternate, and if things went well with their potential donor, whoever that would be, they planned on birthing siblings no more than three years apart. Keshni had volunteered to conceive first—here she blushed, picking through glossed and amber crumble with a spoon—as she was older than Chileshe by two years, and felt she had less time. They guessed it wouldn't happen straightaway, Keshni said to her bowl. Their donor would have to understand that it could take anything from a few weeks to a year or more. If they weren't biologically compatible, further options would be discussed at that point. That might involve Keshni trying to conceive with Chileshe's eggs, or finding an entirely new donor.

They would raise the child, or children, by themselves. Markriss was welcome to play as much or as little a role in the children's lives as he wished, on the understanding that they would live with their mothers until they came of age. They would allot weekends so he could be an active part of their lives, or he could visit anytime, even stay over if he liked. They wanted their children to have as stable an upbringing as they could give. Only there would be an additional parent in their lives.

He focused on Chileshe throughout their clarification of terms. She seemed shrunken, hardly able to eat. The usual shadows beneath her eyes were black-rimmed, pronounced. Once everything was said, Keshni took her wife beneath her arm, stroking a shoulder, kissing her temple.

"How are you feeling?" she asked.

"Not good." Chileshe leaned sideways, against her. "Headache's worse."

"You took paracetamol, yeah?"

"Yeah. Think I might call it a night."

"Really?"

"Uh-huh." She pushed back her chair, stood. "I'm really grateful to you for considering this, Riss. I hoped you would. We're pleased you'd even hear us out this far and think about us being a family together."

Keshni's eyes welled. She wiped her eyes with a knuckle, held Chileshe's hand.

"My pleasure. I'm blessed to be asked, honestly."

They touched cheeks, contact minimal. She shuffled toward the bedroom, Markriss trying to ignore the soft tread of diminishing steps.

At the dining table, he and Keshni remained, immersed in tea lights and dimmed bulbs. It was strange how newly bonded he already felt by the simple act of being asked something that was so intimate. The random chance of their disparate lives drawing closer, to become entwined. The intricacy of future moments and memories to come. As Keshni talked, or poured more wine, or they filled the dishwasher side by side, Markriss grew aware that no one had asked such responsibility of him before. Past relationships had been forged to cultivate distance—his doing, he'd always thought, though now, remembering those days, he saw it was his partners' too. Not one of them had offered to share themselves and the possibility of a future with him, at any time. They had not insinuated, or outright asked. Every one, content to let him go. What a morbid realization, the potential of solitary death in his undetermined future, a life of quiet before, days of entropy becoming years. To be asked, fearful as it made him, opened a place he'd avoided much of his life. Dim light became much brighter, the colors of the room sang a quiet vibration of welcome moods.

When their conversation dwindled into benign silence, Markriss checked the time and booked himself an Uber. It was past midnight. He was loath to travel by night tube. At the door, Keshni's goodbye hug possessed fresh tenderness, filled with warmth he hadn't known he might wish for himself. Yet he couldn't stop himself from finding the blind spot of their bedroom door, imagining Chileshe within. He emerged into damp basement, chilled and alone, solid weight at his chest. He gasped air.

4

It was a couple of days before he received the expected text. In the meantime, he did his best to concern himself with details of ordinary moments, to go about daily life. He made food, ate in stubborn isolation. Read his current novel, attended a cinema screening alone. All he could tell himself, which he did on many occasions, was that the shift he felt inside was common, and there was nothing he should do to pretend he hadn't been affected by what Keshni and Chileshe offered. He just had to keep it within, contained. On the streets, or at home looking from his window, he wondered if the people he saw harbored secrets much like his own, masking the turmoil of inner lives with a feigned display of insouciance, hands deep in pockets, expressions solid as they moved through life. He stared into faces, was sometimes caught, yet rarely cared. Men and women alike would drop their gaze, embarrassed. What was taking place beneath the surface? He often wondered. Was he as successful at feigning normality as they?

Markriss didn't share what the women had proposed with anyone. He buried it like a keepsake, to be faced when he was alone. Sometimes, while thinking about it, he realized he was massaging his right side, just beneath his rib, which had begun to ache without cause, a nagging sore point that sharpened whenever he pressed his fingers to it. The pain would ease, always return.

The most difficult part was not telling Nesta, as part of him believed his friend would think he was mad to even consider the proposition. Markriss didn't want to speculate how that conversation would go. A confession and the awkward labor of exposing the women in any form would be a betrayal of trust, even though they didn't know each other and were unlikely to find out. He didn't tell his mother, certainly not Somayina or any work colleagues. If he decided to go through with their plans for conceiving a child, he would choose who knew about it carefully. Nesta and Willow would be first. Until then, undecided, Markriss didn't want to be swayed by the thoughts and feelings of those not involved. It would be his choice, his decision, unadulterated by other opinion.

He became grateful for the leave he'd been granted, choosing not to go back to the office for daily meetings. He used the time to write in his two notebooks, one for the imaginary details of his fictional world, the Ark, the other his personal thoughts and ramblings on life, the real world about him, his emotions, the buffeting waves of energies he felt when he left his flat. So much was going on, inside and out, he sometimes imagined events might drown him if he didn't hide in the sanctuary of his home, waiting for his energy to rise, to feel strong again. At times it seemed every occurrence was an undertow, pulling him down. When the names of the Cambridge graduates killed in the London Bridge attacks were made public, they were found to be volunteers who'd campaigned for hope and change. The right-wing media, despite protestations, galvanized against such ideals. After the frenzied furor of the resulting headlines, Markriss stopped wanting to be among people. Every interaction with the outside world felt like an assault. He resented having to hide, lacking the strength to stay above it. He was morose, in stasis, trying to envisage a future in the world. In those moments, he wrestled between the choices he wanted to make and what he knew was right. How could he bring a child into an existence he could barely handle? What right did he have to deny a living being the joy of connection with souls as beautiful as Keshni and Chileshe? What would a child of theirs look like? Better still, who would they be?

The conflict of resistant thoughts made his nights open-eyed, sleepless, filled with waking dreams of an undecided future.

That weekend brought a new month, sunshine, and chilled winds. Markriss felt more upbeat despite the cold, maybe due to the surge of vitamin D. He emerged from his flat willingly, glad for the tentative sun on his cheeks, wrapped warm against the temperature dip. After all, it was England. A sensation of being reborn made him smile as he braced himself against the breeze, heading for Portobello's Sunday market full of the urge to hunter-gather for that night's meal. Green hearts adorned shop windows and were spray-painted on walls. He lowered his head, not wanting to see. Wandering stalls and supermarkets, filling his Brooks rucksack with vegetables and glossed meat packets, he started at the double buzz in his pocket, drawing the phone into sunlight.

Chi: We should talk? Shouldn't we? Tues 3 @ Tate M OK? We can check out that Kara Walker? Cx

He frowned, sent back "Sure—12 ok? Rx." Continued shopping, returned to the conflicting ambience of that Friday night, open joy undercut with raw nerves.

In the nights before they were due to meet, sleep became a maddening abstraction. He stared at the ceiling, red-eyed, frustrated.

They met outside the colossal doors of the Turbine Hall. Cheek-kissing, her embrace tight. He closed his eyes, heart beating against her. Wondering if she felt it. As they separated, Chileshe pushed for a smile, eyes glazed with effort, the emotion temporary. He rubbed her elbow, feeling worse for her than he did himself, pausing at the slide doors to let her pass. They wandered past the security table, descending the incline, Markriss walking a few steps behind.

They stopped at the first exhibit, the head of an unnamed African boy sculpted in the center of a huge clamshell, a reworking of *Venus*. All porous matte white, like plaster of paris. There they stood for a long time, just looking. Markriss wasn't certain how it made him feel. Without a word, they continued toward the exhibit proper, a colossal fountain in the center of the Turbine Hall, inspired by the Victoria Memorial at Buckingham Palace, called *Fons Americanus: The Daughter of Waters.*

Three tiers of statues, depicting a number of scenarios. On the first tier, facing the doors, a man in a rope-filled boat, the craft tilted to one side, dragged by the attack of a lone shark. On the second, a scuba diver surrounded by larger sharks on both sides, a wide crest of wave breaking behind her. Above that, on the final tier, a grizzled African sea captain in full uniform looking to the sky. Finally, atop the exhibit, a Santerian priestess, head thrown back, arms outstretched, fountain water pouring from the nipples of her huge breasts, and an undetermined wound in her neck, arcing into the second tier, dribbling from its sides into the first.

Separate yet together, they surveyed this side of the fountain until they'd seen enough, deciding by silent agreement to walk around the circumference and view the remaining statues. A dreadlocked Rasta squatted, head and hair fallen over something neither of them could make out. A stunted tree, the large hoop of a noose hanging from a thick branch. An African woman wearing a tall headdress, a man crouching below her wide-open skirt, covering his eyes with a forearm. A flat-capped man cradling what seemed the corpse of a companion, its face a series of featureless holes. Far left, a pleading third-tier figure on their knees, hands clasped, praying to someone, for something unknown. Below them, riding the calm waters of the first tier, a vaguely rendered sailing ship, small and nondescript, almost alone.

Everywhere were sharks. Large and small, leaping from water, breaking the waves, jaws open. Around Chileshe and Markriss, tourists laughed and snapped photos with their phones, exchanging opinions in small groups. Children ran between them counting sharks. Fountain water pattered, gentle rain.

They circled the exhibition a final time and made for the canteen, grabbing a duo of sandwiches, finding a black slab of table. Both had half-filled water bottles, which they drank from almost simultaneously. Markriss noted their mirrored stance—arms raised, bottles poised at lips—with pleasure he kept to himself. They unwrapped their snacks and swapped half with each other as promised.

"What d'you think?"

"Pretty amazing to see, don't you think?"

He nodded. "I really like her use of the sharks. I've never thought of that before."

"Me neither. Isn't that weird? For us not to imagine that? There must have been so many."

"I like that it works factually and metaphorically."

"Yeah, it does."

"What do you think?"

"I love it. It's the most eloquent fuck-you I've ever had the opportunity to see."

"And in here, right? That's the real beauty."

He grinned, loving the ability to watch her at last, to look into her eyes unrestrained. Chileshe smiled back, fully. Took his hands with both of hers.

"This is good," she said. "Isn't it?"

Markriss shrugged. "Sure. You didn't come here to tell me that, I'm guessing."

"Yeah." Squeezing his fingers. "I'm really sorry about this. I know it isn't easy for you. How I've been, things between us—"

"It's cool, honestly. I told you not to worry."

"I feel like I know you well enough to guess that's a cover," she said, laughing as he looked away. "You're finding it tough. Anyone would."

He released her fingers. "Okay, yes. That's true. But you know, I feel like I did this—"

"Uh-uh." Finger raised, wagging. "We. We did it. And it came from something good, I really believe that. Something Kesh recognized between us all . . ."

"I did wonder. Are you sure she doesn't know?"

"No, she definitely does not. I suppose she kind of gets our connection, she knows that, and thinks there's some feeling between us . . . But whether she thinks what happened, happened?" Quick shake of the head. "No. I don't think so, anyway. As open as she is, she'd struggle with that."

"And what did she say about me before I came over?"

"We've been talking about kids, and all the different methods of having them, for ages, as you might imagine. We've been having that discussion since we dated. And then, after you had the gong bath over at ours, Kesh talked a lot about your energy, how connected we were, and I kind of got where she was going, but like, not really. Then the next day, at lunch, that time you came into work, she suggested we talk to you, and I was like, 'Whoa.' I didn't know what to say to that. Cos on the one hand it made perfect sense; on the other—"

He rubbed a palm across his face, wincing. "You wouldn't look at me. Not then, not at dinner."

"I know. I could've handled it better. I've been reflecting on that. I was a shit."

"You weren't a shit, Chi."

"I was."

"Will you stop?" He leaned over the table, looking directly into her eyes. "You're not. Okay? Look. I—" Clearing his throat, glancing at other tables. A waitress wiped a nearby slab down with a cloth and a squeezy bottle of pink liquid. She moved her arm back and forth, unable to remove whatever she'd found. "I've got something to tell you."

He studied all of her. The thin braid hung against her cheek, a purple band nearest its end. Her baggy pink sweatshirt printed with the outline of a cat, loose at the neck, the matching beanie above. Half crescents of eyes. Dual expanse of lips, recalling how soft. Her scent.

"Okay," she said.

"I love you. Not as a friend, or anything. Really. I feel you in everything I do, like what you're thinking and going through. Everything. I always have. You don't have to say anything back, I just want you to know that. No matter what."

"Yes," she said, and he was heartened to see her blush, looking down at the table, unable to hide another smile. "Yes."

She took his other hand. They looked into each other for a time.

"Obviously this complicates things."

He laughed aloud, bit it back. "Sorry."

"I know, I know, massive understatement. And obviously, I am in love with Kesh, right? She's my soul mate. Deeply, truly. So there's that."

Sobering. "Oh, sure, sure. Course."

"I've always believed in people's ability to love without limitation. Like, we have family, don't we? More than one kid, etcetera. I feel like me and you, we've fallen into that thing that sometimes happens through no fault of our own, or anyone's. We can't stop feelings, can we?"

"Right."

"It's like that Erykah song, you know?"

Markriss looked at her, blinking, burst out laughing.

"*What?*" Grinning with him.

"Sorry." Controlling himself, releasing her hands. "I never really took you as one, but that's the most hotep thing I've ever heard you say."

Her expression blanked in a matter of seconds. He stopped laughing.

"What's up?"

"I'm not really into all that hotep chat."

"What d'you mean?"

"I *mean*, I don't get why people say that stuff. It's ridiculous. Why would we take a word meaning 'peace,' or 'to be at peace,' a word used as a term of endearment for thousands of years, and turn it into something derogatory? Worse still, we take an actual derogatory word inherited from the Europeans who despise us, one used to demean us and amplify our wretchedness, and turn *that* into a term of endearment? What the hell's that about?"

It took him time to recover, possibly too long.

"I didn't say that. I hate that word."

Chileshe laughed. "I know, it's just mad when you think about how we use words, and what we do with them."

"Yeah."

They looked at each other from either side of the black table.

"What were you saying anyway?" he asked.

"Oh." Brief smile. "I'd forgotten. Let me get off my soapbox. What I was *saying* was, I care about you so much. You've become so impor-

tant to me. You're in my heart, you know. I can't overstate that. I just
think this thing . . . you know . . . it's a real commitment. Not just
to me, or Kesh, I don't worry about that so much. But the kids. And
given how you feel . . . Scratch that, how we feel about each other.
We gotta be careful, Riss. Real careful."

"What do you mean?"

Chileshe raised her hands, and let them fall to the table. "That's it."

"But I don't understand."

"Just think about it. I'm not gonna say what's right or wrong, this
isn't binary. Just think."

He played with the sandwich wrapper, lips pursed, unable to see
her. Drenched in frustration, or so he felt. The clatter of trays, plates,
and the swirling conversation in the canteen returned, too loud it
seemed. His knee sprang to life, jittering.

"Are you upset?"

"Nah—no," he said, and had to turn her way. "I've just been
finding it hard, I suppose. With this and, you know, everything."

"It's tough," she said. "No matter which way, we all feel it."

He crackled the sandwich wrapper between fingers, head bowed
toward the table, his churn of emotions pulling him low, a child
again.

They walked the riverbank, not saying very much, just to be with
each other, or so he thought. Given every opportunity to go separate
ways, they did not. Chileshe said she wanted to see the water, even
though the breeze that rose onto the walkway was bitter and crisp.
She huddled in her too-large jacket, even smaller, shoulders hunched,
eyes squeezed closed and watering. At one point she raised her hood,
linking arms with him. He had no idea what was happening, couldn't
stop it.

They followed the bend of the pathway, through a tunnel where
the music of an accordion-playing busker echoed, and out the other
side, dodging crowds that took up space everywhere they moved.
Something weighty bumped his leg, knocking Markriss off balance;
glancing down, the elongated body of a dog swam by, black fur,
triangular snout, wading through the crowd with precision beside its

owner. He was reminded of the dog he'd seen in Brixton, twisting to see if it could possibly be the same animal. By then, the crowd surged at him, unrelenting, Chileshe looking back, wondering what had happened. Any view of the dog, if it was her, blocked by surrounding people. He squared his shoulders, moved on.

To escape the rush, Markriss pointed toward an outcrop of jetty by the Oxo Tower Wharf. At its farthest end, he and Chileshe surveyed the expanse of chopping water, sodden wood underfoot slippery with damp. The slap and slop of tide beneath, St. Paul's dome a humped mountaintop, to their right. Vehicles on the north bank and riverboats hauled themselves with the appearance of great determination. Silent, they watched them creep by.

"Kesh said something cool last night about water being associated with reproduction. She reckons our pelvic area, just above our root chakra, is called the water bowl. It's like a crescent moon or something." Chileshe shook her head, braids jumping. "It's a nice thought. I don't get it, to be fair."

He couldn't think of much else to say, so he didn't. Stamped his feet, burying himself deep into his puffer. She turned, shivering, teeth gritted.

"I don't think I'm being totally honest," she said, lifting her glasses to swipe watering eyes. "I'm scared, Riss. I am."

He wasn't sure what she was talking about, although by then that seemed pretty usual. Children or the world? Him or the week to follow? He wanted to give her comfort, unsure whether he could manage such a thing. Half a meter apart, fingers and cheeks numb with cold, they focused on the other side.

In the warmth of his flat that evening, Markriss flicked through mute television channels until he caught one of David Attenborough's many nature programs. First, he couldn't tell what he saw, then realized it was a bundle of snakes, threaded and woven, moving in slippery, presumed accidental motion. Ponderous, blind. When he raised the volume, Attenborough's calm narration informed him that it was a collection of males attempting to raise their temperature from the friction of their fellow bodies, an action that would later become part of their search for a female. He watched, attempting to see where one reptile ended, the other began.

5

The week hurtled by, much as the year. He tried doing what he could to maintain equilibrium in the face of such tender assault to his sense of self, awakened to truth. He was struggling. He needed help. Malaise was vapor inhaled into his lungs and sweated from his pores. It coated his body, enveloping him in a clouded sensation that closed him off from the outside world. He was dazed, unable to see or hear, to comprehend. Even normal tastes were foreign on the tongue, distant and unregistered. It was something like grief, he recalled, thinking of earlier years, his body's account of loss. The impression of absence in flesh once rich with the promise of abundance, now unfulfilled.

He counted moments, the good things he possessed. Health, home, friendship. He traveled to work, put his head down, filed copy. He stayed away from Chileshe, much as he could; there was no use in going further, trying for more. Keshni was good enough not to trouble him with her own anxieties about what he might decide, seeing, or perhaps sensing, the fraught nature of their present days. With the world in turmoil around them, personal issues seemed trivial and secondary. Trained nurses were said to use food banks. A four-year-old boy with suspected pneumonia was photographed sleeping on a hospital floor amid a pile of coats, the mother's claim decried as fake news by Tories and the right-wing media. The father of the first man to be killed in the London Bridge attacks wrote an article for the *Guardian* denouncing hate. Every day, on his journey to the office, Markriss walked by abraded men and women camped out in doorways beside sleeping bags or tents. Sometimes he gave food or coins. Sometimes he passed quickly, avoiding their avoidance of him, the embarrassed glances into laps, their stunted hope. His return to work had helped a little. In the newsroom, a sense of hushed expectance, of getting work done without qualification or banter became the norm. They kept politics to themselves, speaking of celebrity diets and Christmas at the coffee machine. While others went to the pub after their shifts, Markriss took the tube home.

Vague optimism lingered that no one dared to speak into being. Canvassers with red-and-yellow badges would get on underground carriages in high spirits, campaign manifestos and clipboards under their arms. He and his fellow commuters pretended to ignore them. At home, he opened his laptop, searching through hundreds of e-mails Nesta had sent until he found one with "Kinfolk" written in the subject box—a list of names, and links. He right-clicked each, rewarded by thumbnail pics, names, and accreditations—MSc Counseling and Psychology, MA Counseling and Psychotherapy— above four-line bios written in first person. Markriss picked three that he liked, two African women and one Caribbean man, noted their e-mails, then wrote, copied and pasted a general inquiry to all. He'd thought he might feel better after taking direct action. Instead, he was spent.

He listened to Alice Coltrane's *Journey in Satchidananda*, made peppermint tea, and lay on his bed. Thoughts wouldn't stop racing, and still she came into his mind.

He and Nesta WhatsApped every few days, although his friend was engrossed with teaching and numerous Tinder dates. He seemed to enjoy the things Markriss didn't: making plans and dressing up, useless small talk, endless bar menus and meals. The excitement of the unknown, even disappointment. Markriss wrote to tell him he'd contacted the therapists and received promising replies. His phone stirred, and as he looked down, he saw a brown-handed thumbs-up. It had been evening, after all; dinner-date time. Half laughing, Markriss plucked a chip from the golden pile spread across stiff paper.

The flat was dark, the fitful television screen winking before him.

On Election Day heavy rain fell, a ridiculous display of pathetic fallacy. Markriss worked from home, and took a lunch break at twelve, making the short walk up Notting Hill to St. John's Church. Silence was a physical presence. A trio of attendants stood idle, with lackluster attention. He'd arrived without ID and gave his address instead. A slim, almost translucent sheet of folded white paper, a few steps taken toward the open wooden booth among the low collection of others. He made a cross with the squat pencil on a string, folded the sheet again, posting it into the ballot box that reminded him of a paper shredder—not a great thought. The emptiness of the church room piqued his anxiety. He clasped fists, nodded at the trio of attendants, left.

It still rained, the church stones slippery with wet. Stepping carefully, Markriss headed down the hill to the Lebanese restaurant a few blocks from his house, on the Grove.

Inside, the whispered sizzle of grilling meat on skewers, and before him, the jeweled glitter of baklava pieces stacked into strangely neat pyramids, at eye level. He waited to be served, full of hunger pangs, a distant urge for the sweet combination of honey and pistachio. At a table just beyond the queue, a woman ate, head thrust forward, patiently carving into a whole grilled fish. Markriss recognized her tall, thin figure as the local who had taught an after-school club, only for something to happen between her and the kids that involved them attempting to rob her flat, the woman retaliating with violence. Markriss turned away before she saw him. He'd visited the club to give a talk on journalism, years ago, and couldn't think of a single thing worth saying to her.

At home, he met his afternoon deadline, using growing blocks of words to try to forget the stakes as the nation waited. Played Alice Coltrane from the beginning, staring out of his window at passing legs and feet. The warmth of his radiators was consolation. His phone buzzed to life.

Willow.

"Hey, Mum."

"Hello."

"What's going on?"

A sniff of distaste. "Just thought I'd ring is all. Haven't heard from you."

"Yeah, sorry. Been working."

"Gathered. Must be busy. What with today."

"Yeah, it's pretty crazy. Been flat out."

"Thursday twelfth."

"Yeah," he said, understanding what she meant afterward. The following day was Friday the thirteenth. "Oh, man. You think it's intentional?"

"I wouldn't put anything past them, would you?"

He shook his head, remembering she couldn't see. "How's it looking up by you?"

His mother had swapped the Uxbridge two-bedroom council home where he'd grown up for a Wallington equivalent not long after he'd finished university. He often joked she'd moved out on him, instead of the opposite. It was only half meant for laughs.

"I dunno, can't tell. Be shocked if we went Labour."

"Yeah." Sighing. "So how you doing? Feeling okay?"

"Not so bad. I've got some lavender to give you. Please remind me. If you don't come up I'll post it."

"You don't have to do that. I'll come up, Mum."

"Yeah. Well, it's here if you need it. For your sleep."

"Thanks, Mum." He didn't have the heart to tell her lavender hadn't worked, ever.

"You know what next week is?"

"Course. How could I not?"

"Just checking, don't get narky. I'll go and lay flowers. I've been growing them especially."

"I'll come."

"Carnations and sunflowers. He liked those."

"Yeah, I remember."

"Used to take the heads off with his football, remember that? I'd get so angry."

"You smacked his bum once."

"No, I didn't."

"Yeah, you did. Said if we were back home he'd have to pick his own switch from the tree. He bawled the house down."

"No."

"Yeah, I'll never forget. Then you gave him ice cream."

"Ah." Markriss heard his mother's smile. "At least I did."

"Yeah. He stopped crying right away."

"Hmmm." An electronic tick of silence. "D'you think he forgave me?"

"Course he did, Mum. It's what kids do: cry, tantrum, forget about it."

"What about you?"

He frowned out of the window. "For what, Mum? You never did anything to me."

"I could've taken better care of your brother. I could've—"

Sniffling. Crackling movement. He imagined a sleeve wiped across her cheek. Rounded shoulders.

"Mum. Don't be silly. We loved you. Ninka loved you."

The rattle of her breath, the vibrating speaker.

"Stupid."

"No, Mum. Not at all."

She felt a touch better, and so Willow talked of his father, Vendriss Denny, who'd returned to his birth island of Barbados after he attended the patient-liaison meeting that followed his son's death. The consultants and head nurse had been sorry, telling the family that tuberculosis had been on the rise since the late nineties, even more so in the present day, from what Markriss learned years later. Poor living conditions, poor nutrition, and poorer health all said to account for its resurgence. Once Ninka was buried in Kensal Green Cemetery, a family plot his mother bought with the help of their local community, his father had decided he couldn't live in the house, or country. Markriss never blamed him for that.

"I was thinking of joining your dad. I e-mailed him, we talked. What you think?"

"You lot renewing your vows or something?"

"As friends, you daft sausage. Them days long done."

"I'm only teasing. I think it's good, Mum. It'd be good for you."

"So I have your blessing?"

"You don't need it. You should go."

She made a noise of positivity, and was off on a tangent, talking about taking an online DNA test she'd seen on a tube advertisement to find out where she really came from. Something about not being originally from Carriacou, even though it was still back home to her. The arrival of her ancestors from an undefined place. He stopped listening after a while, as it was always the same thing. She'd call to check on him. Possibly wanting to discuss his mental health, unable to face the enormity of the task. Too fathomless, impervious. She covered up the inadequacy by talking of her own concerns. Markriss didn't mind, he just had limits.

"So you're fine about me buggering off and sit on the beach with your old man? Dunno when, but soon."

"Course, Mum. Then I wouldn't have to worry about you."

Willow spluttered a few unintelligible sentences, blowing kisses down the phone.

"I'll meet you down the cemetery, ten o' clock. Bring the lavender, yeah?"

"Love you, son."

"Love you too."

He put the phone down, ducking his head to look from the window. Spotted rain on glass was drifting mist, the clouds a sea of cotton gray.

He'd known he wouldn't sleep through the night, unsurprised to open his eyes to the void of his flat, the lazed grumble of a night bus, a temporary flash of jittering lights, fallen dark after. He groped for his phone, unable to find it, assailed by remnants of dreams. A ballet of clustered snakes, writhing, desperate for heat. Unable to tell each other apart, in search of the female among them. Constant motion, the quiet murmur of scales. He was cold in spite of radiator heat, searching until his fingers came across sterile plastic. Lifting the iPhone, he fumbled for the home button. Impromptu light caused his eyes to ache, squinting at the screen.

Friday 02:59 13 December.

He tilted the phone to ease discomfort. Typed "election results UK 2019" with a finger. Waited tense moments for it to load.

Wincing at the too-bright screen, he saw that Conservatives had taken eighty-one seats and Labour seventy-three, with a 41.3 percent and 37 percent share of the vote.

He fell onto the pillow. Searched the dark ceiling.

By the time the exit polls were announced the previous evening, hours before he eventually fell asleep, it was already predicted the Conservatives would garner a majority. Fearful, he logged on to the *Ark*, where their boilerplate was designed and ready: "A Blue Wave," the headline foretold. Richard, working a late shift, had landed the breaker. Unable to face the disappointment of watching the vote develop as it happened, Markriss tried to sleep, knowing he'd probably wake hours later racked with runaway thoughts, nothing else left to do. Trapped with the knowledge of what was to come.

Between swipes, he propped a pillow against his headboard and sat up, phone grasped tight, watching the screen in hope something would change, scrolling through windows with a terse finger. An *Indie* article published an hour before he'd woken bore the headline "How to Leave the United Kingdom." Though focused on the wider population, the piece directly addressed the intense worries people of color had about their incumbent PM. He tracked his finger downward, anxiety becoming a gnawing sensation, sinking blunt teeth in his lower gut.

He got up, pulling on his tracksuit and hoodie. Made a cup of peppermint tea and played "The Blessing Song" at low, after-midnight volume. Let music wash his body, standing at the window. The pavement beyond spotlit white, glistening with sharp monochromatic enchantment. Bare trees shivered, stiff and naked in soft breeze.

He frowned, leaned forward, squeezing his eyes tight. A vague shape beneath the minor shadow of the slight tree, a humped form.

The dog.

She sat on muscled haunches, facing his window. Jaws open, tongue lolling, otherwise at rest. A swipe of her tail brushing concrete the only indication that she was real. This time he knew. It was her.

Anu. Anubis.

Elegant head raised, dim yellow eyes peering into his, Markriss's jaws slackened without feeling. His shoulders fell, breath huffed from him. In her eyes, the swirl of infinite existence forming scattered galaxies, each spiral a journey of a million possibilities. In the center of his body, the vibrations of a singing bell. A dark plain of circumstance and the branching flow of decisions. In the far reaches of his mind, the sound of ever-present running water, offset by the farthest hint of irregular wind chimes.

Casual yet deliberate, Markriss raised his puffer from a coat hanger, slipping his arms inside. He put both feet into a pair of slippers, pushing his toes against carpet to make sure they were properly on. Picked up his imitation notebook and put it into a pocket, doing the same with his keys. He opened the flat door, stepping out.

The moon, a brilliant searchlight, full and round. The hush of predawn and shush of dried leaves twirling and spinning, a globular dance.

He caught the scent of marijuana, searching the central steps that led to upstairs flats. Sirus, puffing spectral smoke. Markriss raised a hand; the elder responded with a lifted fist, placed against his heart. As he walked to the steps, Markriss watched the street to check if the dog was still poised, panting.

She was.

When he looked back at the flats, trotting up basement steps, the smoke and Sirus were gone.

He slowed, unfazed by the elder's disappearance, turning to the main road. Perhaps he'd been an image of another time, perhaps a figment of his own making. Markriss didn't care. By the time he reached street level, Anubis had maneuvered to face him. Her tail swished once more, perhaps as greeting, maybe impatience. There was no barking or urgency, only solemn countenance. It was difficult to tell what she thought.

"Good dog," Markriss said, the words barely meeting his teeth. He was unsure whether he'd expressed them at all.

Anubis remained still, red corduroy leash placed on the pavement to her right in a serpent's curl, as though arranged. He bent to stroke her head. She was still, a work of art. When he picked up the lead and stood, she rose to her feet, wet nose pointing at the rise of hill.

"Let's go," he said, through stiffened lips.

He sleepwalked his way up Notting Hill, Anubis pressing forward, tugging the lead into a straight red line, nose angled at the space before her, jaws open, baring teeth. Past the yellow-brick church of St. John's, the locked and chained back gardens of Ladbroke Square, the rise of expansive sash windows.

His eyes blurred, so he swiped at them, though his sight continued to grow hazy, and he was blinded for a moment. When his vision returned, nothing was as it had been. Rising high above his head, a gargantuan metal framework of blue towered miles into night, too far to see where it might end, an impure landscape of pulleys and giant cogs, ropes of steel thicker than the width of his thighs, stark lights projecting powerful beams into darkness. Stenciled and faded white numbers impossible to interpret, a foreign language. A gagging stench of oil coated his nose and throat, making his lungs flinch, and he coughed. Men scurrying and climbing its heights, trivial as aphids on stems, the echoing noise of clanking tools a continual rhythm, though he couldn't see the point at which it originated.

Anubis shivered and stopped, cowering, whimpering. As rapidly as it appeared, the construction began to fade, blown apart like paper shreds in a breeze. Markriss knew he'd seen the gateway he'd imagined for so many years. How and why it had materialized as a living apparition, to become his fleeting dreams made real, was too much to comprehend, and made him fearful of his own mind.

Then it was gone. He was returned to the present moment. He crouched, ruffling Anu's fur for comfort, to feel something solid. She growled in acknowledgment, pulling the lead. Once his legs regained their strength, he stood and allowed Anu to pull him up the steep incline. The infamous former police station angled on a corner, where so many battles were fought. Antique stores, estate agents' bright advertising photographs, the Mitre pub.

On the other side of the hill they waited at the crossing. With no cars to stop them, they moved on.

Another steep rise, contained by a narrow strip of pathway. Night concentrated, shadows grew. Thin mist escaped from Markriss's and

Anu's mouths as they breathed hard. The glitter of dusted frost decorated the ground, reflecting stark moonlight.

They pushed on upward, until his legs burned and breath shot
from their lungs in longer, sharper bursts. Nothing of the city about
them. No sound of vehicles, people, not even the scurry of nocturnal
animals. Still everywhere, theirs the only movement. On their left,
blank walls of houses, to their right thickening branches and a growing
chorus of fluttering black wings as they reached the edges of Holland
Park.

Metal-railed fencing trailed the pathway. Whispers and fumbled
bodies connected in chilled air, alert to the quiet sound of their feet,
their harshness of breath. Men would meet among the trees, something Markriss learned walking this pathway years ago. A cinema had
existed not far from the southern edge of the park and he'd left a
late-night screening, Raymeda's hand in his, returning to her hostel.
Anubis's head twitched as though scenting something on the air, even
as she kept moving, and Markriss followed in her wake. They reached
a portion of fencing where there was a small gate, a braided chain
and padlock.

Anubis stopped, resting on hind legs, contemplating the height
of the gate. She turned to him, then the gate. It took three attempts
before he got the message.

He climbed, rapid though ungainly. At the top, he swung his leg
over. Dropped to the other side with a grunt.

Anubis snaked her body through a gap and sat by his heels until
he kneeled, grasping the red lead from the grass.

The full moon gave all the light they needed. Led by the dog,
Markriss angled right into the depths of trees, and from the corner
of his eyes he saw others note their presence, before rapidly looking
away. Lovers, the homeless, insomniacs like himself perhaps—gave
them the benefit of peace, left them alone. Soon, the canopy of
intertwined branches above their heads blocked all but the slimmest
beams of light. Markriss lost any sense of time, all linear meaning.

Anubis pulled harder. Around them, a dark clearing formed by
the oldest trees of the park by hundreds of years. At the center of
that circular space, emerging from a bed made of gravel, dust, long-

dead bark, the dissolution of material bodies that came before, was a strange trick of light. A silver glitter of eternal, starred moments. An outpouring of energy, vivid as moonlight, spouting high into the limbs of trees, through emaciated branches and beyond, into the very clouds. A vibration hummed through his soles. He craned his head upward and still couldn't see the end of the silver stream, just ink sky around it.

Anubis stepped closer, one paw after the other, lying just in front of the light. Her forelegs lit pale, nose low to earth, watching. Markriss moved to join her, gazing around the clearing in a slow circle, seeing in every direction. With the old trees gathered around him, the tacit wisdom of their energy, he felt overwhelming sadness. In the stillness of a moment where all was time, he knew beauty, and loss.

Markriss took one final look, reaching out a hand, his fingers touching light. Pleasure flooded him, like all he had known.

6

He rose into night gradually, bitter taste flooding his tongue. From liquid to air, arms at his sides, alive to feeling. His eyes closed for a long moment, nerve endings intensified, connections with the elements heightened. The rush of water loud applause in his ears. Atmosphere swirling at his fingers, arms, hair, body, neck, and chest, the feel of lenient material. The aroma of earth and river came as a rich balm he breathed into his lungs as far as they would expand. Higher, eyes opening, and he was there again, in the land he'd dreamed without awareness, not alien, somewhere he knew.

He moved his ethereal body across the landscape, hovering at a height from which he could see the Taut. Everywhere, before him and behind, was the river, blackened earth at its side. There was an escape of vital force from him—not air, though much like breathing, expelled into the atmosphere as blue energy swirling from his body.

Markriss saw a rock close by, and sat to rest. Thighs pressed against the solid stone face, knees bent and protruding, back straight—reassuring physicality. He felt a presence at his shoulder, a hand.

Take time, Wallace said, intention streaming through consoling touch. *You have it.*

Markriss stared into dust. *I've never experienced sadness like that.*

They are immersed in the depths of a period known in Hindu tradition as Kali Yuga, the age of iron. A period of extreme spiritual conflict and war. Meditation and chanting can help a sense of balance on the physical planes, but it takes much practice.

What about my original plane? The place I came from, or the one where I was an Outsider? What were they?

They are all Kali Yuga, to greater or lesser degrees.

So who am I?

He looked into the hood. Wallace was barely visible as a physical entity. His ka moved like illuminated smoke.

All of them, Markriss. You are all.

He set his gaze to the land once more. If every person he encountered or had been was himself, that meant Wallace had told him truth in the beginning. This ethereal being, on this plane, was his one true form. Who he was meant to be.

I'm never destined to find Keshni or Chileshe, am I?

The hood moved its shoulders in the semblance of a shrug.

There are rivulets where such possibility occurs. You simply chose another way.

I should have been happy. It was everything. I wasn't content.

The feeling at his shoulder was gone. Wallace had turned, considering the sky.

Every action has a reaction. You cannot gain without compromise.

His ka emptied a thin stream of blue smoke from his mouth.

You've almost completed your journey. I'm not sure whether the body you claim will live or die. The only chance to avoid certain destruction is to follow the Rogue.

He's on Geb?

We have found him. The decision is yours. Will you confront him, or go back where you began?

I want to be here. I want to be free, Markriss said, and brightness emerged from the edges of Wallace's hood. Silken pink tendrils floating into gloom.

Meditate on what you've experienced. Take to the river where you feel it best. There's no need for me to lead further. You have arrived. Take the next step, Markriss. Go where you should.

He nodded agreement, calming his spirit. He allowed energy to flow through him and connect with gloss-black earth, the corresponding air, the subtle forms of being that traveled above. The expansive universe in continual rotation beyond that place. Chakras spun in motion from his base, coursing upward in cumulative spirals to his crown. He gasped at the electric feel of all that passed through him, from the dust to ether and back. And then, shockingly, there was liquid. Elemental water, the force of life surrounding him until there was nothing else, no awareness of time and space except lapping tide against the place where his ears had once been, no touch beyond the essence that buoyed him, no taste other than bittersweet brine, no sight, only the motion of distant light patterns, fluctuations of the water itself. Rather than sink or rise, Markriss widened the space where his arms had been, releasing control. An eternity passed in that place.

Part Four

The Upper Room

"Awareness is consciousness. Thus, reality will remain a matter of choice."
—Reginald Crosley, MD, *The Vodou Quantum Leap*

13 December 2020

During REM sleep, Markriss returned to Burbank Park, where he walked a redbrick path, the black dog at his side. Nocturnal creatures stirred above his head, occasional shadows swooping low, possibly bats or owls. He saw a lake in the far distance, although with the breeze getting cold, he probably wouldn't walk that far. He was searching for someone he'd been alongside for a length of time, who'd left him with Apnu on . . . That was it, he had left him and the dog on a small rug they placed somewhere behind him. Ninka. Yes. He was looking for Ninka. He'd said he wanted to explore, and he wouldn't go far, and then he'd disappeared into the bushes and not returned. Markriss had waited, listening to the hesitant calls of owls and flutterings of bat wings, shivering cold. He decided to go in search of his brother.

He had thought it was summer for some reason, yet the chill said otherwise. He was quite young, he knew that too, as his sneakers were child-sized. The grass was silver with dew, the moon a pale eye. Apnu panted at his feet. The world seemed to have emptied. Like disintegrating smoke, Ninka was gone.

Apnu took an abrupt left and he followed, stepping from the path to cross wet grass, pushing knotted bushes and branches away until he entered a small clearing.

There was Ninka. Tiny, in shadow, wearing simple shorts and a T-shirt, neck craned back toward the canopy of treetops.

In front of his brother, silver light as wide as an oak tree gushed from a carpet of dry earth and leaves, higher than the trees themselves, into night sky. A roaring waterfall rush erupted around them. Markriss reached out for his brother, almost touching him.

The simulation ended, he was awake.

He lay still a moment, acclimatizing. It was useful not to rise too quickly after a program; users had stumbled and injured themselves, a few elderly users even died. His heart raced from the beauty of what he'd seen and the joy of breathing outside air, the feel of wind, the sound of the creatures wheeling above, the pad of dog paws by his feet. His corresponding chakra ached from loss, a pulsing heaviness he hadn't felt for so long. Strange and painful as they were, Markriss let himself relive the sensations, trying not to question why his simulation had selected a localized Nocturna program at random. He'd never owned a dog, nor visited Burbank Park with his brother. In fact, before he slept he'd programmed the sleeper to take him to the pitzball fields of Chichén Itzá to relive the experience of ancient matches, not remain within Dinium, even if he relished the opportunity to experience the outer world again.

He thought the covering open, watching it slide left with a mechanical gasp, then climbed out to crouch by his podside and inspect the settings. The sim trajectory was correct, his sleep clock primed to the selected duration. According to the pod, nothing was wrong. Markriss double-checked the programs, finding the trajectory seemed normal. He thought-scrolled through controls until he realized all he'd achieved was base-level angst that became stronger the more he thought of Ninka. He slammed the protective display cover shut with vague annoyance, rose, and closed the pod.

Standing, hands on hips, Markriss pondered the issue. It wasn't the first error his Nocturna program had made. He watched the sleeper, biting at his inner cheek.

Two chimes came from his slide. Simi pinged the message, her soft metallic voice like a thought of his own: "Keshni Roberts, *Ark News*."

A pause, then: "We're here. He's going to start in an hour. Are you still coming?"

Markriss pinged back: "Yes. On my way. Don't start without me lol."

Quick strides took him into the kitchen. He grabbed a packet of pea and bean snacks, one orange, one apple, and his water bottle, stuffing them all into his backpack. He left the house.

Day-Lites had entered the first segment of midphase, brightening everything beneath them, spreading warmth and good feeling. Markriss loved his zone at this time of day, though he usually left for work earlier, when the Lites were dim and trams bustled with commuters. Around this time on weekends, he'd sit on his porch, a slide on his lap, playing music and watching the neighborhood pass like the progression of time. The street, one of several affluent blocks that made up Hegarton West, was tree-lined and grass-verged, the sidewalks bleached white. Kids' trikes stood dormant in front gardens, awaiting noisy passengers. The roads were clean, the houses neat and well ordered, wooden shutters at windows and elaborate designs set beneath the fascia boards of flat roofs, mainly roses and papyrus, or the elegant stone heads of jackals and lions.

He walked to the end of the block, muttering good mornings on his way, to join a clutch of neighbors waiting at the D stop. Ready for the working day in sober dresses for the women, plain suits and wide-brimmed hats for men, uniform even though they performed a wide range of jobs: banking, accounting, finance, insurance, management—nothing menial. He forced himself to smile, even as loss coursed through him, a long-forgotten ache. Grief for his brother smothered him like he'd not felt in years.

"Morning."

"Morning, Mark."

"Morning, all."

Murmured greetings. A moment of quiet waiting. Tight, gleaming shoes squeaked as men rocked on their feet. One gentleman, wearing a tan Eurasian designer suit, broad head, broad shoulders, unnecessary raincoat folded over his arm, most likely for show, rocked on his feet and smiled back. He stepped forward.

"Tell us when they've got the buggers, won't you?"

Markriss smiled, though he wearied of the question. "Any day now, my friend. Any day now."

The broad man stepped back. The tram, a golden D at its pineal, trundled forward. As a group, men stood aside to let the women, one with a halo-Afroed child of seven or eight, board the tram. Markriss went last.

The journey was pleasant, in spite of the overhead advertising displays, which he found distracting most of the time. Companies had started experimenting with hologram technology, and it was no fun to be shocked by the illusion of being splashed with speedboat water, or sprayed with fine earth from a quad bike. Most mornings, he sat with his arms folded and eyes closed, rocked into his morning meditation by tram motion. By the time he reached his stop, the L4 center of Tibisiri Square, Markriss would be ready to tackle whatever his editor had in mind.

This morning, undeterred by the squeal of tram wheels, Markriss began to meditate, breathing interrupted breaths for ten-second counts of five successive intakes, until the floor opened beneath him, and he descended.

The rattling of the tram became louder, cutting into his trance, making him wince, its frenzied rock becoming so violent he was nearly thrown from his seat. As his eyes opened with a start, Markriss blinked surprise. Instead of sitting relaxed, his simple visualization had resulted in him riding a dirty, rusted goods lift, the only passenger inside. His stomach plunged as though he were on a roller coaster, something he hadn't felt since he was fourteen, or falling through a pocket of air during an Outer City helicopter tour, a feeling of his innards left somewhere over his head, plunging with nothing to stop or catch him. That clogged physical presence of loss, balled in his chest, felt greater, overwhelming. He hacked and coughed, alive to abject grief.

Another visual jolt. He was back inside the mildly rocking tram, his jaws wide open as though he'd screamed. He almost thought he had; looking around, he saw no evidence of having caught anyone's attention, except for the halo-haired boy watching from across the aisle, eyes crinkled with amusement, the action figure in his hand forgotten, having found a better source of entertainment.

Markriss sat back in his seat, heavy-breathing, ignorant to the buildings rolling by outside the tram windows. Heart a steady thump of muscle at his chest, mucus clogging his throat. He thought back on his morning, the weeks before. The park visualization. The goods elevator. The hooded figure of the old man who'd begun to appear in his dreams for the last few days, for no reason he could decipher. There was no such thing as coincidence, the Cartesians said. Physical became mental and vice versa, they were inexorably linked. If he'd begun to actualize visions on the astral plane with the power to override his sleep program, it was because his former experiences on the physical plane had taken paramount importance. The past, no matter how successful he was at evading it, had changed his circumstances forever and finally caught up with him. The visions could be taken as a need for acceptance. Perhaps he needed to learn how to be open to them, no matter how painful or intrusive they might be.

His fingers rested on the soft plastic seating either side of him. The boy across the aisle poked out his tongue. Markriss responded with an upward thumb, meant as a joke, although it made the boy uncertain. Eventually, sneering, he looked away.

The D trundled toward the busy square, already full of people. Markriss got up, grasping the overhead handrails, heading for the door. The tram eased to a stop, emptying steadily, leaving only the mother and child. Hissing doors closed behind Markriss, the vehicle rolling toward the L4 Eastern Gateway, where it would terminate.

Tibisiri Square, better known as the hub, or "brain," of the level—indeed, the Ark as a whole—was Inner City's epicenter, the location that stood for everything the building was and had ever been. The name Tibisiri derived from a traditional fiber woven by Arawak women in what was the modern-day Caribbean, previously known to the West as the Southern Isles. Used in the context of the square, it suggested the threading together of unions and corporations that created Inner City.

The secondary buildings were set in a quincunx, each on a separate corner, like dots on dice. In the center of the square, the dominant and largest of the buildings was the headquarters of E-Lul, founders of the Ark. To the north was Ark Media, where Markriss was employed, and Ausares Corp, the E-Lul subsidiary whose primary concern was the manufacture of sleeper pods. To the south, just across from the D tram stop, were Kyba Network, who ran neural communications, and the Inner Dinium Architects' and Builders' Union, comprised of designers and construction planners alike. In the early days of the Ark, neural communications were part of the Kemetian Temple and formed one faction, until the Temple moved to a separate building two streets away. Religion and scientific technology struggled to make peace ever since.

He walked the pathway leading to E-Lul Corp. The square was animated with playing children, dog walkers, young couples, and workers eating lunch-hour sandwiches on benches. Between each building, playgrounds had been built. Markriss was overcome by the bittersweet white noise of preschool enjoyment, stung by thoughts of Ninka doing similar things. He watched the children play as he passed along iron railings, fascinated by their leaps from roundabout to climbing frame, slide to seesaw. The inevitable tears of an infant being comforted by their parent, hugs and promises of later treats. Markriss wished he could stop to learn more; temple priests advised that children had the ability to divine the future inadvertently via play. He found he was struck by the contradictions between his silent dream of his brother and the constant flux of thudding sneakers over screaming joy. Yet he was already late.

E-Lul rose above him, broad as a temple and twice as large, equally imposing, lion-brown brick and onyx statues on the grass beside the path. A wide flight of stone steps in front of the building took visitors and workers to the reception, and elevated ramps were built on either side. On the grass, a few yards from the swing-door entrance, a raised platform was set with slim speakers and slide-screens, a translucent lectern at its center. While the stage was empty, the rows of plastic seats beyond were full of chattering people.

A wide slab of a man. Black tunic and black visor, jawline rigid. He stepped in front of Markriss, blocking his way.

"If you'd like to come this way, sir."

He gestured at two upright metal poles three meters apart, sidelights blinking white. Another slab of a security guard waited at their rear, a woman. High-level Corps soldiers, no doubt.

"Oh. Sorry."

Markriss walked between the machines. A loud beep. Red light.

"Can I look at what you've got in your bag, sir?" the woman said over the first guard's shoulder.

"Oh, sorry, sure. I know what it is. I forgot to take out my slide."

"Let's have a look anyway, shall we?"

They riffled through his bag, finding the snacks and the sliver of plastic. The woman ran a handheld scanner over his slide. It beeped green.

"Okay, go and try again. Take your bag with you."

Markriss did as he was told. No beep.

"Perfect. Enjoy the rest of your day, Mr. Denny."

Apologizing, smiling in all directions, Markriss slipped into the front row, nodding hellos, easing his way between knees and too-full bags, trying not to hit anybody with his. He fell into the seat beside Keshni.

"Bloody hell, you, about time! Thought you'd decided to stay in bed."

Keshni looked impeccable as usual, pale slacks and a brown shirt that gleamed, tied-back hair and sunglasses. He could almost believe it was summer.

"Nearly did. Thanks for the wake-up call."

"What are you like?"

"Seriously, I was getting up, promise." Markriss laid the slide on his lap. He thought *voice memo*, primed to record.

"Anyway, no worries, you're fine. It's absolute calamity on L1 apparently. They've bought you time."

"Oh, good," he said, kissing her cheek. She offered the other with a grin. "Sorry, didn't even say hello."

"Typical Mark, too busy to notice I'm here."

"Oh, come on. That's never happened in your entire life."

"Really?" She gave him a theatrical look over her glasses, eyes rolling. "Anyway, what do you think the odds are of getting the Corps to go total lockdown?"

"Haven't they done that?"

"Partially. I mean the whole package, completely ransack the place, evict the lot, or bury them in the Blin. It's what the animals deserve."

Markriss shrugged, crossing his legs. "How far can they go? No more than they have, surely? The Temple is already up in arms."

Another look, Keshni peering over her sunglasses longer this time. "Mark, you're not trying to suggest they're being excessive, I know you're not. If they have to kill them all to get things back the way they were, then it's a done deal, surely. Just don't tell us about it; give us some old crap to write like they sued for peace or some such nonsense. Say no more."

"Yeah, but—"

Cameras flashed, people stood, Keshni and Markriss with them. A moment's wait before Hanaigh E'lul paced onstage, a supplicating palm waving over the crowd. He was short and athletic, glacial eyes and swept white hair, seemingly closer to sixty than the late forties he actually was. Gaunt, with the impression of someone who had lived many lifetimes in one body. Markriss was drawn to his composure, the stillness with which he held himself. He'd seen Hanaigh speak on many occasions, at press conferences and public meetings and on the slide-screen when he hadn't been able to make events, always with that dedicated, confident energy, those quick-fire bursts of life the CEO-governor could barely contain. Nothing like he seemed at that moment, without his usual charm and care-for-nothing bluster, clutching toughened plastic, devoid of a smile.

He stood behind the lectern, right eye blinking twice to switch the microphone on. The twitching silenced his audience.

"Ladies, gentlemen, members of the press. Thank you all for coming, we greatly appreciate it. I know how difficult it was for some of you to make the arrangements at such late notice." Keshni elbowed Markriss in the ribs, grinning. He ignored her. "Please, sit."

They followed his request, Hanaigh taking a moment to look over the crowd, uncharacteristically stern. A distance away, Markriss heard an elongated yell that sounded like a young girl. Possibly from one of the four playgrounds. The retinue of plainclothes security, some ten guards keeping varied positions around the stage, moved their heads in multiple directions like the blind.

"As you're no doubt aware, unrest has plagued our lower levels over the last few weeks without pause, or any chance of communications with the offending factions. What started as a vicious bomb attack on one of our most prized media outlets has escalated into a threat more serious than any of us could have anticipated. Everyone knows the details, I'm sure, but I'll repeat them for those watching at home. A little after 2:25 a.m. on the twenty-eighth of November, a series of three gas explosions took place within the L1 media building 1322 that houses *Ark News* along with a number of other multimedia subsidiaries. Unfortunately, a menial worker, Pious Majeed, was killed in the attack. On-the-ground surveillance, animal and tech spyware told us the attackers were an organized street team–cum–terrorist group, fledgling, yet numerous and hugely influential, calling themselves the Outsiders. While our combat teams sought to bring the leaders to justice, and managed to take down one of their most prominent members, the majority of the terrorists escaped.

"At 11:33 a.m. on the thirtieth of November, the leaders were apprehended at the Eastern Gateway, where they launched an attack on our soldiers. After a vicious battle those leaders were taken down. Now, we don't know what they planned, but from IDs found on their persons it can only be assumed that they were attempting to escape to one of our upper levels, not trying to attack the gateway. That much, I think you all know."

Hanaigh turned right and then left, indicating the slide-screens on either side of the stage.

"Early this morning, after the series of bomb attacks on media outlets on multiple levels—which I'm sure you've all heard about, and I'll go into more detail on later—we had a meeting where it was decided to release the names and identifications of those involved in the original attack, so we might engage the public in tracking down who they are affiliated with, and have a chance of stopping whoever might strike next."

Slide-screens burst into life. A studio photo of a relatively young man grimacing with distaste, narrow, wizened eyes. The surrounding press teams murmured loud. More flashes sparked. Keshni muttered a few words to Markriss, although he barely listened. He pushed forward, slide forgotten on his lap.

"If you'll permit me to continue." Hanaigh's voice rose, waiting for chatter to die. "Please, if you'll permit. Thank you so much. To my right, we have Nesta 'Ayizan' Sahu, Outsider captain and, from our gathered intel, a prime instigator of the first attack. Well respected, highly intelligent, charismatic, and dangerously violent, Sahu dominated the street teams of his quarter by subverting the teachings of the *Metu Neter* and Temple, which proved extremely popular with his surrounding Charlton community. A highly dangerous man."

Hanaigh turned to his left. Another photo, a woman. Her stare dark and unbroken, even in death. A martyr's gaze.

Markriss began to shake. He sat on his hands to still himself and stop anyone from noticing. His slide fell onto the grass with a soft thud. He left it. Keshni looked down, then away, busy typing notes.

"This is Sahu's accomplice and spouse, Raymeda 'Isirah' Khuti, killed with Sahu when he and three other followers attempted to storm the gateway. Strong-willed, very well regarded, particularly by the women of the quarter, Khuti was a former Outer City teacher and facilitator before she turned to agitating for reform. She was long known as an aggressive voice of protest against the Ark, and was involved in numerous politically inclined groups before she entered. As I speak, we're still piecing together how she managed to infiltrate our protocols to gain access to housing, menials, things of that nature."

Much as he wanted to look away, Markriss could not. He saw a dance of stars in Raymeda's eyes as she spoke of the undernourished moon and romance: how dissimilar from the death gaze in front of him. The cries of owls and rustling of leaves, the heat of her body against his skin and static of her fingertips, rough blanket threads beneath their unclothed bodies. They were young and unwise, it was true, yet had there been hope? He couldn't remember. His mind continued to assert that there were no coincidences, which he accepted as an actuality because he was seated among his peers, staring into eyes he knew, and a woman he did not, knowing the pod had projected his astral body into the park where they consummated their relationship, though not the reasons for him encountering things that were not there, and had never been: that streaming light, his brother. He remembered what happened between himself, Raymeda,

Misty, and Nesta in Burbank Park, how it changed him forever. Most of all the bitter fact that he'd forced it from his memory ever since.

Hanaigh E'lul continued to speak, Markriss struggling to retain what the CEO was saying as he listed the remaining Outsiders killed by Corps soldiers—Temujin and Vyasa Broin, Xander Lewis, T'shari Nefer. Too much, way too much. He didn't recognize the others besides T'shari, him only with a vague recall that he almost discounted as mistaken, although the cold eyes of each face stirred him regardless. Markriss couldn't keep still. He was jittery, it was difficult to concentrate. After a time, Keshni noticed his unease. He sensed her glances and pretended he hadn't seen her.

His attention was only roused when Hanaigh spoke of that morning's attacks on L1, 2, and 3. Ark News buildings on each had been the main targets, although TV stations and subsidiaries such as equipment suppliers and pod stores were also targeted. Six bombs in total were detonated within minutes of each other, largely in buildings closed and unoccupied for the night, although seven people had been injured and one additional death was recorded, a security guard doing his rounds in a media establishment. No one had claimed responsibility for the attacks, yet the homemade devices and gas canisters set off by wireless detonation meant the most likely suspects were either Outsiders themselves, or Outsider affiliates—although it was far too early for copycats, and so the latter theory was unlikely. So far, no one had been apprehended for that morning's explosions. Part of Hanaigh's reason for holding the press conference was to announce a number of measures to combat terrorist assaults on Inner City buildings. First, the immediate lockdown of lower-level poor quarters, including a blackout, evening curfew, and martial law until the assailants were caught.

Raised voices, camera flashes. Keshni pressed against Markriss's shoulder, clouding him in Burban perfume, whispering, "Didn't I say?" The heat of her breath and the clamor of bodies as journalists got to their feet, firing questions, made him tense with claustrophobia. Hanaigh pushed his hands downward, without answers. Waiting for them to acquiesce.

"One more thing," he said. For a moment, an echo of the death gaze Markriss had witnessed in the eyes of his old friends marked Hanaigh's. "I have one more thing to say. Given that so many events have been mishandled, and the criticism I've faced from the day I inherited this task—rightfully, some may say, though I'd counter that I inherited many of the problems—I've thought long and hard about what I can do. A leader must lead, I've always believed. And when a leader strays down a wrong path, who should be blamed? The followers? No. I believe in truth, and I stand by that to this day. 'As above, so below' has been our mantra for centuries, and will be for centuries more, yet have we made it so? We have not. We see that truth today, in the admittedly vile actions of others, although it is no less apparent in spite of what they've done. With that in mind, I hereby tender my resignation . . ."

Uproar, bodies rising around Markriss: Keshni, his peers, everyone. The noise of a thousand questions, the jostle of legs and movement forcing past him. Markriss remained seated. On the grass, his slide was buried in mud at one corner. He picked it up. Brushed the screen. The machine was still recording. He placed it on his lap once more.

"I will tender my resignation forthwith. In my stead," the CEO shouted over the noise, "I will be replaced by my daughter, Isla E'lul, whom many of you already know. Isla is strong, resilient, fully capable of heading the company. She's of diligent mind, and one of the smartest people I know. She'll make a worthy leader, of that I'm sure. Thank you, everybody, for your time, and for allowing me to be of service to you. It's been my greatest privilege. Now, I'll take questions."

Markriss got to his feet. The forest of arms around him, desperate for attention, almost knocked him over until he righted himself, lifting the slide high above his head. He couldn't hear anyone, and so he stared at the man on stage grasping the lectern with the clasp of a person who feared they may be lost if they were not anchored. Pale eyes, the color of a sky Markriss knew only from childhood stories, darting to one place then another, finally resting on him.

Hanaigh raised his hand to point at Markriss.

"Mark, go ahead," he mumbled low, rumbling speakers.

Markriss lowered his slide to hip level, gasps and complaints firing overhead, Keshni's tut of annoyance gunshot loud.

"Thank you, Governor. What I'd like to know is how you justify keeping so many people in so many zones across Inner City, and even under our feet, in conditions that are barely humane, only to act with surprise when they refuse to live that way. Seventy people were killed in the L1 poor-zone raid you ordered after the first explosion. Only a handful of those were involved in the original attack. That just doesn't make sense. It's not justice, it's execution without due process, or trial. It's murder. How dare you step down, full of condemnation for the terrorists but not a word for the suffering your company has caused the destitute and menial, bringing everyday terror to *their* lives, never mind the people belowground who never see light. How can you leave that all behind, knowing it exists because of decisions you've made, and just blank it from your mind, move on? How can you live here, far from everything you've done, and not feel complete and utter shame?"

He sat. The following roar washed over him like an elemental force, Markriss jostled even harder than before. People screaming close in his face, spitting, out of focus, necks stretched in anger, pointing, bony fingers stabbing flesh. Work colleagues. Security guards eyeballing hate yards away, faces red and swollen. Even Keshni, glasses snatched from her head, glass-bottle eyes bulging fury, the arm of her shades jerking at him. Markriss couldn't hear the words.

He had not planned to speak, and could not say why he did after so many years of saying nothing at all. He considered the ease he suddenly experienced in his chest and throat. The notion of an object dislodged, seemingly from nowhere. Despite the elements from outside his body, outside his control, inside was a silence that felt new. He rested, listening. Head bowed, examining its quality.

He stayed that way for a time and then, satisfied, raised his head, a touch of a smile pressing at his lips. Hanaigh E'lul blinked in his direction. Nothing to say, or so it seemed. Just looking. He may have smiled with him, though if he did it was inconsequential and Markriss couldn't tell.

Standing, loose backpack clasped between his fingers, body held sideways, Markriss edged along the row. At its far end, free of stiffened bodies, and chairs loosened by overexcitable press members, he noted

Chileshe. She stood with a crew of rival photographers left of the stage, camera lens pointing down at the grass, posture equally limp. She brought her hands together, softly enough for him to question the reality of what he'd seen. Head tipped in acknowledgment, he turned away.

Markriss walked toward the D tram stop, and never looked back.

An empty bench, protruding beyond a playground gate. He sat, turned away from climbing frames and children. There was the inevitable rain of pinging messages he chose to ignore; having no answers himself, it followed that he had none for anyone else. All he knew was lightness, the removal of a weight he hadn't understood he carried. He heard trickling water somewhere in his deepest imagination, pleased for no reason. He allowed himself to watch the press conference run its relatively stable course at the center of the square, small and distant, amplified words echoing, as Simi's metallic voice intoned a predictable list of contact names and organizations he'd worked with since his time in the Ark. He flinched a little when people walked by. Wondering if any were disgruntled L4 residents who'd watched him on their slides, or in offices, who might have already seen what he had to say and harbored a grudge. Soon, he became distracted by Simi's irregular litany, a dubious poetry.

One softly voiced name caught his attention: Willis Bracken, editor, *Ark News*.

Markriss blinked his right eye.

"You're fired."

He waited for more.

"Message end."

Head back, chin raised toward the Lites, Markriss took short breaths, expanding his lungs until panic receded. The steady thud of a pitzball beneath the yells and laughter over his shoulder calmed him. Immersed in the freedom of unknown children, a lack of misbegotten cares. He would stay with the playground at his back, absorbing their energy, and when he felt good enough to leave for home, he'd return and meditate on what he should do. Had done.

He lowered his head between knees, the moment in the square

forgotten, as another scene from his memory played in his mind's eye. The chill breeze of the park. Emotionless orb of the moon. Lifting from his physical self without warning, looking down on Raymeda, sleeping below. The quick snap of a moment like a balloon burst into formless shreds, to see Misty and Nesta, flailing at each other. His friend's eyes bloodred, moving backward as Misty advanced, until Markriss fell.

He trembled, a cold embrace of shame tightening. Hands flat on knees, deep breathing. Blinked his right eye.

Simi, message Misty Amen.

Messaging . . .

"Have you seen the news? VT me."

He glanced around. Nothing. No one close enough for him to care. Another normal day in Tibisiri Square, where the midday Lites were soothing, the warmth a balm, the calm reassuring. Markriss bathed. A home he'd never believed he deserved, unable to admit he'd felt that way before now.

A ping, a name breathed by Simi: "Hanaigh E'lul, E-Lul Corp."

Markriss jumped, staring at his slide.

"Mark? I'm not sure you'll even answer, but I had to try. I'm entirely intrigued by your questions today. I think we need to talk. Come and see me in my building tonight, say six? All this kerfuffle will have gone. Just intro yourself at reception, they'll do the rest. Hope you can make it."